FORGED IN EMBER

Also by Trish McCallan

Red-Hot SEALs Novels

Forged in Fire
Forged in Ash
Forged in Smoke

Red-Hot SEALs Novellas

Bound by Seduction
Bound by Temptation

Other Novellas

Spirit Woods

FORGED IN EMBER

A Red-Hot SEALs Novel

TRISH McCALLAN

Published by Montlake Romance, Seattle

www.apub.com

ISBN-13: 9781503945555
ISBN-10: 1503945553

Cover design by Eileen Carey

Printed in the United States of America

FORGED IN EMBER

Cast of Characters

Commander Jace (Mac) Mackenzie—commander of SEAL Team 7

Lieutenant Commander Zane Winters—SEAL Team 7

Lieutenant Marcus (Cosky) Simcosky—SEAL Team 7

Lieutenant Seth (Rawls) Rawlings—SEAL Team 7 corpsman

Beth Brown—Zane's fiancée

Kait Winchester—metaphysical healer, Cosky's fiancée

Faith Ansell—scientist working on the new energy paradigm

Wolf—Arapaho Special Forces warrior, unknown team, Kait's half brother

John Chastain—FBI agent, murdered in *Forged in Fire*

Amy Chastain—the widow of John Chastain, kidnapped in *Forged in Fire*

Benji Chastain—John and Amy's youngest son, kidnapped in *Forged in Fire*

Brendan Chastain—John and Amy's oldest son, kidnapped in *Forged in Fire*

Russ Branson (aka Russell Remburg)—facilitated the attempted hijacking and kidnapping of Agent Chastain's family in *Forged in Fire*, killed by Zane

Jillian Michaels—sister to Russell Remburg, kidnapped in *Forged in Fire*, antagonist in *Forged in Ash*

Detective Pachico (aka Robert Biesel)—hired mercenary who was instrumental in the attempted hijacking of flight 2077 and the kidnapping of Faith's coworkers

Eric Manheim—one of the men funding the attempted hijacking and the kidnapping of Faith's coworkers

Marion Simcosky—Cosky's mother

Clay Purcell—FBI agent, Amy Chastain's stepbrother

Aiden Winchester—SEAL Team 7, Kait's brother, hero of *Bound by Seduction* (a Red-Hot SEALs novella)

Sitrep

Lieutenant Commander Zane Winters and his fellow SEALs thwart the hijacking of flight 2077. During the resulting investigation, they are approached by FBI agent John Chastain, who enlists their aid in finding and rescuing his kidnapped family. The hijackers demand that Chastain turn over seven passengers from the flight, or else they'll kill his wife and children. But upon returning from the successful rescue, the SEALs find Chastain dead and the list of passengers missing.

Through Amy Chastain, John's widow, they learn a top-secret lab was recently bombed. Seven of the scientists affiliated with the lab had been booked on flight 2077. Convinced there is a connection to the aborted hijacking, the SEALs raid the lab and find Faith Ansell, one of the purportedly dead scientists, on the premises. Before they can question Faith, they are attacked. They capture one of the mercenaries, who goes by the name Pachico, and haul him to a safe house with Ansell. Ansell tells them that before the bombing, her lab had been working on a new energy paradigm that would have replaced every form of energy known to man—and that her coworkers had been kidnapped, and their deaths faked, in order to duplicate the research. When the cabin is attacked, everyone flees into the woods. During the ensuing battle, Lieutenant Seth Rawlings is near fatally injured.

As Rawls recovers from his injury, Amy Chastain meets up with her stepbrother, Clay Purcell, to pick up her children. Her stepbrother, however, is working with the men behind the attempted hijacking—men who are desperate to silence the SEALs. They've injected Amy's children with an experimental tracking isotope in order to follow them back to the SEALs' hideout. When the compound where the SEALs are staying is bombed, they are rescued by new associates, who take them to their base in Alaska. Through their new allies, they discover they share a common enemy known as the New Ruling Order, a group of super-rich men who intend to destroy humanity in order to save the planet.

Chapter One

Up until five months ago, Amy Chastain had never hated anyone.

She flinched as the needle pierced the inside of Benji's small arm and her son's wail ripped through the exam room, ricocheting off the clinical white walls. The hatred burned hotter. Darker. More violent.

"It hurts," Benji sobbed, lifting brown eyes brimming with tears to her face.

"You're almost done, baby. Almost done." Her heart a raw, aching mess, she brushed the tears from his damp cheek and stroked his sturdy back.

The syringe slowly filled with his rich, red blood. There had been far too many syringes of blood over the past week. Far too many teary-eyed wails. Far too many blood tests, X-rays, MRIs, CAT scans—virtually every test known to man.

How could anyone—*anyone*—purposely poison a child? He was only a baby—barely seven years old.

The hatred settled deeper, a raw, pressurized force bubbling and brewing and spitting plumes of rage.

Sure, there had been people she disliked in the past. A person didn't reach forty years of life without disliking *someone*. And when that person was a woman, fast-tracking her way to the top of the White Collar Crime Division in the good old boys' club called the FBI, there had always been someone intent on sabotaging her career. Add in the constant rumors of sleeping her way to the top after she'd married John, who'd been special agent in charge of counterterrorism in Seattle's field office, and, yeah, there had been plenty of individuals to dislike in her old life.

But not hate.

Hatred hadn't entered her life until the insanely rich Eric Manheim and his cronies from the New Ruling Order had kidnapped her and the boys in order to force John to comply with their demands. Hatred hadn't become part of her biological makeup until those bastards had killed John when the hijacking of flight 2077 had been circumvented, thanks to the intervention of Commander Mackenzie and the three SEALs who'd served beneath him. Hatred hadn't become a living, breathing dragon seething inside her until Eric Manheim had detonated her children's lives in service to his dual gods of power and greed.

He'd injected her children, for God's sake, filled them full of this damn biological tracker just so he could follow them back to Mac's safe house and blow the compound to hell and back.

And judging by the grave look on Dr. Zapa's face when the woman had asked to speak with her—alone—Manheim's avarice didn't just threaten the lives and careers of the four SEALs who'd rescued her and the boys all those months ago. No, the bastard's mechanizations threatened Benji's and Brendan's lives now too.

If ever a group of men deserved to be gutted and staked out on an anthill, it was Eric Manheim and his buddies in the New Ruling Order.

"There. See?" Amy dropped her voice to a soothing croon as the nurse smoothly slid the needle out of Benji's flesh and pressed a cotton ball to the injection site. Amy took over applying pressure through the cotton ball as the nurse turned to the stainless-steel counter to tube and label the blood. She stroked her son's back again, a long, soothing glide up and down his spine. "We're all done."

He hiccupped on the tail end of a sob and stared up at her, nutmeg eyes drowning in tears and suspicion. "Are they gonna poke me again?"

"Nope. You're all done." *For now.* Amy fought for a reassuring smile.

"Not only are we *not* going to stick you again today, but also look at this," the nurse said in far too chipper a voice.

Benji stared at the bandage the nurse held out, his mouth dropping open in awe. "It's a dinosaur!"

"Not just any old dinosaur," the nurse told him in a conspiratorial whisper. "It's a T. rex."

"That's my favorite!" The clouds in Benji's eyes cleared, and his voice climbed in excitement.

"It is?" the nurse asked, her eyes rounding in pseudo astonishment. "How about that."

Why in the world would there be children's Band-Aids in Shadow Mountain's clinic? Although the compound wasn't a US military outpost, it was still a military base, packed full of Special Forces soldiers and other essential personnel. She hadn't seen one civilian or child since arriving the week before.

She frowned as Benji's previous appointments rolled through her mind. He'd had at least a dozen blood draws in the past week, and none of them had come with a dinosaur bandage. The clinic must have ordered the kids' bandages specifically for him. She smiled her appreciation at the nurse. The clinic staff had been remarkably kind and helpful, considering that she and the boys had been thrust on them when Wolf, Shadow Mountain's military commander, had hauled them to Alaska and dumped them on the base.

"Look, Mom! I'm a dinosaur!" Benji bounced in place, his gaze fixed on the thick tyrannosaur-shaped Band-Aid that decorated the inside of his elbow.

"I see that," Amy murmured absently as she turned to Brendan.

Unlike Benji, who fought the blood draws with every fiber of his stocky body, her oldest son accepted the procedure with calm stoicism.

He held perfectly still, without making a sound, as the nurse pushed the needle into his arm. After tubing and labeling Brendan's blood, the nurse returned with a collection of bandages to choose from.

Brendan chose the plain brown one.

And wasn't that just like her oldest. Brendan was so busy being the man of the house since his father had died, he'd forgotten how to be a child. She smothered the splinter of grief as John's face rose in her mind.

No time for that.

"All that's left is getting a weight on you two, and then you can go and fill those rumbling bellies," the nurse said after taping the plain brown bandage across the cotton ball she'd pressed to the inside of Brendan's elbow.

Amy glanced at the clock shining black against the white wall of the exam room. Marion should have arrived in the waiting room by now. "Would you mind taking them to get weighed and bringing them to the waiting room when you're finished?"

"It would be my pleasure." The nurse sent her an understanding smile. But then, she'd been there when Dr. Zapa had asked to speak with her . . . alone.

Amy's throat tightened, a cold, hard block of ice hitting her belly. Dr. Zapa's face had been so grave—defeated, even.

As she exited the exam room and hurried down the long, peach-tinted hall, she took deep, slow breaths, trying to calm the nerves tightening her chest. But the scent of disinfectant, fresh coffee, and carpet cleaner hit her lungs, constricting them even further.

Marion Simcosky—Lieutenant Marcus Simcosky's mother—pushed a cloud of silver hair out of her eyes and rose from one of the blue-and-peach waiting-room chairs as Amy walked through the door next to the receptionist desk.

"I can't thank you enough for stepping in like this, Marion, and taking the boys to the cafeteria." Amy forced a smile as she approached Cosky's mother. The woman had been a godsend over the past week, willing to babysit every time Amy had an appointment with their doctor.

"Don't you worry about us." Marion Simcosky's gaze softened, sympathy brimming in her dove-gray eyes. "I'll take good care of your boys while you talk to the doctor."

"Benji will fill up on pastries and cookies, given half a chance, so make sure he eats more than just sweets." She forced a matter-of-fact tone.

"Of course, dear." Marion reached out to pat Amy's hand, her soft face folding into lines of commiseration. "Try not to worry. I'm sure everything will work out. In the meantime, Benji and Brendan will be safe with me."

Another smile was beyond her acting ability, so Amy forced a murmur of appreciation instead. Of course her boys would be safe with Marion. That wasn't the concern. No—what scared her to death, what held her immobile in a raw, terrifying choke hold, was the beaten look on Eve Zapa's face.

Benji's loud, hyper voice barreled down the hallway and burst into the waiting room well ahead of her boisterous son. Amy turned. That was Benjamin for you, announcing his presence by voice way before his thunderous, two-footed arrival. His over-the-top albeit normal entrance *should* have steadied her, eased some of the anxiety. Instead it tightened the lump in her throat and increased the icy churn in her belly.

He's only seven. Just a baby. How could anyone—

She strangled the question, forcing the panic down deep and burying it there. Such questions were pointless. The injection had already been given. The unidentified biological agent had already multiplied and flooded her sons' bodies. Now she had to deal with the consequences—consequences forced on her children by a triad of heartless, unconscionable bastards.

The hatred bared its teeth and snarled. They would pay. Every single one of them. She'd make sure of it.

Commander Jace "Mac" Mackenzie drained the last dregs of coffee as he spied on the three Shadow Mountain men sitting at the cafeteria table in front of him. The distinct, sickly sweet stench of hydraulic fluid drifted from his targets, mixing with the thick scent of cooking that escaped from the kitchen behind him. The men's oily cologne and stained gray overalls marked them as grease monkeys.

He'd hoped his subtle surveillance while they shoveled back mountains of biscuits and gravy would provide some intel on the mysterious military base he and his men were currently calling home. Simple conversation between colleagues could convey a multitude of information. But not this time. When one of the bastards did talk, it was in an unfamiliar, guttural language that Wolf used off and on—Arapaho, according to Kait Winchester. He couldn't understand a damn thing they said, which meant lingering here was a fucking waste of time.

Scowling, he set the white mug on the plastic tray next to the ceramic plate with its smears of gravy. The chicken-fried steak and eggs he'd ordered for lunch had been considerably better than the fare he'd existed on during various deployments. Not only did the Shadow Mountain brass provide their operators with top-of-the-line medical and military equipment, but they also fueled their bodies with edible and *enjoyable* rations. Something virtually unheard of in the US military machine.

He swung his legs over the bench and carried the tray to the dirty dish station. He took his time stacking the dishes, silverware, and tray in their requisite bins. For the first time since he'd entered the United States Naval Academy as a hardened eighteen-year-old, he was uncertain of how to occupy his time. His position as commander of SEAL Team 7, at HQ1, had generated an ever-evolving list of tasks that required attention: ops in need of review, strategies in need of refinement, operators in need of training. Even off time came with responsibilities. Home ownership alone fed on free time like politicians fed on corruption and greed.

He shook his head and grimaced. Hell, when it came right down to it, he'd had every minute of every day spoken for long before he'd entered the USNA. With his old man comatose drunk 90 percent of the time after Davey died and Mommy Dearest split, Mac had taken care of himself and the house since the age of ten. Not that he'd given a rat's ass about the house or his old man, but at least he'd had a bed to sleep in and hot water for a shower—two things that had made it easier to attend school and grab the odd job when the opportunity arose.

The jobs he'd snagged hadn't paid for much beyond food to fill his belly and the occasional new pair of shoes or pants. But the old man's retirement check had taken care of the utilities—assuming Mac had been able to wrestle the money away before the motherfucker dropped the whole damn wad on booze and gambling. He'd been lucky the old man had owned the house outright, thanks to an inheritance from a great-aunt who'd died long before Mac had arrived on the scene. At least he hadn't been homeless. By the time the county seized the property and auctioned it off to pay the property taxes, he'd already joined the navy and settled into his new life as if he'd been born and bred to it. Which, as a third-generation career navy man, he *had* been. The Mackenzies were career navy through and through.

Which made it a bitter pill to swallow to have the navy goatfuck him twenty-six years later. Just goes to prove what wearing the white hat led to. Instead of kudos for preventing that damn hijacking, they'd been wrung out and left to swing in the breeze by their own damn command.

Mac scowled, frustration cinching the muscles of his chest like a straitjacket. He did a one-eighty and headed toward the cafeteria's exit. The lack of progress on bringing to justice the men who'd murdered Admiral McKay and John Chastain—or, hell, even clearing his men's names and proving their innocence against the laundry list of federal crimes riding their asses—was maddening. Almost as irritating as being shut out of the intel and preparations taking place in Shadow Mountain's war room. He didn't even know if Wolf's command had located Dr. Ansell's doomsday device or whether they were gearing up to retrieve the damn thing.

It fucking blowed to be locked out of the loop like this.

No doubt Zane, Cosky, and Rawls were handling this information blackout better than he was. After all, the three were bunking with their respective significant others—code for they were otherwise engaged and didn't give a rat's ass about the intel embargo.

Why the hell that train of thought would give rise to Amy's image was something he had no intention of examining too closely. So far, over the past week, he'd managed to avoid his redheaded albatross almost completely.

As he closed on the cafeteria door, it slid open, revealing the dark heads of Amy's children. Son of a bitch, the woman was like Beetlejuice. He just had to think of her, and boom—there she was. Except . . . the woman who followed the two boys through the sliding door wasn't a short, athletic redhead. Rather, a soft-bodied, grandmotherly type with uncontrollable silver hair.

He frowned, unease stirring as he stepped aside to let the trio pass. Amy Chastain was protective as fuck when it came to her boys. She wouldn't pass them off to Marion Simcosky without a damn good reason.

Not your circus. Let it go.

Advice that might have taken hold if Benji hadn't spotted him and charged forward.

"I'm a dinosaur," he shouted, stopping within inches of Mac and letting loose an enthusiastic roar.

Mac stumbled back, narrowly avoiding a collision with the child.

"See?" Benji extended his arm with another ear-splitting roar.

Holy fuck, the kid could be used as a sonic weapon, crushing the eardrums of enemies far and wide.

Tilting his head, Mac scanned the small limb presented to him. A Band-Aid in the shape of a T. rex shielded the inside of the boy's elbow. "A T. rex, huh? They were pretty bada—fierce."

"*Roar!* I'm fierce too!"

Mac winced. "You know that the T. rex was the most ferocious predator in the history of our planet?" He nodded sagely as Benji cocked his head, his face suddenly slack with fascination. "But what made them so dangerous was their silence. They'd sneak up on their prey in absolute stealth. Attack before anyone realized they were even there. Their silence is what made them so fierce."

Marion Simcosky snorted, amusement sparkling in her eyes. "Nice try, Commander." She turned to the older child. "Brendan, why don't you take Benji to the counter and get him some of that pizza he's been carrying on about. I need a word with Commander Mackenzie."

"But I'm talking to—"

"You can talk to him after you've eaten, Benji. Now skedaddle." She waited for Brendan to herd his brother across the cafeteria floor before turning a suddenly grave face in Mac's direction. "The boys' doctor asked to see Amy in private, and I suspect the news is less than good. Nobody should have to face something like that alone, but she needed help with the boys, so I couldn't stay."

Ah hell . . . Stiffening, Mac took a step back. "Beth or Kait—"

"Aren't here. You are. The meeting with the doctor will be over by the time I find them. Amy needs someone now."

Mac took another step back. "I'm sure Mrs. Chastain would prefer to have a woman with her."

"The only woman available is me, and I promised her I'd take care of her children. Trust me, she'd be much more comfortable with me watching over her boys than holding her hand. Which means you're currently the only person available to step up." She leaned toward him, a militant look sheening her gaze.

Fuck.

"She's at the clinic, Commander. Alone. She needs you." The resolve shifted to entreaty in her eyes and voice.

Double fuck.

He spread his feet and tensed his muscles, powering up for an uncompromising refusal. No way in hell was he taking on Amy Chastain's troubles.

"Fine." The surrender grated as it rumbled up his throat and out his mouth.

Where the hell had that come from?

Mac scowled, regrouping. Time to nip this in the bud and retreat to safety. "Look, I'll check in on her. That's all I'm promising."

He groaned beneath his breath. Agreeing to check up on the damn woman wasn't exactly retreating.

Marion's expression softened in relief. "I'm sure she'll appreciate that, Commander."

Grunting an acknowledgment, Mac brushed past Marion before she talked him into doing anything else. Of course, just because he'd agreed to check on Amy didn't mean he had to do so. It would be easy enough to skirt that duty by heading in the opposite direction. Except his feet developed a mind of their own and carried him two streets to the right and through the clinic's sliding glass doors.

Chapter Two

Amy waited until the clinic doors had closed behind Marion and the boys before turning to the short, perky nurse behind the receptionists' desk. "Dr. Zapa said she wanted to talk to me?"

"That's right, Mrs. Chastain." The girl stepped around the counter. "If you'll follow me, please."

Amy followed the woman down the carpeted hall and through the open door to Eve Zapa's office.

"If you'll take a seat, Dr. Zapa will be with you shortly. Would you like some coffee? The pot's fresh."

Amy swallowed hard, her stomach threatening to climb her throat, and shook her head. With a perfunctory smile, the nurse turned and disappeared through the door.

She wandered toward one of the plush chairs facing the glass desk. Apart from the lighted X-ray reader next to the door, the walls were bare. The surface of the desk was just as sterile. Perhaps the overall austerity of the space fed into the atmosphere of desperation that choked the air. Or more likely it was her own emotions suffocating the small room.

She lifted her chin and squared her shoulders. Enough with the pessimism. There was no reason to feel so defeated. It didn't matter what Dr. Zapa had to say. She'd find a way to save her children. Anything short of a complete cure was unacceptable.

"Ah, Mrs. Chastain. Please take a seat," Eve Zapa said from behind her.

Amy turned, watching as the slender, white-coated figure of her sons' doctor glided into the room. As usual, Eve Zapa looked like she'd stepped out of the glossy pages of *Vogue*. Even the casual swing of her black hair, in its fashionable bob, looked exquisite and expensive.

The good doctor would have been easy to dislike on general principle, if not for the compassion gleaming in her dark eyes and the obsessive commitment she'd shown to Benji's and Brendan's health.

Eve made her way around the pristine glass desk. She placed a manila folder thick with reports and lab results on the glass surface between them, neatly seated herself, and folded her hands.

"The healing didn't work, did it?" Amy forced a matter-of-fact tone, but her legs went weak and wobbly. Fearing they might not support her, she sank into the chair across from the desk.

When Western medicine had failed to neutralize the genetically modified biological isotope proliferating in her sons' veins, she'd turned her hopes to alternative—even mystical—possibilities. Shadow Mountain had three strong metaphysical healers on its payroll.

"No. It didn't." Eve's dark, steady gaze shimmered with empathy. "There was no change to the cellular structure in their blood. The markers are still present. The isotope is still active."

Amy nodded, steadied her voice. "All three healers were there? Kait? One Bird? William?"

With a solemn nod, Eve shattered Amy's final hope. "Yes, all three were present this time. The healing went as expected. It simply didn't have an effect."

Disappointment swelled, wrestled with her hard-fought optimism. She'd held such high hopes that this healing would work. Kait's talent alone was miraculous. By Rawls's account, she'd brought both him and Faith back from the brink of death. But even with Cosky there to boost her healing ability, Kait's attempt at removing the isotope from Benji's and Brendan's cells had failed. That's when Dr. Zapa and Dr. Kerry had discussed the possibility of a combined healing—one utilizing all three healers' talents at once.

It had taken almost a week to arrange the ceremony. The Shadow Mountain healers, along with Cosky, had been gearing up to rescue Faith's coworkers. They'd had to wait for the healers to return, and since the mission had incurred injuries, which had required healing, they'd had to wait several additional days for One Bird's and William's psychic energies to recharge.

If Kait's gift alone was of such biblical proportions it could bring the dead back to life, shouldn't all three of them together be able to perform something even more miraculous?

Apparently not.

Amy squared her shoulders and lifted her chin. Yes, this was a major disappointment. But there had to be other avenues to explore. Other things they could try.

"So what's next?"

Eve looked down. It was a fleeting gesture, but Amy's heart froze and then slammed into triple time. The fierce throb of her pulse flooded her ears. She knew what Eve was going to say before the other woman lifted her head or opened her mouth. That simple, instinctive response had told her everything.

"I'm afraid we've run out of options. Our attempts to neutralize the isotope have failed." She paused to sigh. "Let's back up. How much do you know about cellular biology?"

Fighting the panic fluttering in her belly, Amy shrugged. "Next to nothing."

"Then let me give you a quick rundown of how cells acquire energy. It will give you a better understanding of our problem." She ran a hand through her sleek black hair. "Within each cell there are adenosine triphosphate molecules—or ATPs. These molecules are made up of three chemically bonded phosphate molecules. When the chemical bonds between the phosphate molecules break, a flash of energy is released. The cells use this energy to power their processes."

She paused to scowl and shake her head. "The isotope that was injected into your sons binds itself to the ATP molecule by mimicking the phosphate bonds. When the phosphate energy is released, the isotope siphons it off and uses it to power its signal. We still don't understand how this signal is produced, but—" She broke off, frustration touching her face. "In any case, every attempt to disrupt the bond between the isotope and the ATP molecules has failed. Until we identify this compound and disrupt its bonding mechanism . . ." Her hands separated, going palms up in the universal gesture of helplessness.

"And if you can't identify it?" The muscles in Amy's jaw tightened at Eve's silence.

It was time to explore other avenues, like how the compound had been delivered. Knowing who'd injected it would give her someone to hunt down, someone to demand answers from. "Do you know whether the isotype was delivered through a flu shot?"

"It's certainly possible. H3N2 antibodies were found in both boys' blood. We found traces of thimerosal as well, which is a preservative found in flu vaccines—so there's no question the boys were given a flu shot. What's less clear is whether the biological agent was delivered through the vaccine or whether the timing of the two events is coincidental."

"The flu vaccine is the only injection the boys received." Frowning in thought, Amy settled back into the armchair across from the gleaming desk. "Could the compound have been delivered in a different manner? Through food or drink? Or through the skin, like shampoo? Soap?"

Both scenarios meant someone close to them would have had to slip the isotope into their food or personal hygiene products. She shied away from the implications of that thought. The only people with such access to the boys were her mom, her dad, and Clay.

No. Her parents and brother were not behind this.

They couldn't be.

Dr. Zapa shook her head. "My *best guess* would be that it was delivered through the flu vaccination. If the compound had been taken orally, stomach enzymes and acids would have neutralized it. As for absorption through the skin, the components of the isotope are too large to allow for transdermal absorption. It had to have been administered via injection."

If the compound had been delivered through the flu shot, then the doctor who'd administered the vaccine would know where it had come from. Which gave her a place to start.

With a deep, calming breath, Amy refocused. "If this biological agent is siphoning off the cells' energy, what will happen to the cells? How long will they continue to function normally?"

"We don't know." Eve's dark eyes softened. "As of now the boys' cells appear to be receiving enough energy from the ATP molecules to continue their normal cellular processes." She shifted uneasily in her chair, her lab coat rasping slightly against the cloth upholstery. "How long this can continue is an open question. It would be wise to restrict their activity. The less energy they burn, the less stress on the individual cells. We'll need to monitor them closely, but until we know what we're dealing with, that's about all we can do."

"Restrict their activity . . ." Amy echoed wryly, her stomach constricting. "Have you met Benji?"

But some of the ache in her tight chest eased. The news could have been worse. Much worse. While the danger was still present, Benji's and Brendan's cells hadn't started deteriorating yet. She just had to find a way to neutralize the compound before they did. Clay was the logical place to start since he'd brought in the doctor who'd injected the flu vaccine.

Commander Mackenzie's darkly handsome face flashed through her mind. Mac was certain that Clay had been instrumental in shooting her boys full of that damn compound, and he wasn't shy about bombarding her with his suspicions. His belief that her brother was involved with the NRO meant the commander would step up and accompany her when she confronted her brother—whether she wanted him to or not.

Mackenzie was a pit bull when something mattered to him, and finding a conduit to Eric Manheim, one of the men responsible for setting up Mac and his buddies, as well as for killing his friend Rear Admiral McKay, was of vital importance to him.

She wanted to see Manheim pay as well. Not only was the NRO directly responsible for injecting her children with a life-threatening isotope, but they'd also taken the life of the man she'd loved—the father of her children.

That earlier splinter of pain sharpened, but not as much as she'd expected. Although it had been only five months, John's death already felt like a lifetime ago. With a careful breath, she pushed the residual pain aside and focused on the mission at hand.

Mac's certainty that Clay was involved made him the perfect partner. He'd back her play because confronting Clay would benefit him as much as her.

She frowned, remembering the menacing byplay between the two men back when they'd picked up Benji and Brendan. While she preferred Mac's in-your-face confrontational style to Clay's sneering and mental games, Mac was an expert at escalating tense situations. And God knows her brother was already feeling defensive and unappreciated.

What a fun meeting this was going to be. Clay could be a stuffy, pretentious ass when his back was up, and Mac would make sure his back was up. Still, it had to be done. She needed to find the doctor who'd injected her boys.

Benji's and Brendan's lives depended on it.

Mac swore beneath his breath as he headed across the clinic lobby. It wouldn't hurt to offer support, which she'd turn down, thereby alleviating him of this unwelcome chore. With that in mind, he approached the reception desk only to stop short when Amy suddenly appeared in the doorway. Her pace faltered when she saw him but quickly picked up tempo again.

He studied her tight face, which was a chiseled mask of resolve. Whatever news the doctor had imparted hadn't skewered her. Rather, it had forged a spine of steel. Admiration stirred. Hands down, she was the strongest woman he'd ever known.

"What are you doing here?" she asked, stopping in front of him.

Mac shrugged. "Marion was worried about you. Didn't want you to be alone. What did the doc have to say?"

She frowned slightly, scanned his face, and then rolled her shoulders before squaring them again. "The last healing didn't work."

He caught the barest hint of a waver at the beginning of the sentence, which indicated that she'd pinned a hell of a lot of hope on the outcome of that healing. An insane urge hit—to lean forward and drag her into his arms, to offer her the comfort she so clearly needed. Before he had a chance to act on the horrifying impulse, her voice firmed. She stepped back, retreating into her habitual mask of capability.

Thank Christ.

"With Kait?" He fought to keep an even tone and his hands to himself.

He still found it damn near impossible to believe that Kait Winchester had healed the double tap to Rawls's chest and dragged him back from the dead. Sure, he'd witnessed the miracle with his own eyes, but he still had trouble wrapping his brain around it.

Metaphysical healing? Hands-on healing? No shit?

Even now, a voice deep inside him insisted that he'd misinterpreted what he'd seen or that Kait had somehow tricked them. A Penn and

Teller performance, if you will. Although how in the hell she'd managed that and then continued to fool the Shadow Mountain brass . . .

"Kait, William, and One Bird," Amy corrected, her voice so steady it sounded wooden. "Their three strongest healers. But it didn't work. The compound is still active."

Sympathy stirred. The circumstances had to be unbearable for her. Christ only knew what that toxic shit inside her kids was doing to their bodies or how long they'd survive if the isotope wasn't neutralized soon.

"What's the next step?"

"There isn't one." For a second her voice went breathless and high. She stopped talking to clear her throat.

That earlier insane impulse to wrap her in his arms struck again. His arms twitched. His fingers flexed. He held his breath and took a careful step backward, relaxing as her breathing stabilized.

"They've explored every avenue available to them. Until they identify the compound, there isn't much they can do." Resolve hardened her face again. "Dr. Zapa believes the compound was delivered through the flu shot, as you suspected." She held Mac's gaze unflinchingly. "That gives me a place to start looking for answers."

She meant Clay Purcell, her brother. He'd been the one to arrange the flu shot. Mac cocked his head, studying her face. She'd been damn resistant to that possibility earlier.

If they were to believe Pachico, the tracking isotope had been developed by Dynamic Solutions and given to the NRO by James Link, the company's interim CEO. Of course, the information had come courtesy of a fucking ghost, since Pachico had been dead at the time of his interrogation. Considering the circumstances, it was kinda hard to put much faith in the information. Hell, Pachico had been sketchy with the truth when he'd been alive, and they'd gone and questioned his ghost?

Yeah, right. He shook his head in disbelief. It would be nice to get some collaborative evidence that Link and Dynamic Solutions were behind the isotope.

"You're going after your brother?"

Her eyebrows pulled together. "I'm going to *ask* Clay to put me in touch with the physician who administered the shot. Whoever gave the boys the vaccine knows where it came from, which makes them my best chance of tracking the compound back to its source." She paused to take a deep breath, held it for a few seconds, and then slowly released it. "Clay would never endanger the boys on purpose. He loves us. I have absolutely no doubt about that. However, I do recognize his weaknesses. Clay can be short-sighted and impatient. It's quite possible he listened to the wrong people, which opened up the opportunity for someone to inject the isotope."

Mac grunted, locking his instant disagreement down. His bullshit meter—which had served him well throughout his life—had warped into the red zone during the rendezvous to pick up Brendan and Benji. The moment Purcell had opened his mouth and started needling Amy about her kidnapping and subsequent rape, he'd known the bastard was involved. The verbal attacks hadn't been those of a devoted, protective brother, but rather a narcissistic blowhard. The woman was too loyal to see what was right in front of her nose.

How fucking ironic. He'd finally found a woman who was loyal to her core, and that integrity could easily get her killed.

"What's your plan?" It would accomplish nothing to confront her about Clay . . . again. Besides, she was on the right track.

Her asshole of a brother was involved in this whole mess. If they could force him to give up who'd administered the vaccine, they'd have a starting place, someone to point them toward the entity behind the isotope. Knowing who developed it was crucial in their efforts to neutralize it.

"You calling him?" Mac prodded. They'd have to play the conversation on speaker so he could listen in.

"No," she said slowly, a distant look on her face. "I need to see him. Face to face."

Mac's forehead wrinkled. Why face to face? Maybe she wasn't so certain of Clay's innocence after all. Her questions could be asked and answered over the phone. To insist on a physical conversation almost had to mean she wanted to see his expressions, judge his truthfulness. Which indicated her family loyalty might be wearing thin.

Scrubbing his hand over his head, Mac simply nodded, more than happy to play nice with her plan. He too wanted to see the bastard's face when they interrogated him. Amy might believe her brother had been tricked into betraying her, but he was equally certain the sadistic bastard had been in on everything from the very beginning.

"I'll get hold of Wolf." Mac pivoted, suddenly energized. "See what he can do about getting us down to Seattle."

Amy matched his pace. "Normally I'd point out that you should remain here since you have a price on your head. But you'll just ignore the warning, so I'll refrain from pointing out the sheer foolishness of you accompanying me."

Mac slid her a quick sideways glance. "A warrant, not a price."

Shrugging, Amy walked through the clinic door beside him. "Do you honestly think that the NRO hasn't put a contract out on you and your men? They can't afford to have you taken into custody."

Yeah . . . Mac frowned. She had a point there. Manheim and his buddies at the New Ruling Order probably did want him out of the way. But then the same could be said about Amy. The NRO couldn't afford her account of events any more than they could afford his. Hell, she was much more dangerous to them. They'd managed to thoroughly discredit him and his boys. But Amy was still a media darling, a victim of flight 2077, the grieving widow of a bona-fide hero. Her account would be credible. She'd be believed.

Adrenaline suddenly surged through him.

Over his dead body would anyone touch a hair on this woman's head. And that included her fucking brother.

His stride increased as boredom fell away and plans took shape. Finally he had something to strategize, something to do. They needed a team, backup. Men he could trust.

Luckily he had the perfect trio in mind.

Chapter Three

EXHAUSTION DRAGGING AT EVERY SYNAPSE IN HER BRAIN AND SINEW in her body, Amy Chastain paused in the doorway. The hall lamp burned bright and harsh behind her, casting a thin wedge of light to the right and left of her body and illuminating two bundles of blanket-wrapped boys.

The small apartment the Shadow Mountain housing committee had assigned her boasted two bedrooms, a bathroom, and a small living area with an attached kitchenette. The larger of the two bedrooms barely accommodated the two narrow beds, which had been pushed against the walls in an L formation. At the foot of each bed was a four-drawer dresser. At best, the small closet behind the door held a coat or two. Her room was even smaller, with a single bed and a built-in wardrobe. Combined, the entire space occupied around four hundred square feet.

But the rooms were safe. Secure. Private.

Qualities that were much more important than space these days.

Upon reaching the bed to the right, she leaned over and straightened the collection of blankets before tugging them over Benji's shoulders. It wouldn't be long before the covers were tossed aside again. Her youngest had always been a restless sleeper, thrashing around in bed as though sleep couldn't contain his enthusiasm or exuberant personality.

She straightened then arched her spine, kneading the tight muscles in her lower back. At least the events over the past few days—or even months—hadn't impacted her youngest. While his father's death had dimmed his sunny personality for a while, he'd treated everything else—from their kidnapping to the flight through the tunnels with the compound exploding overhead—with uncontained excitement. Not even the battery of medical tests he'd endured over the past week had squelched his spirit for long. But then, unlike Brendan, Benji had no idea what the test results had yielded.

Brendan knew even though she hadn't told him. Her oldest took after his father when it came to intuition and rock-solid temperament. Although only four years separated her two sons, Brendan was a millennium older in maturity and perception.

Amy turned to the bed on the left and found Brendan watching her. It didn't surprise her. She suspected he hadn't been sleeping any better than she had.

Unlike Benji's trashed cot, Brendan's covers were neatly folded at his chest, the blankets smooth and straight, as though he hadn't moved a fraction of an inch since he'd climbed into bed.

She settled beside him and reached out to stroke his cheek. "Couldn't sleep?"

He studied her face before answering, as though trying to judge what she needed to hear. Such a subtle, heartbreaking response to a simple question.

"It's going to be okay, Mom," he finally said, his calm, quiet voice filling the darkness.

Yep, he'd found it. He'd pinpointed exactly what she needed to hear. His hand rose, caught hers, and held tight. Something else she'd needed without realizing it.

A wave of sorrow—raw and suffocating—broke over her and threatened to rupture her composure. Sorrow for John, for the life that had been taken that could never be returned, for all the things she wouldn't be able to share with him through the coming years. For Benji, whose losses were still to come when he slowed down enough to realize how much had been stolen from him. But most of all for this child lying so still and silent beside her. This adult in a child's body.

Brendan had lost everything. He'd lost his father and the exceptionally close relationship they'd shared. He'd lost his school, his friends, and his sports teams—which he'd excelled at.

But most of all he'd lost his innocence.

Through their kidnapping and her rape, he'd learned that sex could be used as a weapon, leaving bruises and blood and invisible wounds that cut to the soul. Through his father's death, he'd learned that you could do everything right, everything possible, and still pay the ultimate price. Through this awful high-tech shit those monsters had shot into his veins, he'd learned that there were people out there capable of the most invasive, horrific acts to achieve their own agendas.

While Brendan's quiet, deliberate nature had always been the core of his personality, these past five months had tempered his natural demeanor into something harder, darker—heartbreaking in a child.

Nothing had gone over Brendan's head. Although he hadn't said anything, he understood what those bastards had done to her four and a half months ago while they'd been helpless and trapped.

She shied away from the memories, entombing them deep within her, where they smoldered and swelled and pressed outward like a pus-filled abscess ready to burst forth and spew its rot.

There wasn't time to deal with what had happened to her or work through the aftermath. She couldn't afford to wallow in her own personal tragedy, not when there was another catastrophe looming—one that could swallow her children.

"There was something in that shot, wasn't there?"

Brendan's voice dragged her from the crumbling abyss of her own thoughts.

"Something that lets them track us?" While he'd framed it as a question, the certainty sat flat and hard in his voice as well as in the dark eyes watching her.

She swallowed and tightened her hand around his before forcing the admission through her tight, aching throat. "It appears so."

"They can't get it out of us?" His knowing gaze didn't budge from her face, and acceptance resonated in his voice.

The dark brown of his eyes didn't match hers, or John's either, but then neither did the color of his hair. Both were throwbacks to her father. Her biological father, not the man she'd called Dad for the past thirty-odd years. She didn't remember much of the man who'd fathered her besides a quiet voice and strong arms. But she'd seen enough pictures to know where her sons' dark hair and eyes came from.

"Dr. Zapa is working on it, but they aren't sure what we're dealing with yet. In the meantime we're safe here. The signal is blocked by Shadow Mountain." She paused to instill confidence in her voice. "They can't find us here."

"The healing Kait and the others did didn't work?"

Amy silently shook her head, a lump clogging her throat.

Brendan didn't look surprised. She hoped he hadn't figured out the rest of it. If Eve couldn't find out a way to neutralize the compound, her children would never be able to step foot outside Shadow Mountain again. Not without the risk of being scooped up and used in this deadly conspiracy Eric Manheim and his cronies had embroiled them in.

A beat of silence followed.

"Commander Mackenzie thinks Clay did this to us," Brendan suddenly said, a cold edge chilling his voice.

She flinched, denial instinctively rising. Her dad and mom—and Clay—couldn't have had anything to do with what happened.

They couldn't.

"Commander Mackenzie is suspicious of everyone." Which was nothing less than the truth and had nothing to do with what her son was trying to tell her. She backtracked and tried again. "Mac doesn't even know your uncle Clay."

Mackenzie's suspicious face rose in her mind.

Brendan was right, though. Mac did think Clay was behind the injection given to her sons. But if he was right, that meant Clay was behind the rest of it too. John's murder. Her, Benji, and Brendan's kidnapping. What those bastards had done to her. If Mac was right, Clay was responsible for every single horrific blow since late March.

It couldn't be true. It couldn't. She'd known Clay since the age of five. They'd shared a home and an idyllic childhood. He'd been John's best friend and best man at their wedding. He was Brendan's godfather. For him to be capable of such evil without her or John recognizing it? No. It simply wasn't possible.

Straightening her shoulders, she shook her head. "Clay has nothing to do with any of this."

Brendan just stared at her. "He was there, Mom. He brought the doctor. He's the one who told us we had to have the shot."

"Because someone convinced him you needed the shots to get back into school. He didn't realize what you were being given." She forced conviction into her voice.

"He's FBI, like Dad—and he didn't check with the school? Have the shot tested? Dad would have." Reservation and something darker burned in her son's grim eyes.

"That's why your dad was senior agent in charge, and your uncle Clay isn't," Amy said. "Clay misses things sometimes."

"Commander Mackenzie would have checked." There was no give in Brendan's voice.

Yes, Mac would have. The man never took things for granted.

"We've already established that Commander Mackenzie has a suspicious nature," Amy said, exhaustion crashing over her in an emotionally draining wave. Not that she'd sleep, or at least not for very long, if she headed to her bed.

"I think Commander Mackenzie is right. I think Clay knew what was in that shot. I think he gave it to us on purpose."

"Oh, Brendan . . ." Amy's voice failed.

Another wave of sorrow washed over her, only this time it was tinged with rage. Apparently they'd taken even more from her son than she'd realized—they'd stolen his trust in family too, the security of knowing that those closest to you had your back.

"He's never liked us, Mom." Brendan tilted his chin and set his jaw.

That gave her pause.

Never?

Never spoke of long rather than short term. *Never* referenced a lengthier pattern than five months.

Brendan had stopped calling her brother Uncle Clay years ago. When she'd questioned him, he'd told her calling him uncle was a baby thing and he was too old for that now. She hadn't thought much of it at the time, assuming it was something he'd heard at school or through his friends. Had it been more than that? Had he been certain even back then that Clay didn't like him?

"Clay might not always show it, sweetheart, but he loves us." The reassurance sent déjà vu crashing through her. She'd said the exact same thing to Mackenzie—twice now.

Suddenly she felt mired in a case of she-who-doth-protest-too-much.

"He smiled when Benji cried," Brendan said, a flat sheen glossing his brown eyes.

Startled, Amy straightened. "When was this?"

"When the doctor gave us the shot. It hurt bad, and Benji started crying. Clay smiled. He liked seeing Benji hurt. He liked seeing him cry."

She wanted to protest, tell him he was imagining things, but she couldn't. Brendan didn't imagine things, not ever. If he said Clay had smiled when Benji cried—then Clay had smiled.

Nausea rolled up her throat. "Could he have been thinking about something else?"

Brendan's dark brows knitted, but then he slowly shook his head. "I don't think so. He was looking right at Benji, and he didn't smile until Benji started crying."

Amy sat there frozen, a dark, cold shadow pressing into her.

"I know you think of him as a brother, Mom." Brendan sat up and scooted back until his shoulders were braced against the headboard. "But he's never liked us. He might smile with his mouth, but his eyes are mean. He's been like that as long as I can remember."

"Your grandpa's always been hard on him." She paused, shook her head. She was making excuses. But nothing excused this if Brendan was right. If Mackenzie was right. "Why didn't you ever mention this before?"

"Because it didn't matter before."

She thought about that, the cold sinking into her like a thick frost. Even her bones ached. "You really think Clay knew what he was doing? That he injected you on purpose?"

This time he didn't pause to think about it. He nodded solemnly.

If Brendan was right, then what Clay felt for them went deeper than dislike. This rammed right into hatred.

Maybe Brendan was picking up on something that wasn't there. Maybe the past five months had hardwired his natural suspicion, and he was seeing monsters in familiar faces.

Was that what had happened to Mackenzie? Had he lost his innocence during childhood? Had that hardened him into the suspicious adult he was today?

She rubbed at the ache throbbing behind her eyes. She couldn't dismiss Brendan's comments no matter how much she wanted to. Her son was intuitive for his age, with killer instincts. She needed to get hold of Clay and find out. She needed to rid herself of the sisterly bias and discover whether family loyalty had blinded her to the monster her brother had become.

"Hey, Woof Boy. Hold up."

A sizzle of irritation crackling through him, Wolf paused, one thick black boot inches from the cement. With slow deliberation, he placed his foot on the ground, schooled his face to tolerance, and pivoted.

It came as no surprise to find Commander Mackenzie's harsh face and toxic personality barreling down on him. But then he'd recognized the *heebii3soo*'s voice immediately. Well, that and the accompanying flash of annoyance. Mackenzie was one of the few men in existence who could shatter a good morning simply by opening his mouth.

And today was no good morning.

Jude, Wolf's uncle and the leader of the Eagle Clan, paused beside him on the ramp to headquarters. After glancing over his shoulder, he grunted, his shoulders flexing slightly. Without looking at Wolf, he headed toward the looming door of their destination.

"Bawk, bawk, bawk," Wolf clucked beneath his breath.

"Better to run like *nih'oo3ounii'ehiiho'* than drown beneath Black Cloud's *noo'uusooo*'," Jude responded dryly, his boot steps a steady beat against the concrete. The heavy steel-and-glass door opened and closed with a sibilant hiss.

Wolf grimaced as he watched Mackenzie approach. *Storm . . .*

A fair description of the obnoxious SEAL's abrasive personality. Mackenzie's perennial dour mood had earned him the Black Cloud handle, which fit him all too well, considering how often he shed the emotional equivalence of lightning bolts and gale-force winds.

"Commander." Wolf inclined his head as Mackenzie stopped before him, leaning in just enough to invade Wolf's personal space.

"I need access to that nifty experimental chopper you boys like to show off." Mackenzie leaned forward even farther.

"Indeed." Wolf crossed his arms over his chest, refusing to ease away from the not-so-subtle challenge. Only Mackenzie could turn a request into a demand. However, to give the man credit, his demands usually came with valid reasons. "Why?"

Thick black brows beetled over Mackenzie's hawkish nose. Rocking back on his heels, Mackenzie shoved a blunt hand through his short graying hair. "The doc says the isotope those bastards injected into Amy's kids was delivered through the flu shot—which Clay Purcell, her fucktard of a brother, arranged. We need to talk to the asshole, force him to give up the doctor who administered the shot. It's the best lead we have so far. But he's down in Seattle."

Wolf nodded, a scowl quickly following. The ineffectiveness of the combined healing had been a blow. To Amy most of all, but to Kait as well. His sister refused to accept the limitations of her gift.

A wave of fury tinged with disgust rolled through him. The New Ruling Order had much to answer for. They'd proved their willingness to sacrifice their own people through the years, but to endanger the lives of those so young went against everything his people stood for. During the Old Time, they'd lost many of their children to war and disease. After they'd been forced onto the reservation, their children had been taken and sent hundreds of miles away to schools meant to purge their customs and culture. Too many of them had never returned home.

Generations of his people had fought for their children. It was a pity the outside world did not do the same for theirs.

He shook the disgust aside and concentrated on the man practically vibrating with impatience in front of him. Mackenzie had a point. Although Eve maintained that the boys were handling the isotope well, it was uncertain how long the status quo would last. Without intervention, the two boys could very well be the latest casualties in their war against the NRO.

It was of the utmost priority that an antidote be found. Amy's brother was the obvious starting point, as Mackenzie insisted. The timing, unfortunately, was a complete *hoxhisei*.

"Three days. I have no team available until then." Wolf turned back toward headquarters.

"I'm not asking for a team. I'm asking for a bird. Fuck, it doesn't even have to be one of those black op specials. I'll take the Jayhawk."

Wolf halted but didn't turn around. "I can give you the bird *and* a team in three days."

Mackenzie's voice hardened behind him. "We don't know if those boys have three days. We don't have a clue what that toxic shit is doing to their insides."

The commander spoke the truth. If the boys' health deteriorated, Benji and Brendan might need these three days' head start. Turning again, Wolf breathed deeply, burying the frustration and rage. The need to join Mackenzie on his mission and track down the men who'd thrown two *tei'yoonoh'o'* beneath the hooves of their greed exploded inside him like thunder.

But he had other obligations. Sacred responsibilities. Not just to his living warriors but to his dead brethren as well. Grief unfurled and pressed hard against his chest, dampening the frustrated rage. To assure his dead warriors connected with Shining Man above, the smudging ceremony had to proceed. He needed these three days.

But Amy and her *tei'yoonoh'o'* should not have to wait. "You'll take your men?"

Mackenzie's snort and eye roll expressed his opinion of that question. Wolf simply nodded.

"I'll arrange it." Before he could retreat into headquarters, Mackenzie grabbed his arm.

"What the hell's going on with Faith's doomsday device?"

Locking down another spike of irritation, Wolf calmly shook his bicep free. Apparently his capitulation had emboldened the man to demand even more time and answers. Typical.

"Classified," he drawled, knowing the answer would stir the storm clouds again.

Mackenzie's description of Ansell's clean energy generator fit well. Doomsday device, indeed. If Manheim and his cronies activated the machine and managed to mentally link with it, if it augmented their brains' patterns as the machine had done to Dr. Ansell, and if it allowed them to blow up something with a mere thought or kill with a single word . . . yes, the world *would* suffer unholy consequences.

How did one fight such enemies?

That was if they didn't simply rewire it and turn it into some kind of bomb. His mouth tightened. They needed to find the damn thing. Destroy it. Destroy every schematic associated with it. Which was easier said than done when they didn't have a location on the device or the man who currently possessed it.

But perhaps Neniiseti's spirit walking would change that. If Shining Man was willing and the cedar smoke smudged in the right direction, the device's location would be theirs. He forced back a chill of unease. Neniiseti' had plenty of experience navigating the shadow world, but the spirits were capricious and not always to be trusted. They had no way of knowing whether such a journey would prove victorious and give them the location of the device or send them down a rabbit's warren and lure Neniiseti' too deep into Shining Man's web.

"I must go." Before Wolf had a chance to turn, Mackenzie started talking.

"Cos says you lost everyone on that second chopper when it went down." A mix of grimness and sympathy rasped through his voice. "Just wanted you to know how sorry I am—we all are—about that."

Wolf inhaled deeply, breathing through the grief. For a second the agony of dozens of lives ended raged through him again. Although mental linking gave them major advantages during insertions, it carried serious consequences as well. The worst of which was experiencing your brothers' *hiihooteet* through the link, their pain and fear, the sudden absence of their mind followed by that vast emptiness where vibrant personalities had once dwelled. But to lose twelve within seconds . . .

the gray, wintery plains of grief sucked at him, tried to pull him under. He shook off the tide. The vigil would soon begin, followed by the freeing ceremony. Neither would be open to outsiders.

"Appreciate it." Wolf rolled his shoulders, trying to release the tension. Just when he thought he had Mackenzie figured out, the man turned all human on him.

"I know what it feels like to lose men. Good men. Me and the boys, we'd like to pay our respects if you'll let us know when and where."

The mental screams and prayers of a dozen minds as their lives ended echoed through Wolf's mind in a chaotic jumble. The cold, impersonal loss of life in Mackenzie's world was worlds apart from the immediate, agonizing loss of life in his.

"Appreciate it," he said again without extending an offer to Mackenzie or his team. The smudging ceremony would be held in private, void of curious eyes—as such matters always were.

To Wolf's relief Mackenzie's face shifted from sympathy to calculation. "When can I get the chopper?"

"Soon." Which was the best he could do until he spoke to Neniiseti'.

"Soon as in today? Tomorrow? Or three days from now?" Mackenzie demanded, his face collapsing into a scowl.

"You'll be the second to know." To Wolf's surprise, Mackenzie backed up a few paces. But he didn't turn to go. Clearly he had another subject on his mind. He waited a few moments for the man to spit it out, and when the commander's mouth remained shut, he cocked his head. "And?"

"Hell." A grumbling curse shook the air. Mackenzie took a deep breath before continuing with obvious reluctance. "My men's womenfolk are asking about Jillian. They're concerned about her."

Wolf tensed and crossed his arms. "I am aware."

His sister had turned into a veritable shrew on the subject. However, he found it unlikely that Mackenzie shared their worry. Black Cloud was not one to engage in concern for those outside his command. This topic read more like a ruse, perhaps to gain access to Jillian for further interrogation. Mackenzie had made it bluntly clear he still had questions for his *heneeceine3* and didn't believe she'd told them everything she knew about her brother's movements or her kidnappers' agenda. But the last thing Jillian needed was a reminder that her beloved twin brother had been a sociopathic murderer and the mastermind behind the attempted hijacking of flight 2077.

"It is not my call on whom or when Jillian visits. She will step out when she is ready."

Except she showed no interest in leaving her room or in eating, drinking, even showering. He shook the worry aside and refocused.

Everyone needed to practice patience when it came to his lioness. He most of all. He'd known from the moment of their meeting that she wasn't mentally or emotionally stable—in no shape to give him what he needed from her. Understandable, given the circumstances of her children's murders and her brother's betrayal. But the question that haunted him was whether she would ever be ready.

Whether she would ever heal enough to start a new life or take on a new love, even a new family.

Or whether he was doomed to spend his days walking the earth, craving that which could never be his.

Chapter Four

FIGHTING A SCOWL, MAC SHIFTED UNCOMFORTABLY AGAINST THE wood backrest. The chair he occupied had come with his quarters, as had the Formica table, couch, television, and double bed.

The bed was tucked into the corner next to the head, partially concealed behind a four-foot privacy wall that separated the sleeping and living areas. The cramped space and bare walls resembled the dozen or so military barracks he'd lived in through the years—confined quarters that he'd never felt self-conscious about, or uncomfortable in, or any of the other annoying emotions currently squirming through him.

It was just a bed, for fuck's sake. Nothing he hadn't completely ignored while entertaining guests in his small, one-room quarters in the past. Hell, the three huge, battle-hardened men hunkered around the Formica table with their glass tumblers glowing amber beneath their load of Jack Daniel's could have been a replay of that night a week ago, just before the botched rescue attempt of Faith's boss and lab mates. He sure as hell hadn't been focused on his bed back then.

Of course, the light scent of something sweet and fresh hadn't ransacked the air back then either. Nor had the petite, athletic figure of Amy Chastain occupied a fifth chair. Too bad he hadn't considered their meeting place more carefully. If he'd realized her presence in his quarters, so close to his bed, would hype up his imagination and hormones, he'd have chosen other accommodations.

Like the chapel.

He took a deep, careful breath and tried to avoid looking at the woman across the table or the bed across the room. Except that damn fresh scent of hers, which had been driving him crazy for months, snuck into his mouth and down his throat.

His chest seized. A storm of coughing erupted, evicting the air from his lungs.

Christ . . .

It took him forever to get the coughing under control. When he locked the spasms down and turned watering eyes on the faces surrounding him, he found every gaze fixed on him with varying degrees of concern.

Fuck.

He waved a dismissive hand and worked to smooth the roughness from his voice. "Swallowed wrong."

Which would have been an excellent excuse if his lungs had tried to kill him a minute earlier, like immediately after his last upload of JD. Luckily, none of the people circling his table were mind readers.

"As I was saying." He cleared his throat, only to freeze as a tickle dug in, threatening to set off another fit of coughing. Once the tickle faded, he continued. "We've got our bird. The Jayhawk, not their black ops special. But it will get us down there and back in good time."

Concern faded in the eyes surrounding him.

"Where we settin' down?" Rawls leaned so far back in his chair, the front two legs left the laminate floor. "We'll need to file a flight plan. No sense in goin' in dark and raisin' questions."

Nods traveled the table.

"We'll need to arrange a ride from drop-off too," Cosky pointed out slowly. Judging from the distant look in his eyes, he was ticking off items in his head.

"No need." Mac relaxed as his throat and lungs behaved. "Wolf said he'd handle all that once we settled on location." Which had been magnanimous of the big bastard. "Best bet's inserting at 0-dark-100. Let's not give the asshole a chance to arrange a welcome squad."

He forced himself not to glance in Amy's direction. Her brother was an asshole, a first-class one. He wasn't telling her anything she didn't already know.

Still . . . a tinge of shame whipped through him.

"Clay lives on Mercer Island." Her voice was matter-of-fact.

An even stronger flicker of shame zipped through him. Regardless of whether the fuckwad deserved it, Amy loved her brother. It wouldn't kill him to be a bit more circumspect.

Zane picked up his phone and tapped on the screen for a few seconds. "Closest airport that allows private aircraft is King County International Airport." He lifted his head. "That's our set down." As he twisted to look at Amy, the wood feet of his chair squawked against the flooring. "What about your brother? Will he be home? How much traveling does he do for the feds?"

"Not much." Her answer was slow, precise, as though she were measuring each word before she released it. "Most of his assignments keep him close to home." She paused, her forehead knitted. "I still have contacts in the Seattle field office. I can ask around—"

"Fuck, no," Mac broke in. Every muscle in his body tightened at her suggestion.

She had no clue who she could trust and who'd sell her out for a pile of money or a favor down the road. "We know there's a leak in the Seattle field office. We can't afford you contacting the leak."

Amy folded her arms across her breasts. Her chin tilted up.

"What would you suggest? It's not like I can call him and ask if he'll be home, can I? That wouldn't be suspicious at all." She shook her head, sending her short red hair fluttering, a combative gleam glittering in her eyes.

Mac scowled. The woman sure had a sassy mouth on her. It was a source of constant consternation that he found that fault so fucking appealing.

Cosky glanced between Amy and Mac. Slowly, his thick black eyebrows rose. His gaze shifted from cool to amused and knowing.

Fuck.

"Wolf's got impressive connections," Cosky reminded them. "He can probably hook us up with SAT surveillance."

True. Shadow Mountain was remarkably well funded. Hell, maybe they'd hung their own satellite up there in the thermosphere, which would explain how they'd gotten the intel on the lab so fast last week.

"We can use thermal optics on-site as well. Check for a heat signature before inserting," Zane pointed out, his expression as calm as ever. He hit Mac with a dry look. "We're not bananas. We know what we're doing."

With a grimace, Mac let the rebuke slide. Letting his aggravation with himself lead him into stupid territory had been a plebe mistake. Damn it, he needed to get his fucking mind back in the game. Or sit this op out.

"I'll talk to Wolf." He leaned across the table, snagged the bottle of Jack, and dumped two inches of glowing liquid into his tumbler. "I don't suppose you have a key to his place?" He slid a questioning glance in Amy's direction, grimacing when his chest and lungs turned all squirrelly again.

"No. Clay's never been the trusting sort." She reached over and drew the fifth tumbler toward her, nodding when Mac lifted the bottle of Jack. When the whiskey hit the two-finger mark, she waved off the bottle and absently rotated the glass over and over again. "Mom and Dad don't even have a key. I assume that's not a problem?"

Her voice and expression were so calm you'd never know she was discussing breaking into her brother's house.

Rawls snorted and held up his drink to peer into the amber depths. "Nothing an unseasoned plebe couldn't take care of."

Mac eyed his corpsman's glass.

At least Rawls hadn't hit the bottle after that near-death experience had fucked up his head. Too many good men turned to the temporary solace of alcohol, only to drown beneath the constant craving. A face took shape in his mind. Dark hair, haunted eyes, a face far too similar to his for comfort.

But then he wouldn't call his old man a good man. Love had turned him too fucking weak for that description.

"How many entrances are we looking at?" Mac asked.

The skin around Amy's eyes crinkled as she thought about it. "Three. Front, rear, and a door through the garage."

"The place has to be wired." Rawls leaned forward, and the front legs of his chair fell back to the ground with a solid thud. "Considering his career choice, it would be plain foolishness if he didn't have a security system in place."

Amy nodded. "He has an alarm." She shrugged, then added before anyone had a chance to ask, "I have no idea what the disarm code is."

Zane pushed his chair back and climbed to his feet. "Doesn't matter. It should be easy enough to disable from outside. Or, hell"—he stifled a yawn—"there are all sorts of electronics that can disarm with the touch of a button."

Rawls followed Zane's lead and got up from the table. "I'll ask Faith what electronics they have in that candy store of a lab she's been playin' about in." He paused while a yawn elongated his face and squinted his eyes. "Bet she can hook us up with somethin' sweet."

Mac grunted in acknowledgment as Cos pushed back his chair. Apparently the meeting was over. He scowled at Amy, urging her to follow his men to her feet and head for the door. The last fucking thing he needed was an after-meeting chat involving just the two of them.

Not when his bed was all but waving its bedcovers and rocking its springs in an attempt to catch his attention and convince Amy to move the meeting into the bedroom.

When his men moved across the room in a tight herd of big bodies and broad shoulders, and Amy didn't try to join them, Mac jolted up from the table.

"Think I'll hit the gym," he announced, grabbing the first excuse for leaving his quarters that popped into his mind.

"The gym?" His men stopped in unison, but it was Rawls's voice that climbed the air in disbelief. "When have you ever hit the gym?"

Mac fought back a grimace. His corpsman had a point. He should have wrestled up a more realistic excuse. Time to get the cause of his current mental fugue out of the room. To his relief, she seemed to get the hint. With a subtle shimmy of shoulders and hips, she rose to her feet.

Thank Christ.

"This sudden interest in exercise might just throw your heart into revolt." Rawls tossed him a wicked grin. "Wouldn't hurt to have one of us spot you."

Jackass.

"Pretty sure I can handle a couple of sets on my own."

Rawls snorted and shook his head. "I dunno, Commander. You ain't getting any younger."

His corpsman opened the door and stepped into the hallway, flashing Mac a taunting smile before heading down the hall. Zane and Cosky were hard on his heels. As Amy converged on the door, his bed leered at Mac from six feet to the right, reminding him that it was big enough for two.

She stopped for a moment at the open door and held Mac's gaze. "Let me know as soon as you have the schedule. I'll need to arrange for someone to watch the boys."

Mac grunted in acknowledgment. Maybe if his mother had exhibited even trace elements of Amy's concern for her children, his own brother—Davey—would still be alive. But, no, Mommy Dearest had been all about instant gratification and pure selfishness, and Davey had paid the ultimate price.

When Amy finally stepped into the hall, Mac instantly shut the door behind her. A deep, relieved breath lifted and expanded his chest. Big mistake. That fresh, clean scent of hers attacked his lungs again. Light-headed and hungry, he planted his feet and fought the urge to throw the door wide open, thrust out his head, and call her back into the room . . . and sure as hell not for a chat.

Son of a bitch.

A workout might be just the thing to beat his libido into submission. After another breath, shallower this time, he opened the door again.

To the left, Amy's figure was about a quarter the size of normal and quickly getting smaller.

Thank you, Jesus.

He stepped out as quietly as possible, pulled the door shut behind him, and beat a hasty retreat to the right. His route meant he'd have to cross over and then back down to the left. It would also take twice as long to reach his destination—but he wouldn't run the risk of bumping into her in his current horny state.

As it turned out, the exercise was exactly what he needed. An hour and a half later, when he stumbled into his quarters on legs the consistency of fresh cement, nothing was on his mind except a hot shower and some shut-eye. He stood beneath the steamy spray, letting it wash away the stink of exertion until the water lost its heat. After drying off, he collapsed into bed.

Where an all-too-familiar clean scent wrapped around him, liquefying him from the inside out and then sneaking past his defenses to infiltrate his dreams.

The acre of thick brush and towering maples that surrounded her brother's property closed in around Amy, sheathing her in hushed stillness. During the day, with the sun illuminating the landscape, Clay's driveway was long, damp, and thick with shadows. But at two hours past midnight, with night-vision goggles frosting everything an eerie green, the property got downright spooky. Add in the noxious combination of decomposition and dankness hanging in the air, and that creepiness tripled.

Monster-movie creepy.

She looked up when she reached a break in the vegetation. A stream of clouds laced the moon's silver glow.

A monster moon.

Chills prickled her spine, tightening the knot of foreboding lurking beneath her skin.

Not that she believed in monsters. At least not the paranormal kind. But then, according to psychologists, the rampaging creatures that terrified generation after generation across the pages of books and on movie screens were simply metaphors brought to life. Metaphors for the monstrosities that lurked within human nature.

That she believed.

Human nature was the real monster—capable of committing the most horrific acts in the name of greed, hate, fear, lust, or plain old boredom.

A memory seared her mind: the burn of ropes binding wrists and ankles . . . the flash of a tattoo. With a shudder she forced the flashback aside, buried it deep within her mind.

No time for that.

Except she could sense the meltdown brewing. Sense the rage and grief and horror clawing their way to the surface. Sometimes the urge to throw back her head and scream was so strong, it was hard to hold back the shrieks. Anything to ease the pressure shredding her from the inside. Anything to let the grief flood free. Let her screams challenge the sky until her throat was raw and her voice was gone and the memories were . . . absent.

Until the screams purified her.

The sigh that shook her was part frustration and part acceptance. She couldn't let go. Not yet. Not with the boys in danger. No way were those unconscionable bastards who'd orchestrated this nightmare and murdered her husband stealing her boys from her too.

No way.

Setting her jaw, she picked up her pace and focused on the pair of fluorescent-green shoulders fifteen feet ahead. The knot in her belly loosened. The four men fanned out in front of her were all business. They slipped through the brush and trees with tense muscles and fluid strides. One of the men halted for a moment. His torso twisted as his goggle-shrouded face looked over his shoulder, directly at her.

Mackenzie.

From this distance the four men looked identical. Lean, muscular bodies. Smooth, athletic strides. Helmets, with attached NVDs, shrouded their heads, so their hair was covered. Nothing about the man who'd turned pointed to Mackenzie.

Yet she knew with absolute certainty that he'd been the one to check on her. She knew it was him by the way her muscles loosened and the churning in her belly stilled. By the calmness that fell over her, reining in her heart rate and respiration.

The man had a soothing effect on her. His presence acted as a sedative, easing the sharp edges of memories and fears. He made her feel . . . indestructible. Safe. Capable of handling anything, including the men who'd pinned targets on her children's backs.

She had no clue why Mackenzie had such a profound effect on her. It made no sense whatsoever. The commander was a foul-mouthed, misogynistic jerk with a short temper and a chip on his shoulder. Qualities she normally loathed in a man.

In a world gone suddenly crazy, her reaction to such an alpha jackass was one of the craziest things of all.

But then the few times he'd tried to pull that alpha jackassery on her, she'd shut him down fast. Oh, he'd been irritable about it, but she'd gotten her way. He might not bury her in compliments or seek out her counsel, but he listened to what she had to say and acted on it more often than not.

For such a suspicious man, he'd made some pretty stunning concessions for her. This was the second mission he'd led that she'd been included in. And she'd been included in everything from planning to insertion. Which meant he trusted her in the field.

Even back in the beginning, in that horrible house when Mac and his team had swept in to rescue them, he'd trusted her enough to pass her a gun . . . twice. He'd relied on her to protect herself and her boys. For a man like Mackenzie, that spoke volumes.

John had trusted her too—to remain faithful, to take care of the boys and the house. To balance their checkbook. To pay the bills. He'd trusted her with the mundaneness of everyday life.

But he'd shown no faith in her professional capabilities. He hadn't believed she could take care of herself in dangerous situations or use her training and intelligence to return home safely each night. Instead, in the early days of their marriage, he'd worn her down with the constant drip, drip, drip of his passive-aggressive insistence that she take a break from active duty.

She'd done so because she'd understood his fear. Understood that the ghosts of his first family, and their horrifying deaths as they burned inside their car, still haunted his dreams and pulled his strings. For their marriage to work, one of them would have to give in, and with John's history, it wouldn't be him.

But giving up something she'd loved, something she'd excelled at, because the man she'd married couldn't see her abilities or accept her for who she was . . . well, it had pinched something inside her.

Then had come the kidnapping. John hadn't trusted her then either—hadn't believed she could free herself, that she could outwit or outmaneuver the men who'd held them captive. Instead he'd betrayed his office, his oath, and every passenger on that plane by yielding to the NRO. He'd let them use him to hijack that plane, following their directions in a desperate attempt to make sure she and their children survived.

She hated the sense of betrayal and guilt that knowledge brought. Her reaction to his sacrifice made no sense; she knew that. She'd been helpless. Outnumbered. Outgunned. She hadn't managed to free herself, let alone the boys, before Mackenzie had shown up. She had no right to feel so angry and let down by John's actions. He'd given up everything to make sure she and the kids survived. Everything—his reputation, his career, even his life.

But knowing this made no difference. It didn't lessen the ugly mixture of rage and guilt swelling within her. It didn't—

At the sound of a low whistle, her head snapped up. Mackenzie and his men had halted amid the final tangle of brush pressing against her brother's manicured lawn. She joined them.

"Cos and Zane, take the front. Amy and I will take the back. Rawls, keep your eyes on the garage," Mac whispered.

Mac's night-vision goggles swiveled her way again. "You ready?"

She nodded.

Mac swung his head in Zane's direction. "Take out your lock in three. Rawls, hit the scrambler."

In unison, the men broke from the tree line and approached their targets in a truncated lope. Mac crossed the lawn at an angle, with Amy on his heels. She followed him to a spiky metal fence partially concealed by a neat row of eight-foot arborvitaes and waited for him to ease open the metal gate. The springs gave way with a protesting screech, and they slipped through.

The pool looked putrid but luminous through the NVDs as the water reflected the moon's iridescent glow. They flanked the edge of the house, ducking beneath windows and skirting the L-shaped state-of-the-art barbecue station that was Clay's pride and joy.

Mac closed in on the patio's sliding-glass door. From the front of the house came the muffled report of a shotgun. Cosky had just unlocked the front door. Amy watched Mac raise his gun and winced. Clay would give her hell for the damage to his doors.

Squaring her shoulders, she kicked up her chin. If Clay had tried to meet her halfway, this drastic step wouldn't be necessary. Her brother knew who'd injected the boys; it was time he shared that information with her.

"Drop your weapons." Her brother's flat, cool voice sounded from behind them.

Mac froze, then slowly lifted the shotgun into the air.

"I said, drop them." Clay's voice sharpened. "Both of you. Weapons on the ground. Nice and easy. Call your buddies over. I want everyone where I can see them."

She needed to identify herself before someone got shot.

"Clay—it's me. Amy." She kept perfectly still, hands in the air, waiting for him to acknowledge her.

"Amy?" His voice rose in disbelief and anger.

Slowly turning, she watched him step out of the shadows and into her NVD's green glow. His gun was pointed directly at her.

"What the Goddamn fuck do you think you're doing?" His voice climbed with each word.

She kept her hands in the air and her voice calm. He sounded pissed enough to shoot her. "I need to talk to you."

"And you couldn't call? Or knock on my door? Instead you show up in the middle of the night, with guns? Are you fucking crazy?" His voice rose even higher.

Amy chose her words with care. "I needed to see you in person, but it isn't safe to talk on the phone or come during the day."

"Isn't safe?" Clay snorted, his pistol migrating in Mac's direction. "Let me guess—Mackenzie, right? It's safe to pair up with him? He's wanted in a string of murders." A flat, contemplative tone chilled his voice. "Hell, I could take the whole fucking lot of you out right now, and nobody would even blink."

The tiny hairs on the back of her neck lifted. His tone was calculating, like he was actually considering that action. No . . . he couldn't possibly be thinking about cold-blooded murder. "Clay—"

"Shut up." The gun shifted back to her, and she saw his finger tense around the trigger. A flash of hatred flickered across his face.

He's never liked us, Mom. He might smile with his mouth, but his eyes are mean.

Her stomach flipped and then contracted violently. Three dozen years of interactions flashed through her mind. His gaze seemed to get colder and flatter with each passing memory.

"I'd rethink that threat if I were ya," Rawls drawled from the huge azalea bush behind Clay. "While you're at it, how 'bout you drop that gun before I fill you with holes I'll just have to patch later?"

Clay froze for a second, his gun still locked on Amy's chest.

The tight knot in Amy's stomach soured. He wanted to pull the trigger. Even in the green glaze of the NVDs, she could see the ferociousness stamped on his face. Her brother, her only sibling, wanted to kill her.

The acid in her stomach burned up her throat. How could she have missed this?

"Take that fucking gun off her *now*." Mac's voice held a violent edge.

Another long hesitation, and then Clay bent and set his pistol on the flagstone surrounding the pool. Two seconds later, Rawls shoved him to the ground and held him there with a hand on the back of his neck and a knee to his spine.

"Congratulations, assholes." Clay's words were guttural, like they'd been forced through his teeth. "You're just determined to add more charges to the ones pending, aren't you?"

"Yeah, yeah," Cosky said, his voice mocking. He stepped out of the shrubbery, followed by Zane. The two men headed for Rawls, patted Clay down, and then zip-tied his wrists behind his back.

"He's all yours, darlin'," Rawls told her. He and Cosky dragged Clay to his feet.

Amy pulled off her helmet. Clay's face looked statue cold in the moonlight.

Her chest tightened until it hurt to breathe. *He wanted her dead.*

"I hope you have a damn good reason for this insanity," Clay said, icy malice shimmering in his eyes.

"You gave me no choice. You wouldn't listen to me." She moved closer. Close enough to see every facial tic, every flicker of emotion, all the cues from his body language and posture. "There was something in that shot you gave the boys. I need to know what it was. Where you got it from. How to reverse it."

"You're crazy." While his tone was dismissive, an expression flared in his eyes. One that looked an awful lot like smugness. Satisfaction. The expression leaked across his face.

He knows about the compound. He's gloating about the ramifications.

Shock detonated through her, held her immobile. And then betrayal twisted her belly, sent acid surging up her throat.

He knew.

Mac was right. Clay had been instrumental in injecting the boys.

A flood of rage roared through her, cauterizing the shock.

Suddenly she was in front of him, swinging her fist with all her strength.

Thud.

Clay's head snapped back.

A red-rinsed haze enveloped her mind. *He knew.*

Thud.

He did it on purpose.

Thud . . . thud.

Arms wrapped around her waist from behind, dragged her back.

"That's enough, slugger. You want him awake and his mouth working," Mac said, his voice matter-of-fact, maybe even a bit impressed.

Clay spit out a wad of blood and glared at her through a rapidly reddening eye. "Nice, Ames. My hands are tied. I can't hit back."

This time she recognized the hatred twisting his face.

"They're children. Brendan's your godchild. How could you? *How could you do this to them?*" It wasn't what she meant to ask, but the words were out there now, hanging in the air. Too late to call back.

"You can't prove anything." He drew out the words in one long, gloating taunt. "Nobody is going to believe you."

He hadn't denied it. In fact, he'd all but admitted his complicity. Disbelief held her immobile. Struck her dumb.

How could I have missed this?

The wrath swelled again. Demanded vengeance.

She sucked in a deep breath and locked down the fury and disbelief, concentrating on her children.

"I'm not looking to prove it," she said flatly. "I'm looking to undo it, and you're going to help me with that."

He smirked, a laugh slanting his swelling lips. "Seriously? 'Cause I have to say, Ames"—he rubbed his swelling lip against his shoulder—"I'm not feeling inclined to do anything for you."

"Doesn't matter whether you're inclined or not, asshole." Mac shot Clay a look of pure contempt before turning to Rawls. "Grab the med kit." He glanced at Amy. "Wolf gave us some shit that acts like sodium thiopental, only on steroids. We can make him give us the answers we need."

Another unknown drug? Unease squirmed through her. "Is it safe?"

Mac shrugged. "Safer than beating the information out of him." He paused. "Lady's choice."

"Let's get real." Clay's voice was smug. "Ames isn't going to let you shoot me up with that shit."

"Really?" It was Mac's turn to sneer. "You injected her kids with shit far more dangerous. She won't even hesitate."

Mac was right. There was no hesitation. "Do it."

The smugness on Clay's face disintegrated. "You bitch!"

She turned from the frustrated hatred in her brother's eyes to watch Rawls draw clear liquid from a vial into a syringe. "How long until the drug takes effect?"

"Five minutes, according to Wolf." His eyes never budged from the needle.

She squared her shoulders. Five minutes, and she'd have answers. And not just the ones she needed for the boys, but the ones she needed for closure. Why had he done this to her? To the boys? Brendan had been right. Clay did seem to hate them, but why? What had she ever done to him?

"Get him in one of the chairs," Rawls said as he set the vial back in his med kit and flicked the syringe.

Cosky's hand tightened around Clay's elbow, but before he had a chance to drag their captive toward one of the pool chairs, Clay jerked, a startled *humph* breaking from him.

A spot of red appeared on his chest and quickly spread across his white T-shirt. He crumpled.

She was still staring at the spreading stain when two hundred pounds of pure muscle tackled her, shoving her behind the barbecue station.

"Shots fired!" Mac yelled.

Stunned, Amy lay curled on her side beneath Mac's heavy body, listening to the urgent thump of his heart.

"Sound off," Mac said from above her.

"Five by five," Zane and Cosky said, their all-clear indication flowing through Mac's headset.

"Five by five." Rawls's voice.

Amy felt Mac's muscles loosen. He looked down, directly into her eyes, his gaze calm. "You okay?"

She managed a nod. Her body relaxed as his heat seeped into her. Fear, confusion, rage—it all melted beneath his warmth.

"He's using a suppresser," Mac said, his voice a rumble above her head. His chest lifted as he breathed. "It's gonna be a bitch locating his position."

He meant the shooter. The red stain enveloping her brother's shirt bloomed in her mind.

"Clay?" She forced the question out her tight throat.

"He took a round to the chest. Another to the head." Cosky's voice came through Mac's headset. "I'm sorry, Amy. He was gone before I got him to cover."

Gone?

A numb feeling spread through her body, buzzed in her head.

Clay was dead?

"Anyone else hit?" Rawls asked calmly. His question was followed by a string of negatives.

Mac pressed his palms against the flagstone and levered himself off her. Amy fought the insane impulse to drag him back down, to burrow into his hot body and lose herself in his arms. Even amid the chaos and danger, there had been something comforting about his weight pressing her into the ground.

Mac cleared his throat. "We need to move, boys. We can't afford to be caught here. Sure as hell we'll catch the blame for Purcell's murder."

Murder . . . her brother had been murdered.

A wave of unreality swamped her. Clay was dead. She forced herself to think. Everyone had been visible on the patio. The assassin could have taken any of them. But he'd chosen Clay. Shot him twice.

"The shooter was after Clay." She spoke the realization aloud.

Had her brother been meeting someone? Was that why he'd been armed, dressed, and outside at two in the morning? If so, whoever he'd been meeting had killed him. It was the only thing that made sense.

"If he was after Purcell, he could be gone." Mac's tone was calculating. "There's been no action since the original shots. Regardless, we need to move. The boys will cover us. Once we get in the house, we'll cover them."

With a short nod of agreement, she rose to the pads of her feet, her hand grabbing his. He froze. Slowly, his goggle-shrouded head turned in her direction. His fingers tightened around hers, and a spark jumped between them.

The tingle in her fingers spread all the way up her arm and down her spine.

"Cover us," Mac growled into his mic, and gunfire broke out.

The earlier shots had been suppressed, but the current ones were loud enough to wake Clay's neighbors. They needed to vacate the area ASAP.

Mac pulled Amy in front of him. They raced for the door as gunfire ripped into the night from behind them. With each step Amy listened for a grunt, groan, or startled huff from Mac.

His breath was hot and moist against the back of her neck as they closed in on the sliding-glass door. In fact, he was so close his big body heated her from ankle to shoulder.

Something about that niggled at her.

Then they were through the door. Instantly Mac pushed her to the left, behind the safety of a solid wall, and stepped in front of her. That's when it hit. He'd used his body as a shield to protect her on the race to the door. He was doing the same thing now, defending her from possible danger.

Good Lord, the misogynistic jackass persona he presented to the world was nothing but camouflage. Who would have thought it? Commander Mackenzie was a white knight at heart.

Chapter Five

MAC TWISTED IN THE BUCKET SEAT ON THEIR RIDE TO THE AIRPORT, watching Amy. She sat with her body curved toward the door, forehead pressed against the passenger window. She hadn't said a word since leaving Purcell's place.

He shifted uneasily, the fabric backrest of his seat making a *shushing* sound. Which was so fucking applicable, since platitudes hovered on the tip of his tongue. Nothing he said would help. He knew that. So yeah . . . *shush* . . . *shush* . . . Excellent advice, even if it came from a seat cushion.

Except . . . there was something isolated and lonely about her rigid figure staring out the passenger window. Something lost.

Defeated, even.

To watch her brother die . . . that had to be hard enough. But to lose him essentially twice in the span of minutes—hell, that had to be much worse. To find out he'd betrayed her, betrayed her kids, only to watch him die before she could get any answers. Before she could find out how to save her children.

Jesus.

The urge to lean over and wrap her in his arms was a constant burning itch. To provide the comfort and support she so clearly needed. Prove to her that she wasn't alone. That the battle to save her children sat on all their shoulders, not just hers. She had people in her corner, people who cared about her. Who cared about her kids.

The only thing that saved him from acting on the impulse and looking the fool was the empty space between their seats and the three pairs of watchful eyes studying him from their various corners.

"I need to call Mom and Dad," Amy suddenly said, her voice low but steady.

Mac winced. "You'll have to wait until news of his murder goes public. You can't afford to announce he's dead before his body is discovered."

When she lapsed back into silence, Mac grimaced. Hell, the last thing she needed right now was the king of common sense. The voice of reason. Cold practicality against her pain. Regardless of what Purcell had done, he'd still been her brother, and human emotions took longer than half an hour to switch off. She had to be hurting, for a multitude of reasons. None of which he could ease for her.

Damn it.

"I'm sorry about your brother." The words stumbled from him with no thought, no preparation. He coughed to clear his throat and tried for a supportive, reassuring tone. "I know this wasn't the end you were hoping for—" Hell, he sounded like a fucked-up Hallmark card. He soldiered on, growing brusquer and more uncomfortable with each word that tripped out of his lame-ass mouth. "But don't you worry about your boys. We still have options. We'll find the antidote. You aren't alone. Okay."

Christ. Could he have mangled that any worse?

A round of muttered agreement came from the front and back seats.

To his surprise, Amy straightened, drew back her shoulders, and turned to face him. He wanted to lay claim to her renewed confidence, but the woman had proven she was molded from sturdy stuff.

Unbreakable stuff. She'd probably needed only a few minutes to regroup before dusting off her hands and squaring up again.

"With Clay gone"—her voice caught—"our best chance of finding out what they injected in the boys is with James Link."

Relieved that the conversation had turned to strategy, Mac nodded. "Agreed. Link's our best bet."

Pachico's revelations aside, the isotope was exactly the kind of scientific breakthrough Dynamic Solutions was known for. Hell, even if Link wasn't involved with the NRO, as Pachico had claimed, he should still know who had created the tracking compound.

But the relief quickly turned to frustration. Agreeing that Link was their most viable target didn't do them a lick of good. They didn't know where the damn man was. Hell, even if they located him, they didn't have the manpower or resources to mount an effective interception.

He scowled. Damn it to hell. He could sense another round of favor-asking in his future.

"As the acting CEO of a multibillion-dollar company, Link will be tricky to get to." Zane turned to look at them from the passenger seat up front, his calm gaze shifting between Amy and Mac.

"Grabbing him will be damn near impossible," Cosky agreed as he merged onto I-5. "A guy like that? He's bound to have a state-of-the-art fortress. Bodyguards. We'll be lucky if we get within a hundred feet of him."

True. Mac frowned. "None of which makes him invulnerable. We'll have to get creative. Grab him while he's on the move."

"If Link is involved in the New Ruling Order, as Shadow Mountain intel suggests, they have a vested interest in grabbing him too," Amy said slowly, staring at the back of Zane's seat. "We can probably count on them for help."

Mac nodded, biting back another scowl. Fuck, he hated like hell groveling before Wolf, even if Shadow Mountain was after the NRO themselves. Lately it seemed like all he did was beg for favors.

"We won't be able to move on Link immediately. Wolf doesn't have a team available," Mac said, resignation setting in.

They'd have to wait until Shadow Mountain could assist. They needed more men, more support, and more intel. They needed Shadow Mountain's resources. It would be worth it, though. Link was their best bet, both to save Amy's kids and to track down the men responsible for the past six months of death and betrayal.

He just had to convince Wolf of that.

"A few days will give us time to do some investigatin', track down Link's movements, check his protection detail," Rawls said from the back seat.

Amy nodded, turning to the window. She went back to her silent staring, her profile hazy in the shadowy interior of the car. She looked more fragile than Mac had ever seen her.

His gaze tracked the vulnerable curve of her neck and spine. It was the darkness, he realized. It blurred her strength, masked the expression on her face and the acuity of her eyes. He'd never realized how the calm control of her face and the sharp intelligence in her gaze had combined to give her that impression of capability.

Which was the real Amy? This indistinct, fragile woman—or the one who radiated confidence and ability?

Maybe neither. Maybe both. Or maybe there was an Amy in between.

The urge to reach for her hit again. To fold her in his arms and anchor her against his chest. To just hold her, protect her, support her until she was ready to face the world again. Although how much of the urge was altruistic and how much was based on the primeval impulse to feel her against him again was open to question.

She'd felt so good back there on the patio. Perfect. Firm and feminine. Her curves pressing against him in all the right places. Even with the bullets flying and death surrounding them, he'd been intimately aware of the woman pinned beneath him.

He'd been wondering for weeks how they'd fit together. Would she be firm and strong, or soft and pliable? Would her body give beneath his, or wrestle for dominance?

Well, he had the answers to those questions now, along with a new memory to taunt him. He'd been far too focused on the perfection of her body pressed to his. He'd wanted to lie there on top of her, soak her in. Fuck, if he was going to die, this was the way to do it. Except his death meant hers too. And there was no fucking way he would let that happen.

Still, it had taken every ounce of determination he possessed to roll off her. How insane was that? They'd been under fire, for Christ's sake. In the midst of a battle.

The very last place to give in to carnal obsession.

Which just went to prove that the woman was pure poison to him.

Dangerous to the nth degree.

"What say you, darling? Should we put in an offer? Yea? Or nay?" Eric Manheim asked his wife as he stretched back in the patio lounge chair and linked his fingers behind his head. "I must admit, the view is unparalleled."

On the other side of the wrought-iron railing, Cannes Bay stretched before them, the azure canopy dotted with dozens of brilliant-white yachts. The boats sparkled in the summer sun like fallen stars bobbing amid a liquid bed of blue. A beautiful sight from above the water. Below the surface was another matter.

The fuel, oil, and garbage those boats had dumped into the water through the years was part of the reason the ocean was dying. The Global Ocean Commission had proposed an eight-point program to rescue the ocean before it became irreparably damaged. Not that anyone had paid attention. Not that anyone had taken steps to correct the ongoing damage. Not that anyone had shown the slightest hint of concern for the bleak future the report presented.

But then the human race's gluttony and shortsightedness didn't just threaten the oceans—Earth itself was at the mercy of humanity's greedy appetite. If this planet was to continue to shelter his children, and grandchildren, and great-grandchildren, something needed to be done now, before it was too late to reverse the current course toward annihilation.

Thank God the New Ruling Order had the resources and the courage to make the necessary corrections to ensure Earth's survival.

"How much are they asking?" his wife, Esme, asked from her poolside seat. She trailed her fingers through the water of the Olympic-size pool and kicked her feet, creating mild turbulence in the calmness.

"Fifty-four. It just hit the market today." Eric turned an appreciative eye toward the villa. The house really was a work of art. Built of sleek steel and glass, it sat high on a bluff east of Cannes, with unobstructed views from all but a few of its windows.

Esme peered between the railings and sighed. "It's certainly beautiful." She sighed again, her fingers playing with the water. "It's close enough to Cannes to take advantage of the nightlife but far enough to avoid the crowds and stargazers."

Eric nodded in agreement. "I'll have Thomas put in an offer."

"It seems awfully extravagant, don't you think?" Esme smiled at him, her hair flashing platinum beneath the sunlight. "The *Esme* is perfectly fine for the amount of time we spend in Cannes."

"Perhaps." He smiled back. "But a house would be safer for children. It will give them more room to run and play, to work off that endless energy children seem to possess."

"We'll have to childproof this place, as well." Esme's gaze shifted to the gap between the railings. Pulling her feet from the water, she stood. "But there is plenty of time for that. And I quite like this place."

Eric nodded in agreement. It would be nice to have a home base in the area. A place to entertain and relax.

"So we agree then?" Eric asked quietly, and he wasn't just referring to the house. They'd been discussing the possibility of parenthood for months now.

She stared out over the bay for a moment, a pensive look on her face, then turned and walked toward him. "I believe we do."

As she settled into the recliner beside him, Eric reached out and twined his fingers with hers. He lifted her hand to his lips and brushed a gentle kiss across her knuckles. "You will make the most amazing mother."

Her laugh was barely a whisper on the warm breeze. "You realize everything will change now, yes? Everything."

"For the better, I am told." He brushed her knuckles with his lips again. "I'll have Stevens look into clinics."

They'd been trying to conceive naturally for years, in no hurry, willing to let nature take its course. But nature wasn't cooperating. It was time to find out why and rectify the problem.

"No need." Esme met his gaze, her blue eyes as calm and mysterious as the water spread before them. "I've been researching. Bernabeu in Spain has an eighty-two percent live birth ratio. I'll call tomorrow and make an appointment."

"Spain." He'd expected the top fertility clinics to be in France or the States, even the UK. But Spain? He shook his head.

"Is there a problem, darling?" Esme lifted a perfectly contoured eyebrow.

"Of course not. I'm just rather surprised the clinic is in Spain."

Her laugh this time was louder. "Careful, darling, some might call such surprise prejudice. There are top clinics throughout the world, but the Bernabeu has the best live birth rate, and since that is our ultimate goal . . ."

"Of course." Before he had a chance to continue, his cell phone rang.

He glanced at the screen and scowled. The number belonged to David Coulson—the NRO council member who'd been charged with reverse engineering Dr. Benton and Faith Ansell's clean energy generator. Of the nine members on the council, Coulson was the only one he truly despised. The American was an uncouth barbarian who preferred the bloodiest, most violent path to success.

The council had been conceived as a true democracy. Equal authority to all its members. It had worked for dozens of years—the power of democracy at its finest. Active operations were decided by majority rule. Everyone worked seamlessly, hand in hand, toward their ultimate goal, although that objective had changed through the years. And then David Coulson had wedged his way onto the council and immediately set about trying to take it over.

Somehow the bloody sod had managed to collect crucial and incriminating evidence concerning the NRO, the council members, and various operations. He'd used this evidence to force his way onto the board and protect himself from a complete family cleansing.

The only reason the damn American hadn't bulldozed his way to the head of the council was because of the incriminating evidence *they'd* collected against *him*. They'd documented several examples of Coulson's scorch-and-murder approach to business practices.

They had each other over the proverbial barrel, which meant he had to work with the man.

"Oh dear." She sighed. "Our American colleague certainly knows how to ruin a moment, doesn't he?"

"He does indeed," Eric agreed dryly. He hit the Talk button and lifted the cell to his ear. "David."

"Purcell is dead," a harsh voice said without preamble.

"What?" Eric straightened sharply. "When? How?"

"Early this morning. He was shot. A hit."

"A hit," Eric repeated, only to freeze. "You wouldn't have had anything to do with that, would you?"

The American had been lobbying to take out Purcell for weeks. Claiming the man had used up his effectiveness.

"He was of no use to us any longer. Nor could we trust him to keep his fucking mouth shut. He was a liability."

Eric stiffened. The arrogance of the man. "We discussed this at length during our last meeting. We needed him to remain in position to run interference with the FBI. The council agreed—"

"Fuck the council," Coulson growled. "He was a Goddamn liability. It's a damn good thing I moved on him when I did. Guess who he was entertaining when my man put a bullet through his head? Your SEALs."

"Mackenzie?" Eric frowned. That damn navy frog had a habit of popping up in the worst places at the worst times.

"You have any other SEALs riding your ass?" Coulson asked dryly.

Eric scowled at the dig but let it pass. "Did your guy take them out?"

He suspected not; otherwise Coulson would have led with that news.

"Unfortunately, my assassin lacked initiative. He took out his paycheck but left the other five standing." A combination of disgust and anger rumbled through the speaker.

"Five?" If you excluded Mackenzie, there were only three other SEALs on his team.

"From the description it sounds like the extra was a woman. Purcell's sister, perhaps?"

"Perhaps," Eric repeated slowly. "You said Purcell was entertaining them? They were talking?"

"Yeah, but it didn't sound like the conversation was friendly. One of Mackenzie's guys pulled a syringe. That's when my guy took his shot."

"A syringe?" The news caught Eric by surprise. Amy Chastain had been okay with them drugging her brother? Everything he'd read about the woman indicated she was loyal to Purcell. "If they were going for a syringe, Purcell didn't give anything up."

"Purcell didn't know jackshit anyway." Coulson's voice grew faint, as though he'd turned his head away. "The good news is we can swing this hit toward Mackenzie. If we can get video of them in the area, they can take the fall for Purcell's murder."

"That would work only if we had a man inside the FBI to implicate them," Eric snapped, his earlier irritation rising.

"Which won't be a problem," Coulson said, smugness rounding the syllables.

Interesting . . . "You have someone inside?"

Coulson's silence neither confirmed nor denied that possibility. It wouldn't surprise him, though. God knew the man had his hands in everything—the dirtier and more violent, the better.

"What about these SEALs and those damn Indians? Any luck running them down?" Coulson asked.

"We know they are in Alaska. Near Denali National Park."

Coulson snorted. "That's not fucking news. We knew that over a week ago. What the fuck are you waiting for? An invitation to visit?"

"I have men working on it." Although Eric's voice remained bland, his fingers cramped around his phone.

"Tell them to work faster," Coulson said. "We're hitting critical mass. We can't afford any interference."

"Production of Eden is on schedule?" Eric asked, adrenaline spiking. They were so close to reaching their goal. Something he'd only recently begun to believe was possible.

"If production levels continue at their current rate. We'll hit completion closer to the three-, then six-month marks."

"That soon?" Surprise echoed in the question.

A sharp laugh traveled through the speaker. "We promised the production team some pretty impressive bonuses, plus quadruple time, if they completed the run in half the estimated time. It's too bad none of them will live long enough to enjoy the fruits of their labor."

Eric scowled. The damn man sounded far too disgustingly pleased by the prospect of all those deaths. "Murdering an entire production line of people is bound to raise questions."

Another laugh, only this time the derision was directed at Eric. "There will be a hell of a lot more questions after the bombs go off and take out most of the earth's population, don't you think?"

Good point.

Eric turned to look out over the bay. He should save one of the devices for Cannes.

This place would be even more peaceful once they'd washed away most of humanity. Hell, maybe he should hold off on making an offer on this place.

He could probably pick it up for a penny on the million in four months' time.

Chapter Six

AMY'S PACE SLOWED TO A CRAWL AS SHE WALKED TO THE APARTMENT she shared with the boys. It had taken seven endless hours to fly back to Shadow Mountain on the Jayhawk. Seven hours of replaying the events at Clay's house over and over in her mind.

She'd hit him. Not once, not twice, but *four times.*

In her last exchange with him, she'd hit him. And then he'd died.

As she'd done for the entirety of the long trip home, she waited for the shame to rise, for the grief to swallow her. But neither emotion stirred. His betrayal, what he'd done to her sons, had burned away whatever feelings she'd had for him.

All she had left were questions. When had he turned into a monster? How could she not have noticed? For God's sake, her eleven-year-old son had recognized the monster in Clay. Mac, who'd met him—what? Once? Twice? He'd recognized the rot as well.

Yet she hadn't seen it until it was too late.

Trying to relax, she kept walking. It was 10:00 a.m. Benji and Brendan would be up, full of breakfast, awaiting her arrival.

Her head started to throb. A chaotic jumble of panic, anger, and helplessness pressed against her chest.

What are you going to tell them?

Benji would hammer her with his rapid-fire questions and a full-blown account of everything that had happened that morning.

Her steps slowed even further.

Marion would question her with grave eyes and carefully nuanced conversation in an interrogation every bit as effective as the techniques used in the FBI.

Her breathing started to hitch.

And Brendan . . . Her feet fell still. Her oldest wouldn't ask anything. No, he'd simply watch her instead with those ancient, dark eyes. Which, of the three reactions, was by far the worst.

How could she tell them that she'd failed in her quest? That Clay had died and taken to the grave with him the key to neutralizing the isotope?

She couldn't. At least not yet.

She needed a few moments of quiet. A silent haven to process what had happened, to come to terms with Clay's betrayal and death, and to accept her total failure at saving her sons. She needed a safe harbor.

Her feet started moving again but not toward her apartment. When Mac's door appeared in her line of sight, she wasn't surprised. Her subconscious had known what she needed long before her rational mind.

He already knew what had happened, so he wouldn't ask questions. And after that oh-so-awkward attempt at comforting her in the car, he'd avoid that land mine too. Although . . . there had been something sweet about his bumbling attempt to soothe her.

The man constantly surprised her.

When she reached Mac's door, she squared her shoulders and gave it a good rap. It opened immediately. His short hair was wet and tufted, and there were damp patches on his olive T-shirt, as though he'd just stepped out of the shower and dressed without drying off.

"Am I interrupting?"

He scanned her face and shrugged. "I'm headed out to grab some grub."

Something must have registered on her face because he suddenly frowned. "Or—" He stepped back, pulling the door open in a silent invitation to enter. "I can fry up some bacon and a couple of eggs."

He turned and headed for the counter in the far corner of the room, with its hot plate and coffeepot.

"Where did you get bacon and eggs?" She followed him into the room and shut the door behind her.

Instantly the chaos inside her stilled. Her breathing eased. The tension floated away.

"The cafeteria." He bent to open the minifridge tucked beneath the counter and removed a carton of eggs and a bundle wrapped in white butcher paper. "If you want something, just ask them."

Amy cocked her head thoughtfully. She suspected that was his motto. If you want something, demand it.

As he unearthed a frying pan, she made her way to the couch and settled against the corner cushion. The minute she sat down, the pressure in her chest faded. Her muscles went soft and pliable. With a silent sigh, she drew her knees to her chest and relaxed against the cushion, absently watching Mac line the pan with strips of bacon.

Her stomach rumbled as the rich scent of frying bacon saturated the air. She inhaled deeply. "According to every nutritionist out there, bacon is terribly unhealthy."

Such a pity.

He shrugged, expertly turning over the strips. "We all got to check out sometime."

Which reminded her of Clay, who'd avoided bacon, red meat, and anything linked to health risks and early death. Clay, who'd maintained the healthiest diet and lifestyle of anyone she knew. Clay, who'd checked out at forty-two thanks to a bullet to his brain.

A breath escaped her. A quick huff as disbelief hit again.

"Ah hell." Mac turned to face her, self-derision on his face. "I'm an ass. Forget I opened my damn mouth."

There he went, being all sweet again.

Amy smiled up at him. "I'm okay. Really. But you better be careful. I might forget you don't have a heart."

He scanned her face intently and then turned back to the hot plate with a rigid cast to his shoulders.

"Believe it or not, I get what you're going through," he said quietly as he ripped off a couple of paper towels and covered a plate with them. "I lost a brother too."

The news caught Amy by surprise. Lifting her head, she stared at him. "You did? How?"

"He was hit by a car." His shoulders tensed. He stood there for a long time, staring down at the hot plate, before shaking himself. "Happened a long time ago."

He scooped the bacon onto the plate, drained some of the grease from the pan into an empty coffee mug, and moved on to the carton of eggs.

"How many eggs can you handle?" he asked as he started cracking eggs and dropping them into the skillet.

"Three," she said, watching him.

He regretted bringing up his brother; she could sense it. But he'd aroused her curiosity. She knew next to nothing about the man, which shouldn't matter, yet it did.

"How old were you when he died?"

The tightness in his shoulders migrated through the rest of his body. The silence stretched on so long she didn't think he was going to answer. When he finally did, it was in a flat, measured voice devoid of emotion.

"Ten. Davey was six."

So young . . . so young to experience such a profound loss. Amy's heart ached for him. "That must have been rough."

His shoulders rolled, not quite a shrug but close enough. "I survived."

Survived? Maybe. But he obviously hadn't flourished.

"How did your parents handle your brother's death? If something like that were to happen to Benji or Brendan—God." Her arms tightened around her knees.

"It won't, because, unlike my mother, you never put your own pleasure above your children's welfare." A grim, lethal fury vibrated through each word.

She froze at the raw ferocity in his voice. Obviously she'd opened an ugly can of worms and stumbled onto the root of his misogyny. Although . . . a true misogynist wouldn't treat her the way he did. Would he?

Mac slid three surprisingly fluffy eggs onto a clean plate.

Backing away from the tension and bad memories inherent in their conversation, she turned to a new, more innocuous subject. "Where did you learn to cook like this?"

He avoided her eyes as he transferred the remaining three eggs to a second plate. "I've been cooking since I was a kid. Bacon and eggs were a main staple."

Amy mulled that over. What had he been like as a kid? Serious? Grim? When had the cynicism that rode him like a protective skin taken shape? Had Davey's death hardened him into the skeptic he was today?

Information he'd not part with easily . . . if at all. Mac was about as closed off as a person could be. Maybe that was the attraction. He was such an enigma—a dynamic combination of tenderness and rage.

"Don't forget the bacon," Amy said.

"That's my girl." He shot her a forced grin and split the bacon between the two plates. After adding a fork, he handed one to Amy.

His girl.

She mulled over her surprisingly amenable reaction to that turn of phrase.

They ate in companionable silence and then washed the plates and skillet in perfect step. Once the dishes were air-drying on the towels she'd laid out, Amy retreated to the couch. She was full, plus exhaustion was settling in, but she wasn't ready to go home. Wasn't ready to look into Brendan's eyes and admit she'd failed him. Twice. It had been her job to protect him from monsters—both real and imaginary—but the worst monster of all had had free access to her home, to her children.

How had she not realized what Clay had become?

"I was five when Mom married Dad. Clay was seven. He was small for his age; so was I. We both had red hair. We looked so much alike we could have been siblings. Mom said it was a sign, proof we were meant to be a family."

Mac frowned, an uneasy expression crossing his face. As though he could sense the turbulence in her measured words and wasn't sure how to calm the waters.

"He was a quiet kid. Eager. Always trying to please. But nothing he did was good enough for Dad. If Clay hit a double, he got, 'Why wasn't it a home run?' If he got a B on a test, it was, 'Why wasn't it an A?' Life for Clay was a constant stream of 'You gotta try harder, son. You gotta give more.' Eventually he simply stopped trying. He gave up sports. Only did what he had to in school." She caught his flat expression and blew out an exasperated breath. "I know what you're thinking, that I'm still making excuses for him . . . I'm not, honestly. I'm just—" She broke off.

Just what? Explaining? Justifying? Trying to pinpoint how her brother had turned into a monster without her noticing?

"Was he like that with you? Your dad?" Mac asked, leaning a hip against the counter and crossing his arms across his chest. He looked like a man who was super uncomfortable but determined not to show it.

"No. That was part of the problem, I think. I was good at sports. Good at school. Everything came easy to me. Dad would hold me up as this shining example of success while Clay always came up short."

Maybe that's why Clay had hated her. When had the frustration and hurt in Clay's eyes turned to something darker? When had her brother shifted from a demoralized child to a cold-blooded monster? How could she have missed that ugly metamorphosis?

Scowling, Mac pushed himself away from the counter. "What Purcell did, what he became, was not your fault. He chose his path. He's responsible for that choice, where it took him, and what it turned him into."

She laughed, a tight ironic chuckle without humor. "You sound like Dad. He's big on personal responsibility too."

The two men had other things in common as well. Like intense loyalty to their small circle of family and friends. Like a core of impenetrable honor. Their inclination to do the right thing, no matter what it cost them. Their sheer stubbornness. No matter how often they got knocked down, they'd come back up swinging. They didn't know how to give up.

They'd either get along great . . . or beat each other to a bloody pulp.

"Maybe your dad recognized the rot beneath Clay's surface," Mac said quietly. "Maybe he rode him so hard in the hopes of stomping it out."

The insight caught Amy by surprise. Had Dad recognized what Clay had the potential to become?

"You think Dad knew what a disgusting piece of human excrement Clay would turn out to be?"

The venom in her question took them both by surprise.

Mac's eyebrows lifted.

A flush heated her face. "That was unkind under the circumstances, wasn't it?"

"Hell, no." Mac stalked toward her. "What he did was unforgivable. You'd be freaking Mother Theresa if you weren't furious."

She looked down at the floor, fought the burn in her eyes. It was the oddest thing. His immediate support made her want to cry.

"How could I not have seen the monster he turned into? You saw it. Brendan saw it." She wasn't aware she'd asked the question aloud until Mac answered.

"Because you're loyal. Family matters to you. You give those you love the benefit of the doubt. There's nothing wrong with that." His voice was rough, stumbling again.

Amy's heart clenched, throbbed to the point of breaking. He was making excuses this time. Excuses for her. Excuses she didn't deserve. "I was a fool. I should have seen it. I should have stopped him."

"No." He settled on the couch next to her and took her hand. "Loyalty is never foolish. It's one of the things I admire most about you."

There was something in the roughness of his words that pulled at her. In the firm yet gentle grip of his hand. Slowly her gaze rose. Their eyes met. She saw strength in the darkness of his eyes. Protectiveness. Trustworthiness. And something more . . . elemental. Attraction. Maybe even desire.

It didn't surprise her. She'd seen it in his eyes before, back in the tunnels and while lying on the patio beneath his hot, hard body.

Without thinking it through, she reached for his face. Cradled his hard cheeks with her palms. Pressed her lips to his. An explosive breath flooded her mouth as his opened under hers. She slipped her tongue inside his lips, delicately tasting him. Oh God, did he taste good—like bacon and coffee and raw, unabated masculinity. Like honesty and trustworthiness and unashamed hunger.

She relaxed, a hum of pleasure and relief rising. Warmth spread through her, dampening the anxiety and anger. She'd been afraid those horrible days of captivity had ruined her chances of enjoying sex again. Of seeking pleasure. Of accepting intimacy and offering it in return.

She'd worried that she'd never feel this kind of closeness with a man again.

Her mouth opened wider, her tongue tangling with his. Quicksilver chills raced up and down her arms, prickling her spine. Her arms fell to his waist, wrapped around him, and drew him closer.

Which wasn't close enough, not for either of them.

With an urgent groan, he slid his hands around her hips and pulled her onto his lap.

Uneasiness stirred and stiffened her muscles. Memories pressed against the wall in her mind.

The warm, lazy desire chilled.

No . . . no, damn it . . . no.

Reaching for that earlier pleasure, she closed her eyes and pressed against his chest, flicked the inside of his cheek with her tongue, and took his groan into her mouth.

Those bastards weren't going to take this from her too. She wouldn't let them steal this pleasure or the anticipation.

He moaned, the sound a loud rumble in her ears. His hands tightened on her hips, dragging her closer. Subtly he lifted his hips and stroked her with his erection, letting her know exactly what he wanted.

The flash of a tattoo. The burning, invasive assault between her thighs. Lights spinning overhead. A harsh, mocking laugh as she gritted her teeth, locking the scream inside her throat.

The warmth vanished. The prickles faded. Her desire shifted to horror. The flashback still reeling through her mind, she shoved her palms hard against his chest.

He released her instantly, his hands falling from her hips.

Scrambling, she fled his lap.

"Amy." His voice was thick . . . raspy. His eyes were heavy-lidded with hunger. He pressed his fists against the couch and pushed himself to his feet.

"I'm sorry." She backed up, her muscles locked and trembling, the memories boiling over, smothering the passion. He took a cautious step toward her—like you would with a wounded wild animal. She took an even longer step back. "I shouldn't have done that."

"Hey, it's okay. Deep breaths, deep breaths, sweetheart."

She wondered what she looked like to have him so worried.

"I'm okay." But the raw, rattling breath she drew belied the claim. "I better . . . I better go." Another step back.

"Sure." He remained absolutely still, his dark, concerned gaze locked on her face. "But just so you know, you're safe here. Okay? Nothing will ever happen unless you want it to."

The rough apology in his words broke her. She spun and fled. The image of his stark, frozen face followed her down the hall.

Chapter Seven

WHEN THE KNOCK STRUCK HIS DOOR, WOLF OPENED IT WITHOUT hesitation. But he'd expected Jude, who intended to accompany him to the smudging ceremony. The *Hiihooteet* ritual—or death ritual—stirred strong emotions. Such burdens were shared easier between friends . . . and clansmen. Jude was both.

It wasn't Jude's face that greeted him when he opened the door.

"Hell." Sometimes the white man's curse fit the moment more accurately than anything from the people's language. He shifted forward, blocking admission lest Black Cloud decided to enter without welcome. "I have no time for you."

"Nice to see you too. What's with the feathers?" Mackenzie's gaze lingered on the four eagle feathers dangling from Wolf's thick braid.

Wolf crossed his arms across his chest and ignored the question. The death ritual was not for outside ears.

Although there'd been a caustic edge to the commander's tone, the harsh voice was more tempered than Wolf had ever heard it. And there was an odd, tight, maybe even confused look in the black gaze eyeing Wolf's hair.

Something had thrown Black Cloud off his game.

"I know you've heard of the hit on Purcell. His death narrows our chances of finding the cure for Amy's boys." Mackenzie smoothed a palm over his shorn head and cupped the back of his neck.

Wolf tamped down his impatience and simply nodded.

"James Link is our best bet now. He's in charge of Dynamic Solutions' advance technology department, and that shit they injected into Benji and Brendan is as experimental as hell. We need to move on him, A-SAP." The midnight gaze that fixed on Wolf's face glittered with grim determination.

James Link . . . Wolf frowned. Mackenzie had a point. If the compound originated from Dynamic Solutions, as they suspected, then James Link was their best prospect for finding a cure. However, as the acting CEO, he'd be impossible to access.

Not that inaccessibility had ever stopped them from acquiring a target before.

Nevertheless, this topic could not be debated now. There were other priorities. Priorities that had already been put off too long. It had been ten days since the chopper crash. The *Hiihooteet* ritual was not meant to be stretched this far. The delay had been unavoidable. Many of his warriors had been deep in missions and difficult to retrieve.

"I will take this under advisement." Wolf spread his feet, willing Mackenzie to depart. Per usual, Black Cloud ignored the hint.

"You boys have as much reason to go after Link as we do. As a member of the NRO, he's spinning in your wheelhouse. A joint mission to grab him would benefit both of us." Mackenzie's voice hardened and rose. A direct challenge.

Hell—he wasn't wrong.

The timing was.

"I will bring this to the council," Wolf said, willing Black Cloud's boots to start moving.

"Good. That's good." Another swipe over his bristly head, and Mackenzie stepped back and turned.

Wolf locked down his surprise. How about that? The SEAL was leaving without trying to bully his case forward. Atypical behavior to be sure.

"We shouldn't wait too long." Mackenzie spun back to face him, a tired slump dipping his shoulders. "The sooner you take this up the ladder, the better for Amy and her kids." With that he turned and walked away.

The second knock on his door came moments later.

This time he opened it to Jude's placid face. As the elder of the Eagle Clan, his *nesi* wore traditional garb—soft hide trousers and a hide vest over his painted chest. Red and yellow feathers dangled from Jude's graying braid.

"What demands did Black Cloud make this time?" Jude asked, glancing to the right, where Mackenzie had disappeared.

"He wants men and equipment."

"For?" Jude eased back, giving Wolf space to enter the corridor.

"James Link." Wolf fell into step beside his uncle. Silence fell as Jude considered the matter.

"This would not be a bad thing," Jude finally offered with a lift of his shoulders.

Wolf huffed softly in agreement.

By the time they reached the *Hiihooteet* chamber, everyone had assembled. Caged lanterns burned along the craggy walls. The cavern was shaped in a circle—as were all things sacred. Its rock walls and ceiling bore an endless chain of interlocking white circles, denoting that all things were related. In the middle of the dirt floor sat an ancient pot, smoke leaking from the lid like wreaths of breath on a cold morning.

Neniiseti' stepped forward and nudged off the lid to the pot. Smoke boiled up, a steady flood that hit the ceiling and spread out in an undulating wave. Neniiseti' grasped the pot by the wood handles, lifted it above his head, and beseeched Shining Man to allow the smoke to light a path to the spirit world so their dead warriors might find their way to the ancestors. He turned and approached Jude, who leaned forward until his head was immersed in the billowing gray. By the time the pot was offered to Wolf, the ceiling was a sea of smoke.

After the last warrior had partaken of the purification smoke, Jude stepped forward. He halted before each warrior and chanted the recall prayer—words spoken only by the *beniinookee* of the Eagle Clan—and painted a red circle on each warrior's forehead and cheeks. The sacred red circles were physical pleas to retrieve the pieces of their spirits that had torn loose at their brothers' deaths and followed them into the spirit world.

After the last warrior had been prayed over, Jude joined Neniiseti' at the fire. Normally a warrior's totem pouch was used to illuminate their path to the ancestors, but the helicopter crash had left no bodies or totems. They'd had to improvise.

Neniiseti' glanced at the name taped to the back of a toothbrush and threw it into the fire. His voice filled the cavern as he beseeched Shining Man above to show Abe White Horse the path to the ancestors.

A broad face with deep-set black eyes flashed through Wolf's mind. Abe had smiled easily and often. A practical joker, he'd always known what to say or do to break the tension. A fist of loss grabbed his chest and squeezed the air from him. Abe's death was a throbbing abscess among them all.

After the last word fell away, the warriors stirred against the walls, the rustling of their clothes muffled and eerie in the filmy air.

"Hooxei. Walk with me," Neniiseti' said, his voice disembodied within the hazy chamber.

Wolf stopped at hearing his name in the people's tongue and waited at the exit for Neniiseti' to reach his side. The elder exited the chamber before him, as was tradition. Neniiseti' stopped outside in the ancient tunnel, watching the warriors ahead gain distance. Wolf planted his feet and locked his hands behind his back, waiting.

Once the men ahead grew indistinct, the elder turned to face Wolf. "Friends on the outside speak of strangers asking questions about local Indian tribes with military aircraft."

Wolf straightened, the haze from the smudging ceremony fleeing his mind. There was only one organization that would be interested in the answers to such questions. "The NRO?"

They'd known discovery was a possibility when they'd ferried the boys to Shadow Mountain. But the choice had been given. Children were never abandoned . . . at least not among the Arapaho.

"This is unknown but likely," Neniiseti' said. "It would please the council if these strangers were brought before us."

Wolf nodded his understanding. The base was well hidden, protected from curious eyes. The question seekers would hear nothing of value. However, they might hold value themselves. If they knew where Faith Ansell's clean energy device had been taken, the effort to acquire them would be worth the trouble.

"As you wish, Grandfather," Wolf said with a respectful half bow. "In other matters, Mackenzie asks the council's support to go after James Link. There is evidence Link is involved in the NRO. If so, his answers before the council could prove enlightening."

Neniiseti' frowned slightly, his gaze unfocused as he stared down the tunnel. "If the evidence is misguided, and Link is not involved—" He broke off to shake his head. "In such a case, an offensive would be foolish, perhaps even dangerous, exposing our warriors."

"Perhaps." Wolf kept his tone calm and respectful. "But if he is involved, stepping aside would be foolish, perhaps even lethal for the Chastain children."

The elder sighed, his head lifting and falling slightly in agreement. "I will bring this before the council."

Wolf murmured his appreciation and waited. The old one had not walked on yet, which meant there was more to discuss. His intuition proved correct when the spirit walker locked fierce eyes on him.

"Last night a *heneeceine3* walked in my dreams. A caged *heneeceine3* with the stink of infection."

A lion. A wounded lion.

Every muscle in Wolf's body seized. The elder was referring to Jillian; the dream lion made that crystal clear.

"The *heneeceine3* paced the cage. With each pass the stink grew stronger, the *heneeceine3* grew weaker. The rot spread. Slowly the *heneeceine3* crumbled until it was no more. Until the cage stood empty." He paused, the fierce black gaze softening. "Your woman cannot heal here. You must let her go."

Let her go.

Wolf's chest contracted, his muscles aching. "She is not strong enough. She needs more time."

"She grows weaker, not stronger here. She cannot stay."

The gasp of air Wolf took burned all the way down his throat and set his lungs ablaze. "She is not safe on the outside. You know this. She cannot leave."

There was no give on the elder's face. "She cannot stay. The spirits have spoken. She must go." With the finality of his words echoing between them, the elder walked away.

Wolf stood there, his boots frozen to the ground, his muscles locked and shaking, his *beniinookee*'s order ringing in his ears.

He knew of the weight Jillian had lost since arriving at Shadow Mountain, noticed the fragility that increased with every day. Unless he brought her food, she didn't eat. If he left her to it, she'd sleep all day . . . every day.

He recognized the emptiness in her eyes, her disinterest in everything around her. He knew she still wept in her sleep, cried for her babies, stained her pillow and cheeks with tears.

Neniiseti' was right. He knew that. She was not getting stronger. Indeed, her spirit grew weaker each day.

But to let her go . . . his entire body ached at the thought.

She was protected here. Safe. If he sent her away, even to the *heteiniicie*, to those he trusted, she could wander away, disappear from his life. She could be targeted by enemies and taken, or killed.

He could lose her.

You're already losing her.

Frustration burned a path across his lungs and cinched his chest tight. She slipped further from him with each passing day; this he knew too. Her spirit was in a death spiral. If he could not pull her out of this, he would lose her. But if he sent her away, he could lose her then too.

He could lose her either way.

After talking to Wolf, Mac headed for the gym.

Maybe he could torture his body into submission and get some sleep tonight. Fuck knows he hadn't gotten it the night before. The fatigue was extra annoying since he'd gone to bed at a decent hour only to toss and turn. He was too damn old to awake with his cock at full salute and his balls as blue as those moronic aliens in *Avatar*.

The replay of those moments on the couch with Amy's hands burning against his face and her tongue sweeping inside his mouth had been bad enough. But the dreams didn't stop there. They had to flash forward to her glazed, terrified eyes as she fled his arms.

His gut clenched.

Christ, the look in her eyes had hit like a bullet. Took the air from his lungs and the strength from his legs. Amy was one of the strongest people he knew, and for those raw, agonizing moments she'd looked broken.

How could he have been so fucking blind? How could he have missed what she was going through? She'd been kidnapped, for Christ's sake. Raped—repeatedly. Of course she carried major emotional scars. Just because she didn't paste the pain on her face so the world could gawk didn't mean the emotions weren't there.

Christ, he could kick his own ass.

Rage stirred, added spit and fire to his stride. Most of the men who'd held her captive were dead, but two were still awaiting trial in Seattle. What he wouldn't give to track them down, take out every ounce of her agony on their worthless hides.

Amy buried 90 percent of herself below the surface, projecting calm competence while hiding her pain. Which was the opposite of his ex. Hell, Piper wielded emotions like nuclear weapons, scorching everything in her path.

He hadn't known it at the time, but finding Piper riding Martinez had been the best moment of their marriage. He'd walked out of that bedroom minus a wife and the world's softest pillow-top mattress, which he'd fucking hated but agreed to just to shut her up.

The moment he stepped through the gym door, his image was reflected from mirror to mirror; he appeared to be everywhere. He skirted clusters of machines and scattered benches where men were working legs and arms or various other body parts. The place smelled like sweat, dirty socks, and multiple jocks in need of a shower.

He breathed deeply . . . grimaced.

Ah, all the feel of home.

In the far corner were the free weights—and three familiar faces.

Eyebrows arched, he approached the three men who'd staked out a six-by-six-foot matted section. The spot included a bench with a standing rack and a set of weights. Rawls was currently on his back on the bench, working a loaded barbell that weighed as much as he did.

Cosky spotted him first. "You look like hell."

Mac grunted, too tired to work up a snappy rejoinder.

As Rawls completed his set and shoved the barbell on its rack, Zane straightened from his position as spotter and studied Mac. "Cos is right. You look like shit."

Mac flipped the pair a double bird.

Rawls sat up. After using the bottom of his T-shirt to mop his sweaty face, he cocked his head toward Mac. "No offense, Commander, but maybe you should sit down. You're wobbling around like a babe taking its first step."

Mac knew Rawls meant the dig as a joke. Problem was there was enough truth to the taunt that it stung.

Zane shoved Rawls off the bench and took a seat himself. Cosky moved into the spotter's position.

"You should leave the big-boy stuff to us," Rawls drawled as he stretched an arm above his head.

"Really?" Mac snorted. "You haven't kicked the bucket enough already? You looking for another shot at it?"

"Only if Kaity's around with those hot hands of hers." He batted his eyes and directed kissing sounds in Cosky's direction.

Cosky ignored the comment. Even if Rawls had been unattached, he wouldn't move on Kait. Everyone knew that. Rawls lived by the code. You didn't poach a teammate's girl. Ever. Too bad Martinez hadn't figured out that core principle.

"You talk to Wolf yet?" Cosky asked, watching as Zane lifted the barbell and started doing reps.

Mac smothered another yawn. "Just now. He's taking our request to their council."

"You want in on reps?" Cosky asked.

Mac shrugged. "Might as well."

"You're next then."

Silence fell as they watched Zane work the weights. When he finally settled the barbell on the rack, sweat stained his chest and armpits. Mac took Zane's place on the bench.

The weight of the barbell when he took it solo almost drove Mac's arms into their sockets. "What you got on this thing?"

"One-eighty. Why? You want to downgrade?" A definite taunt lingered in Cosky's voice.

Asshole.

"Surprised. That's all," Mac said, lowering the bar to his chest. The motion burned all the way down his arms and into his shoulders. "Thought you pussies could handle more than that."

"This is just warm-up," Zane said dryly.

Greaaaaat.

The second rep burned even worse than the first. By the fifth, his arms didn't burn anymore; they were numb. He held his breath as he settled the bar in its cradle and sat up.

Cosky and Zane added a twenty-pound weight to each end of the barbell.

Two hundred and twenty pounds.

Mac scowled. His arms might just shrink during this next set.

While Cosky stretched out on the bench and Zane moved behind to spot, Mac turned to Rawls. "Has Faith figured out how these bastards are hiding that airstrip up there?"

The question had been bugging the hell out of him since they'd arrived. True, choppers wouldn't need much runway since they could lift and hover. But there were several jets in the hangar, and those suckers needed space for liftoff. Hell, the fucking Grizzly Airbus they had tucked in the corner of the hangar needed a good ten thousand feet of flat, even asphalt.

How in the hell were they hiding three klicks of runway?

Rawls shook his head. "They ain't talkin'. The Shadow Mountain tech guys are mighty partial to their secrets. She's feelin' lucky they let her in on their newest baby. Sweetest little EMP cannon you've ever seen. Once it's operational it'll fry all electronics within a thousand feet."

"That'll come in handy." Mac watched absently as Rawls traded places with Cosky and started lifting and lowering.

After finishing his reps, Rawls thrust the barbell onto the rack with a crash. After a couple of deep breaths, he sat up and turned to Mac. "How's Amy doing?"

"How the fuck should I know? I'm not her therapist," Mac snapped, but the memory of cool hands and a hot tongue followed him onto the bench.

The burn wasn't as bad this time. Maybe because he was distracted. Halfway through the repetitions, the memory of terrified hazel eyes slipped into his mind, interfering with his breathing and his count.

Twenty more pounds were added to each end of the bar. This time Cosky hunched over the bench, ready to catch the bar if Zane's strength gave out. Not that his LC's steady reps and intent expression gave any indication of stalling.

Rawls frowned as he watched Zane work. "Faith says the airstrip ain't even the real mystery about this place. She reckons Shadow Mountain is using a *ton* of energy, enough to power a major city. If they're pullin' the juice from the outside, someone must have noticed. Shit like that's hard to hide. Yet the base remains hidden . . ."

Cosky took Zane's place on the bench but paused before lying down. "No fuck? Where does she think they're pulling the energy from?"

"Hell, she don't know. Lots of questions, not much in the way of answers." Rawls watched Cosky finish his set, then moved over to spot for Mac.

Mac locked down his misgivings as he took his turn on the bench. Two hundred and sixty pounds sat on that bar. All three of his men had managed the weight with no apparent struggle. If Rawls had to rescue him . . . He grimaced as he lifted the bar. He'd never hear the end of it.

Maybe if he got lucky, a heart attack would put an end to his stupid-ass pride and this moronic competition.

Chapter Eight

Amy awoke with the taste of bacon on her lips, the feel of hard muscles beneath her palms, and the memory of a hot tongue stroking the inside of her mouth. Flutters spread through her belly, her nipples were peaked, and the flesh between her legs was throbbing and damp. Eyes closed, she stretched languidly, the sheets sliding erotically against her hot, sensitive skin. It felt sweet to awake to arousal rather than terror, to memories of pleasure rather than nightmares of pain.

Too bad she hadn't maintained this languid sensuality while she'd been lost in Mac's arms.

She frowned, going over the incident in her mind. She didn't understand why she'd reacted so negatively the night before, yet not on Clay's patio. She'd been trapped beneath Mac's body by the barbecue, his hard, heavy weight pressing her down, and she'd felt just fine. Protected, even. There had been no urgency to flee, no terror. So why last night? What had been the difference?

Adrenaline? Rage? Fear?

She shook her head and sighed. The real question was: How was she going to face him?

With a soft groan, she stretched again. She'd have to summon the courage to apologize. She could hardly avoid him. Of course, after shifting their relationship from platonic to sexual, getting him all hot and hungry and then tearing herself from his arms and running away . . . he probably wasn't in any hurry to see her again.

Not cool, Amy. The very definition of not cool.

"Mom?"

Amy bolted up in bed, her son's voice ripping her from that hazy border between sleep and consciousness. Her gaze scanned the dark bedroom. "Brendan?"

"Benji's sick." Brendan's worried voice drifted through the darkness.

Throwing back the sheet, she slid out of bed. The floor was icy against her bare feet, the air cold against the legs her sleep shorts exposed.

"What's wrong with him?" Amy asked as she headed across the room toward the child-size gray blur lurking in the doorway.

"He's hot and he's crying." Brendan stepped back from the doorway, allowing her to pass through.

Hot? Like a fever? Worry dug in. Benji was never sick. There was a running joke between her and his pediatrician—that her son bolted through each day in hyperdrive, moving so fast germs and viruses couldn't keep up.

When Amy flipped on the light switch in the boys' room, a whimper came from the bed to her left.

"Turn it off! It hurts." Benji's face turned toward her. Even from the doorway she could see the dull redness in his cheeks along with the drying tracks of tears.

"What hurts, baby?" She rushed to the bed and knelt on the floor beside him. His forehead felt blistering hot beneath her palm; so did his cheek.

"I'm hot." His voice was fractious as he rolled his head away from her touch and hunched into the wall.

"I can see that." She forced a calm tone even while anxiety took hold.

After seven years of never having a fever, why now? Had the isotope started to affect him? Or was the timing coincidental?

"Brendan?" She partially turned to scan her oldest son's face. Unlike her youngest, he wasn't flushed. No obvious signs of a fever. "How do you feel?"

"I'm fine," he assured her. "I'm not hot."

Brendan wasn't sick, so maybe Benji's sudden fever didn't have anything to do with the isotope. She forced the worry and questions aside and concentrated on comforting her son.

"Brendan, get a washcloth and soak it with cold water." She listened to his footsteps cross the room.

"You hang in there, baby. We're going to make you feel better, okay?" She kept her voice soothing and her touch light. But even that was too much. He whimpered and jerked away from her hand.

She glanced at the clock beside Brendan's bed. It was 5:00 a.m. Too early for doctor's hours, but the base clinic was open twenty-four-seven. She scanned Benji's flushed face. He was obviously running a fever, but she didn't have a thermometer to check how high. Nor did she have any aspirin to bring it down. If it was a case of the flu, the clinic could treat him. If it was something else entirely, they'd reach out to Dr. Zapa regardless of how early it was.

She rose to her feet and stripped off the sheet and blanket he'd kicked aside.

"Brendan," she yelled. "I'm taking Benji to the clinic."

She backtracked to her room to shove her feet into her sneakers and debated about changing her clothes. She opted for speed rather than presentation. Her sleep shorts and top covered everything that needed covering.

"I have the washcloth," Brendan said when she returned to Benji's bed.

"Hang on to it." She leaned over and slid her arms beneath Benji's chunky frame. The muscles in her back protested as she straightened.

He radiated heat like a small furnace, instantly warming her. The fear intensified, tightening her belly and skin. Exactly how high was his temperature?

"Drape the cloth across his forehead."

Benji sighed as soon as the cloth touched his skin. His eyes fluttered closed. "Whatcha doing?"

"Taking you to the clinic." She kept her tone soothing.

"I don't wanna go." His voice warped straight to querulous, and he thrashed weakly in her arms.

She tightened her hold and made shushing sounds. "They'll make you feel better, Benj. They'll take the heat away."

"Uh-uh." He thrashed again, the cranky tone giving way to a sob. "They'll poke me with needles."

Her heart squeezed. She couldn't deny that assertion, since there was a good chance Dr. Zapa would want to draw blood. "But you'll get another dinosaur bandage or maybe even a spaceship."

"I don't care. I don't wanna go. I wanna stay here." His voice started out low and whimpering before escalating to a shriek.

She almost dropped him when he started struggling in earnest. Benji was a solid sixty pounds and difficult to hold when he wasn't cooperating.

"Do you want me to get Commander Mackenzie?" Brendan bent and caught the washcloth as it went flying.

Surprised, she shot a quick look at her oldest. Mackenzie? That was the first name that jumped into Brendan's mind when they needed help. Not Zane or Rawls, but Mackenzie? When had that happened?

"We don't need to bother the commander." Amy injected confidence into her tone. "Between the two of us, we can take care of Benji just fine."

Which was easier said than done when her youngest started writhing like a fish on a line.

"Benjamin Jonathan Chastain." She sharpened her voice. "That's quite enough. You have two choices. I can carry you, or you can walk. Either way you're going to the clinic."

Another sob was followed by a muttered, "I hate you." But he stopped twisting.

I hate you.

She masked a flinch, her heart contracting again. Of course he didn't mean it, wouldn't even remember saying it, but if this sudden fever had anything to do with the isotope . . . Panic tried to break through. She forced it aside by focusing on the child in her arms.

The trip to the main corridor seemed to take forever with Benji's burning weight getting heavier and heavier with each step. They lucked out when they reached the throughway. One of the base's motorized carts was charging along the wall. She lifted Benji inside, recoiled the electrical charger, and pushed the button to start the vehicle. After a tight U-turn, they were on their way.

The sight of the clinic's bright lights brought an avalanche of relief, an easing to the tension cinched around her chest. "We're almost there, baby. Just hang on a little longer."

His weak chuff of pain as she carried him from the cart through the sliding doors slashed at her heart. Was he hotter? Or had the stress and his hot body increased her own temperature?

She was still several steps from the receptionist's counter when a woman dressed in green scrubs appeared in the doorway next to the desk. Her sharp gaze scanned Amy and then dropped to Benji's nodding head.

"Fever?"

"Yes. I don't have a thermometer or aspirin." Or the slightest idea of how serious this fever was.

"Let's get him into an exam room." The woman turned and led the way down the hall.

Amy carefully settled Benji onto the exam table, wincing as he sobbed and curled into a tight ball.

"Doctor Pauli to room B." After waiting a few seconds, the nurse pushed the button again, repeating the message, before crossing to Benji. "Hi there, Benji—isn't it?" At her son's truculent nod, the nurse smiled cheerfully. "Well, Benji, my name's Danielle, and I'm going to take really good care of you."

Amy retreated slightly to give the nurse room to work.

"When did the fever start?" Danielle asked softly. She crossed to the counter next to the exam table and opened a middle drawer. When she turned back, she had a digital thermometer in hand.

"He was fine when he went to bed at nine. I'm not sure when it started. Brendan woke me up, and I brought him right over," Amy said tightly, watching Danielle slide the thermometer between his lips.

"Have you noticed any other symptoms?" the nurse asked as she scribbled on a sheet of paper attached to a clipboard. "Aches? Pains?"

"No, but I didn't spend much time asking him questions. I brought him straight over."

When the thermometer beeped, Danielle pulled it from Benji's mouth.

"What was it?" Amy asked, leaning in for a closer look.

"One hundred three point nine," the nurse said, neither her expression nor tone giving anything away.

Amy's chest tightened. Was a temperature of 104 considered dangerously high? Her boys had rarely been sick and never with a fever this high. Could the isotope be causing it? If so, why wasn't Brendan sick? But then maybe his temperature was elevated too, just not as high or as noticeable.

"Nurse?" Amy waited for the woman to look at her. "Could you take Brendan's temperature too?"

The woman's smile was understanding. "Certainly."

"I'm fine, Mom," Brendan said, although he obediently opened his mouth and accepted the thermometer.

When the instrument beeped, and was removed with a 98.8 reading, Brendan shot her an I-told-you look.

Relieved that Brendan didn't appear to be sick, Amy looked again at her youngest son. Benji still lay curled on the exam table, lethargically enduring the stethoscope and the blood pressure cuff. His lack of response was a clear indication of how sick he felt. His prior exams had been an exercise in patience followed by explicit threats.

This was not normal. Not for Benji. Her son threw himself through life with every fiber in his body. He didn't just lie there and let people do things to him.

A sense of foreboding mushroomed through her until it choked out any sense of optimism. Benji's life was in danger. She could sense it. Every maternal instinct she possessed screamed it.

There was something very, very wrong with her son.

The knock that struck Mac's door was demanding, far too forceful to have come from Amy.

Thank you, Jesus.

Not that she had any interest in pounding on his door, anyway—at least not anytime soon . . . probably.

His scowl as he rose from his seat at the table had more to do with the shredded, aching muscles of his chest, shoulders, and arms than thoughts of Amy. A spasm ripped through his back. He froze, his breath catching as the muscles clenched into a charley horse.

Jesus fucking Christ!

He gritted his teeth and rode out the spasm. He could add his back to the litany of body parts he'd fucked over the day before that were returning the favor today. He had to stop letting those bastards he called friends goad him into paralyzing himself.

The next round of pounding was so thunderous, it shook the door.

What the fuck?

Someone was having a worse day than he was. Or, to be more accurate, someone was about to have a worse day.

Snarling, Mac stalked to the door, trying to keep his torso, shoulders, and back as still as possible. He flung it open to Wolf's rigid, icy face. Startled, he backed up a pace. He'd never seen the big bastard look so aggressive before.

"You couldn't find a punching bag to throw some of that hostility at?" Mac drawled with a raised eyebrow.

From the irritated glitter in Wolf's black eyes, his visitor was considering using Mac as the punching bag. Normally Mac would be down with draining off some of the antagonism with their fists and boots, but not today. Fuck, he wasn't even sure he could raise his arms high enough to land a punch.

Wolf visibly reined himself in. Crossing his arms, he planted his boots and rocked back on his heels. "I've things to do. I've no time to wait for your lazy ass to climb out of bed."

Something had sure put a bug up the bastard's ass. "Seems like you're the one wasting time here."

Wolf's nostrils flared and the glitter in his eyes sprouted crystals of ice. The big bastard was beyond pissed . . . the question was why.

"The council has agreed to the mission you requested," Wolf said through tight lips.

Mac straightened, only to freeze at the burn through his chest and shoulders. At least his back didn't seize this time. "You're green-lighting our op to grab James Link?"

Wolf's nod was rigid, like he'd lost all flexibility in his neck.

"When?"

"Soon," Wolf said grudgingly, swiping a palm down his face. "In light of Benji's illness, the sooner the better."

Mac froze again. Benji? Sick? "Wait. Back up. What's wrong with Benji?"

Wolf cocked his head slightly, his gaze sharpening on Mac's face. Some of the rigidity in his expression eased. "A fever. Amy brought him to the clinic this morning."

"How bad's the fever?"

The question was so fast and sharp it scorched the air between them. A wave of acid hit his gut. *Goddamn it.* The kid was just a baby. He didn't deserve this.

And then the damnedest thing happened . . . Davey's chubby face and bleached-blond scruff of hair burst into his mind. The image was crystal clear, as if he were looking at a photograph.

What the fuck?

He hadn't thought of his brother in years. Too many to count. He'd locked that first quarter of his life behind mental walls of steel and concrete. Bolstered them periodically to make sure the memories didn't break through.

"Dr. Zapa . . . brought . . . fever down."

Mac forced his attention back to the conversation, relaxing as Wolf's words registered. If the boy's temperature was coming down, it might not be as bad as he'd feared. But, Christ, under the circumstances, Amy had to be going out of her mind.

"Do the docs know if this fever is a reaction to that damn isotope they were given?" Mac asked, rage unfurling. The fucking NRO would pay for what they'd done to Amy's boys. He'd make Goddamn sure of it.

"Unknown. But likely." Wolf's voice was suddenly tired.

The rage thickened, clotting in his chest and restricting his lungs. Mac forced it down so he could think. They needed to grab Link and find out what he knew about the isotope and the NRO. And they needed to do it now.

"Set up a meeting with your CO for this afternoon," he said, urgency hitting hard. He'd get hold of Zane and the boys ASAP . . . after he checked in with Amy.

Suddenly that kiss and the awkwardness that had followed didn't mean shit. She had to be scared out of her fucking mind. There wasn't much he could do to help, but at least she wouldn't be alone. That had to count for something.

"Is Benji still at the clinic?"

"Far as I know," Wolf said, a shadow of grimness filtering through his voice. He turned and walked away.

Mac followed him into the corridor. If Benji was there, Amy would be too. She wouldn't leave her son.

By the time he reached the clinic, the muscles in his shoulders and chest had loosened enough that he could walk and swing his arms at the same time . . . without swearing.

The woman at the reception desk was blonde with a huge—and likely fake—rack. He ignored the flirty purse of her lips and faux wideness of her eyes.

"Benji Chastain?" he demanded. "He was admitted this morning."

"He's been moved to extended care." She tilted her head, shooting him a seductive glance through her fluttering eyelashes. "Hang on a minute. Once Jannette gets back from break, I'll show you where he is."

He scowled at her. Nothing about the woman appealed to him. Nothing. Apparently he liked his women less flirtatious, much subtler, and sometimes terrified.

"No need. I'll find him myself." With that, he helped himself through the door and headed down the peach-colored hall.

"Hey. Hey. You can't just barge in without an escort," the blonde sputtered.

A moronic and incorrect statement, since he just had. He increased his pace in case someone tried to stop him. When he came to a fork in the hall, he stopped to glare down one path and then the other.

Luckily a mature woman in green scrubs appeared in the hall to the right.

She stopped in front of him. "You look lost. Where you headed?"

"Extended care. Benji Chastain?"

"Ah yes." She smiled. "Stay to your left. Extended care is shaped like a giant horseshoe. He's in the second cube to the left." With another smile, she brushed past him.

Following her directions, he stayed to the left. He stopped when he entered the extended care wing. Damn if the room wasn't exactly as the woman had described—a giant horseshoe with—he stopped to count—twenty cubicles clinging to the outside walls. The patient stalls were ten by ten and separated by nubby gray eight-foot walls. A fabric curtain across the front of each unit was someone's bright idea of privacy.

The curtain for the second cubicle was closed. As Mac started toward it, he was surprised how quiet his boots were on the tile floor. The slightly spongy flooring appeared to absorb the sound of his feet. He peeked around the gap in the curtain. If Amy or the boy was sleeping, he didn't want to wake them up.

Benji was curled on his side, sound asleep. A standing fan oscillated at the foot of his bed, blowing air over him. A basin of water and a wash rag sat on the cart next to the headboard. Amy looked up from her armchair next to the bed, relief flashing across her face when she saw him. Yeah, he'd called it.

The woman needed someone on her side.

He pushed the curtain ajar just enough to slip through, relieved when Benji didn't stir.

"Hey." He kept his voice to a low rumble. "How's he doing?"

"His temperature's come down, thanks to the fan and the cold-water baths. If it goes back up, they said they'd use the cooling blanket on him. But he's still feeling horrible. Mostly sleeping." Her haunted eyes turned toward her son.

Mac shifted uncomfortably. Now that the obligatory "How ya doing?" or, in this case, "How's he doing?" was all used up, he had no idea what to say.

Fuck, he was a wuss at this.

His gaze dropped to the computer on her lap, and he winged it. "Where'd you get the laptop?"

The tension in her shoulders vanished, and humor softened the exhaustion in her eyes. "I followed your lead and asked for it."

It took an instant to trace the comment back to the bacon and eggs. When it finally registered, he released a soft bark of laughter. "Hell, if I'd known it worked on electronics, I'd have picked one up days ago." He glanced around the cubicle, his gaze lingering on the second armchair. "How's Brendan?"

"He seems to be fine. No temperature or other signs of sickness. He's at the cafeteria getting some lunch." She scooted her chair around to make room for him. "Do you want to sit down?"

He didn't. He was too damn antsy for that. Instead he walked to the bed. Benji was sleeping with his face scrunched and his fists clenched, every muscle in his slight frame tense. Was that normal? Or part of what ailed him? "Do the docs think the isotope is affecting him?"

Amy shook her head. "They don't know for sure, but they suspect it. They said . . ." Her voice bobbled, and she stopped long enough to clear it. "They said that Brendan's blood work hasn't changed. But Benji . . . the compound is proliferating through Benji's cells. It's spreading. They're running more tests."

She shook her head, and the hazel eyes that glimmered off his were bright with fear.

Son of a fucking bitch.

He almost reached for her hand but caught himself in time. He had no clue how she'd react to his touch, even if it was meant in support and comfort. His words would have to do.

"The council's approved the op to snatch Link. We'll grab him. We'll find out what was injected into Benji and Brendan. We'll figure out a way to reverse it."

Assuming the isotope came from Dynamic Solutions, and assuming James Link had anything to do with its development, and hell—assuming they could even get close enough to grab Link.

Some of the tension left her face, and she eased her death grip on the armrest of her chair. "When do you move on him?"

Her gaze drifted to the bed, and Mac knew she was thinking they needed to move fast. As fast as possible. Benji's life could depend on it.

"We're working up a plan now. We go to Shadow Command this afternoon."

"Okay." Amy's voice calmed, her eyes sharpening. "So you need more information on Link, his residences?"

Such research would be right up her alley. She must have run similar searches on her targets back when she'd been in the FBI.

"That would be helpful." He'd offered her the perfect distraction. She already looked less stressed.

Which reminded him of the terror on her face in the aftermath of that kiss. Should he bring that up? Assure her it would never happen again? Before he had a chance to broach the subject, Amy turned the laptop until the screen was facing his way.

"I've already started researching Link, and I found something interesting." She hit a key. A collage of pictures popped up on the screen. All were of the same two men. One was a tall, lean man with dark hair, and the other was even taller but heavier with no hair.

Amy pointed to the one with dark-brown hair. "That's Link on the left and Leonard Embray, Dynamic Solutions' founder and CEO, on the right. These photos were taken between one and ten years ago. Look at their body language. The way they laugh together. Lean into each other. They even clasp hands in a couple of them. I think they were close friends. Like Obama-and–Joe Biden close."

Mac took a seat and leaned in for a closer look. She was right. The pictures did remind him of all the memes he'd seen through the years of Obama and Biden.

"They have known each other since high school. Went to the same college. Once Dynamic Solutions took off, James Link was the first person Leonard Embray brought on board." She narrowed her eyes at the screen. "But as of six months ago, Embray disappeared. There are no photos or public accounts of him since last March. He seems to have vanished. In fact, Link has taken over numerous obligations that Embray handled in the past."

She paused to tap another key on the keyboard, and another picture popped up. "Take a look at this. It was taken about six months ago, around when Embray disappeared." A picture of Link wearing what was obviously a designer suit filled the screen. She moved her finger on the mouse pad and clicked. "This one was taken last week."

The same man in a similar suit, but the difference was instantly discernable. "He's lost weight."

And a lot of it. Hell, he looked like a fucking scarecrow.

"Exactly," Amy said as she turned the screen back toward herself. "But it's not just his face and not just the weight. He looks terrible. Like he isn't sleeping."

Mac glanced at her. She could have been describing her husband's appearance all those months ago, before the poor bastard had lost his life to a knife blade in an airport closet.

"The timing of the weight loss is suspicious, don't you think? I wonder if it's connected to Embray's disappearance. I wonder if Link was somehow involved." She shrugged. "I know it doesn't make a difference when it comes to grabbing him, but if he is feeling guilty, maybe you can use that somehow."

Her husband's appearance had certainly been caused by guilt. Well, that and terror for the safety of his family. But then, John Chastain had been a good man. An honorable one. Sure, he'd made a couple of nasty mistakes when it came to his cooperation with the NRO. But, hell, the guy had been dealt a crummy hand. Damned if he did . . . damned if he didn't. He'd stepped over the line to give his family the strongest probability of survival. He hadn't taken that step by choice.

Mac looked at Amy and then at the child in the bed next to him. He'd have done the same damn thing.

But that didn't mean Link had the same sense of morality.

"Luckily we won't need to rely on a guilty conscience to get him to talk," Mac said, catching Amy's gaze. "Once we get him back here, he'll tell us everything we need to know."

Their eyes locked, and *bam*, the memory of that kiss and its aftermath flared between them. Just like that, the awkwardness was back.

Mac stiffened in frustration. Enough already. They needed to exorcise that damn kiss and get back to basics. "Look, about yesterday morning . . ." Mac squared his shoulders and leaned forward in his chair, his hands balled into one big fist. "I don't have any expectations, if that's what you're worried about. You don't need to fear that things will progress further, okay?"

A long, vibrating silence fell. She finally stirred but avoided his gaze by staring at the ground.

"What if I want them to?" she asked, her voice soft.

He froze. She was still avoiding eye contact. He must have misunderstood her words. "What?"

Her face lifted, and this time her eyes locked on his face. "What if I want things to progress further? What if I want to revisit that kiss?"

"Uh—" His mouth remained wide open, but no further words escaped.

She closed the laptop and stretched to put it on the rolling cart in the corner of the room, then scooted her chair forward until they were sitting knee to knee.

"I'm sorry I ran. But it wasn't because of you. You know that, right?" She leaned forward and wrapped her hands around his fist. "I liked the kiss, Mac. I *enjoyed* it." Her gaze shifted slightly, as though she'd almost looked away. "At least until the nightmare interfered. I wasn't running from you. I was running from the memories."

He turned her hands over and squeezed. "I get that. I do. As long as you know I'd cut off my"—he glanced at Benji's sleeping face and frowned—"junk before I'd ever hurt you."

She squeezed his hands back. "I know that."

The glazed terror and horror that had been stamped across her face ran through his mind. He shook his head. "Maybe you're not ready for this step yet."

She clutched his hands again. "Just hear me out, okay?"

Frowning, he nodded slightly.

"They stole something vital from me in that house. Something I never thought I'd get back. Something I want back."

Rage flushed his muscles. She meant when those bastards had kidnapped and raped her. Too bad Tattoo was dead. The motherfucker deserved so much worse than the clean, easy death Amy had dealt.

"That kiss yesterday? It was the first time I've felt pleasure in months. The first time I've felt sexual attraction. The first time I've felt alive. And damn it—I don't want them to steal that from me too. I want those feelings back."

Okay . . . where exactly was she going with this? He stirred uneasily.

She must have sensed his discomfort because she offered a lopsided smile. "Relax, Mac, I'm not asking for a commitment."

Okay?

"What are you asking for?" The million-dollar question.

"I don't know. More kisses, maybe a one-night stand . . . or two . . . or three."

He stared at her in complete astonishment. A one-night stand. Did the woman know herself at all? "Yeah, I think you need to rethink this."

"I dreamed about you last night." She shot a quick look at Benji and dropped her voice. "Erotic, sweaty dreams. And the nightmare didn't invade the dreams or ruin the pleasure."

Her expression was pure challenge.

Mac backtracked, cleared his suddenly thick throat. "Have you talked this out with anyone? Maybe you should—"

"I have eyes, Mac, and good instincts. I know you're attracted to me."

"That's not the point. The point—"

"I know what the point is." Her voice started to rise. She stopped talking and eyed the hospital bed again. "They can't win, Mac. Not when it comes to my kids. Not when it comes to my body. Not when it comes to my mind. I won't let them." The hazel eyes that held his were full of determination. "I won't let them steal my sexuality. I won't."

It was a fucking miracle the nurse drew back the curtain at her last word because he had absolutely no clue what to say. No fucking clue.

"Benji needs another temperature check and dose of medicine," the nurse said with a cheerful smile.

Mac shot to his feet, mumbled an excuse, and fled the cubicle, for the first time in his life grateful for a nurse's take-charge bedside manner.

Chapter Nine

AMY PICKED APATHETICALLY AT THE SCRAMBLED EGGS BRENDAN HAD brought her from the cafeteria, her appetite cooling as rapidly as the food on her plate.

So that went well.

She winced at the memory of Mac's face after she'd dropped her bombshell. She'd heard the term *shell-shocked* before, but this was the first time she'd watched it happen before her eyes.

She'd totally blindsided him. But then she'd blindsided herself as well. She hadn't planned to spill all those emotions out loud. She hadn't planned to practically *demand* that Mackenzie have an affair with her. Good God, could she have sounded any more desperate or pathetic?

Flinching internally, she tried to maintain her outward calm. Brendan didn't need to know what a twit his mother had become. Or that his mother was rapidly becoming obsessed with a man who wasn't his father. Although she suspected her feelings for Mac wouldn't bother her oldest son.

Brendan was mature for his age—mature enough he might even have picked up on her attraction to Mac. If he had, she would never know. Brendan, like his father, kept his thoughts and feelings internal. Ninety percent of Brendan existed beneath the surface. John had been the same way. It had taken years to burrow under his surface, to connect with the man she'd married, the man she'd loved, the man who'd been a wonderful father to her sons.

Grief whispered through her. Loss. A deep, aching sorrow. But they felt like old emotions—faded by time and distance.

It felt odd to feel this way. Lusting after one man while grieving for another. Yet there was no sense of guilt. Or betrayal. Sure, the two of them had had their problems; every couple did. Yes, even now, she sometimes felt frustrated that he hadn't trusted her enough to feel comfortable in her choice of career. But she'd loved John with every ounce of her heart. She wouldn't change one moment of the years they'd shared. She'd been faithful to him. Would have remained faithful to him for the rest of her life—for the rest of their life together, if he'd lived.

But he was gone.

It felt like he'd been gone forever. Lost to her for years, although she knew her sense of time was warped by her experiences over the past five months. These days Mac was the man who haunted her thoughts, and she couldn't throw the kiss-and-run routine at him again. She had to make sure she was ready for Mac's . . . attention. It was time to do some research and find out how she could counter the flashback and stop it from ruining the moment.

"How come Benji isn't waking up?"

Brendan's voice brought Amy to attention. "It's the medicine they're giving him to keep his temperature down. It makes him sleepy."

Or so the nurses and doctors had told her . . . repeatedly.

"Oh." Brendan got up and wandered to his brother's bedside. "He's never quiet like this." A tense tone entered his voice. "I don't like it."

She knew exactly what he meant. It wasn't natural to see her youngest so still and quiet. There was almost an ominous portent to his stillness.

She rose to her feet and joined Brendan at the edge of the bed. The arm she settled over his shoulders was as much for her as it was for him.

"It won't be long now. The doctors will figure out what's wrong with him and how to make him better."

When she raised a hand to Brendan's cheek and then his forehead, he released a long-suffering sigh and looked up at her. "I feel good. Okay? I'm not sick."

Yet.

But she swallowed the negative response.

Brendan turned back to Benji and frowned. "Commander Mackenzie is going after the people who did this to him. To the both of us." The words weren't a question. They were stated as a fact.

"Where did you hear that?" She hadn't told him the news yet. She'd wanted to make sure the mission went off as planned. Lots of things could happen between planning and launch.

"At the cafeteria. William asked how Benji was doing and said Commander Mackenzie was going to bring back the man who'd done this to us. So we could get answers on how to fix things." His face was solemn. "Is it true?"

"For the most part," she admitted.

"When?"

"I'm not sure. When they—" Her words were cut off by the sound of the curtain being drawn back.

Mac poked his head around the edge of the curtain, his gaze on the bed before scanning her with guarded eyes. "How's he doing?"

He came back.

Relief swelled. Her chest went light and bubbly.

"The same." Amy pushed the words past her tight throat. He'd come back. She hadn't driven him away.

He scowled as though he didn't like her update.

"Here's the plan." His gaze shot from Brendan to Benji and back to Amy's face. "We're about to start brainstorming this"—he shot another look at Brendan—"thing. All that intel you gathered on our target would come in handy."

Amy's heart lightened even further until it felt like it could float right out of her chest. He was asking her to join their prep session. Except . . . her gaze flew to her sleeping son. Her heart turned heavy and sank. She couldn't leave. What if he woke up? What if he needed her? What if he got worse? Or better?

"Yeah." Mac's voice was rougher than normal. The hard planes of his face blurred with understanding. "That's why we decided to hold the meeting in here. Bring in some chairs. There's room for the five of us." He glanced at Brendan. "Or six. You have the laptop." He shuffled his feet, suddenly looking uncomfortable. "Unless you think it would disturb your boy?"

"No, he'll sleep right through it." Amy swallowed hard, the swell of gratitude so strong her chest ached.

He'd known she'd want to be involved in the prep and planning but couldn't leave Benji's side, so he'd brought the prep and planning to her. It showed an understanding of her nature she hadn't expected.

"Good, that's good. Hang on." He ducked back out, the curtain falling shut behind him.

A few seconds later the curtain was swept back again, and Mac stepped in carrying a chair identical to the one she occupied. He placed the chair so close to Amy's, the arms touched. Seconds later Zane arrived, identical chair in hand. He was followed by Cosky and Rawls.

In no time the room turned claustrophobic. The chairs were pressed arm to arm and marched around the edge of the bed. But they got all of them in, by God, and the curtain closed behind them.

"We're looking for possible entry strategies and identifying potential opportunities." Mac cast an unreadable glance her way.

His forearm brushed against hers as he claimed the armrest. Chills swept her spine. Tingles tickled her fingers. He froze next to her, and his breath caught. It was subtle, but she was so close to him she heard it.

"Do you want me to leave?" Brendan asked, his voice carefully neutral. So neutral Amy knew he was dying to stay.

"Amy?" Mac cocked an eyebrow at her, his heavy-lidded gaze dropping and lingering on her lips.

"He already knows you're going after Link." She hoped her voice didn't sound as husky to the rest of them as it did to her. "And he's not going to accidently spill the details to someone who can use them against you."

When Mac's eyes sharpened on her mouth and started to glitter, the tingle attacking her fingers jumped to her lips.

He's going to accept my offer.

Every look he gave her told her so—the way he sat so close, the press of his arm against hers. He shed clues like electricity shed sparks. A sudden spike of nerves hit her belly. She hadn't really thought he'd take her up on it. His no-trespassing signs were posted so high and so often, she hadn't expected him to step outside them and meet her halfway.

"In that case you might as well stay." Zane sprawled back in his chair and winked at Brendan.

Rawls cleared his throat, his attention bouncing between Amy and Mac. "Anyone have any ideas on how we're gonna get up close and personal with Link? Close enough to grab him?"

Cosky's forehead furrowed. "Hell, it's going to be a bitch getting close enough to grab him. As acting CEO of Dynamic Solutions, he's bound to have full security detail."

"Watch your mouth," Mac barked with a meaningful look at Benji and Brendan.

The warning inspired choking, exaggerated disbelief from his men. Amy fought back a giggle too. Of all the men to sound off about swearing in front of her children . . . But still, the attempt to police his men for her sake was awfully sweet . . . and totally unexpected.

After a moment of pulsing silence, Mac cleared his throat. "What did you find on Link's upcoming activities? Anything look promising?"

The glow diminished instantly. "Nothing, unfortunately. The only public appearances he's scheduled for are a month out, which is too far when it comes to our time line."

She barely stopped herself from looking at Benji. Not that her restraint mattered. When she scanned the assembled men in the room, everyone was focused on the bed . . . and the child in it. They all knew why it was essential the mission take place as soon as possible.

Rawls pushed himself up from his chair next to Mac's and stepped up to the bed. "When's the last time they took his temperature?"

"Just before you guys joined the party." She shook her head at his inquiring glance. "No change."

Nobody said anything, but faces hardened and eyes turned cold. Sheer menace crawled through the room.

Their silent but immediate response lifted some of the burden from her shoulders. They cared about Benji and Brendan, and they cared about righting this injustice. She wasn't alone.

Her chest started to ache.

Zane cleared his throat and leaned forward in his chair, running his palms down his thighs. "Okay. If we can't target public appearances, we'll have to look at other avenues. What about residences? Offices? Gyms? Favorite restaurants."

"Restaurants would be easier." Cosky's eyes narrowed, went out of focus as though he was flipping through possibilities in his mind. "Less security. More opportunities to set up an ambush."

Cosky was right, but . . . "I haven't been able to find any restaurants he frequents. Same for gyms. He does have several houses that he spends equal time in—and two office buildings." Amy swatted back a surge of disappointment.

Rawls lifted his hand from Benji's cheek to roll up his eyelid. "Sounds like we're looking at houses or offices, then. We've worked with less."

Had they? Really?

Even if they had, those missions had been conducted on foreign soil. Which meant they hadn't been breaking US laws. It wasn't just Link's security they had to worry about. They had to worry about local police, the FBI, the sheriff's department—heck, they had to worry about every law enforcement agency, period.

"Where does he live?" Cosky asked. "You said he has several houses."

"He has four places. London, Hawaii, Seattle, and close to Naples. But he splits his time for the most part between Hawaii and Seattle."

"Then those are the ones we focus on." Mac leaned back, locking his fingers behind his head.

"Right." Amy opened the laptop. An aerial view sprang up of a sprawling estate bordered on three sides by water. She turned the laptop around and lifted it so everyone could see the screen. "His estate in Hawaii sits on the point of Hualalai, and boasts four hundred feet of private beach access. The house sits back from the water, secluded among the palm trees. It's three stories. Forty thousand square feet. Reportedly twelve bedrooms and sixteen baths. Two pools, one indoor. Weight room, theater."

Rawls whistled. "Nice digs, if you have a hankerin' for overindulgence."

With a slow frown, Cosky rubbed a hand over his face. "It would be easy enough to insert from the water. There's no perimeter fence along the beach."

Nods traveled the room.

"I think you'll find the same vulnerability with his Seattle estate." Turning the laptop around, Amy clicked on another photo. "It sits on Lake Washington, not far from Bill Gates. It has a thousand feet of beach access." She rotated the screen to show them.

A pleased hum swept the room. All four men leaned back in their seats with varying degrees of satisfaction on their faces.

Zane smiled—a slow, gratified stretch of his lips. The skin around his eyes crinkled. "The man does like his beachfront property. It's like he's making it as easy as possible for us." He paused, his gaze steady on Amy. "Any idea which one he's currently at?"

Sighing, Amy lowered the laptop. That was the rub. "No clue. The man takes privacy to an extreme. I didn't find anything current on his movements."

Nobody looked surprised. Nor did they look disappointed.

"Wolf can help us identify which target is most promising." Mac sent her a reassuring smile. "He's got all kinds of nifty little spy toys. We just need to know where to aim the satellites. Don't worry. We'll find him."

We just need to know where to aim the satellites.

Something niggled at her brain, something to do with Mac's comment—something important.

It took a minute for the realization to click into place.

Shadow Mountain had surveillance abilities, even satellites to boost the surveillance. Everything she'd just detailed was likely already known to them. Already under consideration. Her research had been unnecessary.

Indeed, this whole meeting was unnecessary.

Mac had to know that . . . which meant what, exactly?

He'd staged a meeting simply to include her in the planning? Why? To give her a distraction? Make her feel like she was contributing to her children's rescue?

Could he really know her that well?

Chapter Ten

WOLF LEANED AGAINST THE FAR WALL OF THE COMMAND CENTER, waiting for Mackenzie and his men to leave. While Winters, Rawlings, and Kait's fiancé were okay, at least for *nih'oo3oo*, Mackenzie set his teeth on edge.

Like now, for instance, Mackenzie had barreled up to Neniiseti' before the elder had even made it out of his chair and immediately started flapping his jaw. Where was the patience? The respect? Elders were due the honor of directing the conversations, yet Mackenzie had barged in with questions, concerns, and demands.

However, Mackenzie's behavior also gave Wolf the perfect opportunity to slip out of the room unseen. Escape from questions he found no pleasure in answering and demands he found no pleasure in performing. He'd ignored his *beniinookee*'s order regarding Jillian, a rebellion that had carved a gaping, seething wound in his mind and soul.

He straightened and pushed himself off the wall only to find Jude at his side.

His uncle stared at Mackenzie questioningly. "Perhaps Neniiseti' requires rescue?"

If the circumstances were different, Wolf would have launched a rescue himself. But worries of dreams, lions, and spirit warnings kept his feet still.

"Hooxei." Neniiseti's voice filled the room. "I would speak with you. Now."

Wolf looked up at his name and grimaced. Mackenzie had left, and Neniiseti' stood tall and fierce. Forbidding black eyes locked on his own.

Perhaps his *beniinookee* was not the one in need of rescue.

With reluctance dogging his steps, Wolf slogged forward, each step heavier than the last. By the time he stood before Neniiseti', his flesh felt tight and itchy, as though he were a snake about to shed his skin.

He already knew what the spirit walker wanted.

"Grandfather." He bowed his head in respect, aware Jude had tagged along and waited by his side.

Neniiseti' ignored Jude, focusing solely on Wolf, his face sterner than Wolf had ever seen it. Wolf shuffled his feet beneath that flat, disapproving stare, feeling as small and defensive as an errant child.

"Your *heneeceine3* walked my dreams again last night. Her dying shrieks still echo in my ears. I tell you again. *She cannot stay here.* If you will not send her away, I will do so." Without giving Wolf a chance to respond, he turned and stalked away.

Dead silence fell in the wake of his exit.

Wolf fought to unlock his fists and slow the hard, uneven pounding of his heart.

"I tell you again?" Jude broke the silence, his voice climbing in shocked disbelief. "*Again?* You ignored a direct order?" He didn't add "Are you crazy," but the question hung there in the air.

Wolf unlocked his jaw. "I will not speak of this." Forcing his boots to move, he headed for the door.

"Too fucking bad."

Wolf stopped cold. Shock whipped through him. He'd never heard his uncle use the white man's swear words before.

"You do not ignore an order from the *neecee*. You do not. *Not ever.* For any reason. You know this. I taught you better."

Wolf ground his teeth and spun, fighting to hold back the rage, the resentment, the hot flush of panic. "This does not concern you."

"Fuck you." Jude's voice was guttural, his face almost incandescent with rage. Another first. "You *are* my concern. Everything you do is my concern. You are my son by blood, by my sister's body, by my teachings. By the hours and hours spent by your side. Do not dare dishonor me with such lies."

Wolf dropped his head in shame, hearing the hurt and shock beneath the rage in Jude's voice.

What was he thinking? Of course Jude had a stake in this. As Wolf's uncle and mentor, as head of the Eaglesbreath family and the *beniinookee* of the Eagle Clan, every action Wolf took reflected on Jude.

A deep breath calmed him. He took a second for good measure before lifting his head. "Forgive me, *nesi*. I spoke with the mind of a child."

Jude accepted the apology with a single nod. "You will apologize to Neniiseti'."

Wolf simply nodded. An apology was a given. Whether it would be accepted as easily by his chief as it had been by his uncle . . . that was not a given.

Jude's sigh sounded like it rattled all the way up his throat. He settled a heavy, comforting hand on Wolf's shoulder. "Where will you send her?"

Rage stirred again and beat like war drums against his chest. Jude expected him to concede immediately. To send Jillian away. No hesitation. No questions. Just instant acceptance followed by instant action.

Yet everything inside him, the very core of him—that which had recognized Jillian as his mate the instant he'd seen her—wanted to challenge that assumption. Revolt against it. Keep her by his side.

But he couldn't. He wouldn't. Because Neniiseti' was right.

Jillian's hollow face and blank eyes filled his mind. He thought of the brittleness of her bones. The thinness that grew every day. The silent, endless grief. The craving for sleep.

Neniiseti' had spoken it, but they both knew it. Jillian couldn't stay.

Shadow Mountain was killing her.

She hadn't deteriorated until he'd locked her inside this steel-and-concrete prison. In trying to protect her, he was killing her.

The rage vanished, leaving barrenness in its wake. A spirit-sucking, desolate void spread throughout him.

He had to let her go.

"I will lose her." He could hear the raw ache in his voice.

"Maybe," Jude agreed quietly. "Maybe not. You cannot see the future until the future is on you. What *is* known is that she cannot stay here." He paused as though to let that sink in before asking again, "Where will you send her?"

"I don't know." The emptiness spread to his heart. He could hear the hollowness in its beat.

"The reservation, then. We have many there to protect her." His voice was reassuring. "We will keep her safe."

"Safe?" He shook his head, exhaustion crashing through him. "From others? Perhaps. But from herself? Who will make sure she eats? Walks? Showers? Who will show her how to live again?"

How to love?

"Do you forget where you come from?" Jude's tone turned disapproving again. "We have family there. Clan. They will care for her until she returns to you." He paused, his gaze raking Wolf's face. "You must have known she couldn't stay here. Shadow Mountain does not welcome civilians."

True enough.

While the Athabaskan people had lived and hunted in the lands surrounding Denali for thousands of years, the caverns and tunnels within the Great One had existed since the very oldest of the old times. In their prehistory, when ancient migrations were honored by tribal myths and oral histories, the catacombs inside Denali had been held sacred and close to the people's hearts. So close that the network of caves had never been discovered by the white man.

Perhaps they would not have been rediscovered by the Northern Arapaho either, if Samuel Oleska, an elder from the Ahtna tribe, had not visited the Wind River reservation in the 1930s and recognized the white symbols of the Northern Arapaho. Similar symbols, he'd said, were painted across the walls and ceiling of the sacred chambers within the Great One.

Oleska's words had resonated with Amos Two-Worlds, Neniiseti's grandfather and one of the Arapaho's most venerated spirit walkers. Amos had spirit-walked the catacomb of caves that Oleska had described. After multiple vision quests in the sacred chambers of the Great One and mediation with the local Athabascan tribes, Shadow Mountain had been conceived.

Its purpose remained true even today: a base for the war against the NRO, the ruthless, deadly enemy shown to Amos by Be:he:teiht—the creator. Shadow Mountain was meant to house warriors—and only warriors.

In the old times, thousands of women and children had been sacrificed to war. The *hinono'eiteen* had learned to keep their battles and people separate.

"Your *heinoo* will welcome your woman. You know this." Jude's words rang with certainty.

His *nesi* had cause for his certainty. Wolf blew out a beleaguered breath. His mother had been after him for years to take a wife and settle down. To return to Wind River and take a position on the tribal council, as his grandfather had done before him. Of course, as the elder of the Eaglesbreath family, the duty fell to Jude to step into that responsibility. Not that he was any more interested in settling down than Wolf was.

According to his mother, her son and brother were identical berries on a chokeberry bush. The assessment might even be true. Jude had been his only male influence growing up. It was doubtful Wolf would have survived his turbulent adolescence without his uncle's influence. Jude had taught him everything a father instilled in his son. He'd forged the warrior Wolf was today. It stood to reason he'd share similar ideologies and goals with the man who'd sculpted him.

"Do you want me to come with you?" Jude asked.

He meant to the reservation. His uncle had read Wolf's silence on the subject as affirmation he'd take Jillian there. He wasn't wrong. While he'd rather stash Jillian closer to base, he didn't know the local Athabascan tribes well, certainly not well enough to trust Jillian to their safekeeping. Besides, with strangers asking questions about local Indians and military craft, hiding Jillian locally was too dangerous.

The reservation was his only viable option.

With that decided, his mind went to work. With their current mission's urgent time frame, Shadow Mountain could not afford to lose both him and Jude.

"You will be needed here," Wolf said, running scenarios through his head.

Jude simply nodded. While his uncle was semiretired, and Wolf had stepped into his shoes as team leader, Jude still ran the units when necessary.

"I will return once Jillian is settled."

"I would not expect your *heinoo* to release you before the eleventh moon," Jude said dryly.

Wolf grunted in agreement. His uncle knew his sister—Wolf's mother—well.

Jude slapped him on the shoulder as they passed through the command center's door. "Maybe you can invite that half brother of yours down to Wind River. Introduce him to his people. His keeper's gift would be most welcome."

A frown on his face, Wolf kept walking. "Judging by Kait's account and the money they inherited, John Winchester, their father, was a keeper too."

"He was your father as well," Jude reminded him quietly, easily keeping pace. "Keepers run heavy in your father's bloodline."

Wolf grunted. Although he carried the knowing within him, it did not extend to wealth building. Those with the keeper's gifts were prized for their ability to amass fortunes. Without their gifts and the income they generated, Shadow Mountain would not exist. Nor would many of the programs that the Arapaho enjoyed.

But the creator had not bestowed such gifts on the keepers with the intent that they reap the harvest themselves. The gifts had been given to fund the ongoing war against the NRO. Possibly, Aiden understood this at an instinctive level, as Kait said his talent brought him no pleasure.

"No worries." Jude slapped Wolf's shoulder when they reached the bottom of the ramp to headquarters. "I will babysit your teams while you are gone. Give my regards to your mother."

Wolf absently watched him walk away. First order of business was to arrange a ride to Wyoming.

And then he'd tell Jillian.

It took no time to arrange the flight. With departure set for an hour, he grabbed a motor vehicle and took the direct route to Jillian's quarters. When she didn't answer the battery of knocks on her door, he punched the access code into the control panel and let himself inside.

"Jillian?"

No answer.

The interior was pitch-black. He slapped the light switch and waited for his eyes to adjust.

"Jillian," he called again.

Still no answer.

Hesitant to invade her quarters without an acknowledgment of his presence, he waited near the entry. But when she failed to respond to his third hail, he shed manners in favor of action.

He found her in bed . . . again. Fragile shoulders curled toward the wall. She looked so damn thin, anorexic even. His chest aching, he sat down on the edge of the bed and gently shook her shoulder. "Jillian."

Still she didn't respond.

He knew she was alive; at least her body was. He could see the rise and fall of her breasts under the thin sheet.

"Jillian." He sharpened his voice and shook her again, harder. "Wake up."

She stirred beneath his hand. Lethargically turned over. Her eyes were vague—dark lenses wreathed in emptiness. He could feel her dreams pulling at her, feel her longing to return to them. To reunite with her lost children.

His heart bleeding for her, he pulled the sheet down to her hips and slid an arm around her waist. He lifted her into a sitting position. Worry pierced him. She was far too light against his arm. Her body was limp and fragile. Her spirit was all but gone.

He should ask Jude to perform the recall prayer again, to try to recall the broken pieces of her spirit. But Jude had already done so twice to no avail. There were far more pieces of her soul drifting than present these days.

When the spirit broke into a thousand pieces and went wandering, it was all but impossible to call it back.

"What?" Her voice was slurred. Uninterested.

"We must leave this place." He forced the words past his rebellious tongue and helped her off the bed. She wore sweats and a loose T-shirt, both of which stank of too many days of wear against unwashed skin.

"Why?" There was no interest in her voice, her face, or the empty gaze that drifted past his own.

"Because we must." The throb in his chest grew stronger.

"Okay."

Still no interest. Or resistance. But then she could dream anywhere.

"Take a shower." After making certain she could stand on her own, he collected underwear, socks, a shirt, and pants from the wardrobe and pressed them into her arms. "Change clothes."

"Okay." She walked to the bathroom like she was sleepwalking, trailing the dark emptiness of grief behind her like the blood of a dying deer.

He found a gym bag in the closet and packed what few possessions she had, including the knife on the bedside table. The one he'd given her by the river all those weeks ago, when her spirit had been sharp and bent on revenge.

Long minutes later she came out of the bathroom, clothed but with dripping, tangled hair. He relaxed slightly. He'd almost expected her to return to him naked, her thin, weak body on display. The reluctance to see her like that sank deep. When they crossed that bridge, she would come to him healthy. Glowing with vitality and life.

Her spirit restored again.

He'd hold on to that image in the dark days ahead.

"Where are we going?" she asked in a voice that didn't care. She sat on the bed and methodically pulled on the shoes Wolf handed her.

"To Wyoming, the Wind River reservation."

"Oh." Shoes in place, she stood before him, a vacant sign bright in her eyes.

"I won't be staying with you," he told her, struggling against the urge to shake her, wake her up. Bring her back to him. "I must return to Shadow Mountain once you've settled in."

He waited, urging her to react, to show him that he mattered to her, that she didn't want to be left alone and undefended in a strange place.

But her only response was a slow, blank blink and an uninterested "Okay." And then she turned, wandered away, her steps the uncoordinated shuffle of a dreamer.

Leaving his heart to shatter all over the cold floor.

Chapter Eleven

"Reduce speed. We're at one hundred feet." Zane's words came quietly through Mac's radio.

The Zodiac Hurricane H-733 rolled over a moderate swell, its speed slowing as Cosky pulled back on the throttle. Mac leaned over the side of the skiff, trying to see past Zane's and Rawls's broad shoulders and helmet-wrapped heads, but a face full of cold spray as the wind kicked up convinced him to settle back and wait for beaching.

Taking second position in the Hurricane held advantages and disadvantages. While the guys in front took the brunt of the wind and spray, they also had the best view. A full 180-degree vision of what lurked ahead. Mac, on the other hand, had stayed drier and warmer in the middle, but he could see only to the right and left. Hell, he couldn't even see their wake. Cosky, the big bastard, blocked that direction.

Being all but blind lent an uneasy chill to the ride. This was where trust came in. Trust in the men blocking your view, in the training that turned a boatful of individuals into a weaponized, synchronized team.

It had been a long time since he taken second position in a Hurricane, a long time since he'd had to lock on to that kind of trust. It was both satisfying and frustrating being back in the boat after all these years.

"Fifty feet." Zane's voice drifted through the radio again, and Cosky eased back on the throttle even more.

In the green glow his NVDs cast, the dark shadow of the second Zodiac rode the swells beside them. Jude's boat. Jude's team. There was a third boat somewhere in the darkness behind.

He shook the unease off. Fuck, it wasn't like the men accompanying them were total strangers. He'd already fought beside them once. He knew they were professionals, well trained and as disciplined as his own men. But . . . they weren't his men. Team trust was forged through endless hours of training together, followed by hundreds of missions.

Still, it almost felt like old times out here on the waves, bobbing under a moonless sky, the wet rubber of the Zodiac beneath his fingers, the oily stench of diesel fuel drifting past his nose, the sting of spray hitting his face and hands. Hell, even the wreathed moon playing peekaboo above was reminiscent of his stint on the teams.

Of course, there were some major differences. Like the fact that they were inserting within the good ol' United States of America, alongside teams from another nation. If he remembered his long-ago civics lessons, Indian nations were sovereign nations within the boundaries of the United States. Which meant they were launching an attack within the United States, on a US citizen, accompanied by a foreign power.

If they got caught . . . fuck, the consequences would make the fallout after the attempted hijacking five months ago look like a light sprinkle next to a category 5 hurricane.

They'd never see the world beyond the view of bars again, and that was assuming they weren't summarily executed for treason.

Wouldn't hurt to pray you don't get caught.

He grimaced, adjusting his weight on the bench seat stretched across the Hurricane as the boat swayed over another swell. If he believed in a higher power—which he didn't—he'd use all his prayers on the small child engulfed by that huge hospital bed. Those prayers would perform a two-for-one miracle, saving both Benji and the woman worrying herself to death over her little boy.

"Fifteen feet," Zane said.

Cosky cut the engine. The skiff's velocity along with the waves would push the Zodiac the rest of the way forward.

They'd been fortunate so far with this mission. The trip down from Shadow Mountain had proved uneventful. The boats had been waiting for them exactly where they were supposed to be when the Eagles had landed. Mac had no clue who Wolf's stateside support was, but they'd been on the ball. They'd found the perfect little cove—secluded and flat—to land the chopper and ground the boats. Everything had gone according to plan.

The best time to launch a water insertion was during wind and waves and a shrouded moon. From a distance—say a window or computer monitor—the boat simply looked like a slightly larger swell. Waves and wind created noise too, which drowned out the sound of the boat's engine. Conditions had been perfect tonight.

If he'd been a religious man, he might have decided the good Lord was on their side—everything had lined up that tidy. The satellite images placed Link at the Lake Washington beach house. They had pictures of him arriving two days before and nothing of him leaving. Up-to-date imaging indicated he was still there, all tucked away, waiting for them. What the satellite had picked up had been a stroke of almost unbelievable luck. It wasn't uncommon for the intel on mission prep to take weeks to come together. Hell, sometimes months.

Based on the worry lines stacking under Eve Zapa's eyes, Benji didn't have weeks.

He eyed the gray, shrouded sky, and tension ballooned. The pressure just kept building and building until it felt like his skin was about to split. He'd like to believe the anxiety was due to the mission, but he knew it wasn't. He'd ridden in enough beach boats to recognize the feelings attached—which was a mixture of adrenaline and caution.

This was different. This was more like helplessness and worry. And it was linked to Amy. His fixation on her had escalated tenfold these past few days. A natural progression thanks to all the time he'd been spending with her lately.

That off-the-wall request of hers sure as hell hadn't helped. Fuck, he should be running insertion scenarios through his head. Instead he was running her words through his mind. Had she really asked him to seduce her? Had she really asked for a sexual relationship?

To show just how fucked up he was these days, he could even understand her point of view. Understand why she'd made the offer, or request, or whatever the hell it had been. Fuck, he wanted to take her up on it too. Spend a couple of hot, heavy hours—

The boat suddenly stopped—hard—throwing him off his bench. They'd landed.

"Jesus, Mac," Cosky snapped from behind him, pure disbelief in his voice. "Have you forgotten how the fuck to hold on?"

Fuck.

Mac righted himself and rose to his feet, then settled in a crouch. He could hardly excuse his inattention by explaining where his mind had been. Sex wasn't an excuse.

He slid out of the Hurricane and into a foot of icy water. By the time he'd exited the lake, the second and third boats were already disgorging their teams.

As they joined Zane and Cosky on the beach, Cosky looked him over. "Maybe you should think about babysitting the boats and let us take care of the big boy stuff."

Yeah. "Fuck you." He shot his lieutenant the double finger salute to reinforce his rebuke.

Zane glanced between him and Cosky before offering a shrug. "Remember," he said, his voice quiet but clear through the headset. "No shooting unless absolutely necessary. Subdue."

Nobody bothered to nod. They were all crystal clear on that salient fact. The inhabitants of the house they were crashing were American citizens. Ironic, really . . . they'd spent a good share of their lifetimes protecting the citizens of the great ol' USA from foreign nations inserting into their homeland. A lifetime protecting them from terrorists and keeping them safe, comfortable, and alive to carry out their hate rallies and counter-hate rallies.

Alive to kill each other in the name of whatever religion or movement was the flavor of the day.

Christ . . . to go to war against your own people was something he'd never even considered five months ago.

The enemies . . . they were a-changing.

They'd mapped out the insertion details in Shadow Mountain's war room, using wall maps, projection screens, computer simulations, and satellite images, so each team knew exactly where to go and what to do. By now Jude would have taken out any computerized devices and cell phones with that handy-dandy device they'd used on Clay Purcell's house.

The distance from the beach to the mansion was thick with towering, leafy, overgrown trees. Great for Link's privacy, but great for camouflage as well. There was plenty of cover. Zane took point on their way to their target—the mansion's beachfront entrance—with Rawls and Mac in the middle and Cos bringing up their six. They skirted a huge swimming pool and a pool house. Charlie Team had been assigned to clear the pool house, so they kept going.

They split into two groups at the giant marble patio. Zane and Rawls took the left side, slipping along the raised flower beds. Mac and Zane took the right side of the courtyard, with its fountain and pool full of glowing—no fuck, *glowing!*—fish.

Link's mansion gleamed even in the moonlight, and in the green glaze of his NVDs, the dozens of windows imbedded in dark wood shimmered. Mac held his breath as Zane tried the long curved door handle. It didn't budge. Out came the suction cup and glass cutters.

The name of the game was stealth. A shotgun blast to the lock was loud as fuck and would wake the whole house. Of course, if Jude hadn't killed the electronics, the alarm would wake the whole house too.

In a normal assault, they'd have taken down doors and stormed through the place, taking out anyone who drew arms. But the US government frowned on such tactics against its own people, particularly extremely wealthy citizens with a penchant for charitable donations.

Zane hesitated before removing the circle of glass and sticking his hand through the opening to unlock the door. Apparently he wasn't the only one who lacked the requisite trust in their new team members. But no alarm sounded, proof their trust had not been misplaced after all.

They assaulted into the room in their standard predatory crouch, rifles up and sweeping, and scared the holy fuck out of a bunch of couches and chairs—not to mention the grand-fucking-piano. Yeah . . . a total waste of badassery and testosterone and the tight muscles in Mac's chest.

Shadow Mountain command had acquired the blueprints of the place, so they knew the bedrooms were on the second floor, up a staircase that followed the curve of the walls. The assumption was Link occupied one of those bedrooms.

Four huge, green-swathed figures were already climbing the stairs by the time Mac and his team reached the middle of the house. From the look of their ballistic vests and clunky helmets, they were Shadow Mountain warriors, Jude and Alpha Team. Zane fell in behind them, followed by Rawls and then Mac.

Where the fuck was the security team?

The absence of any retaliatory force was fucking weird. Link was rich as hell and utilized some of that money for protection. The satellite images had shown half a dozen men who'd carried themselves like professionals with the bulk of weapons beneath their jackets.

Where the hell were they? The moment the alarm died and the surveillance equipment malfunctioned, whoever was on duty should have kicked into high gear and hightailed it to their client. Maybe that's where they were—covering Link. They'd find out soon enough. The master bedroom was right around the corner.

Mac kept his rifle up and aimed to the left, away from Rawls's back. When they reached the second-floor landing, he followed Zane and Rawls to the right. Alpha Team had gone left, heading to the bedrooms lining the left side of the stairway. Zane and Rawls took up position beside the first bedroom on the right. Mac and Cosky slid along the wall to the second bedroom.

As Zane and Rawls headed into their bedroom, Mac and Cosky assaulted through their assigned door. They went in low and fast, guns up and sweeping. The room was empty. Mac held his position while Cosky swept the bathroom.

"Clear." Cosky's calm voice came through Mac's radio.

They retreated into the hall, emerging in time to see Rawls disappear into the third bedroom. Taking up position along the wall to the fourth, they headed inside. Rinse and repeat, except for the figure sitting, hands up, on the edge of the bed.

"On the floor. On the floor," Mac shouted, his rifle zeroing in on the bastard's chest.

"I'm not armed," a male said quietly as the figure slid down to the thick squishy carpet—his hands still up. Cosky was on him before he'd straightened out on the floor. Mac held position while Cosky anchored the guy's hands behind his back with the flex-cuffs and dragged him to his feet.

It wasn't until the bastard was up and facing him that recognition hit.

They'd just introduced themselves to James Link.

"Target acquired," Mac said into his mic, watching as Cosky checked arms, legs, and torso for weapons.

Their mark stood passively. No struggling. No questions. Just a resigned, maybe even relieved expression on his green-glazed face.

Fuck . . . Mac scowled. This had been way too easy.

"Where's your security?" Cosky asked as he shoved Link toward the bedroom door.

Looked like he wasn't the only one wondering about that.

Link shook himself and cast a confused look around the room, like he expected to see them hiding in the corners.

"Most of them have the night off, but Burns, Capos, and Owens should be around."

Cosky relayed that information to Alpha and Bravo teams.

So they needed to keep an eye out for three bodyguards. Look at that; maybe Amy was right about the guy. Maybe he did have a guilty conscience. He was being so damn helpful—if you could trust what he'd told them.

They joined Zane and Rawls in the hall and headed for the stairs, where they got in line behind Alpha Team. Jude stepped in front of them before they could start down the steps and stood there with his head tilted listening to his radio. After several seconds of stillness, he stepped between Zane and Link.

"Go," Jude said through the radio. "Everyone look alive. There's still no sign of our three security guards."

They descended the stairs in formation, Zane on point once again with Cos holding their six.

Link went submissively. Still no struggling. No trying something stupid, like jumping the rail. No rescue attempt from a bodyguard either. Which seemed the height of incompetence when you were protecting one of the richest men in the world.

They reached the bottom of the stairs and spread out, Jude's team taking the lead. Jude, Zane, and Rawls clustered Link, making sure he was in the middle of a small mob.

No way in fuck were they going to lose him after going to all the trouble. Those missing security guards had everyone antsy. Had they set up a trap? Were they waiting for them?

If they had set up a trap, it wasn't in the house. Mac's team was out of the house and across the patio in no time. They skirted the pool and pool house again, more widely this time with Link in the middle of their protective huddle. Mac swept the silent courtyard, the hair on his arms electrified, eyes and ears tuned for any sign of danger.

Nothing.

Fuck, they just might make it to the boats unscathed. This whole mission had been ridiculously easy.

An assessment he immediately regretted.

Suddenly Jude stopped moving. He froze for a beat of two and suddenly spun, driving his shoulder into Zane's chest. "Down. Down."

His violent shove drove Zane into Link, and they both went down, which saved their lives.

The crack of a rifle sounded from above and behind them.

Jude went down . . . hard. Unmoving.

Chapter Twelve

BENJI WAS GETTING WORSE.

Amy was certain of it. The clues were everywhere. Benji's fever was creeping up even though they'd increased the cold baths along with the dosage of the drugs. Even the cooling blanket wasn't bringing it down like it had at first. The nurses' cheerful mood had warped into downright jolly and overly encouraging, yet they avoided her eyes. Dr. Zapa had become a near constant presence and was ordering blood tests and medical scans every day. And then there was Benji himself, who slept most the time—thank God—but when he did awaken, he complained of pain in his side, or his head, or his chest—virtually every area of his body.

Except for this last time, when he'd awoken screaming.

They'd given him something for the pain, which had knocked him out. He was still sleeping. Something she'd prayed for while he'd been in such pain, but something she hated now.

His stillness in that bed sent flares of panic through her, flickers of foreboding. She was constantly bolting to his bedside to make sure he was still breathing.

Her chest so tight she could barely breathe, Amy threaded fingers through her hair, massaging her tight, aching scalp. She was so tired it was hard to think, but not tired enough to douse the fear or ease the constant throbbing pressure under her skin.

Benji was getting worse, and nothing the doctors did was helping.

It felt like she'd been camped beside his hospital bed forever, although today marked the third day since she'd first sat down in this chair. One day since Mac—along with his men and twelve Shadow Mountain soldiers—had left to kidnap James Link in the hopes of saving her son.

Because that's what this operation boiled down to—kidnapping.

In some ways this horrible helplessness sapping the courage from her veins was similar to that terrible powerlessness of six months ago. She'd been helpless then too, constantly aware that the monsters holding them prisoner had no intention of releasing them alive. She'd known that she alone had to figure out a way to save everyone—an impossible feat with no weapons, no help, and no strategic plan.

And then Mac and his men had burst in, providing the strategy and weapons, giving her the break she needed to save her sons.

She frowned. Could that be part of the pull she felt toward him? The fact he'd been there when she'd needed him? That he'd given her the opportunity to save her children?

Now he was out there again, risking his life for a second time, determined to save Benji again.

God help her, she needed that second miracle. Because she couldn't protect him from this. Couldn't protect *them*, since Brendan could fall sick at any moment. She was helpless again. Terrified. Unable to do a damn thing to save her children.

The curtain slid back, and one of the night nurses bustled in, a horrifyingly cheerful expression plastered over her too-bright face. Amy rose to her feet, releasing the grip she had on Benji's small hand.

As the nurse slipped the thermometer into Benji's mouth and gently held it closed, Amy waited. They were taking his temperature every hour now, but they'd stopped telling her what it was. She knew they didn't want to worry her, which was insane. The simple fact that they didn't want to scare her told her exactly how worried she should be.

"What was it?" she asked the woman point-blank once the thermometer was removed from Benji's mouth.

"Why don't you head to your room and try to get some sleep? It's been three days, and you've barely left his side. You need to rest so you can stay strong for him. We'll call if anything changes."

She'd taken that advice twice through the past seventy-two hours, only to lie in bed, wide awake, terrifying scenarios plunging through her mind. At least her fear didn't seem to be affecting Brendan's sleep. He was at the apartment now with Marion.

"I wouldn't be able to sleep anyway." Amy turned back to the iron-railed hospital bed with its white sheets and pillows. Benji was a tight curl under the covers. God, sometimes it felt like that bed was trying to swallow him whole. "Look, I know he's getting worse. I know his temperature is going up again. You aren't protecting me by keeping his temperature a secret."

The nurse, who was attaching a blood pressure cuff to Benji's small arm, stopped and studied Amy. For the first time since she'd entered the room, the cheerful mask fell from her face. Amy held herself still during the scrutiny, knowing she'd passed the woman's test when the nurse nodded.

"It was 104. Slightly up from an hour ago, but not by much."

That at least was comforting. Some of the nerves chewing their way through Amy's belly stilled. The fact his temperature was still climbing was much less comforting. She silently watched the nurse work the blood pressure bulb and cuff. When the woman frowned and took his pressure for a second time, Amy tensed again. She wouldn't have taken a second reading unless there was something off about the first.

"What is it?" Amy forced her voice to remain steady even though she wanted to scream.

"His pressure and pulse are climbing as well." She caught the expression on Amy's face and hastened to add, "Both can spike when a patient's in pain. Try not to worry, Mrs. Chastain. Dr. Zapa will be stopping by shortly to check on him."

Amy forced herself to breathe. "Have you heard anything from Jude or Mackenzie?"

She needed them to bring James Link. She needed to know what those bastards had injected into her sons. She needed an antidote, and she needed it now.

The woman shook her head. "We haven't heard anything. No warning to expect casualties either, so I guess that's something."

"Okay. Thanks." Amy forced a smile of appreciation and stepped up to the bed, vaguely hearing the rasp of the curtain closing. Leaning over the mattress, she brushed a strand of hair off Benji's forehead. His skin was hot and dry, stretched taut beneath her fingertips. His eyes moved restlessly beneath creamy, blue-veined lids. He looked small and fragile and too damn young to be locked in this bed, this room, this damn illness.

Too damn young to be dying, because instinctively she knew he was.

Her baby was dying.

Please, please, please, Mac. I need you. I need you to bring Link to me.

Taking hold of Benji's hot, dry hand, she collapsed into the chair beside his bed. What would she do if Link didn't have the answers they needed? What would she do if he didn't know how to save her son? The base healers couldn't help him—they'd tried repeatedly and failed.

The hot tension inside her expanded, pressing against her heart and her spine until it felt like the entire world was sitting on her chest.

She welcomed the sound of the curtain drawing back and Eve Zapa's quiet entrance. At least the company would drag her from her own mind and the escalating terror of her thoughts.

Dr. Zapa scanned Benji's face before pulling the clipboard from the metal box attached to the foot of the bed. After reading for maybe a minute, she dropped it back in its holder and turned to Amy. "How 'bout we take a walk? I'll fill you in on the latest test results."

The news wasn't going to be good. Amy knew that without doubt. Eve's grave face broadcasted that loud and clear. Amy took a deep, shaky breath and slowly rose to her feet.

For an instant she wanted to say no, that she didn't want to hear, didn't want to know. She wanted to bury her head in the sand and allow herself to believe that Benji was fine, just sleeping, on the road to recovery. That there was nothing wrong with him at all.

But fantasy wouldn't save her son, and he couldn't be treated if she didn't know what was wrong, so after stroking her knuckles down her baby's hot cheek, she followed Eve Zapa out of the cubicle.

At least Eve didn't make her wait long. As soon as they cleared the curtain, she turned to face Amy.

"I'm told you're aware his temperature, pulse, and blood pressure are rising." At Amy's tight nod, Eve went on. "I'm afraid his blood work is showing signs of abnormality too. Liver, kidney, and pancreas levels are all elevated. The good news is the increase is slight. The levels are on the high side of normal. The bad news is that they *are* elevated. On admission, the blood work was normal."

Amy's heart rate bobbled and then slammed into quadruple time. "*What* . . . what does this mean?"

Eve hesitated, gave a slight shake of her head, which sent her short hair swinging. "It indicates his internal organs are under stress."

Amy swallowed hard. "But you can give him something to help, right? To bring those levels down?"

Dr. Zapa sighed and raised a hand to rub her eyes. "The levels on their own aren't the problem. They're merely a symptom. The issue is the underlying cause. We know the isotope is multiplying. But we don't know what it's doing to his organs. Something is obviously changing. We'll be doing a whole range of tests today to try to pin this down. If we know what the isotope is doing in his body, we can try to combat it."

Try. Eve kept saying *try*. Such a subtle but significant choice of words. There were no guarantees that anything Eve tried would have an effect. There was only one course of action that was certain to save her son.

They had to neutralize the isotope.

Amy squared her shoulders. "Have you figured out why Brendan isn't being affected by the isotope?"

Maybe if they could figure out what was keeping Brendan from getting sick, they could duplicate it in Benji.

Dr. Zapa shook her head. "We haven't. It could be as simple as his age or his immune system."

Disappointment crested. Age and immune system couldn't be duplicated in Benji.

She swallowed hard and asked the question that had been haunting her all day. "Once the isotope is inactive, he'll get better, right?"

"I don't know." Eve's grave tone was lacking the comfort Amy so desperately needed. "Even if Mr. Link is the key, even if he provides the cure, it still may not be enough. It will take time to develop the antidote. Time and equipment. Both of which we may not have. There is also the possibility that the damage the isotope has already done to Benji's body will not be reversed after the antidote is administered. I'm afraid we just don't know much of anything right now."

While Eve was careful to avoid admitting that Benji could still die—even with the antidote—Amy knew that's exactly what she was implying.

How do you go about preparing yourself for that? How do you prepare for the death of your child?

You didn't. That was the truth of it. There were some things you just couldn't prepare for.

The possibility of Benji's death was one of them.

"Alpha One down! Alpha One down!" The shout came through Mac's radio from one of the Shadow Mountain guys.

Crack . . . crack . . . crack.

Mac hit the ground and spat out a mouthful of dirt.

Shit . . . they'd found the security detail. Or the security guards had found them.

Crack . . . crack.

The dirt exploded maybe two feet in front of him. The good news—there was only one rifle, only one shooter. The bad news—there *was* a fucking shooter, and they had no Goddamn clue where the bastard was. He wasn't after Mac, though; otherwise he'd be dead. Like the rest of his team, he was stuck out in the open, completely vulnerable. Easy pickings.

He chanced a lift of his head. Link was still down, Zane on top of him, Jude partially covering Zane.

None of them were moving.

Fuck.

Were they dead?

Even as the question hit, Zane crawled farther up Link's body until he was covering him completely. Rawls dove on the pair, adding his body to the pile.

Crouching, their eyes scanning the courtyard and tree line, Alpha Team formed a protective barrier around the four men on the ground.

Crack . . . crack . . . crack.

The warrior closest to Zane jolted and went down.

Fuck.

The shooter was aiming for Zane and Link . . . and Rawls, since he was on top.

Mac shoved down the rush of adrenaline and focused. The shots were coming from above and behind. They needed to find and neutralize that damn shooter. Rolling onto his back, he scanned the tree line.

A flash of light hit the corner of his NVDs, and he swung his head to the right. There, on the pool house roof, light reflected from a rifle barrel.

Swinging his rifle up, he sighted on the reflection and fired.

"Hot spot on the pool house roof." He shouted the location into his mic and took another shot. Then another. A cacophony of gunfire erupted behind him as Alpha Team bombarded the location.

"Bravo Two down." Cosky's calm voice came through Mac's radio.

Bravo Two was Zane. Fuck. Zane had been hit? How badly?

"Bravo One, go . . . go . . . go," Cosky said.

Vaulting to his feet, Mac sprinted for the beach and his wounded buddy as Alpha Team laid down fire to cover him. He passed Jude's still body. One of the healers was hunched over him, but the only glow he saw was the liquid sheen of blood glazed green by his NVDs.

The healing wasn't working.

Christ . . . that looked bad. Really fucking bad.

For an instant he considered swinging over and—

But, fuck, there were plenty of Jude's buddies surrounding him, and Mac's priority was getting Link and Zane back to Shadow Mountain alive. He caught up with Cosky, who had Zane's arm over his shoulder and an arm around his waist while his buddy hopped along beside him.

Relief shoved the air from his lungs. His LC must have caught the bullet in the leg, but at least he was alive—moving and aware. He grabbed Zane's right arm and anchored it over his shoulders, and then he wrapped his left arm around his LC's waist. In unison, he and Cosky lifted him and ran for the boats. He searched for Rawls and Link as they closed in on the water and found the pair in the Hurricane.

Link's alive.

Thank fucking Christ.

Another storm of gunfire rocked the night, still up high but not from the rooftop.

"Hot spot neutralized," a calm voice said through his radio. "Alpha Team, go."

"Rawls," Mac said, relaxing at the news that the shooter was dead. He and Cosky slowed, lowering Zane to the sand. "Patch Zane up and then head over and see if you can do anything for Jude. He's not moving. Didn't look like their healing was working. Maybe you can help."

He doubted it. He suspected nobody could help Jude now.

Chapter Thirteen

Wolf kicked back in the rocking chair, bracing one booted foot on the porch railing, letting the soothing darkness of early morning wash over him. The porch was attached to the double-wide modular house his mother still called home. It had been his home once too, back before Jude had shown him a whole new, often violent world.

He'd fitted right into the life Jude had introduced him to. Took to the lifestyle like he'd been born into it—which he had. Born and bred for war. His ancestors had been warriors for hundreds of years, as far back into the old times as written and spoken accounts allowed.

Wolf lifted a glass of iced tea to his lips, imagining the endless vista daylight would reveal. The wide-open prairie with knee-high grass that bowed in the hot wind. The flatness of the land was broken by only the distant bulk of cattle, and the clusters of trees and shrubs that were given life by the Little Wind River.

The hoot of an owl echoed through the darkness, followed by the distant knicker of a horse. The scent of manure, grass, and dust filled his nostrils. The sounds and smells were familiar yet not. Images from a dream or a life lived eons earlier.

His mother's father had owned this land, all seventeen hundred acres of it. Back then they'd raised cattle and horses. With his grandfather's death, the land and house had passed to his mother . . . and to Jude.

But his *nesi* had chosen a different life, one inside concrete walls and tunnels instead of endless, wind-scuffed grass. One of adrenaline highs and midnight ambushes instead of long days under a blistering sun.

The last of the Eaglesbreath cattle had been sold before Wolf left high school. His mother leased the land now, collecting monthly revenue without working the land herself. Between the lease revenue, the monthly checks from the oil companies, plus the money he funneled into her bank account, she got by okay.

Taking another sip of his tea, he set the rocker gliding. It was still warm on the porch even though it was more night than morning and borderline fall. The scorching, dry wind was gentler in September—known as the tenth moon, or the moon of the drying grass.

The porch light came on, the light so bright it burned his eyes. At the squeak and flap of the porch door opening and closing, the honey-colored mutt lying beside his rocking chair lifted its head, golden eyes alert.

"I see you've met Molly," his mother said. "You should be honored. She avoids most people."

Wolf dropped a hand and scratched the dog's ears. "Golden retriever?"

"Who knows." With a shrug, his mother dropped into the second rocking chair beside him.

This he remembered too. The two of them rocking on the porch together.

It was a memory that pleased him.

With both sneaker-clad feet braced on the porch floor, she set the rocker moving. The tail of her thick graying braid, which hung over her shoulder and across her breasts, flickered with each push of her feet. "She's a stray. Found her way here a few months back."

Of course she had. His mother's house was twenty-four klicks from the nearest neighbor and forty-three klicks from Horse Tail, the nearest town. Yet dogs and cats, along with the occasional goat, pig, and horse, constantly found their way to her door.

"How many strays you taking care of now?" Wolf asked, glancing at the half dozen dogs and cats napping on the porch. The dogs ranged in size from squeak toy to miniature horse. Long and short hair. Solid to mottled colors. The only things they had in common were full bellies and content eyes.

"Counting the one you just brought me?"

Wolf turned his head and scanned his mother's high cheekbones and oval face. Her comment had been a tease, but she wasn't wrong. Jillian was a stray.

"I knew you would care for her as well as you care for your four-legged children." He looked around the packed porch, filled with the canine and feline lives she'd saved.

He could only hope she'd save Jillian as well.

She laughed, a deep belly laugh, and sent her chair rocking again. His mother never held her emotions in. She loved hard, laughed hard, cried hard, screamed rage when the anger needed releasing. What you saw was what you got.

Half Eastern Shoshone and half Northern Arapaho, her heritage had combined to forge a beautiful woman. She'd inherited the oval facial features from her Shoshone mother and the high cheekbones from her Arapaho father. The dark, liquid eyes had come from both, as had the thick, gleaming black hair. As a boy he'd recognized her beauty more by the constant stream of admirers than by his own eyes.

Her hair was streaked with gray now, her face weathered by sun and wind, but she was still a beautiful woman.

She rarely spoke of Wolf's father. He'd broken her heart when he'd left her behind. He'd almost broken her spirit when he'd married the white woman—Kait and Aiden's mother. What he'd learned of his father had come from Jude, Kait, and Aiden.

She'd never remarried, never bonded with another man. If she'd had sexual relationships with other men, he'd never been aware of it as a boy.

Had she loved only the once?

"She will fare well here, this woman of yours." She shot him a sly and satisfied smile.

He hadn't told her what Jillian was to him, but she knew. He'd never brought a woman to his mother before. Never shared his childhood home with an outsider. His mother didn't care about the color of Jillian's skin or her heritage. She cared only that the son she'd feared would never gift her with grandchildren had committed to someone.

Even if that someone was white and locked in the spirit world.

She'd waited eighteen years for this day, and he could see the joy brimming in her. Feel her expectations.

Perhaps bringing Jillian here had been a mistake. If they couldn't tempt her from the half life, his mother would carry the pain alongside him. It had taken him eighteen years to find Jillian. There would be no other woman for him. He knew this. Just as there had been no other man for his mother. Just as there had been no other woman for Jude after his fiancée's murder.

Jude's Rachel had died well before Wolf's birth, but he'd heard what had happened. The vengeance his *nesi* had rained down on the drug dealers who'd taken his Rachel was still legend among the *hinono'eiteen*.

Those of the Eaglesbreath family loved hard and once.

There were no second chances.

His head turned at the squeak of the screen door opening, and Jillian stepped onto the porch. She'd come out to join them on her own! A jab of hope hit him. Until he saw her eyes. Her hollow, lost eyes.

"She wanted out," Jillian said, her voice that dead monotone. She waved an absent hand at the furry, golden bundle pressed against her knee.

The dog, a carbon copy of the one lying beside his chair, had attached itself to Jillian's side the moment they'd climbed out of the car. You couldn't even slip a sheet of paper between the two.

"Come, sit with us." Wolf got to his feet and led Jillian to his chair, his stomach knotting at the frailty of the bones beneath his fingers.

She didn't protest, just sat down with apathy, the cherrywood of the rocker swallowing her slight frame. Folding her hands, she stared out at the cattle in the distance, her expression vacant. Her canine shadow of golden curled into a fluffy ball at her feet.

"I'll get you some tea," he said, forcing the words through his tight throat.

It's been only two days. Two days. This is not a failure.

Except doubt ate at him.

He'd showed her around Horse Tail, then took her swimming at his boyhood swimming hole out on Little Wind River. He'd introduced her to Billie Two Thorns and Ryan Helmsteader and the other Shadow Mountain warriors who'd left the base when the call of family had grown too strong or their injuries had been too severe to continue serving their teams.

She'd greeted each new experience, each new person, with complete and utter apathy.

Silence and darkness closed around him as he stepped through the screen door. He didn't bother turning on the lights, simply made his way through the house relying on memory and touch. The kitchen hadn't changed since the last time he'd been here. The middle cupboard, which held the glasses, still wobbled when he opened the door. The tile counters were still chipped but scrubbed spotless. The table tucked against the east window was still ringed by three chairs. His childhood captured in perpetuity.

He'd just filled two glasses of sun tea and returned the pitcher to the fridge when Jude died.

He didn't realize for two . . . three . . . heartbeats that Jude was gone, that the link connecting their minds had ruptured. His *nesi*—no, *father*—his best friend was agonizingly absent from his mind. There had been no pain, no fear, no goodbye, nothing to warn him—prepare him—for the greatest loss of his life.

Just sudden, complete emptiness where the connection to Jude had been.

His body reacted instinctively. Every muscle clenched. His breath caught. His head swam. His mind screamed in denial.

No. Damn it. No. Not Jude.

He frantically searched the emptiness of his mind.

Nothing.

Jude was gone.

Through the mental web that connected the Shadow Mountain warriors' consciousness, a roar of disbelief built. A howl of grief. A hundred minds mourning a loss that reverberated so deep it diminished them all.

Eric pulled back Esme's chair and waited for her to seat herself. It was a simple gesture but one he took great pleasure in performing. Esme deserved the very best of care, and that included small but significant gestures like opening doors for her or seating her at tables.

"Thank—" She tilted her head to direct an appreciative smile up at him, but her words were drowned by the scream of an airliner overhead. He glanced up with a disgusted shake of his head. The noise pollution these days was out of control. He looked forward to when the sky would be reserved for migrating birds rather than these endless airplanes and military jets.

As she lowered her head again, he eyed the vulnerable curve of her neck. He smiled. Sometimes good manners came with perks. Bending, he nuzzled the sweet spot at the nape of her neck.

She shivered, her fingers stilling on the napkin in her lap.

His smile grew. He knew all her sweet spots, the places that made her shiver or sigh—just as she knew all his. But before he could get creative and show her just how well he knew her, his cell phone buzzed against his hip.

He knew who it was before reaching for it.

"That can only be our American friend," Esme said dryly, echoing his thoughts. "Once again proving his terrible timing." She sighed and went to work spreading the napkin across her lap. "You might as well take it. It's for the best, really. I'm famished, and if lunch had continued in the manner it was headed—well, I'd likely perish from malnutrition and overexertion."

"Yes." He leaned over to kiss the hollow just below her left ear. "But what a way to perish."

With a laugh she brushed his mouth away, and Eric straightened, dragging the phone from his pocket. Sure enough, Coulson's phone number was emblazoned across the screen. After punching the Talk button, he lifted the cell to his ear.

"Coulson." He shot Esme a conspiratorial smile. "What a surprise."

"Do you get the West Coast news channels?" Coulson demanded immediately, not bothering with niceties.

"The United States' West Coast?"

Like most Americans, David Coulson was completely unaware of geography outside his own little neck of the woods. There were dozens of west coasts in the world. America didn't corner that market by any means—not that you'd know it from listening to its clueless citizens.

"Yes, the US West Coast. Seattle specifically." Coulson's voice rose impatiently, totally missing Eric's subtle message.

"Yes, I can get Seattle's news, but it will take a few minutes to access the channel. Why don't you just tell me what you want me to hear? It will save us both time."

For once his American counterpart didn't launch into one of his smug, self-aggrandizing sneer campaigns. "Someone broke into Link's estate last night. Link is missing, his security detail dead."

Eric froze, the ramifications of the news racing through his mind. "All of his security is dead?"

"There were three on duty, correct?" Coulson said, impatience growing thicker.

"Per shift, yes."

"Then they took out the night shift. The news is reporting three security officers dead. And Link missing."

Eric swore softly, rubbing at the sudden throb behind his temples. One of those security officers had been his man. He'd installed someone loyal to him on each shift for exactly this scenario. "My man was under strict orders to take out Link if something like this were to occur."

He'd also been under strict orders to take the rest of the security team out first, in case they questioned his targeting or agenda. The deaths of the other security guards and Link himself would be shuttled off on the people doing the breaking and entering.

God knew they couldn't afford to have Link in enemy hands, not with everything he knew about the NRO, the people involved, and their upcoming agendas. Christ, he even knew the date and location of the next meeting.

"Well, it looks like your man failed," Coulson snapped. His tone implied it wasn't a surprise—that Eric failed so often it was to be expected.

Eric stiffened, his fingers tightening around the phone. Too bad it wasn't Coulson's thick red neck. "We don't know my guy failed. He could have taken out Link."

"Right." A definite sneer rode the tone. "And they decided to make off with Link's body. For what exactly? You can't interrogate the dead. There would be no reason to take him unless he was alive."

Damn it.

There was nothing worse than admitting when someone you despised was right. "I'll activate the protocols."

"I've already done so," Coulson said, with gloating satisfaction. "Link has been wiped from the system, and the board is voting on electing Poussey as interim chairman until Link or Embray is deemed fit for duty."

The protocol, which had been designed to prevent anyone from making a run on Dynamic Solutions if Link were to be assassinated or kidnapped, had been Eric's baby. His responsibility. A duty that Coulson had apparently usurped.

"Excellent." Eric forced the word through gritted teeth.

It didn't matter who pulled the trigger on the protocol. What mattered was that the company was protected. That whoever had kidnapped Link wouldn't be able to use him to ransack or investigate Dynamic Solutions creations . . . such as clean energy generators that could be repurposed as clean energy bombs.

"We'll need to alter our plans for the next meeting. Link is aware of the location and host."

"Agreed." Coulson sounded bored. "I'll take it. Since I hosted it last time, it's unlikely they'll suspect me of doing so again. Assuming Link is alive and leaking like a damn sieve." Which his tone said they should both be assuming.

"Who do you think went after him?" Eric asked, his mind turning to the underlying problem.

"Who the fuck do you think?" Coulson retorted. "Either those fucking SEALs or those fucking redskins. Or, hell, both. The attack on our lab indicates they're working together."

Eric nodded. His instincts insisted this as well, even though it didn't make sense. "How would they know Link was working with us?"

Hell, it wasn't like they sent announcements out when someone joined their organization. Nor did anyone, ever, announce their involvement in the council. The whole damn point of a clandestine organization was to keep it *secret.*

"How the fuck did they know where the lab was or that we even had the new energy device?" A cold front formed in Coulson's voice. "We have a fucking leak somewhere."

After another prolonged massage of his temples, Eric had to agree. "We need to find it and plug it. Permanently."

Coulson grunted his agreement. "In the meantime, how is the hunt at Denali doing? Any word from your men on the ground over where these bastards are holed up?"

"Nothing." Eric forced himself to stay calm. No sense in alerting Coulson to his building frustration on that front. "There's no sign of a non-US military base. And although there is sign of military aircraft, there's a fucking army base in Anchorage."

Another grunt traveled down the line, this time a thoughtful one. "I have a guy. He's motivated. I'll send him up to poke around."

Eric shrugged. "Fine."

The only good thing about adding Coulson to the council was his effectiveness. While brutal, his methods did tend to get the job done. If Coulson's man could track down the Shadow Mountain crew—or, hell, even Mackenzie and the rest of his damn SEALs—more power to him. They couldn't afford much more of this interference.

"How's the manufacturing going?"

"It's going. We're on schedule. We need to wait until we have enough in stock to hit everywhere at once. We don't want a regroup and counterattack."

"Agreed." It was the strategy the council had developed as soon as Link had informed them of the clean energy generator's potential. It was their very best chance of removing enough of the population to make a difference—of achieving what the council had been created to do: to reset the planet, thus preserving it for all the future generations that wouldn't exist without the sacrifices made in the here and now.

Chapter Fourteen

MAC LEANED THE BACK OF HIS HEAD AGAINST THE CHOPPER'S PADDED wall. From the decrease in the vibrations numbing his ass and thighs, he could tell they were slowing down, which indicated they were closing in on the base. Bulky shadows stirred in the dark interior of the chopper. He stretched, rolled his neck, avoided looking in the far corner at the black vinyl body bag.

Sharing the bird with their dead, after a mission gone sour, wasn't exactly new. The trident promised that no man would be left behind. It didn't promise that everyone would return alive. Just that the same number of bodies would return on the chopper as had left on it.

Still, a body bag was something nobody wanted to sit next to on the return trip. No one liked losing a friend. A buddy. Someone you ate with and joked with and talked with mere hours earlier . . . it was never an easy thing.

The grim silence in the chopper was edged in grief. In thick yet unspoken sorrow.

Mac recognized the atmosphere all too well.

Rawls and the healers had tried to save him. They'd worked frantically, but a shot to the neck meant he'd been dead before he'd hit the ground.

Zane's wound had been bad but treatable. Jude, on the other hand . . . Jesus. Eventually it became painfully obvious that nothing the healers or Rawls did was going to make a damn bit of difference. They'd halted their high-speed retreat so One Bird could climb over and heal the hit to Zane's thigh.

That wild flight across Lake Washington, the Zodiac flying over white-tipped waves and the moon leering down through patchy clouds, merged with dozens of other missions in his memory. Different bodies of water, different teams, but identical imagery.

A snatch and run was a snatch and run whether you did the snatching in Seattle, Washington, or Herat, Afghanistan.

And a dead warrior was a dead warrior whether he came from Shadow Mountain or HQ1.

The chopper slowed again. Mac glanced at James Link. Their prisoner was barely visible in the darkness between Zane and Rawls. Just a dark, indistinct blur. He'd been the perfect captive so far. No attempts to escape. No bravado. Just calm, quiet compliance.

The bastard's submissiveness raised questions. Did he know who'd kidnapped him? Had he shut down to avoid retribution, or did he not care what happened? Maybe Amy was right. Maybe the guy was so riddled with guilt he'd already checked out of life.

It would have been nice if they'd had a chance to question the man prior to arrival at the base. Been able to give Amy some immediate answers. But the chopper was too noisy to carry out casual conversation, let alone an interrogation. Pantomime and hand gestures weren't exactly conducive to grilling a suspect.

Mac rubbed an exhausted hand down his face, feeling the slime of grease paint and dirt on his palm. Jude might have been irritating sometimes, even a downright pain in the ass, but he'd been a good man. An honorable one. A warrior to respect. His instinctive, selfless move as he'd thrown himself over Link and Zane had saved their lives. He'd sacrificed himself so that they would live.

Without that one act of courage, he'd be mourning Zane's death right now, and likely Benji's and Brendan's down the road, if Link had died in that courtyard.

Jude had saved multiple lives with the giving of his own.

Once the bird set down, the cargo lights came on. He caught Zane's grim gaze, the green eyes so dark they looked black rather than emerald. Link stirred, straightening against the padded wall, but he didn't try to get up.

Good little NRO asshole.

The Eagle's engine slowed and finally cut completely, and the bird slowly descended as its lift drew it into Shadow Mountain's gut. It was the third time he'd taken this journey, but the descent, without the engines going, still felt wrong. Abnormal. Like they'd experienced engine failure and were in a free fall.

After so many hours of the rotors beating the air, the sudden silence was surreal. He levered himself to his feet, waiting for his ears to stop ringing. Cosky rose to his feet too, then reached down to haul Link up beside him.

The bastard came quietly, as he'd reacted to everything so far. But this time his compliance was no surprise. He had no place to run.

When the cargo door slid back, they waited for the Shadow Mountain team to disembark, only to find themselves waved forward by the copilot, who'd stepped forward and waited in the cockpit doorway. Mac hopped from the bird and straightened. Then he froze. The chopper was surrounded, as far as the eye could see, by grim-faced, silent men and a few scattered women. Everyone was there: mechanics with their grease-stained overalls next to cooks in their grease-stained aprons next to doctors and nurses in their hospital scrubs.

Jude was returning to a hero's welcome.

Neniiseti', his face more lined and solemn than Mac had ever seen it, stepped forward as Cosky dragged Link from the chopper. He paused before them, raked Link's shrinking form with eagle-bright eyes. "I hope what this one reveals is worth the one we lost."

So did Mac.

"I'm so damn sorry," Mac said, his voice rough and halting, the ability to find the right words foreign on his tongue. Offering condolences to the bereaved never got easier.

A single, dignified nod greeted his words.

Mac searched Neniiseti's eyes, expecting condemnation. He'd been the one, after all, pushing for the mission. Wolf wouldn't have taken the request to his CO if Mac hadn't convinced him to. But there was no condemnation in the black eyes. No anger. Just an eternity of sorrow.

As Neniiseti' stepped up to the chopper, Kait pushed her way through the throng of men and women. Her hair caught in a tousled, untidy braid, she reached for Cosky's hand.

"We can try to heal him, right? We can at least try." Her red-rimmed eyes clung to Cosky's. Drying tracks of tears were visible on her cheeks.

"It's been six hours, sweetheart," Cosky said, his voice a gentle rumble as he drew her into his arms.

"But it won't hurt to try!" she mumbled into his chest, her voice thick with tears. She turned in Cosky's arms to face Neniiseti', her face raw with grief.

"Such efforts will do no good. His spirit already roams free."

"Maybe. Right? It will do no harm." When Neniiseti' didn't agree, she reached out and caught his hand, entreaty in her eyes. "Please. This is going to kill Wolf."

A pulse of silence fell, and Mac could see Kait's chest still, as though she were holding her breath. An audible *whoosh* escaped her lips when Neniiseti' finally nodded agreement. She didn't wait for him to change his mind. Grabbing Cosky's hand, she bolted for the chopper, her long golden braid flying behind her.

"Any chance they can do it?" Rawls asked, his gaze locked on Kait and Cos as they climbed into the chopper.

Mac heard the hope in his corpsman's voice.

"No."

Neniiseti' dashed their hope with that one word mired in certainty.

"They're pretty damn powerful together. They brought me back from the dead. Faith too."

"You were not six hours gone," the old man reminded him. "Jude already seeks the path to the ancestors."

Silence fell once again. A grim silence devoid of hope. From the fresh tears on her face, when Kait finally emerged from the chopper, Neniiseti's negativity had been proven true.

Four Shadow Mountain warriors stepped down from the Eagle, each gripping one of the body bag's handles. As they carried their fallen warrior home, Neniiseti' moved forward to greet them, his voice raised in a rhythmic, deep-chested chant. The words were foreign to Mac but Arapaho from the sound of them.

He shifted to the side along with Rawls and Zane, who tugged Link back as well, as Neniiseti', still chanting, slowly walked toward the hangar's exit. The four warriors carrying Jude's body followed behind him. Slowly, the rest of the men in the hangar fell in step behind them.

When he and his men and Kait were the last ones left in the hangar, Mac stirred, indicating Link with a jerk of his head. "Where are we supposed to take him?"

"Hell if I know," Rawls said, turning to stare at the empty exit. "Hate to ask, as our hosts are kinda busy right now. Suppose we could take him to your quarters?"

Fuck, he sure as hell didn't want to intrude when they were mourning the death of one of their own. But they needed to get some answers.

Amy's kids' lives were depending on it. Might as well question the asshole in his quarters. They could ask their questions anywhere.

"I don't understand," Kait said, her voice still thick with emotion. "One Bird's and William's healings should have worked. Why didn't they?"

Cosky caught her fingers with one hand and stroked her cheek to wipe away her tears with the other. "You know the healings don't work all the time, sweetheart. Maybe he falls into that percentage that can't be healed."

"But that's just it," Kait said, pure bewilderment on the face she raised to Cosky. "He'd been healed before—multiple times, from what he told me. He wasn't in the percentage that can't be healed. So why did he die?"

"One Bird and William were able to heal him before?" Rawls asked, an uneasy expression skittering across his face. "Are you sure?"

"Yes. Positive."

Rawls raked visibly tense fingers through his hair. "Have to admit, Kaity, I'm not fond of this news. Here I was thinking you healers were our own trio of angels, keepin' us from kickin' the bucket and all. But if Jude was in One Bird's and William's thirty percent, and he still died—"

"Then nobody is safe," Kait whispered. Her gaze clung to Cosky.

Mac watched fear edge the grief in her red eyes. He still found it hard to believe in the miracle of Kait's hands, but the rest of them obviously did, and this monkey wrench to their sense of invincibility had rattled them.

Time to give everyone something else to think about. He made a big production of clearing his throat, satisfied when everyone turned in his direction.

"There's a couple of lives right now we might be able to save," he reminded everyone.

And a desperate woman who was waiting for some answers.

He turned to Kait. "You mind going to the clinic and letting Mrs. Chastain know we're about to question Link? Tell her to head to my quarters."

They watched her leave, her blonde braid swinging against her back.

Once she was out of earshot, Rawls turned to Mac, his eyebrows climbing so high they merged with the hair brushing his forehead. "Mrs. Chastain?" He smirked. "You ain't foolin' anyone there, Skipper."

Mac ignored him.

"Mrs. Chastain?" Link said, sudden awareness darkening his eyes.

"That's right." Mac took a step toward him, anger loosening muscles stiff from inactivity. The bastard had recognized her name. "Amy Chastain. Mother of the two kids you bastards poisoned. Widow of the FBI agent you fucktards murdered."

Link flinched, his face blanching, guilt so heavy he could have drowned in it, and Mac knew they were right. James Link was up to his balls in the NRO—complicit in their murderous, violent attacks on innocent people, complicit in whatever horrific plans they had for Faith's doomsday device.

"I see you're familiar with her." Mac balled his fist, fighting the urge to slam it into the bastard's face long enough and hard enough to require some major cosmetic surgery.

But they needed the bastard awake and lucid enough to answer questions.

He shoved Link forward instead. "He was aiming for you, you know that? Your buddy on the rooftop. You were his target. He could have slaughtered the rest of us easy enough. He had the position and the time. But the only men who got hit were the ones protecting you. Jude died because he knocked you down. Zane got hit because he was covering your worthless hide." He shoved Link forward again, his words gaining momentum. "The assholes you're in bed with would rather kill you than rescue you. Shows how much they value your services."

Zane nodded, matching Mac's pace and tone. "I wouldn't count on them coming to your rescue."

Link turned his head and caught Mac's eye. "You're Mackenzie." It wasn't a question. More like an internal confirmation.

"Glad you've heard of me," Mac drawled.

They held their questions until they reached Mac's quarters. Cosky shoved their captive into a chair, circled the table, and casually unholstered his MK3 knife. After dropping into his chair, he laid down the weapon in front of him. Mac followed suit, removing his blade. He considered driving the knife into the table, but, hell—the surface was Formica—with his luck the blade would glance off and stab someone. After pulling their knives, Rawls and Zane took their seats too.

Link studied the knives, with their lethal tips and serrated edges, and shook his head. But rather than appearing terrified, worried, or even smug, he looked exhausted.

For the first time, Mac looked at him. Really looked at him. It had been too dark in the field to see him clearly. In the chopper, Link had been stashed between numerous men, his body and face completely hidden in the darkness. Once they'd disembarked, the reminder of Jude's death had consumed everyone.

But in the bright light of Mac's quarters, the guy looked a thousand times worse than the pictures Amy had dug up.

The man was a fucking skeleton.

Link's passivity combined with his appearance could mean one of only two things. Either the guy was sick as hell, or Amy was right—he was consumed by guilt.

"You aren't going to need the knives," Link said quietly, holding Mac's gaze. "I'll tell you everything you want to know."

"How accommodating of you," Zane said, his level tone in direct contrast to the ice in his eyes.

Link glanced at him then back to Mac. "How are the Chastain boys?"

Mac froze against the urge to maim. As the fury surged in a red-hot haze of murder and mayhem, he bolted from his chair and took a couple of tight turns around the room.

You can't kill him . . . not yet.

He took another tight walk around the room. "You don't have the fucking right to ask that question. Got it?"

"Look, I'm sorry about what happened to those boys. But I had nothing to do with that. When I gave them the technology, it was under the promise that they'd use it only on their own soldiers. It was supposed to be used to track their men if they went AWOL. It was never supposed to be used on innocent civilians and certainly not children. I had no hand in that."

"Are you fucking kidding me?" Mac spun around so fast he went dizzy. He waited for his head to clear before stalking forward. "You gave it to a bunch of sociopathic monsters. Men who've killed hundreds if not thousands of innocent people, and you didn't think they'd use it whenever and however they saw fit? You gave the technology to them. You enabled them to use it. You're every bit as fucking complicit as they are."

"Mac." Zane's calm voice rose from the table. He caught and held Mac's gaze, his green eyes full of relief.

The rage was so hot and so consuming, it took him a minute to realize why all three of his men had relaxed. And then it hit him. Link had just admitted he'd been the gateway to the crap they'd injected into Amy's kids, which meant Link had the data to reverse the drug.

Relief funneled off the rage, allowed him to breathe again. He'd taken his first step back to the table when a knock sounded at the door.

Amy.

He pictured the relief on her face when she heard the news. The hope.

"You can give your apologies to their mother," he told Link over his shoulder.

Or better yet, he could give her the cure and the means to save her children.

Chapter Fifteen

The door to Mac's quarters opened so fast, he must have been standing right next to it. Amy's gaze found Mac's face and clung, searching for an indication that Link had supplied the information she needed. That he'd admitted to developing the compound killing her children.

She found satisfaction in his eyes, so Link must have told them something Mac felt they could use.

As though he'd read her mind, Mac nodded. "He's admitted to giving the NRO the tracking compound."

She stepped into the room and waited for Mac to close the door. "Has he told you how to counteract it?"

Her focus turned to James Link. Good God, the man looked terrible. Eyes sunken into his face. Deep lines gouging his forehead and bracketing his lips. His skin looked pale, almost gray.

It took her several moments to realize he was studying her as closely as she was him.

"I'm sorry about your kids. I am. Truly," he said, his voice sincere.

Amy felt Mac tense beside her. She glanced over and watched anger narrow his eyes and flare his nostrils. The hairs on her arms prickled, and she swore she felt a blast of heat come from him.

"I've already told you," Mac snapped, stalking to the table. "That doesn't do a fucking bit of good."

Amy followed more slowly. "So Dynamic Solutions developed the compound."

Link nodded. "It's basically a tracking device. It was developed as a long-term means to track endangered species through both land and water."

Amy held her breath long enough to steady her voice. "If Dynamic Solutions developed it, then you must have an antidote, a way to reverse or neutralize the compound?"

Link lifted a skeletal hand and brushed the hair off his forehead. "I wasn't involved in the development. That was Leonard. It was his baby."

Okay . . . Amy forced the impatience aside. The longing to return to the clinic and Benji's side was at war with the urge to stay and find out how to save him. "But you must have access to his data? You can find out what he did, what he used, the protocols he had in place. He must have recorded everything that went into the compound. The recipe for the antidote."

Even if Embray hadn't developed an antidote yet, if they had the recipe for the compound—so to speak—they could reverse engineer a way to neutralize it. At least it would give them a place to start.

Link looked away, an expression falling over his face that drove daggers of panic through Amy's chest. He looked defeated. Full of guilt.

"What?" Her voice was hoarse.

"It's doubtful I'll be able to access the mainframe." His gaze gravitated to Mac. "You're right. The NRO doesn't value my services. Nor do they need me to control Dynamic Solutions anymore. They control the board. The minute you took me, I became expendable. If they followed the protocol the board recently approved, the moment they realized I was compromised they'd have wiped me from the mainframe. Voted me out of office. Poussey will step in as acting head."

Frozen silence gripped the room.

Amy felt her lungs deflate.

No. No.

"You're lying." But Mac's voice lacked certainty.

Link shook his head. Scrubbed a hand down his face. "No. I'm not. It will be easy enough to prove."

"How?" Amy asked, her voice tight and breathless, fingers of panic squeezing her lungs.

"If you have a computer handy, I can try to log into the mainframe."

"I've got one." Mac rose to his feet beside her. He walked across the room and through the door to his bedroom. From over the waist-high walls she saw him grab a laptop off his bedside table. He carried it over, lifting his eyebrows when he caught her looking at it. "I took your advice and asked for one."

He set it on the table and pushed it toward Link. "Help yourself."

As Link opened the lid and started working the mouse pad, Mac directed a meaningful look at Rawls. "Doc, why don't you give him a hand with that?"

Translation: *Watch him like a hawk and make sure he's not playing us for fools.*

Rawls took the hint and scooted his chair over until it was right up against Link.

After a few moments of silence while his fingers moved over the mouse pad, Link looked up. "I'm locked out."

Mac bounced a glance off Rawls, who confirmed the statement with a frown and nod. His lips tightening, Mac scowled across the table. "Try again."

Another few seconds of silence, followed by Link and Rawls grimly shaking their heads.

"Again," Mac snapped.

Amy sat back, sliding down in her chair as though her bones didn't have the strength to hold her upright. Defeat crawled through her. It didn't matter how many times Link tried. If he was locked out, he wouldn't be getting in. He wouldn't be accessing the data. Her children wouldn't be getting the antidote they so desperately needed.

A numb disbelief swept over her.

What was she going to do now?

"How do we know you're not using the wrong username or password?" Zane asked.

"You don't." Link pushed the laptop away. "But I'm not lying about this. I'm not faking it. I want to cooperate with you. I want to help you in any way I can."

"You're fucking NRO. What in the *fuck* makes you think we'd believe you?" Mac growled, surging to his feet and circling the room as if he simply couldn't sit still any longer.

Raising his head, Link looked Amy square in the face. "If there was anything . . . anything at all I could do for your boys, I would."

She unlocked her jaw. Forced herself up in her chair. "You must know something about this compound. Something, even the smallest thing. What they used?"

If the doctors here could just get a toehold, something to build on . . .

He shook his head.

"Then Embray? If he developed it."

Link's face seized around the most god-awful combination of regret and pain. "He can't." His voice caught. "He's gone."

She'd been right. The two men had been friends.

"What about Dynamic Solutions? Is there anyone in the company who could smuggle the information to you?"

He frowned, shook his head. "The data is classified. There are only two of us who can access the data. Me and Sheldon Poussey. Sheldon is compromised. He's NRO now."

Amy backed up, trying to look at the issue from another angle. "If we grabbed Poussey . . ."

"He'd be wiped, unable to access the data."

In other words, they'd be in the same boat they were in now.

"What about Eric Manheim?" Mac asked. He tilted his head and narrowed his eyes. "He'd be able to get the information."

"Yes, he would. If you could find him. And if you could grab him."

It went without saying that they couldn't use Link to get to Manheim. Amy searched her mind, desperate for some avenue to pursue. Another way to approach the problem. But nothing came to mind, and they were running out of time.

"There must be something we can do," Amy whispered. She needed to get back to Benji. But the thought of returning to her son's bedside, only to watch him die . . .

Link swallowed hard. His face was full of anguish. "I'll answer any questions the doctors have, but I'm afraid nothing I say will make a difference. If I could go back, change what I did, I would. Unfortunately Dynamic Solutions has not developed a time machine yet." He grimaced. "I don't mean to be facetious. Really, I don't. I deeply regret joining with Manheim and the others. I thought . . . I thought I shared their vision, but it's becoming increasingly apparent that I didn't think things through clearly." He paused, his face haunted. "Leonard was right. I should have listened. I wish I'd listened."

"What vision?" Cosky asked, leaning forward in his chair, his gaze sharpening with interest.

Amy bit back a protest. Who cared about the group's agenda? She needed to know about the compound. From Link's answers to her questions, it was clear he didn't know how to save Benji.

"The NRO's agenda is surprisingly pure. They want to save the planet along with the human race."

Eyes widened in disbelief.

Link shrugged. "It's true. At the current rate of human consumption, population explosion, and global warming, it will be a miracle if humankind still exists in two hundred years. Earth can't continue to support humanity. Not when we are systematically circumventing the planet's ability to support life. The NRO's goal is to save Earth and prevent humanity from going extinct."

"How?" Amy asked, trying to reconcile what Link was telling them with actions she knew the NRO had taken.

From what she'd seen so far, the NRO lacked the altruistic attitude James was painting. They'd killed John. They'd had her kidnapped and brutalized. If Mac and his men were right, they'd slaughtered the passengers of two airplanes and planned to slaughter all the passengers from a third. Plus, there was the kidnapping and murder of Faith's scientific team. Everything she'd seen and heard indicated that these people were ruthless, murderous monsters.

Link sighed. "By cleansing the planet of the bulk of its population."

Amy almost laughed. His explanation was so cartoonish, or maybe comic-book-villain-ish was more accurate. There was no way . . . *no way* anyone could seriously plan something so . . . *diabolical.*

Except Link wasn't laughing. Neither was Mac, nor Zane, nor anyone.

"Faith's new energy generator," Zane said slowly.

Link nodded. "The new energy generator accelerated the NRO's agenda. Prior to its discovery, Manheim and the council were taking smaller but devastating steps to reduce the population. Sterilizing hundreds of remote villages in Africa, India, and China. Infecting people with various fatal diseases. The sudden explosion of cancer, for example . . ." He stopped to shake his head. "But the increase in births has overridden the decreases in population. Until the clean energy project, there was no way to easily clear off huge swaths of people without poisoning the land, air, and water."

"Until the clean energy device," Rawls repeated slowly. "You're saying they can use this device to clear the world of humanity?"

"Yes. It's been rewired. Rather than collecting energy and storing it, the new device will disperse a sonic vibration that will travel for hundreds of miles." He shook his head again and closed his eyes as though he didn't want to see his audience's faces when he admitted to the rest of it. "It will kill every human being in its path."

"But that's crazy," Rawls said, his face slack with shock. "You say they're all about saving the planet? If the device releases a sonic vibration that's capable of killing people, it will kill *any* living creature in its path. Don't they realize you can't fuck with an ecosystem like that? A complete kill-off will affect everything. The lack of insects, bats, and birds will affect pollination. The lack of flies and beetles will affect decomposition."

"Of course they realize. For all their faults, they're far from stupid," Link said. "Keep in mind that water, air, and vegetation will not be affected. There will be no residual effect once the devices fall silent. The affected areas will eventually rejuvenate. New animals, insects, and birds will move in. The NRO already has labs set up to inseminate, grow, and repopulate animals and insects en masse. The surviving creatures will spread out; they'll adapt. Earth will reshape itself."

Amy shifted uneasily in her chair. The crisis she found herself embroiled in was bigger than her and the boys. Much bigger. Even if she managed to get the antidote in time, what Link was talking about could easily kill them, along with everyone in this room.

"How many devices would they need?" Cosky asked.

"Thousands. But they are halfway there."

"Do you know where they're producing them?" Zane rubbed a finger along the furrow above his eyes.

"No." Link leaned back in his chair and shook his head. "Coulson's in charge of the devices, along with production and distribution."

"Coulson who?" Rawls asked.

Link glanced around the table. "David Coulson, the head of Care-One Pharmaceuticals."

"We need to take this to Shadow Command." Zane turned to Mac.

"No shit." Mac scowled. "What kind of time frame are we looking at? How soon can they produce enough of these devices and get them in place?"

"They are aiming for January first. A new year . . . a new Earth."

"Sweet Jesus," Rawls whispered. "That's less than four months away."

"We know about it now. We can stop it." Cosky laced his hands behind his head. "Piece of cake."

"Absolutely. What are we waiting for?" Rawls drawled.

"What about Embray?" Amy asked. "I take it he didn't agree with the direction the NRO wanted to take. Is that why they killed him?"

"Lennie was horrified." Link's eyes went blank and his face pinched as though he was remembering something terrible. "He accused Manheim and Coulson of not wanting to save the world—but of trying to control it. To install themselves as dictators. To decide who lived and died."

"So they killed him." Mac's voice was grim.

"No. Much worse." Link swallowed hard. "They couldn't control Dynamic Solutions if Lennie died. So they destroyed him instead. They injected him with a combination of drugs from David's company, which caused an instant stroke. The stroke destroyed his brain stem. With Lennie alive but incapacitated, I stepped in to control the company. They immediately had me appoint NRO sympathizers to the board."

"Wait. Wait." Amy jolted forward, energized again. *Did I hear him right?* "Embray is alive?"

"If you call it living," Link said tightly. "Lennie wouldn't. He's in an unresponsive coma. No neurological activity. He can't answer your questions."

"He's alive." Amy turned to stare at Cosky. "Kait . . . if he's in her thirty percent . . ."

Bodies straightened and eyes sharpened as the possibility made its way around the table. If Kait could heal Embray and he still remembered the science behind the tracking isotope, there was a good chance he could create an antidote.

"Where's Embray?" Mac braced his arms on the table. "What kind of security does he have?"

Link looked puzzled. He glanced among the men at the table, his gaze finally settling on Amy. "He has no security. Why would he need it? He's unable to answer questions. He's in a coma. He's got round-the-clock nurses and a doctor on the premises. That's all that's necessary."

"Where is he?" Mac repeated, his voice hard.

With a shake of his head, Link looked even more baffled. "I had him moved to Wilkes Island, Dynamic Solutions' retreat, a week ago. It's private. Remote. He used to love it there."

If Kait could heal him . . . Amy swallowed hard, the rise of hope so sudden it was almost painful.

Maybe her boys had a chance after all.

Chapter Sixteen

SLOUCHED IN ONE OF THE JET'S HUGE PADDED-LEATHER SEATS, WOLF stared unseeing out the small window next to his head. They'd sent the big bird to collect him. The Citation Latitude. She was Shadow Mountain's most recent baby, and a treasured one at that. Capable of cruising in excess of eight hundred klicks an hour and more than five thousand klicks on a single tank of fuel—she was a wonder of aeronautical engineering and craftsmanship.

The fact that they'd sent her, rather than any of the other birds they had to choose from—planes that would have accomplished the same thing just in more time, like the jet he'd flown down on—well, it spoke of Neniiseti's urgency. The need to have Wolf on base . . . *now*.

With Jude lost to them, Wolf was the elder of the Eagle Clan. He would lead the death prayers and the recall ceremony. He would tie new warriors to the mental web as well as excise those who wished to leave it. He would take up Eagle Clan chieftain tasks and leave the warlording behind . . . for the most part.

A necessity that did not sit well with him. Not well at all.

Jude had been the Eagle Clan chieftain. To fill his *wo'ohno* . . . Grief swelled, followed by a surge of rage. He pushed both down deep and held them there. It was not the time for such emotions.

It felt odd to be returning on the Citation. Black Hawks or the new experimental Shadow Eagles were more his thing. Machines for a warrior.

You are no longer a warrior. Best get used to traveling in style.

It was an annoying mental voice. One full of condescension and unwelcome truths. One that had been growing stronger by the hour since Jude's death, since that moment in the kitchen when his life had crashed to a halt, only to take off on a new trajectory.

An unwelcome trajectory.

It had taken five hours for the Citation to touch down at Riverton Regional Airport. He was two hours into the four-hour flight returning him to Shadow Mountain. Which added up to too many hours and too much distance. Too much time lost in his own mind, caressing vengeful wishes, exploring the uselessness of *if onlys*.

His mother's haunted face rose in his mind. The way her shoulders had frozen under his hand as his words hit her ears and detonated in her mind. The way her body had sagged from the blow. The sudden dimming of her bright eyes. The dullness of shock and flood of anguish across her face.

She hadn't cried. His mother, who wore her emotions as an outer skin, who laughed and cried and screamed without barriers, hadn't wept or screamed at the death of her *hisoh'o*. She'd drawn her anguish in close and held it there. The pain was so raw she couldn't release it.

Had Jillian even noticed their grief? Their sorrow? Had she questioned his sudden return to base? Had she noticed he was gone? Rage flashed, roared through him with the heat of a thousand suns.

He tried to tamp it down.

It was not Jillian the fury clawed at. He knew this. Knew the rage would crest and fall, and he must steer the descent into calmer waters. But it was difficult. Here he sat with too much time to remember and regret.

If only he hadn't allowed Mackenzie to convince him of Link's necessity. There would have been no mission, no ambush. No death.

Maybe not Jude's death, that annoying voice inside him chided. *But there would have been deaths. At least two. Children's deaths.*

He scowled at the reminder.

If only he'd ignored Neniiseti's directive and refused to take Jillian away. He would have been on base to lead the team. Jude would not have died.

You would have been banished. Jude would have led the team. He would have still died.

If only he'd dropped off Jillian at his mother's house and returned immediately to base. He could have led the mission, and Jude would be alive.

This time that annoying voice in his brain remained silent.

He should have returned to base immediately. Jillian wouldn't have cared. His presence had been for his sake, not hers. She'd paid more attention to the stray dog that had attached itself to her than she'd paid to him.

While he'd been shepherding a woman who didn't need him, Jude had died.

That was the crux of it. The root of his rage.

Mackenzie was an asshole, but he'd been right. They did need Link. Not just because of Amy Chastain and her doomed children, but because of Faith's doomsday device. Link was their best shot at running that device down and destroying it before the NRO used it themselves with horrific results.

The mission had been imperative, but Jude shouldn't have been leading the Shadow Mountain teams; Wolf should have been.

Jude was dead because Wolf had let his personal entanglements supersede his Shadow Mountain commitments. His duty to his men. To his people. To Shadow Mountain Command.

Jude was dead because of him.

He closed his eyes. He pressed his forehead against the icy glass window and looked out over the cold white clouds the jet was surfing across.

I should have been there.

The words rolled through his mind, knocking every other thought aside. That little voice that had been annoying him all day remained silent. Because it knew he was right.

Jude had died because of him.

What would have happened if they'd swapped positions was impossible to say. It could have been Wolf who'd died last night and Jude mourning the loss of a son. Or Wolf's warning beacon could have triggered and warned them of the sharpshooter above in time to take him out before any shots were fired.

Why it hadn't gone off anyway was something he didn't want to examine too closely. Jude's sense would not have triggered as his was the death foretold. But for Wolf's not to trigger—such a failing indicated something unforeseen and unchangeable.

Which played hell with his self-accountability.

By the time the Citation landed on Shadow Mountain and taxied to its hangar lift, Wolf had locked the rage and grief down tight. He stepped out of the plane to find Neniiseti' waiting for him.

The elder carried his sorrow in the slight curve of his shoulders and the trenches carved in his face. Wolf stopped before him, offering the half bow of respect.

"Was Link worth it?" Wolf asked, his jaw so tight it hurt to open his mouth.

Neniiseti' shrugged. "There is no measuring such things. However, the *nih'oo3oo* knows much."

"He's sharing what he knows?"

Neniiseti' nodded before turning. Wolf stepped up to his side. "He knows how to help Amy's children?"

"He does not. However, he has opened another path. One we would not have known without his words."

Wolf mulled that over. Not the best outcome, but not the worst either. "What of Faith's machine?"

"He does not know of its whereabouts, but he has given us names. Many names. One of these names is charged with this device and the alterations they have made to it."

Now that sounded much more promising.

"This, at least, is much more than we had before," Wolf murmured.

But Neniiseti' was right. There was no way to measure what they'd gained from the mission to grab Link against what they had lost. There was no equivalency between the two.

"The spirit of the eagle runs strong through your clan," Neniiseti' said without looking at Wolf. "It is imperative you bring in a lieutenant."

Wolf nodded. The elder was right. With Jude gone, they needed to show a second the ways, someone to step in when Wolf was dispatched to the ancestors. If both Jude and Wolf had died at the same time, an Eagle Clan elder from the Southern Arapaho tribe would have been brought in to teach the ceremony to the fledgling chieftain of the Northern Arapaho tribe. And so it had been since the old times.

It was preferred that the ways be taught from within the clan as there were deviations between the Northern and Southern tribes.

Within the Eagle Clan, his mother's family line ran strong. Descendants of the Eaglesbreath family had held the Eagle Clan chiefdom since the old times, but he was the last of the Eaglesbreath warriors. If he produced no sons, his lineage would die with him. It was time to look outside his bloodlines for a lieutenant.

"I dreamed last night," Neniiseti' said. When Wolf stiffened, the elder shook his head. "Not of your woman. I dreamed of two *tei'yoonoh'o'*. One a girl with hair the color of corn after ripening. The other a boy with hair as black as the blackest among the people."

Kait and Aiden? But why dream about them as children?

"Within the bluest of blue skies rode a shadow. It descended closer and closer to the two on the ground. It landed on a fence post near the *tei'yoonoh'o'*. So close they could taste the breath of the creator. See the fierce wisdom of Be:he:teiht in his eyes. It held them there for many heartbeats before flying back to the creator and gifting the *tei'yoonoh'o'* with two feathers."

"They are Eagle Clan," Wolf said, instantly understanding the meaning of the dream.

The eagle was sacred among the *hinono'eiteen*. As the eagle was seen as the mediator between the creator and those who walked the earth, sightings were good luck, something to celebrate. But only Eagle Clan members had close encounters with the spirit bird.

When the *hiinooko3onit* had inducted Wolf into the Eagle Clan, he had done so in the same manner as Neniiseti' had described in his dream. The spirit bird had landed on a fence post next to Wolf's horse. The spirit of Be:he:teiht had radiated from the bird. Wolf had been lost in the spirit eagle's fierce gaze for heartbeat after heartbeat. And then the spirit had screamed and flown up into the sky, leaving a single tail feather behind.

The sacred feather.

His induction into the Eagle Clan.

He'd been thirteen when the spirit had visited him, and he'd never shared the story of his induction with anyone. Not even Jude. Clan inductions were private, but he'd known what to expect. From Jude, from his mother, from the many grandfathers and grandmothers—of both his lineage and outside—who'd passed the traditions down to him. He'd known what a visit from a spirit animal felt like, what it meant, and what to do with the sacred totem it left behind. His hand closed over the bulk of the totem pouch that rested close to his heart. He was never without it.

Kait and Aiden had not been so lucky. They'd had no clue they'd been inducted into a clan. Had they kept the feathers? Had they realized there was something special, something sacred in that moment? They had never mentioned the incident to him. Inductions came to children not long after puberty. Perhaps they had forgotten.

Then the questions arose.

Clans tended to travel within families. As Neniiseti' had noted, the Eagle Clan was strong in his mother's father's family—within the Eaglesbreath lineage.

But Kait and Aiden were not Eaglesbreath. They and Wolf shared the same father, but they had different mothers. Eagle Clan had been passed down to him through his mother—his mother's father, specifically.

"This explains the strength in Kait's hands, although an Eagle Clan healer is rare." *And precious,* Wolf acknowledged silently. "But like my father, Aiden carries the keeper's gift." Precognition—in many forms—was common in the Owl Clan. Aiden carried the gift of fortune; Wolf carried the gift of knowing immediate danger surrounding his friends and family. A gift that had utterly failed him during the night. When the grief spurred rage, he shut down that line of thought, focusing on the conversation at hand. "Kait and Aiden are of my father's blood. They hold no claim to my mother's lineage. The Owl Clan, not the Eagle Clan, is strong in my father's line. Where did this clan claim come from?"

Neniiseti' raised a grizzled eyebrow. "You have the foreshadow of the Owl Clan but were claimed by the *hiinooko3onit.*" Neniiseti' frowned. "We would do well to map your sire's bloodline. For the *hiinooko3onit* to claim all three of his *tei'yoonoh'o'*, the eagle must have been strong in his blood, and we have need of more Eagle warriors."

Wolf nodded. There were more than nine thousand Northern Arapaho on the Wind River reservation. He knew where his fraternal grandparents had resided in Riverton, but he'd had no interest in engaging with them. Or with his various aunts and uncles or cousins. From his mother's accounts of his father's childhood and adolescence, he'd had good cause for turning his back on his family, casting aside his heritage, and never looking back. Alcoholics and drug addicts had proliferated among the Little Horse lineage.

They still did, from what he'd seen.

"Bring your brother to me. The Eagle Spirit has spoken. He calls his lost children home."

"Yeah." Wolf wiped a hand down his face. "Aiden is not all that enamored with his Arapaho heritage."

Neniiseti' shrugged. "You must change this."

Right.

Wolf sighed. Maybe Jude would have some idea . . . The thought fractured as he remembered Jude would not be advising him of anything anymore.

For the first time in his life, he was truly alone.

Mac watched as his suggestion that Kait accompany them into Leonard Embray's room and heal him there detonated around the table.

"No way in fucking hell," Cosky roared, bolting up from the table without pushing his chair back. It crashed to the floor behind him.

Mac winced, and the pounding in his head jumped from a bongo to a bass drum.

Well, that had gone over about as well as he'd expected. Grimacing, Mac rubbed at the throbbing behind his temples. Christ, what he wouldn't give for a few hours of decent sleep . . . or, hell, even some Excedrin.

It had been a long night, and day, followed by night again.

"Since our whole damn plan hinges on Kait healing the bastard, we *have* to bring her," Mac reminded him, forcibly keeping his tone calm and reasonable. Christ knew there was enough shouting going on; he didn't need to add his own voice to the mix.

"Not into the fucking house." Cosky turned on him with the cold intensity of a viper, pure death glittering in his gray eyes. "She can heal him from the fucking chopper."

Rawls turned his chair enough to catch his teammate's eyes. "See, that's not gonna work, Cos. If Embray is hooked to a ventilator like Link says, the minute we unhook him he'll stop breathing. He'll be dead long before we reach the chopper."

"Then bring the fucking machine," Cosky snapped.

"Yeah." Rawls cocked his head, scratching his chin. "They weigh a ton and need electricity. The only way this plays is if Kaity comes in with us."

Cosky's jaw tightened as he set his feet and locked his knees. All go for war. "Not. Gonna. Happen."

"We'll keep her safe." Mac stepped in for a round of convincing. "Hell, according to Link, there's no security." Or at least not much. "We'll go in first, clear the place out. Make sure we're good to go, and then we'll bring in Kait."

Cosky bared his teeth at him. "Sure, 'cause that worked so fucking well last night, didn't it?"

Not quite the same scenario, but close enough. Fuck, Cosky had a point. Mac sat back again, gazing longingly at the last sliver of amber in the bottle of Jack. The fact he wanted it so badly he could taste the bite on his tongue told him, clear as hell, he needed to let the bottle sit.

No way was he turning into his old man. He knew when to let the bottle go.

"If Kait doesn't come in with us, then this mission doesn't happen," Mac said, letting some of his building frustration creep into his voice. "She has to be in that room."

Cosky shot him an I-don't-give-a-shit look. Which nudged Mac's frustration into the pissed-off zone.

"I'll let you explain to Amy why you let her kids die." A low blow, but the stubborn bastard deserved it.

"She doesn't need to heal him in the damn room. She can do it from the chopper."

"He'll be dead by then," Rawls reminded him.

"She pulled you back from the dead. Faith back from the dead. She can pull him back too."

They'd been over this terrain repeatedly and were getting nowhere. It was too bad they couldn't enlist Willie or One Bird, but they were flying solo on this mission. The Shadow Mountain crew were up to their collective braids in their tribal traditions, arranging Jude's funeral.

All Neniiseti' had said was the ceremony would take three days, and all the Shadow Mountain warriors would be attending. Upcoming missions were grounded. At least in terms of Shadow Mountain support. They were lucky they'd been given a pilot, although they suspected their new pilot wasn't entwined in the Shadow Mountain culture.

There was no way in fuck he was gonna complain, though, not after what happened last time. At least when it was just him and his men, there were a lot fewer men to worry about. Of course if they brought Kait, that would bring with it a whole new headache.

Fuck . . . they were damned if they did and damned if they didn't.

"Look," Zane tried again, his tone reasonable. "If there is more security than we expected, we won't take her in. If we take fire, *any fire at all*, we won't take her in. We'll cover every possible angle."

"No." Cosky folded tense arms over his chest, his face so hard it looked carved from steel. "Goddamn it. You know as well as I do that we can't cover every angle."

His furious gaze traveled the table, damning them all.

Mac scowled and slumped in his chair, eyeing the bottle of Jack again. The bastard had that right too. No matter how hard you tried, you couldn't prepare for everything. It was one of the first things you learned when you joined the team.

When Rawls opened his mouth to take another run at his teammate, Mac caught his eye and shook his head. There was another way around this roadblock. Cosky would hate him for it, come after him with all barrels blazing, but it would get Kait Winchester in that room.

The knock that hit his door was a welcome interruption. Tempers needed a chance to cool before more planning could take place. They also needed to get Link back. While they had mapped out most of the retreat where Embray was being held, there had been a couple of questions they hadn't gotten to before Shadow Command had hauled Link to the war room to question him themselves.

At least Link's answers to Neniiseti' and the other Shadow Mountain interrogators had provided useful information. He'd answered all their questions with the same openness he'd answered theirs. He'd given them names, companies, locations, even clandestine operations conducted by the NRO.

He'd furthered their understanding of the organization considerably. What James Link hadn't mentioned to anyone was whether their adaption of Faith's device had interfaced with any NRO members' brain patterns and enhanced their mental capabilities.

A small comfort under the circumstances.

Still, Shadow Command had seemed pleased with the wealth of information Link had given them. Jude's sacrifice had likely saved millions of lives.

Mac shook his head as he reached for the door. He doubted Wolf would see it that way. It was obvious the two men had been close. Wolf was much more likely to react with blame than gratitude next time they encountered each other.

In fact, he half expected Wolf to be at the door with his fists cocked and ready. Neniiseti' had said that Wolf would return by early afternoon, and according to the blinking clock on his coffeepot, it was well past that now. When he opened the door, two flat-faced guards, with Link between them, stood before him.

"We have finished with him for now," one of the sentries said, giving their captive a light shove forward.

Mac stepped back to allow Link inside. "Good timing," he told the men before looking at Link. "We've got more questions for you."

He walked back to the table with Link beside him. The minute everyone was settled and quiet, Rawls launched the first of the questions.

Slouched back in his chair, he was all Southern laziness. "Run through the personnel on-site per shift again."

They'd asked him variations of this question at least half a dozen times so far. It was an important one. A life-and-death one. If the answers offered weren't truthful, they needed to know. Lies could be caught during repetition. If someone knew the answer to a question, it came immediately to mind. If it was false, if they had made it up, they hesitated, trying to remember the details of their answers before. Or they offered different answers. So far Link's answers had come quickly and been consistent.

Mac was almost certain he wasn't lying.

"Day shift has six people," Link said patiently. "The housekeeper, who also cooks; the groundskeeper; the doctor; two nurses; and the helicopter pilot. The helicopter is parked on the pad. After six p.m., the housekeeper and groundskeeper retire to their house on the opposite side of the island. So there are four people in the compound between six p.m. and six a.m. Everyone except the night nurse will be sleeping. The physician and pilot are on call but are required to remain on the premises in case of an emergency."

"How long are the shifts?" Cosky spoke this time.

"Twelve hours."

Mac grabbed the legal notepad they'd been taking notes on and folded the sheets until he came to a fresh page. He pushed it and a pen toward Link.

"Map out the compound. Rooms, bathrooms, closets. Don't leave anything out."

There were two other such maps among the pages. Those two had matched up perfectly. They'd see if this one did as well. Once the map was drawn and rechecked, everyone settled back in their chairs.

"With the compound chopper already taking up the pad, when we call ours in, it'll have to land somewhere else," Cosky said.

Their strategy called for a water insertion—he hoped like fuck this one went better than the last—followed by a helicopter landing once the compound had been secured.

Kait would come in with the bird.

"There is a large courtyard off the library. It's across the compound, so it will be a bit of a longer haul. But there's plenty of room to land your helicopter." Link paused, frowned, and seemed to hesitate before finally shrugging. "You guys understand that Embray is incapable of speech. Incapable of movement. You won't get anything out of him. If you're thinking of using him as a hostage, a negotiating chip, you'll be wasting your time and resources. Eric and Coulson will never negotiate for him. They don't need to. He can't do them any harm now. He can't do you any good. This whole endeavor is rather useless."

Silence rounded the table, and everyone avoided looking at one another.

From Link's perspective, what they were planning would sound foolish and wasteful. But he didn't know about the ace up their sleeve.

Which reminded Mac . . .

He stretched, made a show of looking at his watch before rising to his feet. "I think we're good for tonight. I'm going to take a walk, check in on Benji. One of you boys take Link back to the war room."

A round of amused, knowing looks passed among his men. He ignored them. They were certain he was headed off to visit a woman. He was, but not the woman they assumed. There was another woman on his mind. A woman he happened to know was sitting by Benji's bedside, giving Amy a break to shower and eat.

It was time to get down and dirty—in a conversational way—with Kait Winchester.

Cosky might be adamantly opposed to letting Kait into that room, but Cosky's fiancée had a mind and heart of her own, along with an interesting way of getting Cosky to change his mind.

When he explained the circumstances and consequences to her, she'd insist on joining them in that room regardless of Cosky's opposition. Regardless of the danger. He had to hand it to her: the woman was a warrior at heart.

For an instant, just an instant, a swell of guilt pressed in on him. If anything happened to her during this mission, Cosky would never forgive him. Hell, he might not forgive himself.

It was a hell of a realization—one he wouldn't have had six months ago. But when he thought of swapping Kait for Amy—of walking her into danger—yeah, his perception tilted on its axis.

What the hell were these women doing to him?

Chapter Seventeen

Amy paused before Mac's door, a glaring sense of déjà vu creeping up on her. Hadn't she just done this? Was that her modus operandi these days? Show up at Mackenzie's door in the middle of the night without invitation?

Any other man might take her new hobby as an invitation to a wham-bam-thank-you-ma'am. She frowned. Heck, considering that verbal sexual ambush she'd done on him at her son's bedside, he could be forgiven for assuming that was exactly what she was after.

She wasn't. She just wanted to say thank you, that was all. Let him know how much she appreciated the lengths he'd go to help her son.

When Amy had returned from showering and grabbing a quick bite, Kait had told her how Mac had approached her to explain why it was imperative that she attempt to heal Embray in his hospital room while he was still hooked up to the machines.

The fact that Mac had hunted Kait down in private, rather than having Cosky enlist her aid, was a clear indication that Cosky had been vehemently opposed to the plan. So opposed, he hadn't planned to tell her about the option.

Which meant Mac had gone around his best friend and lieutenant's back. A move that could very well cause a massive schism between the two men—perhaps between the entire team.

But he'd done it anyway.

Because the best chance of saving Benji was bringing Embray back alive. To keep him alive, they needed Kait in that room to heal him before unhooking him from the machines.

Amy wasn't a woman who cried often or easily. She could count on both hands how many times she'd given in to tears. But what he'd done, the possible sacrifice he'd made—for Benji, for her—brought the blur of tears to her eyes.

Mackenzie was not a soft man. Or a man given to extravagant measures. He was an honest man. A good man. One who saw the world in black and white. He moved within his world on the twin principles of trust and loyalty—when it came to his team, anyway. When it came to his life as a SEAL.

Yet he'd broken both of his core principles—Cosky's trust and his own loyalty to his teammates—for her.

She should have been appalled at what he'd done, what he'd sacrificed—except he'd done it to save Benji and Brendan. And she was good with that reason. She'd break every oath, every principle, every law to save her sons.

She needed him to know she understood what he'd done and what his actions might cost him. She needed him to know how much she appreciated his efforts.

How much she appreciated him.

But . . . she glanced down the deserted hallway and listened to the silence. No noise drifted through any of the doors. She'd lost track of time, and the lack of windows in the base screwed with her natural body rhythm, but she sensed it was late. Quite late.

Maybe she didn't need to let him know all this right now.

Maybe it could wait until morning. Besides, Kait—who had agreed to watch Benji for a bit longer—would need to head back to the apartment she shared with Cosky.

As she turned, set to leave, the door abruptly opened. Mac looked as surprised to see her as she was to see him.

"Hey," he said, obviously at a loss for words.

"Hey," she repeated, at a loss herself.

After a few seconds of awkwardly staring at each other, he stepped back and threw the door open wide.

"You want to come in?"

"Sure." The word was garbled and breathless, so she cleared her throat and tried again. "Yeah. Sure."

The awkward silence followed them into the room. Amy cleared her throat again. "I'm not keeping you from anything, am I? Looks like you were on your way out."

He shrugged and ran a hand over his hair. "Nah, couldn't sleep. Decided to get out, stretch my legs."

"Ah." Well, this conversation was sure going nowhere fast. Her gaze settled on his hair. It was quite a bit longer than it had been when she'd first laid eyes on him. Rather than those spiky bristles, it looked soft and thick with the slightest hint of a curl.

Sexy.

The gray at his temples added a touch of dignity to the sexy.

"How's Benji?"

She forced her eyes back to his face, finding concern in his expression.

"The same." Her throat closed, causing another round of throat clearing. "I guess I should be grateful his blood work hasn't gotten worse."

It was hard to feel grateful about anything, though, except possibly the man standing in front of her.

"We're hoping to get the go-ahead tomorrow morning. Head out early enough to hit the San Juan Islands by midnight."

Another midnight operation. He was probably used to them. From what she gathered from listening in on Mackenzie and his men while they talked shop or strategy, these midnight missions were preferred.

It made sense. Most people would be asleep, with slower reflexes and mental fuzziness.

"You're going in by boat again?" Amy wasn't surprised by his nod. He'd mentioned that possibility earlier.

"Too loud and bright by bird. It would wake up everyone on the island, blow the operation. The island's too small to land a couple of klicks away and hike in. So we're stuck with a beach landing."

She nodded again, tried to remember why she'd come. Oh yeah . . . "I wanted to thank you. I mean, that's why I came. To thank you. For everything you're doing for Benji . . . for me."

It was hard to believe he could look even more uncomfortable, but he managed it. All fidgety and awkward.

"It's no big deal," he muttered, staring at his boots instead of her face. "The least I could do."

Her heart melted. He looked like a grade schooler who'd just given his first crush a fistful of wildflowers—if the grade schooler were six feet tall and sexy as hell.

Maybe she wasn't here just because of her appreciation.

"Look, about what I said at the clinic." She glanced at the wall clock. It was after midnight. She couldn't stay long; she needed to get back to Benji. But this needed to be said.

"You don't need to worry about that." He lifted his head, caught her eyes. The gaze that held hers was so earnest it wrenched her heart. "You're under tremendous stress. I get it. I didn't take that conversation seriously, and I don't harbor any expectations. We'll just forget you brought it up."

Her heart melted into a gooey puddle and started dripping all over the floor.

What a complete idiot.

"That's awfully understanding of you," she told him dryly. "But I was serious about what I said. I was also completely aware of what I was offering, regardless of the *tremendous stress* I've been under. Obviously the timing is off right now. But after you get back with Embray and once Benji is back to normal, I fully intend to jump your bones."

He rocked back on his feet, his mouth falling open like she'd hit him with a Taser.

He did a slow shake of his head, befuddlement in his eyes. "Jump my bones?"

"I'm sorry. Is that slang not in your lexicon? How about I fully intend to fuck you two ways to Sunday." She lifted an eyebrow and hoped the jargon came off as smoothly confident rather than uncomfortable and out of character—which was how she felt. "Does that clear it up?"

The shell-shocked look vanished. A mesmerizing glitter sprang up in his black eyes. He cocked his head, studying her intently before *tsking*. "I'm astonished to hear such profanity coming from you, considering your distaste of swearing."

"You mean *fuck*?" The eyebrow she lifted was pure challenge. "I'm not using it as an adjective. I'm using it as a verb—an action verb to be precise; hence it is not swearing."

"How inventive." He took a predatory step forward, meeting her challenge and escalating it. "So do I have any say in this?"

"Of course!" She forced herself to remain still when every instinct insisted on retreat. "If my offer doesn't interest you, I'll move on. I'm sure there are other men on base willing to take me up on it."

The glitter in his eyes intensified. "Fuck that. Nobody on base will touch you."

What? He doesn't think anyone else will find me desirable?

"Course, I might have to neuter your first few choices until the message gets out."

Oh . . .

"What message?" she whispered as he closed in on her.

"That you're taken," he murmured against her lips.

Rather than nerves, a warm, fluffy sense of desirability rose inside her. It had been a long time since she'd felt wanted like this. A very long time.

But then the memory of what happened during their last kiss flashed through her mind. She hadn't planned on passion coming into play tonight, and she hadn't had a chance to start researching rape trauma yet.

It shouldn't matter, though, right? This felt so perfect and immediate. She'd just concentrate on the man before her and drown out the bad memories.

The first kiss had been at her instigation. But this second one . . . this second one was all his.

She expected his lips to seize hers, to blaze across her with the same hunger she saw carved across his face and glittering in his eyes.

Instead they were soft, gentle—seducing instead of taking. His lips stroked. His teeth nipped. His tongue licked. He worked a tingling path across her mouth and cheek, lingered for a thorough exploration of the sensitive spot just below her ear, and then lazily nibbled his way back to her lips. She was putty beneath his mouth by the time his lips finally settled back on hers.

He felt so good against her. Solid. Hot. Pure male animal. At some point during his lazy seduction, her hands had found the hem of his T-shirt and crept up under it, enjoying the sensation of hard muscle beneath her palms. Then she discovered that a light scrape of fingernails down the rigid plane of his back left rippling muscles in their wake. And that if she dug her nails in slightly, the tempo of his heart picked up. He suckled her lips a little harder, a little faster, as some of that laziness gave way to hunger.

She wanted the hunger. She wanted him raw and panting under her hands. She wanted to be devoured as though she were unbreakable—made of steel.

To move him along, she opened her mouth and flicked her tongue along his lips. Her arms tightened, her fingers digging harder into his back.

Tingles spread across her scalp and down her spine, settling into the hot, throbbing junction between her legs. Squeezing her legs together to ease the building ache, she nibbled his lips and teased his tongue with the flirty swipe of hers. Her body subtly stroked his, hips to hips, breasts to chest, as the wicked blast of longing grew stronger.

She could do this. Hunger ruled her. Nothing mattered but Mac and the need unfurling inside her.

Now she wanted—needed—more.

He got the message . . . and acted on it. His mouth opened wide over hers—seduction overtaken by hunger. By claiming. His hands moved down to her hips to drag her against his swollen crotch. As his mouth moved over hers and his tongue swept into her mouth, his arms slid around her back.

Hard arms locked her against him until they were sealed together, pelvis to pelvis, breast to chest, mouth to mouth. Until she was completely helpless and trapped in his arms.

Unease stirred and nudged back the urgency. She concentrated fiercely on Mac. Reminded herself whose arms she was in. When she pulled back, his arms loosened but not quite fast enough.

Flash.

The nightmare roared up, swamping her.

Harsh bright lights. Burning around her wrists and ankles and between her legs. A hot, hard body on top of her. Helplessness. Trapped.

She jolted back. The unease shot straight to panic. Her arms fled his back. She forced her hands between their bodies and shoved.

"Amy . . . Amy, easy . . . easy, babe." His arms loosened even more.

She broke away so violently she would have gone over backward and hit the floor if his hand hadn't snaked out, captured her elbow, and steadied her.

With great gulping breaths, she stood before him. Shaking. Her skin crawled. The nightmare still raked her mind. Once she was steady on her feet, he let her elbow go and stepped back.

"I'm sorry." She forced the apology out on gulps of air.

God . . . oh God . . . how could you do this to him again?

"You have nothing to apologize for." His voice was quiet and firm. "We'll work around this. It will just take time."

That sounded like he hadn't given up on her. The realization gave her the courage to raise her head. She found him standing before her, his face calm, his stance firm. Like he wasn't going anywhere. There was concern in the frown that wrinkled his brow. But no anger. No blame. No defeat.

"We should have expected these . . . aftershocks," he told her in that same quiet, calm voice. "After what happened, after what those bastards did to you—" He flinched as she recoiled.

"Aftershocks," she repeated, the breathless gulps giving way to hoarseness. Her heart and lungs were settling. Her skin had stopped its crawl.

"Aftershocks. Consequences. Whatever you want to call it." Mac scanned her face and relaxed slightly. "The point is, we know what triggers your reaction now."

"We do?" Amy tilted her head, staring back in bewilderment. What was he talking about?

The panic had dissipated, as had the flashback. Her lungs and heart were working again, but the panic attack had flushed the hunger out of her system too. It had stolen her passion. Frustrated anger whipped through her, blasting away the icy touch of the nightmare.

"Yes, we do." Mac's face gentled. He took a careful step forward. "You reacted only when my arms closed around you, when I pulled you to me and held you there. When I wasn't touching you or I touched you only lightly, you were fine. Hell, you were as hot as I was."

Amy thought that over. Could he be right?

She went over the embrace in her mind. She'd been fine during the kiss. Fine while her hands were up his back. Fine when their tongues had been doing the happy dance. But when his arms had slid around her waist and contracted—even the thought of his arms around her brought the whisper of unease.

"You're right," she said slowly, much less satisfied with the realization than he was. So what if they'd identified what caused the reaction and the terrifying flood of memories? It wasn't as if they could make love without him touching her, now was it?

"Relax," Mac said, looking annoyingly upbeat. "Now that we know the trigger, we can avoid it. There are plenty of ways to get . . . physical . . . that don't include my arms around you."

"But—" Amy licked her dry lips.

His gaze dropped, tracking the movement, and desire flickered across his face.

"What if I want your arms around me? What if I want your touch?" she whispered hoarsely.

His focus shifted back to her eyes, and the hunger on his face banked. He remained level and calm. "We'll go slow and work up to it. We have the time. It will just take patience."

Go slow? Amy buried her irritation. He was trying to help. It wasn't fair to unload her frustration on him. But seriously . . . *patience*?

Between waiting for a cure for the boys and waiting for her mind to relax enough to enjoy these moments with Mac, patience was in short supply.

She wasn't sure how much she had left.

Chapter Eighteen

The sky was boiling with thick black clouds that pounded their bodies, the boat, and their weapons with a constant swath of icy rain. Mac wiped the lenses of his NVDs—again—trying to clear his vision as their Zodiac powered through the heavy waves. There was no second boat beside them this time—or third behind them.

They were alone on the choppy seas.

Alone in the relentless rain.

Christ, the Pacific Northwest could be a total bitch sometimes.

They'd been lucky Neniiseti' had loaned them the Eagle. Their experimental birds were more stable in iffy weather. A Black Hawk would have been grounded, which would have pushed the assault back a couple of days. Hell, they were lucky they had a full crew too. Without the magical hands of the Shadow Mountain healers, Zane wouldn't have been fit for duty. A thigh hit during a ST7 mission would have laid him up for weeks, if not months.

Since visibility was practically nil in the heavy deluge, they were relying on compasses and state-of-the-art GPS systems. As they'd done two nights before, Zane and Rawls were in front, Mac was in the middle, and Cosky worked the throttle.

But unlike two nights before, there was obviously something wrong with Mac's LC.

Amid the constant stream of rain running down his helmet and blurring the NVD lenses, he saw Zane double over, hugging his abdomen. If it had been anyone else, he'd have suspected seasickness. Christ, the hard lift and bang of the boat and the endless bounce of the waves were bad enough to give anyone digestive distress. But this was Zane, and his LC had been on much rougher seas without hugging his belly and puking his guts out.

Turning to Cosky, Mac drew his finger across his throat and waited for Cos to cut the engine. Once the boat sat silent, bouncing on the waves, he looked at Zane again.

Rawls had already turned to his buddy and was busy taking his pulse. "Fast and thready," Rawls said through the radio.

Zane doubled over again, his grunted groan following Rawls's voice into their helmets.

Whatever was wrong had hit hard and suddenly. He'd been fine on the trip down in the Eagle. He'd been fine as the bird had dropped to the water and launched the skiff. Hell, he'd been fine as they'd taken their baths and swam over to the Hurricane. It wasn't until they'd climbed aboard the boat and headed for Embray's island that Zane had started to fidget and then doubled over.

"What's the deal? Appendix?" It was the only thing he could think of that would come on so fast.

They were well into their mission, but they could call the chopper back. Airlift Zane out. While the chopper hightailed it to the nearest emergency room, the rest of them could continue the mission. They'd be down one man, but hell—Zane was useless to them now anyway.

Fuck, he was a downright handicap.

"Not me," Zane grunted and followed it with a moment of rigid silence. "Beth. The baby."

It took a second for his explanation to register; when it did, an explosion of startled breaths hit their comm units.

"Ah hell, Skipper," Rawls said, his sympathy stumbling into silence.

Ah fuck.

Over the past few months they'd found a lot of humor in Zane mirroring Beth's symptoms. His morning sickness, complaints of bloating, and swollen feet—hell, even his craving for pickled eggs and avocados had been funny as hell.

Nobody was laughing now.

Fuck, nobody had thought about what would happen if something went wrong with the pregnancy. Nobody had thought about what a handicap that link between Beth and Zane would be during a mission, when their lieutenant commander's focus needed to be on the operation ahead.

Nobody had considered that the link between the two could get them all killed.

"Can you tell anything from what you're getting?" Rawls asked, his worry clear.

"Just that she's in pain—" He broke off, and a hiss sounded through the comm units. "Terrified for the baby."

The raw grimness in his LC's answer told Mac how much Zane hated knowing that she was in pain and fear, and that he couldn't help her.

As omens went, this one didn't bode well for the success of their mission.

The fucking storm, the fact that one of his men was in acute distress—any other operation would be called off at this point. Rescheduled.

But they *couldn't* reschedule this one. Not with Benji's liver and kidneys failing and his chances of survival declining.

No doubt Zane would kill to get back to Beth, but his life wasn't in actual danger. No, they couldn't rely on him, not in his current condition, but that was easy enough to solve. They could bench him, have him babysit the boat, while the rest of them carried out the mission. Link's information had indicated there wasn't much danger.

They should be fine.

He grimaced. Of course the fact that they *should* be fine almost always indicated they *wouldn't be.*

Still, they had to chance it.

Cosky apparently read his thoughts. "It's five hours back to Shadow Mountain. Another half an hour for evac and lift out. If we scrap this and scramble up, Zane won't get to Beth's side for six hours, give or take.

"Embray's maybe fifteen minutes away. We can be in and out of his compound in half an hour. An hour more. That's what we're looking at," Cosky continued calmly.

Tense silence claimed the boat. They all knew that anything could happen in that hour. People died in less than an hour every day. If things were that bad on Beth's end, that hour could make all the difference to Zane.

But if they did pack up and head home, Benji would almost certainly die. Damn it, they needed more information. How bad was Beth? Zane could just be picking up the beginnings of a stomach flu and his gal panicking.

"Alpha One, Alpha One. Copy," Mac said into the headset mic.

"Alpha One, copy." The chopper pilot sounded crystal clear in Mac's ears.

"Radio base. We need a status on Beth Brown ASAP."

"Copy."

The silence grew tenser and tenser as they waited for the pilot to report in. Finally a sputter surged over the line.

"She's in ICU at the base clinic."

"Which doesn't tell us jackshit," Mac snapped, his frustration building. "Diagnosis? Prognosis?"

"All I'm getting is that she's in the clinic undergoing treatment," the pilot responded coolly.

"Fuck." Mac closed his eyes. They were wasting time just sitting here. He had to make a decision.

If he ordered the go-ahead and Beth died, Zane would never recover. Fuck, there was a really good chance that he'd lose both his best friends during this fucked-up night.

From Cosky's attitude, it was clear Kait hadn't filled him in on the change in plans. She was playing her conversation with Mac close to her chest. She probably wouldn't tell him until the bird landed at the compound.

That explosion still loomed ahead.

He looked at Zane, who'd doubled over again. "We'll get in and out ASAP. Get you back on the chopper and back to Beth in record time."

Zane's grim silence echoed through his radio.

"Cosky, light her up."

Mac almost expected the engine to stall. Christ knew everything else that could go wrong was headed in that direction, but the engine immediately sputtered to life, and they were back on their way.

Landing took fifteen minutes, as Cosky had predicted. They hopped off the boat and tied it off on one of the rocks jutting out of the beach. Unlike their last beach landing, jagged rocks, a steep hill, and torrential rain confronted them.

"Stay with the boat," Mac whispered into his mic, knowing everyone would recognize who the order was directed at. The fact Zane didn't protest was proof of the shape he was in. Proof he knew he'd be a handicap during this upcoming snatch and fly.

Cosky took point, Mac falling in behind him and Rawls on their six. They climbed the craggy hill bent double, each step a struggle against wind and rain. Once they crested the top of the hill, the lights of the compound lit up their NVDs. The original plan had called for Zane and Cosky to take the south entrance while Mac and Rawls took the door that led from the east courtyard directly into the master bedroom and Embray.

With them down a man, one of them would have to breach their entry point solo.

"Rawls, Cosky. Go south. I'll take east," Mac whispered.

"Copy," Cosky and Rawls said in unison.

The south entry point was closer to the bedrooms where most of the crew would be sleeping. While his men swept the bedrooms and secured anyone they found, he'd cover Embray's room. Once the bedrooms were cleared, Cos would sweep the rest of the house while Rawls marched their captives to Embray's suite. Mac would sit on Embray. Make sure no one had the bright idea of taking him out once they knew the compound had been compromised.

There would be no fucking repeat of what had happened at Link's place.

As he turned a corner along the brick wall, a pair of windows shining like a beacon came into view. A door stood between them, light filtering through it as well but not quite so intensely. He buddied up to the window, his back against the brick wall.

"In position," he whispered into his mic. He waited for his teammates to echo his readiness. Once they were all in position, Rawls would hit the electronics scrambler, taking out alarms, phones, and cameras.

"We're a go," Rawls said quietly, all business.

"Go," Mac ordered.

There was a momentary flicker in the light streaming through Embray's bedroom window as though the disruption to the electronics had affected the lights as well.

Whoever was in the room would have been distracted by the flicker and likely investigating the cause. Mac chanced a quick stretch and peek only to find the room empty. At least empty from his current viewpoint. Didn't mean there wasn't someone tucked in a corner he couldn't see.

Plus, it wasn't technically empty. There was the still figure in the hospital bed and the thousand or so blinking machines surrounding it. Fuck, Rawls hadn't been kidding when he'd said that Embray would be surrounded by a gazillion machines.

Ducking below the window, he crept to the door and reached for the knob. Son of a bitch . . . it opened easily beneath his fingers. The sheer ease of accessing the room sent disquiet skating down his spine. Nothing ever came this easy, and when it did, there was hell to pay later.

He entered the room fast and low, rifle out and sweeping.

Nobody.

He booked to what should be the bathroom according to the multiple maps Link had drawn, barreling in fast and low as he'd been taught as a plebe. Empty.

Back out to the bedroom. This time he headed to the doorway that led to the rest of the house. He chanced a quick glance outside, exposing as little of himself as possible. Empty halls on both sides.

Where the hell was the nurse? Someone was supposed to be on duty.

He settled with his shoulder two feet from the left of the door, positioned so he could keep an eye on both doors as well as the windows.

He listened as he waited, expecting screams, or gunfire, or a muffled shout. Clues his men were at work. But the place sat still and silent and forbidding as death. It felt like forever before Cosky's voice came down the wire.

"Alpha Two secure."

"Copy. Alpha Three secure," Mac whispered. "But the night nurse is AWOL."

A soft snort traveled down the wire. "We got her."

No shit? What had she been doing in the bedrooms? Yeah, after a bit more thought that question answered itself.

"The lambs are on the move," Rawls said, but it was a few minutes or so later before Mac heard the shuffle of feet moving down the hallway. He stepped out to greet them, rifle up and ready—a silent threat in case anyone got the bright idea to run. With bound wrists, docile feet, and terrified faces, two women, followed by two men, trickled into Embray's bedroom.

"Everyone down on the ground, backs against the wall," Mac ordered.

"Now wait just one damn minute—" One of the men, a tall, balding guy with a condescending purse to his lips, squared off against him.

Mac shoved him to the ground. The minute the bastard's ass touched the floor, the rest of their captives followed suit, and Rawls went to work zip-tying their ankles together.

Their four prisoners jelled with Link's crew count during the night shift. But who the hell was who? An unexpected visitor would give them the same head count, but leave a crew member loose to cause trouble.

"You identify them?" he asked Rawls.

"The two women are the nurses. Meet the pilot." He nodded at the guy he was zip-tying.

Which left tall, bald, and patronizing as the doctor. Figured.

"Which one's the night nurse?" he asked Rawls, half-determined to light into her. Jesus Christ, the whole purpose of having a night nurse was to have someone on hand at night. Not raunching it up in bed.

A terrified gasp and low moan from the short, curvy woman at his feet answered his question.

"We're secure. Call in the bird." Cosky's order traveled through his headset.

Tensing, Mac radioed the pilot, giving him the green light. Shit was about to hit the fan. As Rawls continued zip-tying their prisoners, Mac took up guard duty. Once he'd finished binding the last set of ankles, Rawls stood, stretched, and headed toward the still figure in the bed.

"Look," the bald bastard with the thin lips said. "I'm Dr. Archibald. If you're looking for money—"

"We're not," Mac said to shut him up.

"Well then, what is it you want?" Dr. Pretentious asked with a slight snip, as if he was annoyed they hadn't prostrated themselves in awe over his awesome doctorness.

"We want you to shut up," Mac snapped, keeping his voice low and mean, which wasn't a hardship since tension had tightened his throat, increasing its normal gravelly tone. He scanned the assembled men and women at his feet. "Sit there, shut up, don't move, and you'll be fine."

Rawls checked Embray's pulse, studied the machines, leaned over the bed to roll their target's eye down, checking for . . . something.

"That's my patient," Dr. Pretentious said possessively. "You're not a doctor. You have no right—"

Mac tuned him out as soon as Rawls straightened, and he turned to the blinking and beeping machines. The old plan—the one Cosky had insisted on—called for Rawls to unhook and detach Embray from the apparatuses so they could carry him to the helicopter, where Kait would attempt to bring him back from the dead. Their new plan—which his corpsman wasn't aware of yet—called for him to leave Embray hooked up until Kait tried to heal him in the room.

Christ, was that ever going to cause an explosion.

"Rawls." Mac waited for him to look over before giving him the finger across the throat. With a quick unsnap and yank, he pulled off his headgear. "Change of plans. Kait's coming here."

Rawls froze, then tore off his own headgear. The face that emerged was soaked with sweat, or rain, or both, and full of shocked disbelief. "That isn't what we decided."

"Kait and I adjusted the plan."

Rawls shook his head, then shook it again, as if the first time hadn't been enough to get his message across. "Sweet Jesus, Mac. What the hell have you done?"

"What I had to do," Mac snapped back, pushing aside the creeping sense of remorse.

Rawls swore softly beneath his breath. "You went behind his back and put Kaity in danger. He'll never forgive you for this. You had to know that."

Yeah, he did. Regret stirred. He hardened his resolve. There was no other damn way.

He'd do it again, damn it.

"You better tell him to meet the chopper. If Kait hikes all the way over here by her lonesome, he'll kill you before anyone can stop him."

Mac simply nodded. He'd already planned on alerting Cosky to the change in plans once the bird was in range. No sense in gutting their friendship any earlier than necessary.

Minutes later he heard the rotors. He put his headgear back on and keyed the mic.

After one long, shuddering moment of hesitation—there was still time to switch to plan A—he closed his eyes and set the course. "Alpha Three, head to evac point."

"Repeat?" Cosky's calm question came over the radio. "You'll need help carrying the target."

"You're on escort from the bird. Target will walk out."

There was a moment of confused silence while Cosky deciphered that cryptic comment. Then—"You. Fucking. Bastard." Another moment of silence. Mac could almost feel the wave of volcanic fury rolling down the line, every bit of it directed at him. "You're dead. You get me? Dead."

Yeah, he got him.

But damn it, Kait needed to be here. He'd keep her safe. He'd keep her alive. He'd do whatever it took to ensure her safety. Embray wouldn't survive being unhooked from those machines. That they knew for a fact. They couldn't afford to assume Kait could pull the man back from death. Nobody had been able to pull Jude back. Fuck, if Rawls really had died, like he insisted, he'd been gone only seconds. Same with Faith. Embray would be officially dead for a hell of a lot longer than that—several minutes at least. They couldn't afford to assume Kait could work a miracle and bring him back to life. No, he needed her in this room to heal Embray while he was still living.

Benji's life depended on it.

Plus, there was this whole fucking NRO Armageddon agenda. Embray had been blessed with one of the sharpest intellects in modern times. If they couldn't locate Coulson's sonic bombs, they'd need strategies for neutralizing the devices' effects. Embray's mind, assuming he recovered with it intact, might just be the difference between humanity's salvation or destruction.

Maybe Cos would forgive him for throwing Kait into the hot spot eventually.

Like in a million years.

The minutes ticked by as Mac waited for Kait and Cosky to join them. Their captives were sitting there all nice and quiet, like good little lambs. Embray was lying still and silent, machines expanding his lungs and pumping his heart.

The poor bastard.

Even if Kait—with Cosky's help—did bring the guy back to life, Embray was still going to have a shitpile of work ahead of him. He'd spent months lifeless in that bed; his body was bound to have atrophied.

More minutes ticked by.

Finally, closing in on seven minutes after Cosky's last livid response, Mac heard the muffled sound of boots in the hall.

Cosky's cold, impersonal voice followed through the headset. "Alphas Two and Four, at rendezvous."

"Copy," Mac acknowledged quietly.

So Kait had gotten her way, which meant Mac had too—by default. Mac had suspected she would bulldoze into the room, but he hadn't been 100 percent certain. After all, Cosky always had the option of hog-tying her and leaving her at the chopper.

When the pair reached the room, they immediately made their way to Embray's bed, pulling off helmets and gloves as they walked.

Kait's face, head, neck, and long golden braid were soaked. Her flex pants were as well, and they clung to her legs and hips like a second skin. Cosky was every bit as wet, although his BDUs repelled the water so he didn't look as damp.

After one livid glance, his gray eyes so furious they looked burnished in steel, Cosky ignored Mac.

The pair converged on Embray. Kait leaned over the bed, her hands pressed to Embray's head. Cosky's hands joined them, his hands settling over hers.

One second, two, three—

Was it working? Mac shifted to the side so he could see the two sets of hands pressed against Embray's head, searching for that weird glow that he'd seen in the woods when they'd worked on Rawls's motionless body.

Nothing was happening.

Four seconds, five . . . *come on, come on.*

Still nothing.

Frustration and disappointment stirred. The magic should have started by now, right?

Nine seconds, ten.

Damn it. Damn it. Damn it.

Rubbing a hand down his wet face, Mac leaned forward, urging the magic to flow.

Come on. Damn it, come on.

He was so certain that the power in Kait's hands hadn't sparked that when the bright light suddenly kindled across Embray's face, Mac wondered whether he was imagining it—wishful thinking and all. He shut his eyes, counted to three, and reopened them. The luminescent glow had intensified and climbed up to Kait's and Cosky's wrists.

It was working.

The relief was a raw, shaky rush.

Rawls moved closer to the bed, watching Embray intently. "His eyes are moving."

The bastard hadn't awoken yet, so Mac wasn't sure why the eye movement was important, but from the intense relief in his corpsman's voice, it was.

If Mac hadn't been watching his corpsman for signs of how well the healing was progressing, he would never have seen the narrow, elongated shadow slide across the window behind the bed.

An arm. A hand. A gun.

Fuckfuckfuck.

He couldn't take the shot. If Rawls popped up, it would take out his skull.

"Gun. Down," he roared, swinging up his rifle.

Rawls dropped, opening a line of fire, but neither Cosky nor Kait moved.

Jesus. Jesus. They were in some kind of fucking trance.

The shadow in the window shifted, settling at a direct angle with Kait's head. He had a shot now, but a bad one. There was only an arm. A hand. A gun. No head, no chest. Through a window. Weird angle. If he missed, Kait would die.

With no time to think, he acted instinctively, throwing himself forward with every ounce of strength he possessed. He hit Kait and Cosky, knocking them to the floor as a gun coughed. The window shattered.

An icy pinch hit his chest, then a second. He went down hard, sprawled on top of Kait.

He tried to roll off her, get his feet beneath him, bring up his rifle. But nothing would move. A puddle of ice spread across his chest and around his sides and sank into his back until his entire torso was numb.

Ah fuck . . . this was bad. Really bad.

"Rawls." The name burbled wetly from his mouth. "Gun. Window."

"Got him," Rawls barked. "You just fuckin' breathe. Mac, breathe."

Mac tried to follow the order, but his lungs wouldn't cooperate.

Yeah . . . bad.

A blast of gunfire sounded. His men? Or the other . . . the tango Link hadn't listed?

Fucking bastard.

Vaguely he registered hands on him. Pushing him aside. Dragging off his helmet, ripping off his ballistics vest. The coldness spread down his legs. His mind went fuzzy. Except for one thought.

One thought that kept recycling.

He forced open his eyes, tried to blink the fuzziness from them, but all he could see were black dots crawling across an ocean of red.

"Not me." He forced the words past the blood clogging his throat. "Kait on Embray," he wheezed, praying they understood. "Not me."

Embray hadn't awoken. She couldn't heal both of them. She had to do Embray. Had to.

Exhausted, he fought out one more instruction. "Tell . . . Amy . . . sorry."

No. No . . . not right.

His fuzzy mind tried to focus. Tried to get the words right. "Love . . . her."

He wasn't sure whether the words made it out of his darkening mind. He couldn't feel his legs, arms, torso. Couldn't feel anything anymore. No cold. No pain. Just nothing.

Why hadn't he told her when he'd had a chance? He'd known for a while.

Despair followed him into the darkness.

Chapter Nineteen

For the first time Eric could remember, David Coulson's call hit at the perfect moment. He looked to the clean, bright hallway they'd taken Esme down. He wanted to go after her, to hold her hand through the examination, but she'd wanted to face the procedure alone. Which left him out in the private waiting room . . . alone, vibrating with an odd anxiety. He wasn't even sure why he was so anxious and tense. He wanted to find out why they hadn't conceived. He wanted a baby.

Maybe that was the problem. Maybe he wanted it too much.

Regardless, a distraction was just what he needed.

"David, old chap," he said, forcing a jovial tone despite the itchy, jumpy sensation playing across his nervous system. "It seems like I just spoke with you yesterday."

Well, not quite yesterday, but it hadn't been that long ago. James Link had been taken, when? Two days ago? Three?

"Leonard Embray was taken last night," Coulson said, dropping the news on Eric like one of the bombs he was so fond of utilizing.

"What do you mean, taken?"

"I mean he was unhooked from the machines keeping him alive, hauled out of his bed, and carried to a chopper that flew him off the island."

"Why the devil would anyone do that?" Eric asked in bewilderment. "The man was in a coma. No brain function whatsoever. He's incapable of answering any questions. He's of no use to anyone."

"Any chance his condition improved recently?" Coulson asked, the same puzzlement in his voice that was in Eric's.

"No," Eric said with certainty. "After Link's departure from our organization, I reached out to Embray's physician. As of yesterday, Leonard Embray was still in a coma."

"I see . . ." Coulson's voice trailed off. "I don't suppose it matters. Once they unhooked him from the heart-and-lung machine, they effectively killed him. Everything he knew about us died with him."

"Hmm . . . yes," Eric agreed absently as something else started niggling at his mind. "How did you find out about this so soon?"

The crew on Wilkes Island had reported to Link, and Link had reported to Eric—at least until he'd disappeared. Coulson hadn't been in that loop at all. He shouldn't have known where Link had moved Embray. He shouldn't have known about the island. He sure as hell shouldn't have received this news before Eric.

There was a moment of calculating silence, as though his American compatriot was wondering how much to reveal. When he finally started talking, it was with the vocal impression of a shrug. "Considering how obsessed Link was with Embray's condition and comfort, I suspected he might visit the compound if his disappearance was self-devised. So I sent a man to the island to keep an eye out for him."

"You sent a man," Eric repeated. He didn't bother asking how Coulson had even known about the island. The American had proven repeatedly that he had fingers in many pies and ears in many places. "Let me guess. Your man had orders to take out Link?"

"And Embray, if Link attempted to remove him. They know too much."

Eric had to agree. Link in particular knew enough to do some serious damage to the organization.

It did not matter if he'd disappeared under his own steam or been kidnapped. Under the right drugs or physical encouragement, everything he knew could be made available to outside sources.

The fact someone had logged into Dynamic Solutions' mainframe under Link's username and password and attempted to access the database meant one of two possible things. Either Link had gone AWOL and tried to run from the repercussion of severing ties with the NRO, or he'd been taken and convinced to try to access the databank.

Luckily, they'd had their protocols in place to prevent such things.

"Was your man able to take out Embray before they grabbed him?"

"No. There were multiple agents involved, and access to Embray was limited. He tried to line up a shot through a window but missed. When he was sighted and wounded, he retreated. Since Embray wouldn't survive removal anyway, he didn't feel it was worth the risk to reengage." The sudden coldness in Coulson's tone was a clear indication of how he felt about that decision.

"I see," Eric murmured. He turned at a noise in the hallway and ambled closer for a better view but lost interest when a nurse walked past instead of his wife. "Did your man get a good look at the crew that crashed the compound?"

"Sounds like Mackenzie, Simcosky, and Rawlings. He said there was some blonde gal there too," Coulson said.

"No Indians this time?" Eric asked, glancing down the hall again.

"Doesn't appear so, but my guy mentioned their sweet ride. He said it wasn't a Black Hawk, but it looked military—like nothing he's seen before. Sounds like the damn machine they escaped in up in the Cascade Mountains, so I'd say they are still hooked up with those Indians." He paused, and a deep booming horn echoed down the line, as though he was near the water and a ferry was traveling past. "What about those assholes you sent up to Anchorage? They get back to you with anything?"

Eric debated about passing on his not-so-good news. Coulson would almost certainly blame him for this turn of events. But, hell, he couldn't hide it forever; might as well get it over now.

"They've disappeared. Cell phones just go to voice mail. According to the motel desk clerk, they checked out. Took all their stuff."

"Son of a bitch." Coulson sounded beyond frustrated. "They cut and run?"

"I find that doubtful," Eric said. "Their last money drop has gone unclaimed."

"Just fucking great," Coulson growled. "You can't take care of anything, can you?" He barreled over Eric's denial. "Well, I can't afford to send anyone up there to cover your ass. If Link was taken, we don't know what the fuck he told them or which operations he compromised. I need all my men on security detail, guarding our warehouses and labs. You need to fucking step up and find out where those bastards are holed up."

"It's too bad your man didn't take out Mackenzie and his men when he had the chance at Clay Purcell's house, when he had them under his rifle scope. Or even last night when they were hauling off Embray," Eric drawled, and he straightened as Esme's slender figure showed up in the hall. "Don't lay this fuck-up exclusively at my door. I don't have much more time. What about Link? Is everything in place?"

"Yeah, we're set." Coulson sounded rough and tight, as though he were nursing his fury deep in his throat. "Not sure how Embray is going to play into this. His disappearance will look suspicious as hell. But I've got a top-ass digital manipulations wunderkind cutting images out of previous recordings to place Link on scene when Embray disappeared."

Smart. Eric nodded approvingly. "Excellent. That should back up the files and digital entries nicely."

It had been surprisingly easy to implicate James Link in a violent overthrow of Dynamic Solutions and the attempted murder of its founder and CEO. If things did go downhill and the authorities started investigating what had been happening inside the technology behemoth, Link would be taking the fall, and the evidence that had been planted would lead the investigation away from the NRO.

Hell, if Link exposed them, no one would believe the word of a man accused of trying to kill his best friend and steal his company. Not when the men Link would accuse were behemoths themselves, and squeaky-clean ones at that.

"Hey, how are you feeling?" Amy asked Beth softly, peeking around the corner of the curtain that blocked off her cubicle. The clinic staff had set up Beth in the cubicle next to Benji. Having their two patients close to each other undoubtedly saved time and energy.

Frightened violet eyes lifted to Amy's face.

"I don't know. They say the baby isn't in any distress, and the cramps have lessened, but I'm still bleeding." Beth's gaze, tinged with fear, dropped back to her hands, which were pressed against the fetal monitor strapped across her swollen belly.

The way Beth was pressing her palms against her belly reminded Amy of the way Kait healed by pressing her hands against an injury or wound. Beth looked like she was trying to do the same thing, use her own energy to keep her baby safe. Who knew, maybe it was working, because Beth was in much less pain than when she'd arrived. Of course, that could be the medication she'd been given too.

Amy looked down at Beth's swollen belly and tense hands. No doubt she was wishing it was Kait's hands pressed over her. But Kait was down in the San Juan Islands trying to save another life. Three lives, if the first one was successful.

"Why haven't they called for one of the healers?" Kait might be unavailable, but there were several other healers on base. Surely one of them could help.

"They're holding some kind of traditional ceremony for Jude. Dr. Zapa doesn't want to disturb them unless it's an emergency, and since the baby isn't in distress, they say it's not an emergency."

Yet.

While Beth didn't say the word, it hung clearly there in the air between them.

"But that's good news." Amy worked on an encouraging tone. "If they felt there was real danger to your baby, they'd call the healers in. They must be pretty confident that everything is going to be okay."

Beth's murmur was neutral, neither agreeing nor disagreeing. But she was getting opposing information. The cramps and bleeding were telling her the baby was in trouble while the fetal monitor was telling her it was fine. It would be hard to decide which to believe: your body and instincts or technology.

"Have you heard anything from Mackenzie? About Embray?" Beth asked, her gaze bouncing off Amy's face and drifting left toward Benji's cubicle.

"Nothing." Amy hesitated. According to various conversations she'd listened in on between Mac and his men, Beth and Zane had a mental connection. "How about you? Are you picking up anything from Zane?"

Beth shook her head. Her face and body tensing, she remained silent for a moment before relaxing and continuing. "I've shut the link down as much as I'm able. Zane needs to focus on what he's doing down there. He can't afford to be distracted. Which means no worrying about me." Concern settled over her face. "I hope I've buried the link enough that he's not picking up on the cramps and pain. He's mirrored some of my other symptoms when the link is open. God. I hope he's not feeling this."

Considering that Amy had heard Dr. Zapa give an update to the chopper pilot at the nurses' station phone, she was pretty sure Zane had picked up on something. She decided to take her cue from the good doctor and keep that information to herself. No need to add to Beth's anxiety. Mackenzie hadn't made landfall at that point anyway—so it wasn't like she could offer Beth any good news to relieve her mind.

Or her own mind, for that matter.

"How's your son?" Beth asked after another few seconds of face scrunching and tense muscles.

Watching her, Amy didn't think that Beth's cramping had lessened much.

"His temperature is creeping up again," Amy said tightly. "So are his liver and kidney levels. His doctors are talking about bringing One Bird and William in later today to try another healing."

Beth looked surprised. "I didn't think their healings worked on Benji."

"They didn't last time." Amy's gut clenched. She doubted it would work this time either. The suggestion felt like a last-ditch effort. "Dr. Zapa is hoping that since there is some actual damage to his kidney and liver, the healing might work this time. Last time there was no damage anywhere, so there was nothing to heal."

"Oh, Amy, I'm so sorry." One of Beth's hands lifted from her stomach and reached for Amy. "I can't imagine how awful this must be for you. I'm praying Kait can bring Embray back and he can save your boys."

So was Amy.

Amy looked to Beth's other hand, the one clinging tensely to the fetal monitor. Considering her own panic over the welfare of the child she was carrying, Beth probably had a very good idea of how Amy was feeling.

Stepping forward enough to grasp the offered hand, Amy gave it a gentle squeeze.

"Nothing has climbed to a dangerous level yet," Amy murmured, trying to remain positive even though exhaustion and fear kept cycling up, swamping her, only to be beaten back down again.

Had they reached Embray yet?

Had Kait healed him?

The cooling blanket and fan, along with the drugs they had Benji on, were still working to keep his temperature down and his liver and kidneys working. But their effectiveness was wearing off far too rapidly for her peace of mind. At what stage would Benji pass the point of no return? When would his organs shut down?

At what point would Leonard Embray's antidote make no difference whatsoever?

She was terrified they were on the fast track to that occurring. Even if Embray did know the antidote, would he be able to process it in time?

She returned to Benji's side and dipped a washcloth in the plastic basin on the stainless-steel cart beside his bed. After wringing it out, she gently wiped his face and chest before draping the cloth across his forehead. The cold baths didn't seem to be helping anymore, but at least wiping him down beat the heck out of just sitting here, staring and worrying.

"Shh, you're okay, baby. You're okay." She soothed him softly as he stirred fretfully at her ministrations.

She ran the wet cloth over his face, chest, and arms a few more times. After a spine-popping stretch, she sat down and picked up the laptop. She'd been wanting to research sexual assault and how to recover from it but hadn't had an opportunity. Between Brendan, the nurses, doctors, and SEALs, someone was constantly joining her in Benji's room, and this particular subject wasn't something she wanted an audience for.

Scrolling through the dozens of articles her Google search called up, she quickly discovered that most of them didn't pertain to her situation. She didn't blame herself for what had happened. There had been eight men, and they'd kidnapped her children before they'd come after her. If she hadn't acquiesced, if she'd refused to go with them, they would have killed the boys. She'd taken the only course of action open to her.

Nor did she feel shame or dirtied—like the experience had somehow soiled her. Sex wasn't suddenly shameful to her.

What she did recognize were the symptoms they listed for rape-induced post-traumatic stress: the hypervigilance, the rage, the insomnia, even the flashbacks.

Her chest tightened until it felt like her old friend—that five-thousand-pound elephant—was sitting on her lungs, making it difficult to breathe. Anxiety churned through her belly. A rush of helplessness and panic worked to break through the barriers she'd erected.

The research was dredging up those ugly, unbearable feelings she'd buried all those months before.

She took the advice of one of the articles and practiced deep, even breathing until the tension and panic eased. That blog post, she suspected, was going to be particularly helpful. It even gave tips on dealing with flashbacks.

Several of the other articles gave illustrations of the common ways women dealt with the trauma of rape. Some women buried the experience, pretended it had never happened, and went about their everyday lives as though nothing had changed. That certainly resonated with her. It was exactly how she'd dealt with it.

But then she hadn't had time to process it. She'd been dealing with John's murder, grief at his loss, helping Benji and Brendan adjust to his death. Plus, there had been so many details she'd had to handle: the funeral, the insurance, the bank accounts, the reams and reams of paperwork. Then there had been the investigation into his death, followed by the toxic crap the NRO had injected into her boys, which led to the current crisis.

She'd barely had a chance to breathe over the past five months, let alone work through the aftermath of what those bastards had done to her.

She reread the articles again, paying particular attention to the one with actionable tips for dealing with post-traumatic stress symptoms.

When the curtain slid back, she instinctively closed the link she was reading before looking up.

"Mrs. Chastain?" the tall blonde nurse said, her gaze scanning Benji's hot face and then zipping up to the machines' displays. "The pilot checked in. They're on their way back . . . with Leonard Embray."

Amy's heart skipped a beat and then started beating harder . . . faster. "He's alive?"

"He's alive," the nurse confirmed, looking away.

That was good news. Great news, even. So why wouldn't the nurse hold her gaze? Alarm bells crashed through Amy's head.

"But?" Amy prompted when the woman fell silent.

"The information coming in is spotty. There's been a lot of radio interference. They've reported that they have Embray and he's alive. However . . ." She hesitated.

Amy bolted up from Benji's bed and took a threatening step forward. "What?"

The nurse retreated, caution flashing across her face. "Apparently there was an incident, and Commander Mackenzie was wounded."

Wounded.

Her chest tightened. *Wounded* could mean anything. A splinter. A broken arm. A graze or flesh wound.

Or . . . ?

She stared at the nurse, at the sympathy on her face, and her scalp tingled. Her skin alternated between hot and cold.

"How bad?" she asked hoarsely.

"I don't have the specifics. The pilot said they were pumping a lot of blood into him. Warned us to have a crash cart at the hangar and units of AB positive on hand. We lost the chopper after that, but it doesn't sound good," the nurse said.

A crash cart . . . blood on hand . . . but they were hours away. Hours away. It wasn't like they'd be arriving any second so the ER could provide the treatment he needed.

"Why didn't Kait—" Amy broke off, realizing even as the question parted her lips why Kait hadn't healed Mac.

She couldn't heal both men. Even if Mackenzie was in the 30 percent of the population Kait could heal, she couldn't do two major healings at the same time. She simply wouldn't have the energy for two. She would have to choose: Mac or Embray.

The fact that Embray was alive and headed to Shadow Mountain was a clear indication of who she'd chosen.

Had Mac had anything to do with that choice? Or had Kait's gift simply not worked on him?

"What they should have done," the nurse said, her voice sharpening with accusation, "is take him to the nearest ER. It wouldn't have taken long to fly in and drop him off. Why in the world they would fly him all the way back here instead of seeking emergency treatment is beyond me."

Because if they'd taken him to an ER, any ER, his gunshot would have been reported and investigated by the local police. All gunshot wounds had to be reported. Before he even made it out of surgery, the police would know who he was. He'd be arrested.

She thought back to that night in March when Jillian's brother had kidnapped Beth right there in the Enumclaw hospital. Hospitals were not safe. They were particularly dangerous when the monsters behind this whole damn conspiracy had people in the FBI and local law enforcement. If Mac wasn't killed outright while he was cuffed to his hospital bed, he'd be killed after processing in jail.

But were his chances of surviving any higher on the chopper, hours from home and help?

"How are they giving him blood? Do you have units on the chopper?" Amy asked. Were transfusions so common on these kinds of missions that they had minifridges full of the various blood types?

"I have no idea," the nurse said.

"Please let me know if you hear anything else." Amy raised her voice as the nurse turned around and walked away.

As the curtain closed behind her, Amy stood there trying to beat back the fear. Mac would be okay. They'd get him here. Get the healers on him. Get the blood in him. He'd have the best of both Western and Arapaho medicine.

He'd be fine.

He had to be.

To distract herself she looked around the room. Benji was still in the same position he'd been in an hour ago, two hours ago, maybe even three. It seemed like she'd been sitting by his bed forever—singing to him, reading to him, wiping him down. Beth's admission next door had been a welcome diversion . . . not that she'd wish what Beth was going through on anyone. Which reminded her. She eyed the wall that bordered the two cubicles.

How much of the conversation had Beth heard? The cubicles were right next to each other.

It wouldn't do Beth's anxiety any good to be over there all by herself after hearing the latest round of news. After one last look at Benji, she slipped out of his cubicle and over to the next, relieved she'd decided to check on Beth when she found the woman's purple eyes locked on the curtain, obviously waiting for Amy to arrive with an update.

"How much did you hear?" Amy asked.

"Most of it," Beth responded immediately. "Embray is alive and on board. But Commander Mackenzie was injured?" At Amy's nod, Beth hesitated before bursting out, "They didn't say anything about Zane? Right? He wasn't hurt too."

Amy shook her head. "He wasn't mentioned. I'm sure if he'd been hurt, the nurse would have said so."

Or not. If Zane had been hurt, they might not tell Beth for fear the news would stress her and the baby even more. They probably wouldn't even tell the nurses or doctors at the clinic in case Beth overheard a couple of them talking. If Zane had been wounded, they wouldn't find out about it until the chopper landed.

Time seemed to inch forward unbearably slowly while they waited for more news from the chopper. The Eagle, with Mac on it—fighting for his life, from the sound of it—was at least four hours away. Which gave Amy way, way too much time to think. To guess. To bargain.

The thought of Mac dying, of the chopper landing without his larger-than-life personality on it . . . the thought of never seeing that scowl or bristling acceptance or that glitter of hunger light up his black eyes . . . the thought of him being lost to her broke something inside her. Something fragile and new and hopeful.

It also brought memories of loss and grief and unbearable anger. Benji's hospital bed was hard enough to look at sometimes. The last time she'd been in a room with a hospital bed, she'd been in it. She'd been lying there trapped, helpless when Clay and her parents had told her about John. When they'd told her that her husband was dead and nobody had any idea who'd done it.

The echo of sorrow, grief, and longing rose. John was always in the back of her mind. It was a sense of emptiness that never quite went away—except when she was with Mac. Mac filled the room so completely, there wasn't room for ghosts.

But now he could be dying. Killed by the same bastards who'd stolen her husband and her children's father.

She still didn't know who'd killed John. Oh, she knew who it was in general—that the NRO had been behind it. But she didn't know who it was specifically—the monster who'd stabbed John over and over and then left him to bleed out all over the floor.

Although since confronting Clay, she'd begun to suspect she knew the specific *who* now. The monstrosity who'd killed John. Clay would have had access. He had knowledge of where to stab for maximum damage. He'd been in the marines and trained in hand-to-hand and knife-to-knife combat. Since they'd been friends, best friends even, John would never have suspected him. Wouldn't have been on guard. Would have been easy pickings.

The knowledge brought a wave of nausea. The thought of her brother, who she'd loved, murdering her husband was unbearable.

The idea drew her mind back to Mac. He'd been suspicious of Clay from the beginning . . . and now he might be dying. Dead, even.

Enough. She took a deep breath. This morbid remembering and worrying was doing nothing. She turned back to Benji, dipped the cloth in water, and began to wipe him down again while reciting his favorite book to him. It was a book she'd read so many times she'd memorized it.

> Sam the Cat
> Just wanted to say
> Thank you so much
> For the tuna today

She'd recited the book several times, along with a few other books from Benji's list of favorites, and washed Benji from face to toes at least a hundred times when the sound of boots pounding on the linoleum floor sounded from behind the curtain.

As she shot up from the bed, the curtain was yanked to the side, and Rawls stepped into the cubicle. Vaguely aware of voices in the cubicle beside her, she froze at the sight of his haggard gray face and bloody clothes.

Oh God. So much blood. Way too much blood.

Mac must have died.

She plunged into darkness, desolation.

Not again. Not again. To lose another so soon.

Rawls mouth was moving, but she couldn't hear what he was saying. The ringing in her ears blocked out everything. The ceiling started to spin, and the floor too. Even the walls around her whirled until she was spinning apart into a billion separate pieces.

Nobody would be able to find all the pieces of her again.

There was the sensation of moving. Of her butt hitting something hard. Of her shoulders and head being pressed down. The ringing in her ears subsided.

"Breathe, darlin'. There you go. Breathe."

Amy tried to comply. Tried to force her lungs to move. One breath—exhale. Two breaths—exhale.

The ringing in her ears disappeared.

The third breath came easier. And then a fourth.

Her body stopped spinning.

"There you, go. That's it," Rawls said, patting her shoulder.

He was patting her shoulder, for Pete's sake. Like she was some poor old lady in the middle of a fit of hysteria.

A bubble of laughter swallowed the breaths. Why, she had no idea. Nothing was funny. Nothing was even close to funny.

"Easy . . . easy. Deep breaths now."

He sounded worried. It was enough to stifle the laughter.

She chanced another inhale and then another.

She needed to straighten, to face the world again.

A world without Mac in it.

Nausea stirred, but she forced it aside. Centered her mind on her son. Benji still needed her. She couldn't give up. She couldn't give in to the darkness.

She focused on Rawls. His face looked so gray it blended into the walls. Losing Mac must have devastated him. Did he blame her? For the choice between Mac and her son?

They didn't even know for sure if Mac's sacrifice would save her son.

Maybe Rawls knew. Maybe Embray had given him the antidote on the trip back or told him how long it would take to create it.

"Embray?" It was all she could manage. Her raw throat didn't want to voice the rest of her questions.

"He's alive." He stepped back from her to shove tense white fingers through his hair. "Hell, I'm sorry, Amy. The pilot was supposed to let you know that we grabbed Embray. Got him off the machines. He's alive."

"I know. They told me. Has he said anything?"

"No. He's alive. Breathing on his own. Brain waves are there." He swayed but quickly stabilized himself. "But Kaity quit working on him when Mac got hit."

"Mac," Amy repeated, the grief rising so fast and thick it darkened her gaze. Everything in the room looked dimmer, darker, dirty. "She couldn't heal him."

"No, she—" He suddenly broke off, a startled look of realization in his eyes. "Ah fuck . . . I'm an idiot. Mac's alive. It's a miracle. He's one stubborn son of a bitch, but he's alive."

"But . . . but . . ." Her focus dropped to his chest and legs, the huge swaths of blood covering him.

He followed her eyes down. "I should have cleaned up before I came to see you, but I wanted you to know we have Embray and why he is still out."

Amy paused. "They're alive? Mac and Embray?"

The world brightened.

"Yeah." He swayed again, his face even grayer than before. "Kaity couldn't bring them both back to one hundred percent, so she healed Embray enough to get him off the machines and Mac enough to close up the holes and stop the bleeding. She gave them both a chance to make it to base, where One Bird and William were waiting for us." He shuffled over to lean against the wall. "Mac's was harder, much harder. Wiped out Kait and Cosky completely. But she did it. Got them both on the chopper . . . alive."

Enough to stop the bleeding.

The words echoed through Amy's mind. Her vision sharpening, she scanned Rawls's face. The pilot had said Mac had lost a lot of blood and that they were pumping a lot of blood into him.

Rawls's haggard face and unsteadiness suddenly made much more sense. When he started to slide down the wall, she sprang forward and shoved an elbow under his shoulder.

"You gave him the blood, didn't you?" she asked, steadying him and shuffling him to her chair.

"Some of it," he said.

More than some of it, from the look of him.

"Zane gave too, Cosky a little, even the pilot. Hell, we drained it right out of him while he was flying." He offered her a sickly smile. "It was a team effort."

Holy God . . . they'd drained it out of the pilot while he flew? That could not be safe.

But it had kept Mac alive.

The world brightened even more.

"Where is he?"

"In the ER. They're giving him more blood and calling the other healers in."

Giving him more blood.

Rawls must be talking about Mac. Amy wasn't sure who she'd been asking about. Mac? Embray? Both?

If they were calling in the healers, it meant the docs felt his condition was critical.

He was still in danger.

"You need to lie down," Amy said, the urge to run off to the ER hitting hard and fast. But Rawls needed help too. He'd obviously given way too much blood. When she donated blood, they gave her orange juice and cookies. Something about bringing up the blood sugar.

Of course. Duh, she was in a hospital.

"Nurse," she yelled, yanking the curtain back. "Nurse, I need help here."

"Ah now, darlin'," Rawls murmured, sounding like he was half-asleep. She spun around. He'd slumped down in the chair, and his eyes were closed. She heard movement behind her.

Zane stood there looking every bit as pale and haggard as Rawls. "Stupid bastard," he said, gesturing to Rawls. "I told him to ease back on the damn blood."

When the nurse bustled into the room around him, he stepped to the side, making way. "He overdid it on the blood donation."

Zane swayed as he spoke the words. The nurse had excellent instincts and caught his arm. "Looks like he wasn't the only one. Help me get them into beds. No sense in them hitting the ground and knocking themselves out."

"Can't you do more?" Amy asked, shaking Rawls to wake him. Every cell in her body vibrated against the urgency to get to Mac. Make sure he was okay. She couldn't leave these two until she knew they were being taken care of.

She roused Rawls with a couple of hard shakes as the nurse led Zane away. She had Mac's savior up on his feet and heading for the door when a second nurse—the shorter, darker-blonde one—showed up in the cubicle entrance.

Amy helped her steer Rawls to the bed next door. He fell onto the bed more than climbed and instantly fell asleep. As the nurse slipped a needle into his arm and hooked up a saline drip, Amy zipped out to check on Benji. His face was still hot. Still red. Still precious. Blood pressure and pulse were the same as before. Certain he'd get by without her for a few minutes, she headed to the ER and Mac.

Chapter Twenty

WOLF HAD WEATHERED AT LEAST A DOZEN DEATH RITUALS SINCE HIS arrival as a raw eighteen-year-old recruit. He'd presided over half a dozen of them alongside Jude after his *nesi* had risen to leader of the Eagle Clan and appointed Wolf as his second.

He knew what to do, how to do it—how to set his *nesi*'s spirit free to find the path to Shining Man and take his place with the ancestors.

But nothing . . . nothing before in his life had ever felt so . . . *wrong*.

The mantle of *beniinookee* of the Eagle Clan sat sloppy and raw over his shoulders. It didn't belong to him.

As befitting the leader of the Eagle Clan, Jude's body was wrapped in a buffalo robe. A full war bonnet of eagle feathers sat on his chest. He'd be buried as he was laid out here, in the most sacred of sacred rooms.

Once the death ceremony was complete, Wolf and Neniiseti' would escort the body down to Riverton in the big bird for a second, Catholic ceremony at Saint Stephen's church.

The cavern was full of huge, silent warriors. Above the flickering yellow torches, the smudging smoke swirled across the rocky ceiling as though it were a living, breathing thing, purifying all who drew it into their lungs.

Except . . . Wolf didn't feel cleansed, or purified, or made whole. Rather, the emptiness expanded within him, swallowing huge chunks of his soul. If Jude's death could steal the spirit from him and replace it with such hollowness, how much worse must it be for Jillian?

For the first time, he truly understood the emptiness swallowing her. To lose all her children and the brother she loved in one moment of madness. No wonder her spirit sought escape and turned to those she loved and lost to the spirit realm.

With the smudging smoke choking his lungs and tearing his eyes, Wolf knelt over his *nesi* and best friend, chanting the holy words and painting sacred red circles on Jude's cold forehead and cheeks—counterclockwise this time to allow the trapped remnants of Jude's spirit to break free and follow the smoke to Shining Man and the spirits of their ancestors.

But the words felt hollow, the sacred red paint foreign against his fingers. The silent, stoic eyes of his warriors, with the red circles he'd painted on their faces, seemed intrusive . . . judgmental. Jude's dead flesh against his fingers so very, very wrong.

Had Jude felt unworthy when he'd taken over the duties of *benii-nookee* of the Eagle Clan? If so, he hadn't shown it.

As Wolf stood and stepped back, Neniiseti' stepped forward, a faded and worn red leather pouch held high in his right hand. He broke into the sacred chant, beseeching Shining Man to light a path with the smudging smoke so that their brother Jude Standing Eagle could find his way to the ancestors and take his rightful place by their side. Wolf, along with the rest of the warriors, repeated the chant. When the last word fell into echoes, Neniiseti' threw Jude's totem pouch into the fire.

The sacred prayer was chanted again in unison by dozens of strong warrior voices. Then only the crackling of the fire echoed in the chamber.

Wolf stared into the blaze, the emptiness inside him widening. He watched as the fire enveloped Jude's totem pouch and the talismans inside it. The leather charred quickly, cracked and blackened, as the flames stole Jude's spirit away.

The spirit totems were private and sacred. The only thing Wolf knew for certain was that Jude's pouch had held the remnants of the eagle feather the spirit bird had gifted him.

As did all Eagle Clan spirit pouches.

Lost in his thoughts and memories, Wolf didn't hear Neniiseti' offer the final prayer of thankfulness or the rustle of clothing as the warriors slowly filtered out of the cavern, leaving him alone in his grief.

"Come." A hand touched his arm. "Our duty here is done."

Wolf stirred, turned away from the body at his feet. It would remain here, wrapped in smudging smoke, until they loaded it into the coffin for the trip to the reservation. He followed Neniiseti' from the chamber, achingly aware of the empty place at his side.

Once outside the chamber, in the mouth of the ancient tunnel that led to the base, he paused to shake the disorientation aside.

Neniiseti' waited for him, the fierce black eyes dark with sorrow and secret knowledge. "After Standing Eagle became the *beniinookee* of the Eagle Clan and presided over the first *hiihooteet* ceremony, he came to me."

Standing Eagle had been Jude's Arapaho name, although he'd been christened Jude Eaglesbreath by Father Murphy. The Christian name had stuck, thanks to his mother's insistence that everyone use it. Wolf's grandmother had been a progressive Indian. She'd wanted her son to assimilate into Western society and reap the rewards of Western approval. She'd been willing to give up her culture and heritage to do so. It had been a source of never-ending frustration to her that her only daughter, Wolf's mother, had fallen into the blanket Indian ways and named her grandson Wolf, following the old teachings. The name served as a constant reminder of the culture and heritage of the *hinono'eiteen*.

The light touch of Neniiseti's hand on his arm was a subtle rebuke, a reminder that the elder was speaking and deserved the honor of attention.

"Forgive me, Grandfather, my mind travels." Wolf offered a half bow of penance and forced his mind to focus.

Neniiseti's quiet nod offered acceptance and understanding. "As is expected with the death of one's father."

Wolf opened his mouth to correct the old man only to realize that the elder was right. Jude had been much more to him than uncle. He'd been his father in every way that mattered. The grief dug in again, with claws tipped in poison. He held hard against it and focused on Neniiseti'.

He fell into step beside the elder on the way down the tunnel. For the first time since Jude's death, his curiosity stirred. Many things had been brushed aside to stand steward over his *nesi*'s death, but they had not been forgotten.

Many updates were needed.

With that in mind, he went to headquarters instead of his rooms. Bright Feather, who'd been charged with running the base, met him in the war room and filled him in on the events of the past three days.

The news that Mackenzie had skated across death's scathe, surviving by the thinnest of margins, was followed by the news that he'd talked Kait into inserting into a battle zone.

What had Mackenzie been thinking? If the commander wasn't clawing his way back from death's door, he'd kill the *heebii3soo* himself.

"When will Embray have the antidote ready?"

Although William and Kait were taking turns healing the child, no one knew how long this could continue.

"Soon," Bright Feather said, twisting in his chair to study Wolf's face. It was the third time he'd done so.

What did he see that brought such curiosity? Had Jude's death been stamped upon him in some way he was unaware of?

"What of the *nih'oo3oo* from Anchorage? What say they?"

The two men who'd been asking questions around town about strange military aircraft and an Indian base had been easy to bait and trap. His last conversation with Jude had been after the first interrogation. At the time they hadn't offered anything of value.

"Nothing." Bright Feather sounded disgusted. "They don't know who hired them or what they wanted the info for. Everything was done through paid cells and money wires."

Money wires sounded traceable. Bright Feather was a genius at electronics and computers. If the transfer could have been traced, he would have done so. Still . . . "You couldn't trace the wire."

He received a look of disdain at the question, as though he should have known better and avoided wasting both their time. "The account's been deleted. So far I've had no luck pulling up any information on it."

Wolf nodded. So the men were useless. Time to cut them loose.

"What of Link? Has he given us anything we can use?"

Bright Feather's face lit up. "Yes and no. He's been a gold mine of information. Names. Locations. Schematics. The problem is they know he's been tapped. He doesn't know where they're holding the devices. But even if he did and gave them to us, the locations would be invalid now. All the product has been moved. Yeah, we know who to take down, but getting to them isn't going to be easy. They're covering their asses. There is one thing that could really be to our advantage. One of the NRO quarterly council meetings is coming up. If we could hit them then, we'd get the head and all the tentacles of the beast."

"When?" Wolf asked, his heart picking up speed. Bright Feather was right. If they could hit them during this meeting, not only would the NRO be crushed, but also Wolf would be able to cut out of them the location of Faith's new energy device.

"Twelve days," Bright Feather said. "Thing is, nobody knows where the meeting will take place. The original location is certain to have been changed as soon as Link was taken."

True.

Wolf scowled. While sometimes a spirit quest could pinpoint locations tied to certain people—that's how they'd located Faith's friends—such ceremonies worked best if the location was already in use. It was much more difficult to pinpoint an upcoming location.

In fact, it had been done only once before, and the success there had been solely due to the fact that the target had mentioned the upcoming meeting while Neniiseti' was spirit-stalking him.

The chances of that happening again were slim to none.

They needed to come up with another way to pinpoint that meeting.

Mac awoke slowly, incrementally, his journey to awareness punctuated by the beep of machines, the blinding flashes of overhead lights, the ebb and flow of hushed conversations, and the soothing scent of baby powder and rain. Amy's scent.

He forced sticky eyelids open. The overhead lights all but blinded him, and he tried to turn his head in search of that clean, fresh scent. The pain that dug into his torso convinced him to reconsider the movement. He swallowed a groan and froze, waiting for the discomfort to subside.

"'Bout time ya joined us in the land of the livin'," Rawls said quietly from Mac's left.

The fact that he *was* in the land of the living brought misgiving and expletives. There was no way he should have survived those shots. Hell, he'd been bleeding out. He'd felt it. Kait must have healed him instead of Embray.

Goddamn it.

Although—Christ, he caught his breath as another wave of pain dug into his chest—he wasn't feeling all too healed at the moment. "Sitrep?"

"You took two rounds—armor piercing—to the chest."

AP rounds? *Motherfucker.* Well, that explained the chest hits even though he'd been wearing ballistics plates. It didn't explain why he was still alive, although he suspected he knew the answer to that. Damn it. "Kait healed me? What about Embray?"

If they lost Embray because of those damn shots he'd taken, he'd never fucking forgive himself.

"Embray's alive. Kait healed both of you. You enough to plug up the holes and stop the bleeding. Embray enough to get him off the machines—alive—and onto the chopper. She got you both back to base so you could undergo treatment."

Color him impressed. That had been some damn fine thinking on Kait's part. And it sure as hell beat being dead.

"Where's Amy?" Her scent was still so strong in the air, she must have just left the room.

"She's off to talk to Embray."

No shit? "He's awake? Aware? Does he have an antidote?"

"Yes, he's awake and aware. No brain damage as far as anyone can tell. As for reversin' the isotope, that's what she went to find out."

Ah hell, he should be there beside her. If Embray didn't know how to shut that damn isotope down, Amy would need someone with her. Someone to help her absorb the blow. Girding himself against the pain he knew was coming, Mac dragged the covers and sheets to the side and tried to ease himself up.

Fuck.

The avalanche of ripping, shredding agony dropped him flat again. Yeah, he wouldn't be going anywhere for a while.

"Jesus, Mac." Rawls sounded annoyed more than concerned. "What the fuck? You can't give it a day or two before you undo all the healing Kait did?"

"Amy shouldn't be alone with Embray," Mac said when he could talk again.

"She ain't. Cosky, Kait, and Brendan are with her."

Mac relaxed slightly at that news. Settling back, he carefully rolled his head on the pillow until he could see Rawls's face. More pain—but bearable this time. "Cos still pissed at me?"

Rawls shrugged, his soft snort echoing through the cubicle. "I figure your whole self-sacrifice routine smoothed those waters, but I'm sure Cos will be weighin' in on that himself."

Yeah.

Fuck. Not a conversation he was looking forward to.

Chapter Twenty-One

THREE DAYS AFTER HIS ARRIVAL AT SHADOW MOUNTAIN AND HIS awakening from a yearlong coma, Leonard Embray's physicians finally allowed Amy to talk to him. Her frustration had risen as she'd waited for the clinic doctors to decide that Embray was stable enough to process the information she had for him. Talking to him was imperative. Life and death hung in the balance—her sons' lives or deaths. Waiting for the doctors' okay to talk to him had been excruciating.

It wasn't until she told him what James Link had done with his pet project and watched his face harden, his skin redden, and his eyes widen and bug out slightly that she realized *his* life might hang in the balance too. What if pure rage raised his blood pressure enough to give him another stroke?

She shot Cosky a worried glance, but he just shrugged and settled against the cubicle wall.

"He did *what*?" Fury burnished Embray's brown eyes, turning them more copper than chocolate. "He used the N2FP protocol on human subjects?"

"He gave the isotope to the NRO," Amy told him, watching worriedly as a muscle twitched in his rigid cheek. "And they injected it into my children so they could follow them to our safe house."

"If James gave it to the NRO, then he's ultimately responsible," Embray said tightly, his face twisting. He looked almost incandescent with wrath.

Amy suspected his last comment addressed more than Link's involvement in what had been done to Benji and Brendan. A lot more, as if it touched on James Link's ultimate betrayal—his theft of Leonard Embray's life and company.

Dynamic Solutions' founder and CEO reminded Amy of Jeff Bezos. Not that she'd ever met the Amazon billionaire in person, but she'd seen pictures, and Embray reminded her of those pictures: dark, intense eyes; cue-ball skull; extra-long forehead coupled with extra-large ears that stuck out more than a little; chubby cheeks; and a largish nose. He could have been Bezos's twin brother.

"The N2FP protocol was never, ever, *ever* intended for human trials. James *knew* this! The isotope was genetically engineered for the gray whale. Certainly we had plans to use the tracking isotope on other animals, but the compound needs to be genetically altered for each new species. To inject N2FP into a human subject in its current form would prove catastrophic."

Amy flinched, her skin crawling at his choice of words. "Catastrophic how?"

The word fit what was happening to Benji. What could be more awful than Benji dying?

"The protocol would break down a human host's cells," Embray said flatly, although the look he gave her was sympathetic. His voice gained control, but wrath still marred his face. He took a couple of deep breaths before zeroing in on Amy again. "When was the injection given?"

"About a month ago—give or take." Amy fought to keep her voice steady.

"Jesus . . . James . . . the bastard." Embray's face seized as a guttural edge sliced through the sentence.

"You must have a way to reverse the effects?" Queasy and suddenly way too hot, Amy reluctantly forced the question out. She *needed* to know the answer yet dreaded hearing it at the same time. If he said no . . . if he couldn't figure out a way to reverse the devastation taking place in Benji's cells, her son would die.

She wasn't certain she could bear knowing that.

The healings that Kait and William were doing on Benji were short-term. The fact that they'd helped at all had caught everyone by surprise. Apparently Dr. Zapa's instincts had been correct. Now that there was physical damage to Benji's cells, the healing energy had something to repair. But the fix never lasted long. As soon as the healers stepped away from Benji's bed, the isotope started eating away at his cells again, and his kidney and liver enzymes crept up. The healings weren't correcting the core problem; they only alleviated the symptoms. The only way Benji would survive this was by neutralizing the isotope destroying his cells.

Embray paused to frown. "While I hadn't developed a reversal compound, I had worked up the reversal protocol for one. If you have a laptop, I can download the specifics."

Cosky moved away from the wall. "Do you remember it? It's unlikely you'll be able to access Dynamic Solutions' mainframe. Link was locked out the moment he disappeared."

Embray's smile showed teeth and temper. "Trust me. I'll be able to download it. Dynamic Solutions isn't the only place I backed up my research."

Amy turned to Brendan. "Honey, would you get the laptop in Benji's room?" She waited until her oldest left the room before turning back to Embray. "So you'll be able to create something to reverse the effects of this"—what had he called it?—"N2FP prototype?"

"Yes. I can," Embray said with a curt, confident nod. He narrowed his eyes and tilted his head slightly.

The tension in Amy released in a whoosh, as though she were a balloon and someone had pricked her with a needle, letting the air out. Finally some good news.

"I'll need a lab, and it may take a while to collect the required elements," Embray continued. "But I'm confident that given time, I can come up with a reversal to the N2FP protocol."

Given time?

The relief vanished. Tension filled her again. How much time did Benji have? "How long will it take you?"

"It depends." He glanced at the people assembled in his cubicle. "I was told I was brought to a military base?"

There were questions in his eyes along with faint surprise on his face. He must have wondered why he'd been brought to a military base rather than a hospital.

"There was concern that you'd be exposed at a hospital," Cosky explained blandly. "Considering the NRO's power and reach—" He broke off with a shrug. "This facility is secure. Impenetrable. You're safe here."

Embray seemed to accept that. "I'll need a top-of-the-line lab to create the neutralizer."

"Not a problem," Cosky assured him. "You'll find everything you need here."

Embray shot Cosky a skeptical look. "I'll need to check out the facility for myself, which may be problematic as I'm not quite mobile yet."

An understatement, considering the man had just spent the past six months in a coma and hadn't made it out of bed since awakening.

Cosky shrugged. "No problem. Plenty of wheelchairs to choose from." His nonchalance seemed to put Embray at ease.

Brendan pushed the curtain aside and reentered the room carrying Amy's borrowed laptop. He handed it to Embray, who immediately flipped the lid and started tapping keys. A minute or so later, he gave a tight smile of victory. "I have it. Where shall I print it?"

"I've been using the nurses' station. The laptop is already linked to that printer," Amy said, a tingling sense of unreality sweeping through her.

They now had what amounted to a recipe for the neutralizing agent. Although the neutralizer still needed to be created, at least they had something to work off.

Embray shut the laptop and leaned back against his pillows. He looked exhausted and drained, his face as white as the pillowcases behind his head.

According to the reports she'd read on Embray and Dynamic Solutions, he was on the same financial playing field as Bezos. He was ranked as one of the three richest men in the world—worth more than $89 billion. Certainly he was right up there with Eric Manheim and David Coulson, two of the men who'd taken him down.

It was almost impossible to believe that a man of his intelligence, wealth, and status could have been neutralized so easily by the NRO. But they'd had help, and Embray had been betrayed.

"So tell me what other disasters James has orchestrated since I've been out." The vicious edge to Embray's question was clearly audible.

There was a lot of emotion there. Hatred mostly.

Silence claimed the room in the wake of Embray's question. The man looked beat. Hardly in the condition to take on another life-and-death revelation.

"Tell me." The order came through Embray's clenched teeth.

For the first time Amy saw the determination and fortitude he'd used to carve out his piece of the technological pie.

Cosky frowned, studying the pallid frustration on the face across from him. Finally he rolled his shoulders and ran a hand over his head. "He ratted out the clean energy generator Dr. Benton and Faith Ansell developed. Which led to the NRO kidnapping Dr. Benton and his team. Coulson forced them to recreate the device. Once he had the schematics, he reverse engineered the prototype and created a sonic distributor—or, as Link calls it, a clean bomb."

Embray froze at the disclosure, horror settling over his face. "Jesus," he whispered, his voice suddenly shaky and weak. "If those bastards were serious about what they told me . . . about resetting Earth . . ." He shook his head, disbelief slackening his features. "Well, hell . . . they have the means to do so now." He took a deep breath, and his body seemed to sag into the mattress as if this new revelation had sucked all the strength from him. "What you're describing would kill most of Earth's population and set up the New Ruling Order as less than benevolent dictators."

The next time Mac awoke, he was instantly aware of where he was and what had happened. Eyes closed, he assessed his condition. He wasn't in as much pain as before, but he could sense the worst of it lurking beneath the surface, like a shark circling in the water. They probably had him on some heavy-duty painkillers. That shark would be a hell of a lot closer to the surface, ready to strike, when the current dose wore off.

He sought Amy's scent. It was there but faint, like an echo on the air.

"I see you're awake," a chipper, unfamiliar voice said. "Can you tell me what your pain level is? From one to ten."

Mac carefully opened his eyes. This time the light didn't send shards of pain through his skull.

"The pain level," the nurse reminded him, that perky tone in her voice rasping against his temper.

"One," he said. Which was true if he didn't move or breathe. He'd prefer the lack of breathing to the fuzzy head that was dispensed along with the painkillers.

"One as in no pain and ten as in severe pain," the nurse said, that chipper tilt annoying as hell.

He scowled at the irritatingly cheerful note in her voice, which started the chisel back up in his skull. "I know what the fucking pain scale is."

From the sour expression on the nurse's face, she didn't find his declaration convincing. Probably because of the flinch that had accompanied it.

"Sure." The cheerful tone deflated. "Of course you're not in pain. Why would you be? It's not like you took two shots to the chest or survived a deflated lung or endured massive blood loss. That's just all in a day's work for you big macho warriors, right? Pain? What pain? I don't feel no stinkin' pain. You warriors . . . you're all alike." Aggravation furrowed her brow and narrowed her blue eyes. "Missing the good sense God gave a gnat. But whatever, I'll just leave you to suffer in peace along with your manly ego."

The woman's voice got progressively dimmer but more sarcastic as she exited his cubicle. The fabric curtain snapped shut with a sharp rebuke.

Jesus H. Christ. What the hell had put her ass in such a twist? Quite the bedside manner there. At least she hadn't tried to check his bandages. Fucking with his bandages would raise the pain level to DEFCON 20 on her pain threshold.

When the fabric curtain slid back again, he fully expected to see the once chirpy, now crabby nurse—with something that would hurt like hell. Maybe a series of rabies shots or a full body scrub with a steel bristle pad.

But it was Amy's concerned face studying him from the cubicle's entrance. Her hazel eyes scanned him from head to foot.

"You pissed off Nurse Cheerful. I didn't think that was possible." She stepped farther into the room, twisting at the waist to drag the curtain shut behind her.

Mac studied her as thoroughly as she was assessing him. The dullness of exhaustion glazed her hazel eyes. Her face was pale, the skin tight, with thick black circles rimming her eyes. Even her hair hung limp.

"How long have I been out?" She hadn't looked so run-down last time he'd seen her.

"You're headed into day five." A few more steps brought her flush with his bed.

Shit. Five days? He needed updates on everything, but he'd start with the most important.

"How're Benji and Brendan?"

Her face softened at the question. "Benji is hanging in there. Still sleeping. They have him in an induced coma while we wait for the antidote. Brendan hasn't gotten sick yet. Thank God."

"Good. That's good," he said roughly. "How long before the antidote?"

"A couple of days, from the sound of it. They had to order some of the elements required."

Mac frowned. Something was niggling at him, something she'd glossed over earlier. "Benji's organs?"

"Yeah, that." She shuddered. Hope and fear fought for control of her eyes. "Benji's organs were getting bad fast. In the beginning stages of failure. The meds weren't working anymore. As a last-ditch effort, the doctors brought in William, and his healing worked. They've been alternating with Kait now. So far they appear to be holding organ failure at bay. As long as they keep working . . ." The hands around his tightened.

He wanted to ask her why the healing had worked this time, but the question wasn't important. What was important was that it had. He needed to conserve his strength for the important things.

"What's the catch?" She'd just told him that they were curing Benji, so why was the fear still so bright in her eyes?

"There is no catch," she said, but her face tensed.

Like hell. He turned his hand until he could catch her fingers and squeeze. "Then why are you still worried?"

"Because everything is so uncertain. What happens if the healings quit working before the reversal is ready? What happens if someone gets hurt badly, and they need all the healers for them?" The round eyes that clung to his were full of fear and apology. "They couldn't even heal you the rest of the way because they were saving all their juice to keep Benji going." She swallowed hard, shook her head. "What if this reversal Embray and the lab are creating doesn't work? How long can William and Kait keep this up?"

Well, that explained the fear in Amy's eyes. It also explained why he still hurt like hell. He shrugged it off. He would deal with the pain if it kept Benji alive and the terror off Amy's face.

"How many healers per healing?" A sudden wave of exhaustion rolled over him.

He fought to keep his eyes open and his mind focused on Amy. She needed reassurance. Support. He wasn't going to lie to her; he would never lie to her, even to ease her fear. But he could present some facts that might relieve her worry.

"You mean each time he's healed? One. Why?" She frowned slightly.

"Because there's more than one healer here. There are plenty to go around."

She shook her head, her eyes clinging to his. "With Kait tapped out and reenergizing, they wouldn't even heal you for fear they wouldn't be able to help Benji if he needs it."

The guilt in her expression was so sharp it cut him to the quick. "I didn't need healing. I can heal the rest of the way on my own. Why would they waste their energy on someone who doesn't need it?"

He wouldn't have wanted them to either.

"One day at a time, sweetheart. Let's not get ahead of ourselves." He didn't realize what he'd said until her eyelids flared and her hands flexed around his.

Fuck.

He pulled back reflectively. Their hands separated as he waited warily for her response. To his relief and frustration, she didn't have a chance to reply. The curtain suddenly swung back, and Rawls stepped inside.

"I thought I heard that old-man-raspy voice of yours."

"At least I don't have no prissy accent." Mac shot a quick glance at Amy's face but didn't see a reaction to the endearment.

Rawls shook his head and smirked. "Jealousy. Pure jealousy." As he removed the chart from the box wired to the foot of the bed, the smirk fell from his face. He spent a couple of seconds flipping through the papers clipped to the board before dropping it back in the box.

"So tell me, Doc. Am I going to live?" Mac asked with another sideways glance at Amy. If not for the telltale widening of her eyes and flexing of her hands, he'd have thought she'd missed the endearment completely.

"Near as I can tell."

The slowness of the reply brought Mac's attention to his corpsman. He caught the rise of Rawls's eyebrows.

"Maybe I should come back later."

"No. No." Amy moved away from the bed. "I need to check on Benji." The eyes that dropped to Mac's face were shadowed, the green fire dampened. "I'll stop by later. If you're feeling up to it."

"Sure," Mac mumbled and watched her slip past Rawls and out of the room.

"From that scowl I'm guessing I interrupted something," Rawls said, an apology thick in his voice.

"No. You didn't." Mac scowled harder.

Damned if it wasn't the truth. The exhaustion surged again. He ignored it. It was past time for some more updates.

"Zane? Beth?"

"They're both fine. The baby is fine. The docs are monitoring Beth, but it looks like what happened earlier was a false alarm."

Great. Just fucking great. Zane had been sidelined by a false alarm. How much of that clusterfuck would have been avoided if they'd had

Zane on guard duty too? There was little doubt his absence had played into the downhill spiral the mission had taken. With two eyes on guard duty, maybe that shooter would have been sighted earlier . . . which reminded him—

"You take down the bastard who shot me?"

"I hit him, but he didn't go down. Took off instead. Since we were occupied keeping you breathing, we opted to let him go." Rawls pushed back the chair next to Mac's bed with his boot and dropped into it.

Point taken.

Mac battled another surge of exhaustion. At least the fatigue was muffling the pain.

"You take Link apart for setting us up like that?" That fucking detail still rankled.

Rawls shrugged, muffled a yawn with his hand. "He swears he didn't know about anyone else on the island. Hell, truth be told, I tend to believe him."

Mac snorted. "You always were a Pollyanna."

"Makes no sense why'd he'd set us up. Not when he's stuck here to face the consequences."

Okay. Rawls had a point.

"What's your take on Embray?" Amy had told him the man was alive and awake. If he was already working on an antidote to his compound, he must have awoken with his mental faculties intact.

None of which meant they could trust him.

"My take? He's pissed. Beyond pissed would be more accurate. You should have seen him when we told him his isotope had been injected into Amy's boys. If Link had been in front of him, he'd be dead. No question."

"Can we trust him?"

Rawls paused, pinching his chin as he thought that over. Finally he shrugged. "Don't know. He's saying all the right things. Doing all the right things. Not sure how we can test his trustworthiness at this point, other than waiting to see if his antidote works."

Fuck.

Mac grimaced. What a way to test someone's character . . . by waiting to see if a child lived or died.

On that cheerful thought, Cosky stepped into the room. Mac scanned the flat, cold face. Ice still chilled the gunmetal-gray eyes. Mac couldn't remember ever seeing them that cold—or distant—at least when they were aimed in his direction.

He frowned, the pain in his chest kicking up a couple of notches. Rawls had been wrong. That moment of self-sacrifice—when he'd saved Kait's and Cos's asses by jumping in front of the bullets meant for them—hadn't sweetened his lieutenant's temper.

Of course, Kait wouldn't have been there, in need of ass-saving, if Mac hadn't talked her into that damn room.

Fuck.

He grimaced, shooting Rawls a quick look. "You want to give us a minute?"

Rawls sent him a sympathetic glance as he headed for the curtained exit. Yeah . . . he knew how much Mac was looking forward to this conversation. Once Rawls had cleared the room, Mac grabbed the bull by the horns.

"Look. I'm sorry, okay?"

If anything, Cosky's face turned stonier. "No. You're not. Fuck, if you could go back in time—you wouldn't change a damn thing."

Mac scowled. "Not true." He shrugged. "I'd shoot the bastard before he had a chance to plug me."

Judging by the frustrated anger that flashed across Cosky's face, his lieutenant didn't find the facetious statement amusing.

"Goddamn it, Mac." Cosky raked tense fingers through his hair. "You had no right—"

With his chest throbbing, like someone had reached into his sternum and yanked out a rib without the benefit of anesthesia, and his head aching like an ice pick had gone to work on his skull, Mac abruptly had enough.

"Bullshit." He raised his voice, drowning out his lieutenant's tirade. "Would I do it again? You bet your fucking ass, because it was the right damn call, and you know it. Ask yourself this, you sanctimonious ass: If it was Kait lying in Benji's bed dying and Embray was the only person who could save her, would you want William in that room to revive him from a coma or in the chopper to revive him from death? Which would give Kait the best chance of survival?"

He barked out a laugh at the suddenly frozen look in Cosky's eyes, only to catch his breath as acidic agony washed through his torso.

Jesus . . . fucking . . . Christ.

He wasn't aware of making a sound, but he must have because he vaguely heard the harsh *swish* of the curtain being wrenched back.

"That's enough, Cos. We don't need you gettin' him all riled up and undoin' the magic Kaity put into him."

He fell into unconsciousness straining to hear Cosky's reply. From the icy anger on his lieutenant's face, the bastard would probably be fine with Mac ripping open Kait's magically mended tissue and bleeding out all over the bed.

Chapter Twenty-Two

Amy looked up from Benji's bedside as Leonard Embray wheeled into the cubicle. From clinic chatter she knew he'd started physical therapy and was able to walk short distances, but she'd seen him only in the wheelchair. He looked incongruous sitting in that chair, thin and long—with his knees almost touching his chest when he had the footrests down.

It had been six days since he'd promised her an antidote to the isotope he'd created, and from their discussion the day before, it sounded like they were close to a finished product.

Maybe.

Hope restricted her breath as she waited for him to speak.

"Yes," he said before she had a chance to ask. "Phase one is complete. We have a viable candidate to neutralize the N2FP isotope. We introduced the reversal to Benji's latest blood sample an hour ago. It looks promising so far. The N2FP9 compound does appear to be dissolving the bonds between N2FP and the ATP molecule."

The relief hit her in a numbing rush, but it wasn't long before questions and worries kicked in. "When will this neutralizer be ready to give the boys?"

"A day or two? Assuming there are no problems going forward." Embray wheeled his chair closer to the bed and frowned, his gaze on Benji's still face. "We'll need to monitor the blood samples for anomalies before introducing N2FP9 to a living organism." He turned his body in the chair to look at her. "How are your boys?"

"The same." She tensed, suspecting there was a reason he was asking—other than simply inquiring about their health.

"Has your oldest started showing symptoms?"

"No," Amy said, the tension spreading. "Why?"

He sighed and raised a thin hand to pinch the corner of his eye. "The new compound is highly experimental. You understand this, yes? I'm afraid that after the N2FP9 protocol is deemed viable, you're going to have to make a difficult decision. Normally the next step would be to test the new compound on lab animals. But there are only two living organisms on this base that have been infected with the N2FP isotope."

He meant Benji and Brendan.

Without thinking Amy bolted up from her chair. "What exactly are you saying?"

He dropped his arms to his sides and stared up at her. "I'm saying we have no way to test this other than by giving it to your son. And since it's experimental and has never been tested before, we have no realistic expectations on how it will react in a human host."

"Then inject some lab animals with the tracking isotope and test the new compound on them." But Amy already knew it wasn't that simple. Embray would have already done that if it was an option.

"We could do that, of course, but it would delay our window considerably. The N2FP isotope is much more difficult and time-consuming to create. It would take time to create an exact replica of the compound proliferating in your boys. Then we'd have to wait for the isotope to multiply through the lab animals. It would be weeks before we'd have a viable candidate to test the new compound on." He paused to study her. "My understanding is that time is an issue for your youngest son."

Amy shook her head, turning to Benji. "You're asking me to choose which son to give your antidote to."

"Yes," Embray said very quietly. "The choice doesn't have to be made now."

"But soon?" Amy whispered.

"Very soon," Embray said.

Two days later, when Leonard wheeled into Benji's room and parked his chair next to Benji's bed, Amy still hadn't decided which child she should experiment on. That's what injecting the compound into one of her sons boiled down to—an experiment.

From the sympathetic expression on Leonard's face, her time was up and her decision was expected.

Her head aching from a combination of anxiety and exhaustion, she stared at the small frame stretched out in the hospital bed. Benji was still sleeping. It seemed like he'd been asleep forever. It seemed like months since she'd heard his loud voice and watched his hyper, easily distracted personality ricochet from one interest to another.

The IV bags next to her son's bed were full and constantly dripping, keeping him hydrated and medicated. Just like the feeding tube they'd inserted into his stomach, through his nose, was keeping him fed.

"It's time," Embray said simply. "We've learned as much from the blood samples as we possibly can. We need to move to phase three. We need to test N2FP9 on one of your boys."

Amy flinched.

Phase three—experimentation on one of my children. Benji or Brendan? How am I supposed to choose? If this compound isn't ready, it could kill them.

Amy flinched.

"It's just that he's already so weak," Amy said. Settling beside Benji on the bed, she rested her palm on his forehead. His skin was hot and dry under her hand. The fever was on the rise again. "What if injecting him with this new compound puts even more stress on his organs? What if he's not strong enough to survive it?"

"That's why you should test it on me," Brendan said from behind her. He scanned his brother's face and looked up, his gaze dark and solemn. "I'm serious, Mom. This is the only way that makes sense. I'm not sick yet. I'm stronger. We can test it on me. See if it kills the stuff they injected in me. If it does, you can give it to Benji."

"He has a point," Embray told her.

Of course Brendan had a point. He always had a point. But injecting him instead of Benji didn't lessen her anxiety. Nothing really changed. She was still putting her son in danger. Just a different son.

How could she choose between Benji and Brendan?

She couldn't.

"You have to give it to me," Brendan said as though she'd been thinking out loud when she knew she hadn't. "If you give it to Benji, it could make him worse. It could kill him."

"It could do the same to you," Amy reminded him, rubbing her forehead. She needed to think. Which meant she needed to sleep. For a week solid. Maybe if she got some decent sleep, she could think clearly.

Because she wasn't ready to make this decision. She just wasn't. There had to be another way. One that didn't require her possibly sacrificing one son to save the other. If she got some good rest, maybe she could think of a way out of this.

"Mom—"

"No," Amy broke in sharply. "Give me a chance to think, Brendan. There must be another way. One that doesn't endanger either of you."

From the scowl wrinkling Brendan's face, he didn't agree, but he knew to back off when she used that tone of voice on him.

She turned her attention back to Embray. "Do you have time to talk to Commander Mackenzie? He's been wanting to meet you. I'll get him if you have a few minutes to spare."

The fact that they hadn't met yet was a surprise, but Embray had been spending most of his time in a wheelchair in the lab, overseeing the development of his reversal compound. Mac had been spending most of his time recovering in bed.

The day before yesterday was the first day they'd allowed Mac out of bed. That had been to sit in a chair. After that, when the nurses weren't watching, he'd taken it upon himself to take a few more breaks from his bed. He'd even taken a little walk from his cubicle to Benji's—all by himself—to the horror of the nursing staff.

It was a miracle the man hadn't fallen and broken open his healing wounds.

"How is this new stuff going to be given?" Brendan asked, watching Leonard stretch his legs out on the floor by sliding his heels across the tile squares. "They gave the first shot in my arm."

Embray nodded, grimacing as he slowly, painfully pulled his legs up and settled his feet on the footrests again. "It will be administered the same way—into the muscle by injection."

Brendan must have been wondering whether the new shot would hurt like the last one had. He'd said it had hurt badly. So badly Benji had started to cry. He'd also said Clay had smiled.

He'd smiled because Benji had been hurting.

Rage stirred at the thought, along with disbelief that she could have so blindly looked away from the monster her brother had become. But it wasn't long before grief swept in, followed by confusion. Why did she even care that Clay was gone?

Look what he'd done to her. Look what he'd done to her babies.

"Mom. Mom?"

Brendan's voice drew her back to the present. "I hear Commander Mackenzie's voice next door. He's awake. Should I go help him over?"

Amy winced at that suggestion. She could just imagine how Mac's pride would handle that. "No, I'll go. I need to talk to him anyway. How about you find us a few more chairs?"

The chairs that Zane, Cosky, and Rawls had dragged in the week before had long since disappeared.

"We'll be back in a minute," Amy said, offering Embray a smile before hurrying over to the cubicle next door.

There were ominously rising voices coming from behind the curtain, and only one of them was Mac's. Sure enough, when she peeked into Mac's cubicle, he was trying to force his way out of bed, and the shorter, heavier nurse tried to block his escape.

"You keep this up, Commander, and we'll strap you down to this bed. Honest to God, we will. I've told you. We don't have time to keep an eye on you, and you *cannot* be walking around on your own."

"I'm perfectly capable of walking around on my fucking own."

Yeah . . . Amy coughed. That was not the point.

"Nurse?" She stepped into the room, ready to referee. "I'll keep an eye on him." When his frustrated black gaze snapped to her face, she shrugged. "Try not to be an idiot, Mac. You've been up, what? Two whole days. You can't afford to lose your balance and rip apart all those wounds Kait healed. Like it or not, you need someone to watch you and step in if you get dizzy or you're thrown off balance."

He obviously really, really didn't like her lecture. A full-scale scowl twisted his face.

"I'm . . . fucking . . . fine." He growled the words through his teeth, his furious gaze locked on her.

It didn't look like he'd be calling her sweetheart anytime soon.

Before the regret had a chance to swell or she could tell him he obviously wasn't *fine*, the clomp of boots sounded behind her. She turned as Rawls stopped in the cubicle door.

"Easiest way to deal with the commander when he turns all toddler like this is to give him something to knock him out. Midazolam or Versed will do."

The slow, charming smile Rawls turned on Amy and the nurse indicated he was joking. But when his bright-blue gaze hit the bed, it chilled and flattened. Maybe he wasn't joking after all.

"Fuck you," Mac snapped at Rawls, a clear indication he didn't think his corpsman was joking.

Rawls faced the nurse, hypnotizing her with another megawatt smile. "I'll hold him down if you want to get the Versed."

"All right, damn it. You've made your point," Mac snarled. He pulled his legs into bed and slumped back.

As he thumped his head against the pillows, he looked exactly like the bad-tempered toddler Rawls had called him. A broad-shouldered, far too masculine, grumpy toddler.

Okay, maybe not a toddler at all.

"If you want to get out of bed, call one of us," Rawls told him as he walked to the foot of the bed and pulled the clipboard from its aluminum box. He quickly flipped through the pages, scanning the information, only to drop it back in the box. "That's my blood running through your veins. I'd prefer you protect my investment."

Mac snorted, the scowl slipping from his face. He looked to Amy. "Is that Embray next door?"

Amy pulled back slightly in surprise. Was that why he'd been so determined to get out of bed? To come next door and meet Leonard?

She shot Mac a disapproving look. "Yes, it is."

He had the grace to look slightly abashed. "I want to talk to him."

"I'm aware of that. Which is why I was coming to get you."

The strangest look crossed his face.

"Well, you got me. Might as well take me." Pure blandness glossed the words and shaped his expression.

Okay . . . she was 99.9 percent certain he wasn't talking about Embray now.

"What a smooth talker," Rawls drawled with a roll of his eyes.

Obviously she wasn't the only one who'd picked up on Mac's double entendre.

Then Rawls turned serious. "Embray's next door? Is he finished with the antidote?"

"He is." Just like that the conflict was back.

What am I going to do?

Chapter Twenty-Three

As subtly as possible, Mac shifted in the chair he'd taken after Rawls had walked him over to Benji's room. He'd be the last to admit it, at least out loud, but his chest, legs, and arms—hell, his entire fucking body—was pitching one badass screaming fit.

He could really use one of those pain pills he'd been refusing to take.

Not that he was going to give in to his body's demands. Sure as hell not while Amy sat beside him, shooting him those concerned little looks from beneath her eyelashes.

Fuck. He hated, hated, *hated* appearing so feeble in front of her.

He focused his attention on Leonard Embray, Mr. Fucking Billionaire CEO—the majority shareholder of one of the companies that made the Fortune 500 and *Forbes* magazine's top picks every damn year. By all accounts the man was richer than God. Insanely respected in both the tech and business communities.

Or, in layman's terms, a rich white fucktard.

Mac had known exactly what to expect—a pretentious, self-centered know-it-all. Except . . . Embray blew every one of those preconceptions out of the water. He was quiet. Thoughtful. He listened, took everyone's opinions in, before offering his own. He was respectful of everyone. He avoided stepping on egos. He didn't flaunt his wealth or status, not even his power.

And he was grateful without being overly grateful—which was a hell of a fine line to walk. He'd managed to thank Mac and Rawls for dragging him off that island without creeping them out or making them uncomfortable.

"If *James* isn't lying"—when he said his ex-partner's name, Embray's voice dropped noticeably and took on a guttural, lethal edge—"and those bastards have reverse engineered Dr. Benton's clean energy generator, then we have a problem. A big one." He paused, staring at Benji's bed. "Link said they were reproducing this new device by the thousands?"

"That's what he told us," Mac confirmed.

"We need to find those devices and destroy them." Embray's words sounded flat and cold and very, very certain.

No shit. That was something everyone could agree on.

"Finding them is going to be a problem," Amy said. "Coulson never gave James the locations where the devices are being stored."

"Unless the bastard's lying to you and knows more than he's saying," Embray said.

"He appears to be genuinely remorseful," Rawls offered slowly, carefully.

"Sure he does." Embray's mouth compressed into a thin blue line. "Because he got caught. He sure as hell didn't come forward on his own, did he?"

Fair point.

Hell, the guy had good reason for hatred. What Link had done was unforgivable. He'd fucking watched while Manheim's thugs had held Embray down and injected him with that cocktail of drugs. The bastard had known the drugs would destroy Embray's brain and turn his body into a mindless husk of muscle and bone. It would have been kinder to kill him outright. Instead, Link had set up his buddy for a living hell and made it possible for a cabal of criminals to steal his company.

"In any case," Amy said, as carefully as Rawls, "we have no idea where the devices are."

After a few moments of silence, Embray's gaze shifted to Mac. There was a cold, implacable sheen to his eyes. "You must have something or some way that will force him to talk. To spill all the secrets he's hiding."

There was no wishy-washy play at morality in the question. Embray was perfectly fine with torture and drugs to get the information they needed. Hell, Mac respected that.

"He's been put through the process. Everything he told us after the Sodium Pentothol he'd told us in prior interrogations, under his free will."

Squaring his shoulders in his wheelchair, as though he were metaphorically stepping up to the plate, Embray looked Mac square in the eyes. "I can expose them. I can line up a press conference ASAP, one carried by every news station in the world. I can tell the world what they told me. What they did to me. I can clear your names. But it will take months for the various authorities to investigate my claims. With their wealth and influence, they will remain free while my story is verified. Free to serve their agenda. Free to implement their crazy-ass plan to destroy the world. Free to use the devices they *stole* from me." Rage erupted across his features, writhed in his eyes. He took a deep breath and then another before continuing. "They can't be allowed to regroup to rebuild their network. We need to shut them down. All of them. At once. For good."

Mac stirred, leaning back in his chair to ease the constant ache in his chest and spine. "Link told us the council has quarterly updates. These meetings are held in person at random locations. The next meeting is scheduled for late next week. That's when we need to hit them. Every damn one of them will be there. Including Coulson, the bastard in charge of repurposing your clean energy generator. We can grab Coulson, convince him to give us the locations to the new warehouses.

After we clean the council, we can wipe out every device they're producing."

Embray smiled. A cold, confident, chilling smile. "Then that's when we hit them."

Mac simply nodded. They were way ahead of him there. But, hell, he was starting to like this guy. "That's the plan. As soon as we get a location."

Considering that every single member of the NRO had their own fucking jet, chopper, and yacht, not to mention a trillion estates between them, how the fuck were they supposed to find this meeting? The question was giving Mac a headache.

Embray frowned thoughtfully. "I might be able to help with that. We know who makes up the council. If we can trust James to supply us with the locations of all the quarterly meetings he participated in, I can write a script that will predict possible locations for future meetings based on past ones and property owned by council members or their family and friends."

"You can do that?" Mac's eyebrows shot up.

"I can write the script. I can plug in the previous locations and instruct the program to pull all the necessary information off the net." He shrugged. "It would give us a list of possible locations and rate them from highest probability to lowest. Whether any of the locations will be where they actually meet . . ." He trailed off with another shrug.

"It would be a start," Rawls said. "Give us some locales to check out."

Mac nodded his agreement. "Do it."

Embray released the brake on his wheelchair and started rolling himself backward. "I'll get started on that right now." He looked at Amy as she pushed her chair away to clear a path for him. "We can't sit on the reversal much longer. You need to make a decision."

Brendan shifted in his chair, his mouth open, but a quick glance at his mother had him shutting it again. Smart boy. He'd been so quiet through the discussion with Embray, Mac had forgotten he was even in the room.

As Embray wheeled past the curtain, Mac braced himself. Climbing to his feet was going to hurt like a thousand hells. Maybe a million. One of those pain pills the nurse was constantly trying to shove down his throat was looking better by the second.

The agony was every bit as bad as Mac had feared. But finally he was up—sweatier and shakier than before—but up. By the time he reached his bed, he must have been a little green around the gills, considering the alarmed look Rawls gave him.

"I'm gonna hunt down the nurse. Get you a pain pill. And this time you'll damn well take it." Rawls vanished through the curtain.

Mac lay back, holding his breath, waiting for the chainsaw churning through his chest and back to ease up enough to allow breathing again.

By the time Amy slipped into his cubicle, the pain pill had been in him a good thirty minutes, and the agony had receded behind a fuzzy barrier. He could sense it was there but didn't feel it much anymore.

He'd been waiting for her. He wasn't sure why. She hadn't said she'd stop by.

"Hey." He smiled. The feeling of floating brought on by the drugs was getting stronger.

"You look a lot better." She stepped to his side and reached for his head, then suddenly stopped and dropped her arm.

What had she intended to do? Feel his forehead like she constantly did with Benji? A sharp sense of longing constricted his throat. He would have liked the touch of her hand on his head. Hell—he'd like the touch of her hand anywhere: head, hand, arm, cock . . .

"What do you think of Embray?" she asked, snagging a chair and dragging it up to the bed.

"Seems like a good guy." Mac watched her take a seat.

Too bad she didn't sit on his bed next to him, like she did with Benji. Of course, there was only about three inches of room between his hip and the edge of the bed. He carefully scooted himself over until his right hip hit the steel bars, hoping she'd get the message.

She didn't.

"What's wrong?" Amy asked, half rising from the chair. "You're scowling."

"Nothing." But he could feel the scowl gaining momentum.

"I should go. Let you rest. I'll come back later." She rose to her feet.

Ah fuck.

He caught her hand. "Don't leave."

Troubled hazel eyes scanned his face. "Are you sure? If you don't want company, just tell me."

"I always want your company." His hand closed around hers. He drew her up to his side. "Just closer."

"Closer," she repeated. Her gaze dropped to the space he'd opened on the bed, and understanding registered.

She stood there a moment with the strangest, most solemn expression on her face. She hesitated for so long he was certain she was going to retreat to the chair or flee the room. Then she shook her hand free and turned around.

Ah fuck, you scared her away.

She placed her hands on the mattress in front of his knees and hoisted herself up, then scooted around until she was facing him.

"Like this?" Her eyebrows climbed.

A sense of contentment swamped him. He leaned back, basking in her heat beside him. "Perfect."

"Good to know." She paused. "Sweetheart."

Ah . . . yeah. His contentment disintegrated, unease taking its place. "About that."

She laughed softly. That strange, solemn expression flitted across her face again. "It's okay. I guess we're at that stage now, aren't we?"

The contentment returned. He offered her a lazy smile and reached out to claim her hand again. "We hit it back when you offered to jump my bones."

Another soft laugh. Her hand clasped his. "Looks like that will have to wait. You're in no shape for acrobatics."

True enough. Too bad Kait hadn't used more of her mojo on him. At least to heal him enough for some extracurricular activity.

"Give me a few days. I might not be ready for acrobatics, but I'll still rock your world."

"What ego." Her smile was teasing. "You know I'm going to hold you to that promise, right?"

A turbulent darkness engulfed her eyes, and he knew she was thinking about before. How she had frozen and fled. They had identified what caused her panic. They could work around it. He'd do some Googling too. Read up on rape and the accompanying psychological scars. There had to be women out there who'd detailed their path back to sexuality. Maybe he'd find a roadmap to helping Amy find her way back to hers.

Amy still hadn't decided who to give the antidote to by the time she slid down from Mac's bed. They'd discussed the pros and cons again, but everything boiled down to one thing—uncertainty. While Embray and the lab techs could make assumptions based on testing Benji's and Brendan's blood, nobody had any idea what would happen to a living, breathing human body once the new isotope was given.

"What are you going to do?" Mac asked, squeezing her fingers.

She hadn't asked him who he'd give the antidote to, although she suspected he'd have said Brendan—for all the reasons Brendan had given. But she couldn't ask him to make such a decision any more than she could ask herself.

Maybe she didn't need to make that terrible decision anyway. A third possibility had crept into her mind, and the more she thought about it, the more she realized it was the only option she could live with.

She drew in a breath and let it out slowly. Her decision was finally made. Peace spread through her. "I'm going to talk to Embray. Ask him to recreate the compound and inject it into me. That way I can test the reversal."

Mac's fingers clenched around hers. At her hiss of pain, he released her hand.

"You think this is a terrible idea." She could see his disapproval in the sharp furrow of his brow and the compression of his lips.

"I think you haven't thought this through. What if Benji gets sicker while you wait to test this thing? What if by the time you do test and clear it, he's too sick to recover? What if the compound followed by the reversal kills you? Who's going to raise your boys then?"

All questions she'd asked herself.

"If Benji or Brendan goes downhill, we can switch tactics and give the antidote to them immediately. But as of now, the healings are keeping Benji's body healthy. Kait and William can continue healing him until I test the antidote."

Although she hated leaving Benji in that coma, with tubes up his nose and piercing his arms, and she hated asking Kait and William to continue healing him, until she could test the reversal, this was the only option she could live with.

"Brendan isn't even sick . . . yet," she continued. Was she trying to convince Mac or herself that this decision was the right one? "It could be weeks before the compound starts affecting him. There's time to do this. Time to test it and make sure it won't kill them. If something happens to me, my parents will raise the boys."

The look on his face grew colder. Her stomach flip-flopped. "How am I supposed to choose, Mac?" Her chest heaved. The ache in her head pounded in time with the one in her heart. "I can't choose between them. I can't."

Mac went still. "You've already decided on this, haven't you?"

She nodded. "It's the only choice I can live with."

His face went completely expressionless, his eyes blank.

Her breath caught in her throat as a piercing sense of disorientation hit her. She'd gotten used to his . . . if not warmth, at least openness toward her. But the flat look stamped across his features reminded her of when she'd first met him. Closed, chilly disinterest. It felt like a giant step backward.

She'd just lost something precious. She could sense it. She turned away. "I'm going to find Embray."

As she slipped past the curtain, she expected, even hoped, that he'd call her back. But dead silence followed her out of the room.

What did you expect? His blessing? For him to talk you out of it? Maybe order you not to do it?

Most of all she wondered why. What had caused the change in him? What had he expected of her?

Eventually anger nudged aside the confusion. She'd done nothing to deserve such a cold reaction. And she had enough on her plate without worrying about him. She'd focus on her boys, on getting them cured and healthy. The first step in that goal was finding Embray.

Which turned out to be more involved than she'd expected. When she went to his cubicle, the nurse said he'd gone to the lab. The lab said he'd gotten a phone call and left—but nobody knew who had called him or where he'd gone. She went back to check on his cubicle. A laptop was sitting on the bed, but no Embray. Frustrated, she walked over to check on Benji.

A curly-haired brunette nurse with huge brown eyes nudged back the curtain to Benji's cubicle and poked her head through the opening. "If you're still looking for Mr. Embray, he's visiting next door."

Amy's eyes followed the sideways jerk of the nurse's chin. The woman was indicating Mac's room. She listened hard but couldn't hear anything. Whatever the two men were discussing, they were being quiet about it. When she reached Mac's cubicle, more evidence of privacy presented itself. The curtain was pulled fully across the entrance. She heard Mac say her name.

They're talking about me?

Curious, she eased up to the curtain. The voices were still low but clearer.

"We're agreed?" Mac's gravelly voice.

"If she insists on this," Leonard said. His voice softer and less gritty. "She may change her mind once she realizes how long it will take to recreate the isotope."

"I doubt it. She's damn determined. If she changes her mind, fine. But if she sticks to this plan, I want your word that you'll come to me when the isotope is ready."

"You have it."

What the heck were these two planning?

The obvious answer hit, and good Lord, did it ever pack a punch. Suddenly Mac's complete shutdown made sense. He'd been determined to hide his intentions from her, and how better to do that than by pushing her away.

She shoved the curtain all the way to the side and stepped into the room. "Why exactly does Leonard need to come to you first with the tracking isotope, Mac?"

The two men looked guilty as hell . . . like two grade schoolers with their hands stuck in the cookie jar. Mac straightened and scowled.

"I can't let you do this, Amy. You have no idea what this shit will do to you. You say you can't make a choice between your boys? Well, I don't accept this choice." He thumped the back of his head against his pillows, looking disgruntled and stubborn.

At least he's not cold or closed off anymore.

Amy glanced between the two men. When she caught Embray's eyes, he shrugged but didn't look remorseful. Apparently he agreed with Mac's solution.

"Let me guess." She crossed her arms and cocked her head. "He's supposed to inject you instead of me. Right?"

Mac eyed her carefully and then crossed his arms, mimicking her posture but from a reclining position. Pure determination glittered in his black eyes. "Not supposed to. He's going to."

"For God's sake, Mac—"

"If you insist on this, it's going to be me. End of discussion. You have a family. Children, for Christ's sake. If things go wrong, I'm the expendable one. You're not getting near the fucking isotope."

They'd see about that. "I can't ask you to—"

"You're not asking," he broke in, his voice emphatic. His face hardened. "And I'm not offering. I'm telling you. I'm the one who takes that needle."

Her chest went mushy and warm. He was putting his life and health on the line to keep her and the boys safe. Proof positive that he hadn't shut her out or backed away. Relief shot a giddy fizz through her veins.

Not that she could let him do it. And he was certainly *not* expendable.

"Mrs. Chastain. You need to come with me right now," a woman said from behind her. Pure urgency rang in her voice.

The warmth loosening Amy's chest vanished in a shower of ice. "What's wrong? Is it Benji?"

She spun around and stumbled to the cubicle next door.

"It's not Benji. It's your other boy. The older one. He's locked himself in the lab."

"What?" Amy's voiced climbed in horror because she knew what Brendan was going to do. She whirled back around and hurled herself

into Mac's room, her eyes locking on Leonard Embray's startled face. "Where do you have the antidote stored?"

"N2FP9?" He straightened in his wheelchair, understanding widening his eyes. "In the lab. Shit." He struggled to his feet. "The vials are marked. It won't be hard for him to find them."

"Son of a bitch." Mac bolted up, slid his legs off the bed.

Amy was in a flat-out run before she'd even cleared Mac's cubicle.

"Amy!" Leonard's voice echoed behind her. "N2FP9 needs to be administered in the precise dosage based on body weight. He *cannot* just inject himself. The wrong dose would kill him."

The news hit Amy like a thousand Red Bulls. Her muscles jolted and buzzed. She kept running.

Please, God . . . please . . . please don't let him have injected himself. Please, God.

White walls and closed doors flashed past her. It seemed to take forever—even though the lab was only three rooms over—before she skidded around the last corner, and the glass doors of the lab came into view.

She slowed long enough for the double doors to slide open. Several people in white lab coats were clustered against the windows of a smaller, rectangular glass room at the back of the lab. She headed in that direction and pushed her way to a clear spot against the glass.

Brendan was standing next to a stainless-steel counter with two racks of vials—one on either side of him. She watched him pick up a vial from the rack on his right, look at the label, and move it across to the rack on his left.

Thank God.

Her entire body went limp with relief. If he was still checking the labels, then he hadn't found the antidote yet. She knocked on the window. He glanced up and spotted her. Recognition flashed across his face, but he went back to picking up vials and checking labels.

"Brendan." She knocked again.

This time he ignored her.

"Brendan, hold on." She raised her voice until she was shouting.

"He can't hear you," someone in a white lab coat said. "It's soundproof. There's an intercom next to the door."

The door . . . the nurse had said he'd locked himself in. Someone had to have an extra set of keys, right?

"Doesn't anyone have the keys?" She shuffled along the window, bumping people out of her way until she found the door. Instinctively she tried the handle, but, yeah, it was locked.

"Sally has the keys. She's on her way," someone three or four people back said.

A pause followed and then, "Damn. He found what he's looking for."

Whoever had spoken was right. He'd stopped going through the rack of vials. Her fingers fumbled on the intercom button as he carefully scooted the first rack of vials into the tabletop refrigerator.

"Brendan." She held her finger down on the intercom button. "You can't do this."

The only indication that he'd heard her was the slight hesitation that coincided with her voice as he picked up the second rack of vials.

"Brendan." She paused to steady her voice. "You can't do this. Leonard says that the wrong dose will kill you."

That at least caught his attention. He frowned at her and then came over to the door. He punched something on the wall next to it, and his voice came through the intercom.

"Can you get Dr. Embray for me?"

"He's on his way." At least she thought he was. Some of her panic eased. He'd stopped what he'd been doing. Maybe Leonard could change his mind.

"Move back. Move back. I have the keys," someone among the pack of people yelled.

Amy's finger was still pressing the intercom when the shout came. Brendan must have heard it because he turned and rushed back to the stainless-steel counter.

"Brendan, wait. *Wait!*"

Ignoring her, he scrabbled through a drawer below the tabletop fridge and pulled out a hypodermic needle and syringe. As Sally pushed her way to the door, he fitted the needle to the syringe, inserted it into the vial through the lid, and turned both upside down.

"No. You can't do this. You can't." Amy's voice rose to a scream as Sally inserted her key in the door and Brendan pulled the syringe from the vial and poised the needle near his arm.

"Back off," Brendan said as the door opened. "I can inject this before you can reach me."

With the door still open, Sally hesitated.

Amy turned to her, the nausea churning hot and furious in her belly. "Leonard says the wrong dose will kill him."

Conflict swam across the woman's face, but she eased back slightly. Amy stepped through the open door, partly to talk to her son and partly to block anyone else from making any disastrous moves.

"Look, Brendan. I know you think you're doing the right thing. But you're not thinking this through clearly." Echoes of Mac's voice rang in her mind. "This isn't the answer."

He gave her a get-real look. "Yeah? And what is? You doing something stupid and convincing Dr. Embray to give you the compound so you can test the antidote?"

Either her son knew her better than she'd realized, or he'd eavesdropped on her conversation with Mac. Either way, she wasn't going to convince him not to inject himself. Her safest bet was to get him to delay.

"At least wait until Leonard gets here. He'll tell you the right dose and give you instructions on how to inject it."

"Okay." But he didn't lower the syringe or take his eyes off the door.

By the time Leonard Embray wheeled up to the lab door, Amy's nerves were stretched to the breaking point. She stepped up and to the side and he joined her in the enclosed space.

"The syringe is full," she told him without taking her eyes off her son.

"Damn." The word was muttered under his breath. "Son, it's very, very important—essential, really—that the dosage is correct. How much do you weigh?"

"One hundred and five pounds," Amy and Brendan said in unison. "At least that's what he weighed at his last checkup," Amy added.

"We need an exact current weight." Leonard's tone was absent, like he was doing mathematics in his mind.

Amy relaxed. If they could convince Brendan to come out to be weighed, maybe they could grab him before he had a chance to inject himself.

"There's a steel platform to your right about six feet. Do you see it?" Embray asked, craning his neck to the left like he was looking at something.

Amy shot Embray a confused look. What was the man doing?

Brendan glanced to his right and then back to the door. "I see it."

"That's a scale. Step on it. Tell me what the display on the counter says."

"What are you doing?" Amy hissed, nailing him with a glare. "We don't want him injecting himself."

"Relax," he soothed. "He's not going to give that syringe over easily, so we need to at least make sure the dosage is correct. That way, if things go bad and he injects himself, it's not with the full syringe." He gave her a reassuring glance. "I'm still going to try to talk him into giving it up. But after the dosage is correct."

She nodded, swallowed hard. That made sense. But, damn . . . once he had the correct dosage, what was to stop him from just injecting it?

Silence reigned as Brendan shuffled to the platform, his gaze constantly on the door. "It says one hundred and two pounds."

"One-oh-two," Leonard repeated slowly. He went silent and still for a moment, his gaze narrow and sightless. "Okay. You need three CCs. Bring the syringe to me, and I'll make sure it has the correct dosage."

Amy held her breath.

Her son was too smart to fall for Leonard's ploy. He shot the man a disgusted look. "I don't think so. Do you think I'm stupid? Tell me how to do it."

Leonard gave her a shrug and an I-tried look and then turned back to her son. "On the syringe is a series of lines. Each line has a corresponding number. Do you see them?"

Brendan moved the syringe closer to his eyes. "Yeah. I see them."

"Find the line that says three."

Amy measured the distance between her son and the entry. He was distracted but even farther from the door. He'd still have plenty of time to inject himself before she could reach him and grab the syringe.

"Okay. Turn the syringe so the needle is facing up, and press the stopper until the liquid level inside the syringe is even with the line that says three."

Brendan's eyes flitted from the side of the syringe to the door and back again. "Okay. They're even now."

"That's great, Brendan." Leonard slumped down in the wheelchair—as though, now that his adrenaline rush had subsided, his weakness was catching up with him. "Let's talk about how to inject yourself now."

"You said it needs to be injected just like the first one was."

"Well, certainly. But in that first shot, the N2FP isotope was injected into the flu vaccine and—"

"Because they were trying to hide what they were giving us," Brendan interrupted. He was far too intelligent for Amy's comfort. "You said the antidote was ready to go, so if it needed to be in the flu shot, you'd already have put it in there, right?"

"Well, that's rather simplistic," Embray mumbled, clearly stalling.

"That's what I thought." In a move that caught everyone by surprise, Brendan lifted the needle and plunged it into his bicep.

"No!" Amy screamed as he thumbed in the stopper.

Only it was too late.

Just like that, her eleven-year-old son took the decision away from her.

Chapter Twenty-Four

Wolf added another bundle of chokecherry branches to the fire and sat back on his blanket, listening to Neniiseti's prayers. The old man's voice was weak and tattered, ravaged by the hours of chanting. Breathing deeply and rhythmically, Wolf tried not to think. When attending a vision quest, one sought to quiet one's thoughts, lest they draw the attention of the spirits that are being sought.

There was too much at stake to chance wicking the spirits away from Neniiseti'. They needed the information the old man sought. They needed a location for this upcoming meeting.

Suddenly Neniiseti' stopped rocking. The elder's muffled, frayed voice stopped midchant, and he collapsed onto the dirt. The spirits had released him.

Wolf climbed to his feet. His aching muscles punishing him with each step, he hauled the elder up and helped him out of the chamber. He didn't ask what the spirits had revealed. Such questions could wait until the *beesnenitee* had replenished his body and rested his mind.

Upon driving Neniiseti' to his quarters and half carrying him to the narrow cot he called a bed, Wolf made himself at home on the floor. Vision quests took monitoring—both before and after the spirits released the seeker.

By the time Wolf awoke, hunger coiled in his belly, vibrating like a rattlesnake. He called the cafeteria and ordered two breakfast specials.

Neniiseti' stumbled into the bathroom as the food arrived. Upon his return, the spirit walker's eyes were red-rimmed and vague, filled with dreams and visions.

"Were the spirits forthcoming, Grandfather?" Wolf finally asked, rising from the table to retrieve the coffeepot. He filled both their cups.

"As much as spirits are wont to be," Neniiseti' murmured, staring into the cup Wolf had just poured.

Wolf simply nodded. The *beesnenitee* was still processing the visions. He would share only when what the spirits had revealed was understood.

As it turned out, the spirit walker's sharing came early. "The spirits showed me a white mansion floating on a sea of blue, the word *Princess* on her creamy flesh."

Judging by Link's list of earlier meeting locations, the NRO utilized boats quite often.

But Princess*?*

Wolf cleansed any indication of frustration from his face and eyes. A yacht called *Princess*? Yeah, that wouldn't be hard to locate at all. The spirits could have been a little more forthcoming. Like giving an identification number.

As he rose to his feet to begin the impossible task of locating this yacht on a sea of blue, Neniiseti's scratchy voice stopped him.

"Hooxei, send the healers to Black Cloud. He must be ready."

Ready?

A terrible premonition struck. He turned stiffly to face the elder. "For what, Grandfather?"

"Black Cloud and his *beniiinenno* will fight beside you." The *beesnenitee* must have seen the resistance on Wolf's face, because his red-rimmed eyes narrowed and finality rang in his voice. "The spirits have spoken. It will be so."

Without a word Wolf stalked from the room to arrange the healing as he'd been directed. But the thought of working with Mackenzie on another mission had turned the promise of the new day sour.

During the last quarter mile of his workout with Rawls, Mac kicked his legs into high gear. He still didn't overtake his lieutenant. But, hell—he'd managed to keep up with the bastard without hacking up a lung, which was good enough for Mac considering the circumstances.

Rawls jogged back to him. "Not bad, Commander. Not bad at all."

Mac slowed to a jog and then a walk. "Beats the hell out of a hospital bed."

It was almost impossible to believe that he'd been camped out in said hospital bed less than twenty-four hours earlier. There was sure as hell some nuclear power in Kait Winchester's hands.

"How's Brendan doing?" Rawls fell into step beside him.

"So far, so good." Mac frowned uneasily. Christ, the kid had about given Amy a heart attack. Hell, his own heart might have stuttered there for a moment or two as well. "He hasn't gotten sick, anyway. Embray says it will take a few days before we'll know if the reversal drug is working."

"Sweet Jesus." Rawls shook his head. "That kid's got some balls on him. Glad to hear that little stunt didn't do him any extra harm." He shot Mac a sideways glance. "Cos talking to you yet?"

Mac's jaw clenched. "Not yet."

Frowning, Rawls rubbed a palm down his face. "Give him time. He'll come around."

Yeah. Mac swallowed a curse. He probably shouldn't have gone off on the poor bastard like that. "Got plenty of that."

Silence fell between them for a moment, and then Rawls gave Mac a light shoulder shove.

"I've been meaning to ask." Rawls paused. The faux innocence glittering in his baby-blue eyes held no innocence whatsoever. "Any particular reason you're suddenly so determined to turn that flabby desk-jockey body of yours into six-pack abs and steel thighs?"

Flabby?

Mac instinctively looked down. Fuck . . . he'd never gotten that bad. He gave his corpsman the middle finger. Rawls laughed and laid into his shoulder with a couple of quick jabs. Mac fought back a wince. No way was he giving the asshole another opening to denigrate his desk-jockey body.

After a few minutes of cooling down and getting their breathing under control, Rawls turned the conversation to Kait's unexpected healing.

"Did the big bad Wolf ever get around to telling you why he sent Kait to heal you?"

"Hell, no." Mac suspected Wolf had done it for the sheer joy of fucking with Mac's mind.

Wolf must have known that Mac would refuse the healing. Why else send Kait to heal him while he was out like a light thanks to too many pain pills and too much exertion? The struggle to the lab when Brendan held the whole clinic hostage had been bad enough. But that solo return trip had damn near killed him. By the time the heat from Kait's hands had penetrated enough to wake him from his stupor, she was done, and he'd been miraculously healed.

A fact he should have shown some gratitude for, according to Cosky and Zane and . . . hell, pretty much fucking everybody. Okay, maybe he'd bellowed like an enraged buffalo, as Amy put it. But he hadn't needed the healing. He'd been healing just fine on his own. True, he'd been in pain and slow to get around—but he *had* been healing. They would have been better served to conserve Kait's strength in case Benji took a turn for the worse or Brendan crashed.

Something he'd almost pointed out to Amy when she'd lit into him for his volcanic reaction. But Amy had looked so exhausted and drained he hadn't wanted to remind her of the danger her boys were in.

She needed some sleep and a real meal, and now was the time for both. Benji's condition hadn't changed. Neither had Brendan's, for that matter—although adverse effects wouldn't show up for another day or so. Which meant this might be the only time Amy had available to catch up on her sleep.

Kidnapping the woman and forcing her to bed—only to sleep—was the top ticket on his mind when he walked into the clinic an hour later.

Embray pounced on him before he made it to Benji's cubicle. "The script's finished. We have a list of possible locations."

The news stopped Mac cold. He hadn't expected the computer program to produce results so quickly, but the accelerated timetable was a godsend. The quarterly meeting Link had mentioned was only three days away.

"How many locations did it give us?"

"Too many." Embray's voice was grim. "We need to narrow it down."

Mac took the printout Embray handed him, scanned it, and scowled. Too many didn't come close to describing the sheer volume of properties listed. The computer had split the list into planes, yachts, and estates, but there were dozens listed in each category.

"Can you program the computer to narrow this down any further?" Mac asked, although with only three days to work with, they didn't have much time for another script run.

"Not without stronger data."

Which they didn't have. Link had given them all the information he'd been aware of. Maybe seeing the list would remind Link of something he'd forgotten.

"I'll get hold of Wolf and ask to see Link, see if he can identify a best option from the list," Mac said.

Shadow Command had Link under twenty-four-hour security and locked away somewhere in the bowels of the mountain. So far they'd been good about letting Mac and his team have access to him whenever they needed.

Since Mac didn't have Wolf's phone or pager number—or whatever the fuck people used around here—he borrowed the clinic's phone to contact base headquarters.

The plebe who answered the phone promised to relay the request to Wolf. Mac hung up. He'd give the guy thirty minutes to make good on his promise, and then he'd head over to headquarters in person. Sometimes in-your-face cage rattling produced quicker results. Not in this case, however. With fifteen minutes to spare on Mac's self-imposed timetable, Wolf walked into the clinic.

"Where's the printout?" Wolf asked, stopping in front of Mac.

Mac passed the sheets over. "Where's Link?"

"I'll take it to him," Wolf said, bending his head and scanning the sheet. Suddenly he froze. With a slow shake of his head, he tapped one of the line items with his finger. "This one. *Princess.*"

Mac leaned closer, peering at the listing Wolf indicated. It was a yacht owned by Coulson's wife's family. "What makes you think it's gonna be held there?"

"We received intel recently from . . . a trusted source. They said the meeting would be held on a boat called *Princess,*" Wolf said in a flat, don't-ask-me-too-many-questions tone of voice.

"You don't say." Mac eyed the big bastard suspiciously. "I don't suppose you're gonna share this source with us?"

His question was ignored. No surprise there.

"So why the hell didn't you tell me this earlier, like when I gave you the damn list?"

Wolf shrugged. "All we were given was a boat named *Princess.* No identification numbers. No owner. I asked Link. He wasn't aware of any council member with a boat by that name. Your computer list provided the rest of the identification."

Wasn't that just handy as fucking hell?

"Assuming this is the same damn boat and not a fucking coincidence," Mac said.

"There is only one *Princess* on your list," Wolf reminded him.

True enough.

Hell, Mac wasn't even sure he wanted to know who Wolf's source was. Last time it had been a fucking ghost. Besides, they didn't have all that many options anyway. And so far Shadow Mountain's intel had been right on target.

He'd just pretend that Wolf's current sources were human rather than wisps of ether.

"We still need to find this boat," Mac mused, but that was a minor detail and easily accomplished. With the resources Wolf and his buddies had, they should be able to acquire that information in no time.

Wolf was already heading for the clinic door. "Be ready to bug out. We'll go wheels up as soon as we have the location."

Rocking back on his heels, Mac raised his eyes in exaggerated surprise. "No shit? You're allowing us to join the party."

Without constant badgering. That had to be a first.

Another shrug lifted the enormous shoulders. "Be ready."

Mac snapped him a mock salute and, "Yes, sir." But Wolf was already gone, which made the sarcasm much less effective.

After calling Zane, filling him in on the upcoming mission, and telling him to pass the word to Cos and Rawls, Mac headed for Benji's room. Brendan looked up from the game he was playing on Amy's laptop, but Amy didn't budge from her slouched position in the chair opposite the bed.

Sleeping? Brendan mouthed the word and nodded at his mother.

Yeah. Mac frowned as he stepped into the room. Her position in that chair looked as uncomfortable as hell. Time to whisk the lady off to bed where she could rack up the *zzzs* without crippling herself in the process . . . assuming he could get her to cooperate without pitching a fit about staying with her kids.

"How are you feeling?" he asked Brendan. The kid didn't look any different. No obvious signs of a fever or pain. He even looked rested and fed. Amy had made sure the boy got enough sleep and meals. Too bad she wasn't doing the same for herself.

Brendan cocked his head and paused, as though he were monitoring his body. "I don't feel any different."

"That was a pretty brave thing you did yesterday," Mac told him quietly. "Stupid. But brave."

Brendan shrugged and looked away. "Not really. I had to do it. It was the only thing that made sense."

"That doesn't make it any less brave."

"I guess."

"Your mom needs some real sleep, in her bed instead of this chair," Mac told Brendan as he walked around to the front of Amy's chair. "I'll take her back to your rooms if you'll keep an eye on your brother."

"I'll stay and keep him company. But Mom won't go with you."

The boy was probably right. Amy had proved repeatedly what a devoted mother she was. So damn devoted she was determined to run herself into the ground. The contrast between her behavior and his mother's was so stark it was almost comical. Here Amy would barely take a break from her sentinel duty, as though leaving Benji's side left him open to illness or injury. As opposed to his own mother, who'd been too busy fucking every sailor in port and crashing every party to remember she had kids . . . let alone feed and bathe and tend to them.

Or make sure they were at least locked in her car while she was getting her weekly fuck on so they wouldn't get hit by a Goddamn car.

He wrestled his mind from that direction before Davey's face could bloom in his mind, and he refocused his attention where it was needed—on the woman sprawled out before him.

She had to start taking better care of herself. He bent to slip one arm beneath her knees and the other around her back. He held his breath as he lifted her. She was heavier than she looked. Heavy enough he started rethinking the whole carrying-her-to-her-quarters thing. But then she sighed, cuddled into his chest, and wrapped her arms around his waist.

You can do this. Just dig in, ignore the discomfort, and get her home.

Besides, it felt so good to have her in his arms again . . . without her panicking and pulling away. Everything fit perfectly. Her ass against his left arm, her back against his right side, her breasts against his chest. Even her head snuggled perfectly into the hollow of his throat.

And then she sighed again and her warm breath caressed his bare throat.

The sound and sensation lurched through him like a shot of Jack Daniel's. A burning rush that adrenaline-bombed his veins and jump-started his heart, lungs, and cock.

Oh yeah, standing in front of Brendan with the boy's mother in his arms and a full-blown erection filling the crotch of his loose sweats was not one of his finer moments. He turned a little too hastily and stumbled, caught himself, and froze. But she didn't awaken. If anything, her breathing seemed deeper and more even.

"The door code is one-five-three-five," Brendan called out softly from behind him.

Jesus, he hadn't even thought about how he was supposed to access her apartment. Hell, maybe subconsciously he intended to take her to his quarters. His bed.

By the time he walked through the clinic's sliding doors, his arms were cramping. There was no way he'd make it all the way to her quarters without dropping her. Luck was on his side, though. A motorized cart was parked to the right of the door. He carried her to it and carefully settled her into the passenger seat, then propped her against the backrest. She stayed there until Mac climbed behind the wheel and backed up the cart, at which point she slid down the cushion and plopped her head in Mac's lap.

He caught his breath.

Son of a bitch.

Her mouth was so fucking close to his swollen cock, he could swear he felt her warm breath caressing the sensitive skin down there. Which was impossible considering the heavy fabric separating the two . . .

With his heart beating way too fast and his palms sweating, he backed the transport out of its parking slot. Turning the wheel hard to the right, he sent the cart into a tight U-turn.

Holy fucking Christ.

The momentum rubbed her cheek against his crotch. His cock twitched, elongating, apparently trying to reach her mouth.

By the time he reached her quarters, the lower quadrant of his body felt flushed and heavy and ached like a motherfucker—with no end in sight.

Jesus—he was too fucking old for blue balls.

He pulled the golf cart into the wall at an angle beside her door. Got out, punched in the code, and yanked off his shirt to shove it under the doorframe so the door would stay open. This time when he eased Amy into his arms, she cuddled up against his chest—his bare chest. It shouldn't have made any difference. She was still clothed, for Christ's sake. There was no reason for the heightened sensuality or the damn chills tickling his spine. They weren't even touching bare skin to bare skin.

But possibly, just possibly, removing his shirt had been another subconscious move toward getting himself naked . . . and in her bed.

He seriously needed to rein in his damn libido.

Trying to ignore the way her warmth was heating his naked chest, he carried her into the first bedroom and found two narrow beds. He carried her back out. The second bedroom had a bigger bed. He eyed it as he laid her down in its middle. Might not be big enough for both of them, not for what he had in mind . . .

When her back hit the mattress, she uttered another of those delicious soft sighs and rolled over to hug her pillow. His cock, the bastard, urged him to climb in there beside her . . . give her something else to sigh about, give her something else to hold on to, give himself a chance to rock her world—as he'd promised.

Of course, she wouldn't get the sleep then.

With a frustrated groan, he removed her sneakers, backtracked to the first bedroom, and dragged a blanket off one of the beds, then returned to Amy's side to spread the blanket over her.

And then he fled.

Because that's sure as hell what it felt like. Fleeing the room for fear he'd give in to his primal impulses and climb into that bed with her, only sure as hell not to sleep.

Chapter Twenty-Five

Amy caught Kait's fingers as the long-haired blonde goddess stepped back from Benji's bed. The hand she squeezed between both of hers was still lobster red, hot enough to sting and emitting heat like a cooling stove.

Clearing the roughness from her throat, Amy gave Kait's hand one last squeeze and stepped back. "With luck, this will be the last time he'll need healing. There're not enough thank-yous in the world to express how grateful I am. Without you he wouldn't have survived until the antidote was ready."

Kait waved the gratitude away, her brown eyes softening in sympathy. "That stunt Brendan pulled must have given you a few gray hairs. I bet you'll be ready for a nice long vacation once this is over."

Amy's stomach knotted at the memory. Chills tingled across her scalp. Lord, her son's stunt, as Kait called it, had given her more than gray hair—it had almost given her an aneurysm, her blood pressure had climbed so high.

Amy laughed. "A sandy beach, warm breeze, and clear blue water would be nice."

The mental picture that bloomed in her mind made her smile, partly because there was someone holding her hand in the vision. A dark-haired man with watchful black eyes and a furrowed brow.

Except he really didn't fit with the sandy beach and crystal clear water. She ditched the surroundings but kept the man. She could do without the beachfront vacation. She wasn't sure she could do without the man.

"You're certain the antidote is working on Brendan?" Kait asked carefully as if she didn't want to stoke Amy's anxiety.

"We won't know for sure until tomorrow. But it looks like it." Amy didn't cloak her relief. "The blood test today showed a reduction in the N2FP isotope. The bonds between the isotope and the ATP molecules are dissolving. If this continues tomorrow, and Brendan doesn't show any secondary effects, Leonard says we can give Benji the antidote."

"That's great. This healing should last him for a while. Hopefully at least until Cosky gets back. So far Benji hasn't needed that extra boost of power that Cosky supplies, but it eases my mind to know that he's there if your son needs both of us. Or if anyone else does too, of course."

Kait's face tightened more and more as she spoke. Eventually she stopped talking altogether, took a deep breath, followed by another, and closed her eyes. Amy could almost see her force the worry away.

Amy's tension, on the other hand, rose like a flare. Cosky was going somewhere? Somewhere dangerous, judging by Kait's reaction.

"Where's Cos going?" Amy didn't bother to keep her voice or expression unconcerned. If Cosky was headed off on a mission, then the other members of ST7 would be going as well. Which concerned her deeply.

Kait inhaled another breath and exhaled slowly, but this time the tactic didn't appear to work quite as well. Strain flickered across her face. "Wolf located the yacht the council is meeting on. They go wheels up at oh-two-hundred."

The anxiety jumped a few more notches. "Is Mac on this mission?"

With a slow nod, Kait brushed a strand of hair from her eyes. "They all are. Wolf and his team. Mac and his. They're pulling out all the stops."

Which made sense. The NRO had to be stopped. The civilization-ending device they'd created needed to be destroyed. Shadow Mountain, along with Mac and his team, couldn't afford to take any chances. They had to hit hard and fast.

But did Mac have to go along for the ride? The man had barely recovered from one near-death mission. Did he have to jump straight into another?

Amy closed her eyes and fought to calm her heart and mind. Of course he had to go. Mac wouldn't send his men if he wasn't willing to go himself.

That sense of duty and his loyalty were two of the things she respected about him most.

She reined in her fear and assessed the situation, forcing herself to think past her initial panic. "Are they boarding from the water or fast-roping down from the chopper?"

"I don't know." Kait shook her head. "Cosky didn't say. All I know is that the boat is at sea. Somewhere in the Gulf of California."

Which meant Mac and his team would be in their element. They had trained extensively for waterboarding and roping down from above. The *S* in SEAL even stood for *sea*. Some of her anxiety eased.

Plus, Shadow Mountain had a couple of secret weapons. If Mac or any of his men took a hit, this time they would have plenty of healers on board ready to help them.

"You're going with them, right?" Amy asked. Having Kait on the mission would give the men much better odds. She was the strongest of the Shadow Mountain healers.

Kait couldn't heal everyone, of course. Nor could she heal death—as proved by her attempts on Jude. But at one point or another, Kait had healed all the SEALs except Zane. So if Mac or Rawls or Cosky were hit, she'd heal them, just like she had in the past.

Kait's throat worked. Pure frustration flooded her face and seethed in her eyes. "No. Cosky and Wolf won't let me." She blew out an irritated sigh. "If it was just Cosky, I could work around it. But Wolf runs the whole damn show. With him backing Cos, I can't even get near the hangar and stow away."

Some of Amy's newfound calm expired.

"They'll still have William and One Bird, though. I'm sure they'll be fine," Amy said, trying to convince herself as much as Kait. Too bad she didn't believe her own reassurance.

"Sure." But the strain in Kait's eyes remained. "You should get some sleep while you can. Benji should be good for a day or so now. I'm sure the nurse will keep an eye on him."

"I'm fine," Amy said with a smile. "I got several uninterrupted hours this morning."

After Mac had carried her off to her bed and left her there drenched in his scent, she'd dreamed about him. She'd awoken completely refreshed, with the smell of him still surrounding her. She still wasn't sure whether she was pissed or pleased that he'd left her in that bed alone. On the one hand, she'd gotten some desperately needed sleep . . . on the other he hadn't been around to turn her dreams into reality.

"It wouldn't hurt to get some more," Kait said. "Who knows what tomorrow will bring? You may not get another chance."

Amy thought about that as she walked over to check on Brendan. Dr. Zapa had admitted Brendan after he'd injected himself so they could monitor him. Having the two boys next to each other made life a little easier. She didn't have to ask someone to stay with Brendan while she was with Benji, although Brendan was in and out of his bed so much it was hard to keep track of him.

This time he was in bed, lying on his side, sound asleep. She pressed the back of her hand to his forehead, a new habit. Benji's downhill spiral had started with a fever, so she was fever shy these days.

"I feel fine, Mom," Brendan said, startling her. "No different from how I felt before the shot."

She could have sworn he'd been sleeping, but his dark-brown eyes were open now—clear and focused, as if he'd jumped directly from sleep to mental acuity. His father had been the same way. Fully awake the moment he opened his eyes. No haze, no fading dreams. Just instant focus.

"Are you still mad at me?" he asked, his face more curious than worried.

Amy sighed and brushed a tuft of hair off his forehead. "You scared the hell out of me, Brendan. You had no idea what that stuff would do to you. You had no idea if it was safe to take it the way you found it. It could have killed you."

She broke off. They'd had this discussion already. Multiple times. But she was virtually certain he'd do the exact same thing if he had to do it again. Brendan was positive he'd done the right thing. Nothing anyone told him would convince him otherwise.

He'd inherited his father's conviction and faith in his own ability.

It was so strange. If you counted by days, John's murder hadn't been that long ago. Almost six months now, 180 days—give or take. But emotionally . . .

It felt like forever. Years at least. John felt like a dim, treasured memory. She didn't dream about him anymore. Not like she had in the beginning.

Mac dominated her dreams these days.

Guilt swelled. John had been a good man, a good husband. A wonderful father. He deserved better than this. He deserved to be mourned for longer than six months.

"Are you okay, Mom?" Brendan propped himself up with his elbow.

"Just tired." Amy leaned over him to pull up the thin white blanket.

He apparently bought that explanation, because he lay flat again and closed his eyes.

"You should get some sleep," Brendan said. "I'll watch Benj." But his eyes were already fluttering down and his face was relaxing.

"Don't you worry about Benji," Amy whispered, leaning down to kiss his forehead. "Rest now." By the time she straightened again, he was sound asleep, his breath coming deep and easy.

She peeked into Benji's cubicle to check on him. He'd rolled from his back onto his side, but his face looked peaceful. The fever flush was absent from his cheeks. She hesitated there for a long time. Kait and Brendan were right. She should head to her quarters and get some sleep.

But sleep wasn't what she needed.

The night nurse looked up as Amy approached her desk.

"I'll be away for a while," Amy said. "Buzz me if you need me, okay?"

Dr. Zapa had given her a pager when Benji had been admitted to the extended care unit. So far they hadn't needed to use it, but the medical staff could reach her immediately if Benji—and now Brendan—took a turn for the worse.

"Absolutely, sugar. You go and get a good meal and relax." As Amy walked out of the clinic, the nurse went back to her clipboard and charts.

She must look a lot worse than she realized; it seemed like everyone was trying to send her to bed. She could go back to the set of rooms she shared with the boys. They'd be silent and empty. Lonely. Unappetizing. But she wasn't going there. She'd known exactly where she was headed and why long before she'd left the clinic.

It wasn't home—although she didn't think of this place as home. She doubted she ever would.

Mac was shipping out. Embarking on a mission that might well kill him. She wasn't completely certain what she felt for him, but whatever it was, it was strong. He frustrated her at times, annoyed her at times, made her want to throw things at times. But he also made her feel safe and trusted. He brought her to life.

What she did know for absolute certain was that she didn't want him to bug out. The thought of him dying seared through her like a sword, filling her with pain. She felt something for the man . . . something that dug deep and clung.

She'd lost one man she'd loved. She didn't think she could bear losing Mac too.

She knew, without a doubt, that she would regret it for the rest of her life if she didn't explore this sexual connection between them. Tonight might be the last chance she'd have for that exploration.

Benji was safe and so was Brendan, so she'd take this night for herself and pray that her demons didn't rise up and ruin everything . . . again.

The streets and corridors were quiet around her. The gray walls were a soothing, indistinct blur. It felt good to get out of the clinic and stretch her legs, work her heart and lungs. Not enough to tire her out but enough to limber her up. One of the tips from the articles she'd read was to get plenty of exercise. She needed to make that a priority as soon as the boys were back on track.

She ran through the other tips aimed at preventing flashbacks: methodical breathing, anchoring in the here and now, anticipating triggers, paying attention to her body's danger signals, and the steps to self-soothing.

These were all methods she could use to derail the flashback before it had a chance to strike—before it could ruin the moment.

Because she intended to make love to Jace Mackenzie tonight.

For this night to progress the way she wanted, the way she *needed*, she required his help.

One of the things she'd absolutely *hated* following her kidnapping was how public everything was. Everyone knew about John's murder, her kidnapping, and the rape. The media had fed on the tragedy of her life for weeks. Her parents and friends had been supportive, but they'd treated her like she was fragile, breakable, as though the kidnapping and rape *defined* her or had broken something inside her. The knowledge of what she'd gone through had constantly lurked in the back of their eyes or shuffled across their faces.

She couldn't look at them, interact with them, without being reminded of what those bastards had done to her.

Mac wasn't like that. He knew what had happened in that crappy track house. He'd seen the video. He'd seen the bruises—so she should have felt uncomfortable around him. Yet there had never been any awkwardness between them. Not even in the beginning. Maybe because he'd never treated her as though the experience defined her. He'd simply acknowledged it and moved on.

He'd never treated her like a victim either, or like she was fragile. He'd been more likely to snap at her or yell at her than treat her like she was breakable. She counted on that from him. Needed it.

She couldn't bear the thought of the rape coming between them now, of Mac treating her differently. But to move past the nightmares she was going to need his help.

For the first time, when she reached his door she didn't hesitate. She knew why she was there and what she was doing. There was no sense in pretending otherwise—a sentiment that echoed in the firm rap she gave his door.

When the door swung open, she found no surprise on his face. No questions. She found hunger instead, anticipation mixed with relief. He wordlessly pushed the door wider. She turned to face him as the door closed behind her but stepped back out of reach. Before things went any further, she had to explain what she needed tonight.

"I've been reading up on"—she hesitated—"post-traumatic stress and flashbacks."

He cocked his head, his gaze sharpening. "Anything useful?"

"Yes, actually." She tried for nonchalance. "You were right about the trigger. About how the flashback is prompted by your arms closing around me. Apparently it's quite common. They even have a name for it—trauma triggers."

Mac scanned her face and nodded slightly. "So we avoid that trigger. What else?"

He didn't sound unnerved or worried. Rather, he sounded matter-of-fact. In control. Like it was no big deal. She relaxed, a tickle of nervous excitement racing through her.

She reached out to run her hands up his chest. His T-shirt was soft and warm on her palms. "I'm supposed to ground myself in the moment by doing a lot of . . . touching."

"I can get behind that." He bent his head. His voice was thick and raspy against her lips.

She shivered as he brushed a kiss across her mouth. "And you're supposed to do a lot of touching too. Like my arms and my shoulders, my back. Lots of light touches without any holding."

"Now *that* I can really get behind," he whispered, angling his head to nibble at the soft skin behind her ears.

She quivered as his teeth scraped the sensitive flesh, lost her breath as he slowly, sensually trailed his fingers from her wrist to her shoulders.

"Like this?" he whispered, his breath moist and hot against her ear.

She burrowed in closer, until his hard chest was pressed against her tight, throbbing breasts.

"Just like that. Except . . ." She eased back from him and ran her hands down to the bottom of his shirt. She caught the hem in the curve between her thumbs and forefingers and oh so slowly pushed it up. "All the articles claim bare skin works best for grounding."

Okay, so maybe the articles hadn't actually said that, but bare skin certainly worked best for *her* grounding. Her fingernails lightly scraped his abdomen as the shirt rose. His skin twitched at her touch, and a soft hiss of need broke from him.

Quivers attacked her spine as his muscles bunched beneath her hands. She pushed his shirt up until his patience gave out and he wrenched it over his head. To have so much power over his reaction was rather exhilarating. Heat flared inside her, humming through her veins.

"Who are we to argue with the experts?" His voice sounded raspier than ever, close to hoarse. His fingers traced a casual, light-as-a-feather path down to the bottom of her shirt. "I assume the bare skin mandate is for you as well as me?"

"Absolutely." She swallowed a groan as his hands drifted lightly up her back, taking the shirt with them.

As the sensation registered of his arms sliding up her waist and the sides of her breasts, some of the heat dampened and tension rose. He pushed her shirt up over her head, and darkness fell. The quivers stilled. Her heart began racing.

A section from one of the articles flashed through her mind.

Pay attention to your body's danger signals.

The sudden tightening of previously fluid muscles was a danger sign; so was the diminishing heat and the panicked beat of her heart.

Ground yourself in the present.

Once her shirt was off, her sight returned. She zeroed in on Mac's bare bronze chest. On the puckered scar from the bullet wound he'd taken in the woods after he'd rescued her from the monsters. Before the flashback had a chance to kindle, she pressed her hands against Mac's chest, against his heart, and focused on the hard, steady thump under her palms.

Remind yourself where you are, who you are with.

"I'm with Mac. This is Mac." Her voice was thin, shaky, the nightmare just a breath away.

"That's it, babe. You're with me. Mac. You're safe. Nothing to fear here."

Thud . . . thud . . . thud.

She concentrated furiously on the steady beat of his heart. The feel of it pumping beneath her fingers. On his heat and strength. On his hard, hot muscles. The calm, raspy rumble of his voice sank into her ears, and then her mind held the flashback at bay.

It took her a moment to realize that his hands had fallen from her sides. They were standing torso to torso, her hands on his chest, his arms loose by his hips.

"You okay?" he asked.

She looked up, afraid of what she might see on his face. In his eyes. But his face was still, his black gaze sheathed in tranquility. It was so odd how this man who'd reacted so explosively more times than she could count could face her with such absolute calm when she needed it most.

"You with me, babe?" he asked, his voice as quiet as his eyes.

Her tense muscles softened. She brushed her palms over his nipples, smiling as the muscles of his chest rippled. That earlier current of excitement sparked again, inched through her. "I really need to focus on touching. That appears to ground me the best."

"By all means, touch me." His hot breath steamed the side of her neck, kicking up a flurry of tingles and quivers. He nibbled a path to her collarbone. "I'm a big believer in going with what works."

"Oh, this certainly works." She was vaguely surprised by the sensual purr in her words. By the way her body was softening and heating and liquefying in all the right places. By how easily she'd turned away from the nightmare.

There was obviously something to all that grounding advice.

She ran her hands down his chest and tucked them into the waistband of his jeans. His belly twitched at the move. His crotch swelled. The heat creeping through her mushroomed, expanded, until her skin felt tight and swollen and increasingly sensitive.

"But according to the articles, you're wearing too many clothes." Her fingers drifted to the fastening of his jeans, to unbutton and unzip.

"Can't have that." His voice deepened to guttural, thickened with hunger. "How about we move this discussion to the bedroom?"

He took a step forward, the movement trapping her hands between their bodies. His fingers skimmed down her sides to lightly rest on her hips.

Another step.

His chest rubbed against her breasts. Her nipples peaked. Her breasts swelled and throbbed in time to the beat of her heart. A flash fire swept through her, pooling in a hot rush between her legs.

Another step.

His pelvis brushed her belly, a carnal dance of advance and retreat. The quicksilver tingles spread through every inch of her. Another purr broke from her, a sigh of contentment as the sexual attraction shifted to erotic need.

This was exactly what she needed. The heat. The hunger. The brush of his body against her. Each step a sensual shimmy of hard, hot muscles against her overheating skin.

Raising her head, she focused on his hungry face, on the urgent glitter in his dark eyes. Then his lips took hers, and his tongue surged into her mouth, and the heat inside her turned volcanic. By the time they reached the foot of his bed, every inch of her felt incandescent, lit from the heat boiling within.

"Babe." His voice rasped against her lips. "Unhook your bra for me."

It took a second for the realization to hit.

He can't do it himself . . . not without wrapping his arms around me. He remembered my trigger, remembered what sets off the flashback. Even driven by arousal, he remembered.

Her heart swelled at the realization. He was putting her first. Her needs above his own. It couldn't be easy to keep his hands to himself, to remember not to reach for her. But he was doing it. For her.

Her heart cracked wide open at that knowledge.

She made quick work of unhooking her bra, then shrugged her shoulders until it slid down her arms and fell to the floor. Instantly his hands moved up and filled his palms with her breasts. He leaned back slightly to give himself more room to work. She gasped and then groaned at the caress of his calloused hands on her breasts. Heat surged in places she didn't even know existed.

When his thumbs brushed over her nipples, she shook, her knees going weak and wobbly. The throbbing in her pulse points shifted, intensified, zeroing in at the junction between her thighs.

"How's this for grounding?" he whispered in that gruff, hoarse voice before catching the fleshy bottom of her ear and gently tugging.

"I think . . ." Her words emerged thick and sultry with a hint of a pant. "That I need to do some more grounding myself."

As her hands dropped to the open fly of his jeans, she was vaguely aware that he was turning them, using his big body and a hand on her hip to shuffle them around.

His mouth dropped back to hers, and his tongue darted into her mouth as she slid her hand inside his jeans, into his underwear, and took his penis in hand.

"Jesus." Tearing his mouth from hers, he arched into her hand.

"I see . . ." She tried for a sultry, teasing tone. "You like phase two of grounding."

"Fuck." He pressed his penis into her hand again and groaned. "If this is phase two, phase three might just kill me."

If that wasn't close to the sexiest thing she'd ever heard . . .

She slid her hand down the thick, smooth flesh and wrenched another groan from him.

"Babe—" He broke off to hiss. "It's been a while for me . . . much more of this and we won't make it to phase three."

His voice shook beneath the slow, steady glide of her hand. She smiled against his lips, giving the rigid flesh between her fingers another firm pump.

"Ah . . . *fuck*," he groaned, arching into her hand.

"I'd love to." She punctuated her acceptance by tugging on his nipple with her teeth and simultaneously pumping the straining flesh in her hand.

He said something that was far too garbled to make out. She felt hands on the waistband of her slacks, and then the tension around her waist gave. Since she was all for getting naked as quickly as possible, she toed off her shoes and shimmied her hips and legs until the fabric pooled around her ankles and she could step out of them. Of course, getting naked didn't just pertain to her.

Mac had way too many clothes on.

She let go of his penis in favor of grabbing his waistband and dragging his jeans and underwear down. Once the material had reached his knees, he dropped to the mattress and raised his legs, allowing her to pull off his shoes and from there his pants and underwear. Naked, he pushed himself farther back on the mattress and stretched out, his fists knotted in the blanket above his head.

"Babe," he said thickly, wings of red climbing his cheeks. His eyes were locked on her face and glittered with black fire. "We may need to tie my wrists to the headboard. I'm having a hell of a time keeping my hands off you."

Something whispered through her at his suggestion, a subtle return of the raw, ugly tension that heralded the arrival of the flashbacks. An image flashed through her mind . . . wrists cuffed to a headboard, only they weren't his . . .

No.

Damn it.

No.

She focused furiously on the man below her. On his damp, close-cropped black hair, his tense face, the black fire burning in his eyes, the urgent straining of his penis. The burnished copper of his skin. He was so beautiful stretched out before her. Perfect.

Mac. This is Mac.

He was all hers. If she could find the courage to take him.

Without looking away, imprinting his image in her mind, she crawled onto the bed and over him.

This is Mac's room. I'm safe here. Safe with Mac.

"Mac," she said. The feel of his bare legs rubbing against hers sparked a new flurry of tingles and stoked the waning flames.

"I've got you, babe." His hands left the blanket to skim up her body in a feathery caress. He cupped her breasts and squeezed them gently, then slid his right hand down her abdomen in another of those light, barely there touches. When it reached her panties, it slipped beneath the fabric and between her thighs. She spread her legs wider, giving him deeper access, encouraging him to explore.

The last traces of the flashback dissolved under his touch, at the slide of his finger as he stroked her clit. She froze above him and breathed deeply, drawing his musky, male scent deep inside her, where it drowned the ghosts of her nightmares in escalating pleasure.

So close . . . so close to flying.

That talented finger pushed up inside her, pulled out, and thrust in again. His thumb rubbed her clit, and that delicious, familiar tautness cinched tighter and tighter, drew her deeper and deeper.

"That's it, babe. That's it. Let go." His voice was gritty. Raw.

Let go . . . fly . . . Yes, she needed to fly. But not like this. Not alone. She wanted to fly with him. Together.

She pushed herself up with her knees and shoved her panties down her thighs, vaguely hearing the fabric rip at her urgency. Then she was guiding his rigid length in place and taking him inside.

They both froze as he filled her, dual groans breaking from them at the exact same time. As his hips lifted, driving his thick, hard length deeper into her, filling her completely, his hands rose above his head and fisted the sheet.

To keep from grabbing her.

Even now, claimed by passion, he was still thinking of her.

The knowledge seeded something inside her. Something fragile and new. Something close to the first delicate unfurling of love.

Then the dance was on. The lift and fall of hips. The pounding of hearts, the raw, breathless cries. The tension wound tighter. The sunburst drew closer and closer. They were on their way—flying—together.

Chapter Twenty-Six

TEN HOURS AFTER HE'D SNUCK OUT OF HIS BEDROOM LIKE A MAN ON the run, Mac banged his head against the helicopter's padded wall. Unfortunately it didn't pound any sense into his head.

You're a moron.

A fucking cowardly moron.

Mac shifted against the Eagle's wall, and the vibrations from the engine numbed his back.

You should have woken her—asshole.

You should have told her how you feel instead of sneaking out the door like a fucking loser escaping a drive-by fuck.

Mac grimaced, more disgusted with himself than he'd ever been in his life.

They'd yanked the seats out of the Eagle to scale back on weight and give the extra team of six men room to sit. But even camped out on the floor, this bird was a hell of a lot easier on the spine than the Black Hawk.

Yeah, things could have been worse . . . much worse.

It had been a stroke of luck that David Coulson had stepped in to host this quarterly meeting after the previously scheduled one had gone bye-bye. Coulson, the selfish bastard, had apparently opted for his own convenience rather than his compatriots'—who'd had to fly in from around the world. Good news for Mac and Shadow Command, since the jackass had scheduled the meeting on his wife's family's yacht, which was currently cruising the Gulf of California, a distance of five thousand klicks from Denali or ten hours by Shadow Mountain's experimental Eagle—eleven plus change if you included the two pit stops to refuel. Even with the bulk of their intel coming in just twenty-four hours premeeting, the boat's location had made the mission a possibility.

According to Link, the typical MO of these guys—when the meeting took place at sea—was to chopper out to the yacht at night under the cover of darkness. The actual meeting took place during the day, and then the bastards would depart the following night—once again under the cover of night. Which meant his team would be fast-roping down to the yacht during the middle of the fucking day, in front of God and everybody, in the hopes of rounding up all the bastards at once.

Yippee.

With luck, anyone who saw the choppers out over the water, or even boarding the *Princess*, would assume they were HQ1 training missions from Coronado. The base was only 725 klicks to the northwest, and the Gulf of California was an old stomping ground for team training.

Chances were if this meeting had been held anywhere else, they would have lost their window to take out the NRO, which meant most of humankind would have died a silent, sonic death within a matter of weeks. So eleven hours of joint-stiffening inactivity was a small price to pay when you were saving the damn world.

Mac pulled his knees to his chest for a count of twenty and then stretched them flat again. It had been a long time since he'd been packed like a sardine in a chopper, his ass and legs numb from the constant vibrations under and around him, while his brain spun off in one direction after another, obsessing over things he should have done differently, things he should have done better. Like being a fucking man and waking up the woman who'd just given him the best three hours of his life before he walked out that door. Like doing the adult thing and telling her goodbye, telling her he loved her, while she was awake to hear his damn confession.

What the fuck is wrong with you?

What the fuck were you thinking?

He'd pound some sense into his own skull if he'd thought it would do any good.

Sighing, Mac closed his eyes and fought to focus. They were somewhere around ten minutes from their target—give or take. Which put the bird at somewhere around five hundred fucking klicks an hour. Unfucking believable. That was a hell of a lot faster than the Black Hawk's three hundred klicks an hour. Taking the Hawk would have added another six hours to the time frame.

Still, eleven hours of stiff muscles wasn't something he enjoyed. There were plenty of ways he'd rather be spending his time.

An image flashed through his mind: Amy's flushed face, the sensual glaze burning in her hazel eyes, her high, firm breasts with their rosy nipples . . . the way they'd barely jiggled as she rode him . . . His muscles tightened at the memory—so did his cock.

Yeah, last night was not something he should be thinking about right now. Not when they were about to rope down onto the *Princess*'s quarterdeck and engage the enemy. Fuck, he was already stiff as hell and dreading the slide down the rope. The last thing he needed was to go down with a bazooka packed in his briefs.

Amy had been fast asleep when he'd snuck out of the room, sprawled facedown, her hair a spiky halo of fire against the white of the pillow. The curve of her naked spine relaxed. What he could see of her face was softened, blurred. She'd looked so damn content he managed to convince himself that he was doing her a favor by not waking her up. Christ knew she needed the sleep. The woman had spent the past two weeks taking care of everyone but herself. She could use a few hours of solid shut-eye.

But after five thousand klicks, twelve hours, and an eternity of looking back . . . he could see his retreat for what it was. An act of pure cowardice.

He'd been too much of a yellow-bellied lizard to step up for the after-sex talk. Too fucking scared to admit that he had feelings for her . . . strong feelings. Feelings an awful lot like love.

He was a fucking coward, that's what he was. So damn terrified of making himself vulnerable he couldn't even force himself to utter those three little words. Which was beyond pathetic because he knew—*he knew, damn it*—that Amy wasn't his mother, or his ex, or Jenn.

Unlike Mommy Dearest, Amy would never leave her kid in the car in the middle of a drug district so she could have some uninterrupted fuck time with some guy she'd just hooked up with in a bar. Unlike his ex, Amy would never entertain half the base in their bed while he was deployed thousands of klicks away. Unlike Jenn, Amy would never cry rape or accuse her husband's best friend of that despicable act because she was jealous of the unbreakable bonds between platoon buddies.

Unlike most of her gender, Amy had principles and courage and . . . He paused. Frowned. Shook his head.

Come to think of it, he couldn't see Beth, Kait, or Faith doing any of the things his mom or his ex had done either. Hell, Faith had insisted on inserting with his men when they'd gone after her lab mates in case her clean energy generator was used against the rescue team. Kait had stood toe to toe against Cosky's fury and inserted with them to liberate Embray. Even Beth had faced down armed killers back at Marion's house and rescued herself and Marion using common sense and courage. Hell, all three women were in the same percentile as Amy.

Which just made the four of them an anomaly.

Movement near the cockpit caught his attention. He looked over in time to see the cockpit door slide back and the crew chief hold up five fingers. Five minutes to go. Men stirred, pulled on their ballistic helmets, checked weapons and radios. One of Wolf's warriors checked the fast-rope bags and their attachments to the fuselage.

Mac stared at the two canvas bags, each bulging with their cargo of thick, plaited rope—the rope he'd be sliding down in a matter of minutes. Time to get his head back in the game and stop the damn daydreaming and self-castigation. Distraction was the number-one reason missions went south and operators lost their lives.

No fucking way was he going to be the cause of either.

He pulled his helmet on, tested his radio, and completed one last weapons check on his suppressed MP7 submachine and Sig Sauer pistol. The MP7 wouldn't be his first choice for any other missions. But it was the boss on ship boardings, the quietest gun out there. They may have lost their overall stealth advantage by coming in hot with the chopper, but they still needed near silence while clearing the decks. It wouldn't do to have the security force following his progress by the gunfire. Which meant the MP7 was the way to go. The damn thing was so quiet you could take someone down in one room without anyone next door hearing the shot. Once the radio and weapons checks were completed, he pulled on his heat-resistant gloves. Sliding down the rope fucked with unprotected hands.

The ship they were about to board was famous when it came to ridiculously expensive and overly indulgent boats. Hell, it was listed on multiple sites as number seven among the ten most expensive yachts in the world. Among her many luxuries were six decks, three swimming pools, four hot tubs, two helicopter pads—both of which were currently occupied. All of this on a whopping 520 feet of marine muscle. Her cruising speed was an impressive twenty-five knots an hour, although she could hit peak speeds of thirty knots. She even boasted a fucking theater and ballroom.

Her fame had made it ridiculously easy to track down her blueprints, which had seemed suspicious as hell until word had trickled in of her other, less public enhancements. She came equipped with an antimissile radar system, a deafening L-RAD acoustic device, armor plating, bullet- and blast-resistant doors and bulletproof glass at the bridge and master bedrooms, two mini-escape submarines, antisurveillance equipment, and a couple of citadels—or fancy-ass panic rooms—with enough food and water to last weeks.

Rumors also abounded of military-grade weapons—regardless of maritime law—and security details trained in special operations. Hell, according to the articles they'd pulled up on the Internet, half these damn mega-yachts were crewed by former SAS operators—British Special Air Service.

All those sweet enhancements made her the perfect meeting ground for a cabal of the most powerful, ruthless, and paranoid men in the world.

Boarding this baby was going to be an absolute fuck fest. They'd have to hit the ship's electronics hard, three hundred feet out, to render the missiles, citadels, and L-RAD system inoperable before the captain and crew realized they were about to be boarded and passed on the news to the council. No sense in sending the little bastards scurrying off to their panic rooms before his men had a chance to nab them.

Thank Christ that Faith and Shadow Mountain's tech team were beyond fucking brilliant and had already developed a localized EMP cannon that would fry every electrical circuit, microprocessor, and electronic system within a thousand-foot radius—with the exception of the Eagle's, which had EMP shielding. Fuck, with the cannon being mounted outside the bird on the inboard pylon pair, the crew and teams inside would even be protected from the nasty shock that accompanied an EMP pulse.

Go, Shadow Mountain ingenuity.

Before the EMP cannon had come out to play, they'd considered a two-pronged attack. Wolf and his team would fast-rope to the quarterdeck. Mac and his team would pull alongside in the Hurricane and use a compressed-air launcher to attach a flexible ladder with grappling hooks to the ship's rail and board from the water. They'd scrapped that plan once they'd discovered it was forty-five feet from the water line to the main deck and that the *Princess* could hit speeds of thirty knots per hour. Climbing that flexible ladder while the Hurricane was bouncing around like a fucking rabbit trying to keep up with her quarry would put them way behind the rest of their party. To maximize success, they needed all boots on deck at the same time, and it was a hell of a lot easier sliding down a rope than climbing up one.

Hence, the EMP blast and two choppers, with two sets of fast ropes per chopper. It was the fastest and safest way to deploy their teams. With snipers targeting opposition from above and an operator heading down the ropes every three to four feet, they could safely deploy in minutes. Or at least that was the plan.

They'd see how well that went—the best-laid plans had a habit of getting pretty fucked up.

At one minute to go, the crew chief stepped into the cockpit door again and held up one finger. There was a muted high-pitched whine, and a sudden static charge swept over him, lifting the hairs on his arms. They must have fired the cannon. If their luck held, the *Princess* had just gone dark.

The men surrounding Mac rose calmly to their feet, stretching legs and arms. Two of Wolf's warriors dragged the cargo doors back, and the roar of the engine flooded the cabin, sucking every other sound from his ears. The fast-rope bags were unzipped, the line attachment rechecked and then checked again.

As the wind rushed in, whipping his BDUs into a frenzy, Mac felt the Eagle's forward momentum slow. The bird slowed even more. Went into a hover. Began to drop. Settled into another hover. The coiled ropes were pulled from their bags and tossed out the cargo doors.

A couple of Wolf's snipers took position in the corners of the doors. One by one the operators grabbed the rope and slid down it like firemen sliding down a fire pole.

Wolf's men deployed first, four to five feet apart, sliding down the ropes from one cargo door or the other. Zane went next, followed by Rawls and Cosky, and then it was Mac's turn. Beside him he could see the snipers' eyes scanning the decks below, looking for opposition. The fact that no shots rang out was good news; they'd caught the security detail by surprise.

Maybe. Or maybe all those SAS operators were holed up somewhere, ready to ambush.

The wind was even worse here, trying to tear him from the chopper, but the instant he grabbed the rope, his respiration, pulse, and nerves chilled. Old business, this. Muscle memory. He'd fast-roped down from more birds than he could count, during both training and combat. This was routine, familiar.

Then he was out the door, sliding down, the rotor wash doing its best to tear him from the rope.

Amy awoke to cool sheets and an empty bed.

She stretched lazily and rolled over to check the alarm clock on the bedside table—6:00 a.m. She hadn't slept that hard or that peacefully in months. She felt fantastic. Alert. Focused. Able to face the world and anything it might throw her way.

Like waking up alone in a cold, empty apartment.

Mac wasn't here. The cool sheets had registered the moment she'd gained consciousness. Granted, she'd known he had an early-morning liftoff. She'd accepted that. But he could have woken her up and kissed her goodbye.

She vaguely remembered him maneuvering her pliant, barely conscious body under the sheets. Getting them situated must have been difficult without picking her up. He'd crawled into bed beside her; she remembered that too. Only not to hold her. Instead he'd lain there next to her, his body toasting her from toe to ear.

She'd drifted into sleep feeling warm and secure and wishing with every cell in her body that his arms were around her, cuddling her close, holding her tight.

Had he regretted the lack of after-lovemaking intimacy too? Or had he been relieved? Had it made it easier for him to roll out of bed and leave her behind? Had he looked back on the night and decided she wasn't worth the effort? That she was too much work?

She frowned as she threw back the covers and climbed out of bed. He'd showed her so much care. He'd put her first, focused completely on her pleasure. For a man to treat her like that during the night and then walk out the door come morning, without a goodbye or a kiss or even a "hey, the sex was great; let's do it again sometime"—well, it was hard to reconcile.

Scenarios that she wouldn't have considered the night before started to nibble at her mind, eroding her confidence about where the relationship with him was headed.

Maybe he was tired of her . . . already.

Maybe he'd decided her baggage wasn't worth his trouble or time.

Maybe the sex hadn't been as mind-blowing for him as it had been for her.

He'd been pretty handicapped, after all. He hadn't been able to hold her, or lift her, or even remove her bra without freaking her out. He hadn't been in control either, or on top. She'd pretty much run the entire show.

She groaned, a sinking sensation hitting. He'd seemed to appreciate the grounding—with all their touching. He'd even turned it into a game. But had it worn thin? Had he felt used in the end? Like a tool rather than a participant? Was that why he'd left without a goodbye? Under the circumstances she could see how he might feel like that. How he might think she'd just used him to get off. Although he'd come too, his orgasm could have resulted from simple male physiology.

Shaking her head, she headed for the bathroom.

It was a damn good thing she hadn't confessed her love for him. That mistake would have given her one more thing to overanalyze and agonize over.

The damp towel but lack of humidity in the bathroom indicated he'd been gone awhile—several hours at least. He was probably halfway to California by now. Which kicked up the memory of what he was doing in California. A surge of apprehension mixed with the irritation.

Still, it was early, barely six thirty when she walked through the clinic door.

"Well, you certainly look better this morning," Nurse Cheerful said. "A good night's sleep will do wonders."

The woman was right about that. Although a bout of mind-blowing sex followed by eight hours of solid sleep produced even more miraculous results.

"What were Benji's last temperature and blood pressure readings?" she asked, pausing at the nurses' station.

"Both normal."

Amy smiled in relief. "And Brendan?"

"Normal and normal. Both boys are doing great."

In some ways the update on Brendan was the best news of the morning. Normal temperature and blood pressure meant Leonard's reversal compound wasn't affecting him, which meant they were one step closer to giving Benji the N2FP9 antidote.

She checked on Benji first. He was still sleeping. His face was tranquil. His cheek was cool and smooth to her fingers, proof that his temperature hadn't spiked again. So far, so good.

She found Brendan sitting in the armchair beside his bed, tying his shoelaces. He looked up as the curtain slid back. "I'm hungry."

The sheer normalcy of his complaint brought a smile and sense of ease. Brendan was always hungry. So was Benji, for that matter. "I could use a hot meal myself. Why don't we head to the cafeteria?"

The clock was just hitting 8:00 a.m. when they finished eating and returned to the clinic.

"Perfect timing," Dr. Zapa said from the nurses' station, where she'd been chatting with the nurse on duty.

"Do you want me to come with you?" Amy asked, looking at her son. She didn't have to look down far. He was almost as tall as she was—at eleven years of age. He was going to be tall like his father.

"Nah. That's okay." He stoically accepted the kiss she pressed to the top of his head before walking off with Dr. Zapa.

She eyed the clock as she made her way to Benji's cubicle. When would Mac and the teams reach the Gulf of California? Her breathing accelerated as anxiety dug in.

It was an hour before Brendan joined her in Benji's room. He immediately took over her laptop and began playing games. She tried to occupy herself with a surprisingly current edition of *People* magazine, but with each second the nervousness increased until it felt like her chest could explode from the pressure.

What will the tests reveal?

How long before Mac's boots hit the Princess*'s deck?*

The edginess from just one of those concerns was bad enough, but the two of them in tandem seemed to multiply the apprehension by more than a factor of two. By the time footsteps sounded outside Benji's cubicle, her skin barely contained her nerves. She jerked up from her armchair the moment the curtain was pushed aside.

"Relax." Dr. Zapa's smile was blazing, brilliant with relief. "Brendan's test results look amazing."

The breath Amy had been holding escaped on a whoosh. She looked to the right as Leonard Embray wheeled into view. "The new compound is working?"

"It appears so." He wheeled farther into the space. "There was a fifty-nine-point-two percent reduction from yesterday's blood test."

"How much total?" Amy asked, relief slowly working its way through her.

"Ninety-one-point-seven percent total," Leonard responded readily. He rolled up to the bed and took hold of Benji's wrist to check his pulse. "Brendan has less than nine percent of N2FP left in his cells. At the current rate of dissolution, he should be clear of the isotope by midday."

The news was almost unbelievable. It was difficult to wrap her head around. Dizzy with relief, she turned to Benji. He was so small under the covers. So fragile, with the tubes running down his nose and into his veins. He looked like a distant memory of the child who'd raced from room to room, roaring like a dinosaur.

She wanted her son back.

"What about Benji? When can he get the reversal?" She looked Dr. Zapa squarely in the eyes, searching for a flicker of hesitancy. An iota of resistance. But only relief and confidence shone from her face and gleamed in her eyes.

"Yes, it's time to discuss our options." Slipping past Leonard's wheelchair, she picked up Benji's clipboard and flipped through the top pages. "We can wait for a few more days until N2FP is completely clear of Brendan's system, and we've had a few days to assess how his body is handling the reversal compound. Or"—she looked up, clipboard in hand—"we can give the reversal to Benji now, while Kait's healing is buoying his system. While his organs are strong and his temperature is down. If we wait to administer the antidote until we're certain there are no side effects, we may lose our window. We know Benji's organs will begin failing again. We know the N2FP isotope will multiply even faster through his body the longer we wait. The faster it proliferates, the greater the chances of massive, irreversible organ failure."

Amy nodded slightly and inhaled deeply. "Okay, what do you suggest?"

"My instincts tell me we need to act now. That we can't afford to wait. Every minute we hold off, that damn isotope is spreading inside him. Last blood test showed a fifty-nine percent proliferation rate. We need to kill it now before it gets out of control."

If there had been even an ounce of hesitation in Dr. Zapa's voice, Amy might have hesitated herself. But there wasn't. So she didn't. With a firm nod she made the decision.

"Do it then."

The actual injection was almost anticlimactic. They already had the correct dose for Benji's weight ready and with them. They swabbed Benji's small bicep, slid the needle in, and depressed the plunger, and it was over.

Except for the praying . . . and the worrying.

Chapter Twenty-Seven

Eric Manheim took a sip from his bourbon sour, striving for a polite expression as David Coulson finally blessed them with his presence. The bloody American had been the last to land on the boat the night before, just as he was the last to arrive for the meeting Giovanni was about to call to order. Rather ironic, considering he'd been the one to insist that the summit be held in his territory for a change. Under normal circumstances the man's arrogance would have been loathsome and annoying. But Eric's mood was too good for irritation to set in.

He paused to adjust the Glock in the oversize right pocket of his suit. The garment had been specifically designed to accommodate the weapon. When a man oversaw the bulk of the banking institutions in existence, it was wise to carry personal protection. Leaning back in the big executive chair, he smiled as the leather padding adjusted around him, contouring to the curve of his spine.

"I say, David." Eric dug into his breast pocket and removed six Gurkha Blacks. "These chairs are quite fine. Who sells them?"

"How the fuck should I know." Coulson set the large leather satchel he was carrying on the gleaming rectangular table the council had convened around. "They're fucking chairs. Who cares where they're available? A chair is a fucking chair."

Bloody sod.

But not even the repugnant American could sour Eric's mood. With a benign shrug, he slid a Gurkha to each of the men around the table.

Samuel Proctor, the cigar enthusiast among them, lifted the stogie to his nose and inhaled deeply. A look of pure bliss spread across his fleshy, hound-dog face. "What's the occasion, Manheim?"

"It must be something important," Hasso Albrecht added. "We know how fond Esme is of the cigar."

They all also knew that Eric had flown in alone. Esme had been sickly and tired the past few days. Regardless of whether Esme accompanied him, he generally tried to adhere to her wishes.

"A long-awaited project has finally born fruit." Eric accepted the platinum cigar guillotine Samuel slid his way and clipped off the head of the Gurkha he'd kept for himself.

Everything had progressed much faster than he'd expected. The tests wouldn't confirm that Esme was pregnant for a while yet, but he was certain she was carrying his child. Certain that in nine months or so, they'd welcome a little girl—or little boy—with Esme's beautiful sky-blue eyes into their family. However, he'd wait to announce the next generation of the NRO until the pregnancy test came back affirmative and they were past those uncertain first three months. According to the reproductive specialist, 80 percent of miscarriages occurred in the first trimester.

"How about we stop wasting time with personal celebrations and get down to the business at hand." Coulson unzipped the bronze satchel and plunged both hands inside. He pulled out a large oval object and carefully placed it on the table. The sphere's metallic casing glittered in the sunlight pouring through the unfiltered windows. "This, gentlemen, is Eden, and she is going to reboot our planet."

Eric froze, the Gurkha still caught between his teeth. Slowly he lowered the cigar and leaned in for a closer look. "This is our sonic bomb?"

"No. It's a fucking dragon's egg," Coulson drawled mockingly. "What the hell, Manheim. How about you pull your head out of your ass. You were the one who asked to see the damn thing."

His lips tightening, Eric folded his arms across his chest and sat back. What he wouldn't give to shove that metal sphere up the bloody sod's ass . . . or take out the Glock and put a couple of holes in him. A pity that second option was off the table.

Giovanni, who was sitting next to Coulson, reached across the table to pick up the device. He slowly rotated it in his hands. "How do you turn it on? There's no switch. No compartments. No means to access its internal wiring."

"It's operated by remote." Coulson reached back into the satchel and pulled out a round plastic object with a single red button. "Put it down."

Once Giovanni had returned the device to the table, Coulson pressed the red button. With a soft hum, a three-inch illuminated computer screen slid out.

"The weapon is armed, and the timer set from here." He tapped the plus button at the bottom of the screen, and a bright-red 5:00 appeared on the device. Another tap, and the number shifted to 10:00. "The plus sign adds five minutes at a time to the clock. The minus sign runs the timer down." He pointed at a red triangle in the upper right quadrant of the screen. "Press this icon, and Eden is armed." He pressed the minus sign until the screen went dead and then punched the red button on the remote again. They all watched as the computer screen retreated inside. "Once the device is activated, the panel will automatically withdraw. Since there is no way to access the control panel without the remote, there is no way to circumvent the blast."

"*L'électricité* cannot be cut to them, *oui*?" Alain Pinault murmured, taking a healthy puff on his Gurka.

"Exactly." Satisfaction rang in Coulson's voice. "The metal alloy we used is indestructible. Once the timer is set and the device armed, we destroy the remote. At that point no one can stop Eden from going off."

Feeling particularly benevolent, Eric pointed his cigar at Coulson. "I say, David, excellent job with this."

After so many years of inching their agenda forward, they finally had the means to recreate Earth and pass something on to future generations that was worth inheriting.

Before Coulson had a chance to respond, a voice came over the intercom.

"Mr. Coulson? Sir? We have two helicopters heading toward us, closing in fast."

Everyone but Coulson sat up straighter.

"Relax," Coulson drawled. Sprawling back in his chair, he spread his thighs wide. "Nobody knows we're here. Hell, even if Link did spill the beans about the quarterly meetings, there's no way he'd know we're holding it here. That was the whole point of mixing up locations."

Eric wasn't reassured. Too many inexplicable coincidences had happened recently. Mackenzie and those damn basket weavers shouldn't have known the location of the kidnapped scientists either, yet somehow they had.

They were too close to their objective for complacency.

"Did you mention the meeting to Christy? Her parents?"

A faint *whop-whop-whop* filled the room.

"Don't be an ass." Coulson's eyebrows beetled over his nose. "They know nothing about this. As liberal as that whole family is, they'd be horrified by our agenda. Hell, I even removed their entire crew and substituted a couple of my own men to run the damn boat just to make sure nothing discussed today leaked. The choppers are probably out training. Coronado naval base isn't that far away."

Coronado.

Eric froze. Forgot to breathe. "You don't suppose Mackenzie and his—"

"No fucking way," Coulson snapped, jackknifing up in his chair.

He punched a button on the armrest of his chair, and a panel opened in the wall behind the head of the table. A television screen appeared, broadcasting *The Price Is Right.* The five contestants standing in front of the stage were bouncing up and down.

The *whop-whop-whop* got louder.

Coulson punched another button, and a view of the yacht's stern, as seen from what looked like the bridge, took over the television set. In the distance two ominous shadows darkened the brilliant-blue sky. They looked like some kind of helicopters, but nothing Eric had seen before. Maybe experimental aircraft? Which brought to mind those damn Shadow Mountain Indians.

"Sir?" The voice came over the intercom again. "They're—"

There was a burst of static, and the television went dark, as did the lights above the table and the lamps in the corner.

"Just a breaker," Coulson said after a long, tense silence. But judging by the tendon visibly twitching in his neck, he didn't believe the excuse any more than Eric did.

Eric dug into his pocket and pulled out his cell phone. The screen was dead. Just to be certain, he pressed the power button. Nothing.

The *whop-whop-whop* was much louder now.

"A breaker wouldn't affect cell phones," Eric said, raising his voice.

Other hands plunged into pockets and pulled out cell phones. None of them worked.

"An EMP blast." Proctor jerked to his feet, shoving tense fingers through his thinning gray hair. A sheen of sweat glistened on his forehead. "We need to get to the submersibles."

"The submersibles will be as dead as the phones," Coulson said. He lurched up from the table. Urgent strides carried him to the window. He leaned in and looked up.

"The ship's down. The engine vibration is gone." Giovanni's wide, white-rimmed eyes shot to the windows. He grabbed his tumbler of scotch and dumped it down his throat.

He was right. Eric's pulse started to pound. The *Princess* was dead in the water.

His face ashen, Giovanni slowly rose to his feet. "Where are the panic rooms?"

"The closest is there." Coulson flung his hand toward the wet bar tucked in the corner of the room, exposing the damp stains in his armpits. "It's dead."

His Adam's apple bobbing, Giovanni shuffled to the bar and peered at the walls.

"It's dead, you fucking moron," Coulson shouted. "We need to fucking move."

"Where?" Eric asked, rising to his feet. He forced his voice to remain calm even though everything inside him quaked. There was no doubt who was about to board them. Which meant his life was over.

Within seconds the roar from the rotors overhead was so loud it was impossible to hear anything beyond the thunderous *whop-whopping*. A murky shadow spread across the windows. The room darkened. The crystal tumblers scattered on the table and rattled against the wood.

Eric held his breath, his attention turned outward and upward, praying the helicopter would fly past them, leave them in peace. But the rotor thunder continued to deafen as the damn thing hovered there somewhere above them.

His skin tightened to the point of pain.

There was no question now. The helicopters were after the boat. After them. When he turned back to the window to ask Coulson where the safest place to hide was, the American was gone.

The bloody bastard had abandoned them.

Eric hurried to the door on wobbly legs and looked both ways down the hall. In the distance was the sound of an explosion followed by gunfire. He caught a glimpse of Coulson's back as the man disappeared around a corner. For an instant he considered following him.

Fleeing. Maybe jumping from one of the yacht's rails. But the helicopters still beat the air above. They'd see him abandon the ship and simply haul him out of the water.

He turned from the door. Besides, there was more at stake here than their own lives.

The whole world was at stake. He couldn't let the soldiers boarding the yacht take anyone on the council alive. If the SEALs or those Indians captured even one council member, Eden would be forfeit. The NRO would be destroyed. For the good of the planet, everyone in this room needed to die. Coulson was already gone. But that didn't matter. Eden's sonic blast would make sure the bloody sod didn't live long enough to pass on any secrets.

Of course, once he accessed Eden's screen and set the timer, everyone in the room would know his plan. If their survival instincts kicked in, and they mobbed him, they could prevent him from arming the device. He needed to circumvent any resistance to his plan.

Luckily he was armed and a very good shot, thanks to hours of practice at the shooting range. He had the element of surprise too. Proctor and Giovanni were both armed, so he'd take them out first. The other four wouldn't stand a chance.

His decision made, Eric reached into his pocket and pulled out his Glock 17. Six shots later, he was the last NRO member in the room. The smell of gunfire and blood clogged the air. He closed in on the table and set the pistol down. Eden's remote felt surprisingly tiny in his hand—rather nondescript, really. He clicked the red button, and smooth as pie, the glass screen slid out.

For the first time ever, he was thankful for Coulson's paranoia and insistence on EMP shielding in the alloy they'd used for Eden's shell. Coulson had worried that one EMP blast over a warehouse would take all the devices down. The current situation had never entered anyone's mind.

He hesitated, his finger brushing the plus sign, his mind going to Esme and their baby.

Thank God she isn't on board. She'll continue our cause. She'll make sure our child is raised on a healthier, renewed planet.

Grief rose, thickened in his chest until each breath was an effort. How he wished he could be there to watch his little boy or girl take their first steps or speak their first words. How he wished he could watch the birth, gaze into Esme's beautiful blue eyes as she pushed their child into the world. How he wished he could tell Esme one more time how much he loved her.

Still, there was no hesitation as he punched the plus button and armed the device. For his child to enjoy a better world, he had to protect him or her now. If that meant dying . . . then he'd accept that sacrifice.

A bright-red 5:00 appeared on the screen and started counting down. The screen slid back in, and a pulsing red strobe light circled the top of the device.

He dropped the remote on the ground and stomped it with his boot. Then he bent to scoop up the plastic pieces. He walked to the window, cranked it open, and tossed the pieces into the ocean below.

It was done.

Before he could reach the front of the table and his pistol, a horde of black-clothed men wearing military armor burst into the room. Half a dozen rifles locked on his chest.

"On the floor. On the floor," hard voices shouted.

He caught glimpses of dark eyes and olive complexions as he lowered himself to the carpet. American Indians, from the looks of them. He'd been right. Shadow Mountain had found them.

Lying on his stomach while one soldier bound his wrists and another checked him for weapons, Eric watched his captors shove Coulson into the room. The bloody sod was bound, with a split lip and bruises forming along his cheek and jaw, but he was alive.

No matter.

When the device detonated, it would kill Coulson, along with everyone in a five-hundred-mile radius—including the bastards who'd boarded the yacht. The blast would cripple Shadow Mountain, but the NRO would remain intact. Esme would make sure the devices were distributed and detonated.

She'd survive, along with their child, to rule a vibrant new planet.

Chapter Twenty-Eight

MAC'S GLOVES HEATED ON THE DESCENT DOWN THE ROPE. HE TRIED to control his speed with his boots, but the quarterdeck came up fast. He hit the ground hard, felt the impact in his ankles and knees, but his MP7 was already up and sweeping. The chopper hovered for a few seconds longer and then the rest of the fast ropes came down, hitting the deck with a slight bounce.

Mac settled into position, his weapon scanning. Half the men from his chopper had already gone down to clear decks three and four. Wolf's chopper, which had deployed its team at the bow—assuming it had found enough clear space to toss the ropes between the swimming pool and hot tub—would clear from the lower decks up. The Eagles would loiter above them, dropping again to hover for evac. Which meant ascending the fucking caving ladder to get back aboard the bird.

Something *not* to look forward to.

"Eagle One. Breaching."

The news came over his radio. The voice was unfamiliar, but Eagle One was his crew. The guy must be one of Wolf's men from the breaching crew.

They hadn't been certain whether the door to the bridge would remain locked following the EMP hit. A couple of old-fashioned dead bolts could foil an EMP blast. A breaching team had been assigned to each chopper. Since this was a blast-proof door, the breaching would be trickier, but he didn't doubt that among all their techy toys, Shadow Mountain had something that would get the job done.

His intuition proved correct. A small localized explosion shook the outside entrance to the bridge. The bulletproof glass in the door shattered, as did the window that stretched across the helm. A cloud of dust and debris rolled outward.

With the debris cloud still tumbling through the air, impacting visibility and giving him some cover, Mac headed up the stairs to the helm with Zane and Cosky right on his ass. The door was just hanging there, swinging from side to side, barely attached to its frame.

"Moving," Mac said into his radio.

He hit the door hard and fast, going through low, his MP7 up and sweeping. Three walls. A huge freestanding wheel. Dead instrument panels. A gaping hole where the window had been. A warm, ocean-salted breeze.

POP . . . POP.

Shots rang out to his right. One of the bullets grazed his bicep with a fiery burn. He locked down the pain and swung the MP7 to the right, spraying the corner. A pistol poked out from behind the far right-hand side of the console. Another shot rang out. A portion of wall next to his ear exploded, peppering the side of his head with chunks of debris.

Son of a bitch.

The bastard was tucked nice and tightly in the corner behind the instrument panel, which gave Mac no target to sight on. At least not until he moved deeper into the bridge—which gave the asshole plenty of time to fill him full of holes.

"Shooter," he said into his mic as he ducked back behind the mostly detached door.

Detached. Bullet resistant.

The pistol this fucktard was using looked like a 9 mm Glock, so the rounds didn't have enough force to punch through the bullet-resistant door. Probably wouldn't penetrate the ballistic plates in his vest either.

But then the asshole didn't need to aim for Mac's chest to do major damage. His face, neck, arms, and legs were vulnerable. The door in front of him, however, would cover his entire body.

The damn thing would probably be too fucking heavy to serve as a mobile shield, but he wouldn't know until he tried. He grabbed the tilted door and tore it from its frame. Shock registered. Hell, the damn thing didn't weigh nearly as much as he'd expected. Not much more than a regular door.

Crouching, shoving the door in front of him, he crab-walked his way toward that occupied corner.

Ping . . . ping . . . ping.

Round after round ricocheted off the door and bounced around the bridge or burrowed into the walls. Another round grazed the top of his ballistics helmet, almost shoving it off his head.

Fuck!

He ducked lower, yanking his helmet back into place.

Once the last quarter of the instrument console came into view, he chanced a quick peek around the corner. The move was greeted by wild, terrified eyes, but no return fire.

What was this? Amateur hour?

He sprayed the corner above the asshole's head with the MP7. The moron shrieked and curled into a ball, protecting his head with his arms.

SAS? My ass.

Mac shoved the door aside and was on the guy before the echo of gunfire died. Dragging him onto his belly, he yanked the asshole's scrawny arms behind his back and flex-cuffed them together.

"Clear," he said, rising to his feet.

"Moving," Zane said through the radio.

By the time Mac dragged his captive to his feet, Zane was already through the interior door with Cosky on his six.

Mac handed off his prisoner to one of Shadow Mountain's mop-up crew and took position behind Rawls. His corpsman turned slightly. An intense blue gaze raked him from head to toe, lingering on his arm. Which—Mac glanced down—was oozing blood but not too heavily.

"Graze?" Rawls asked, turning back to the door.

Mac didn't bother answering. Rawls was already easing through the door. Besides, his arm didn't hurt much. His head, on the other hand, was apparently protesting the bullet to his helmet, which was fucking ridiculous. He'd taken much harder hits without feeling any pain. He scowled, pushing the nagging ache aside.

"Deck one clear."

"Deck four clear."

The notifications came through the radio within seconds of each other. He'd heard sporadic gunfire echoing through the yacht, but there'd been no reports of "Eagle down," so the assault was proceeding better than they'd expected. Which didn't engender any sense of relief. Easy access was usually a good indication that shit would hit the fan at some point down the road.

Mac followed Rawls through the door and down a plush, carpeted flight of stairs. Zane and Cosky had taken position at the bottom and were controlling the hallway below. According to the schematics, the fifth deck contained several bedrooms with en suite baths and a separate dining room. Hell, this deck even included a spa, complete with a masseuse.

"Deck two clear."

The report came as they cleared the last of the bedrooms—this one decorated with creamy wallpaper and gleaming, dark-wood floors. The furniture was some kind of white wood that contrasted starkly with the dark floors. The blinds, which were the same color as the furniture, only in fabric, were cinched high, letting the California sun blaze through.

Like the three bedrooms and spa they'd cleared before it, the room was plush, smelled expensive, and stood empty. So far the entire fifth deck had been empty. They eased into the dining room, which was vacant too. The light-wood furniture and trim gleamed beneath crystal clear windows.

His head started pounding like a motherfucker.

What the fuck?

Why the hell was his head acting up now?

All that dazzling light streaming through the windows wasn't helping the damn headache. Too bad the blinds weren't down. Squinting, he spoke into his mic. "Deck five clear."

As he turned toward the door, a whirring followed by a muted thud sounded behind him. He spun, his gun up, eyes sweeping the suddenly dim room, muscles locked and loaded. The abrupt switch from bright sun to muted shadows was disorientating. It took him a moment to realize the sound he'd heard was all the window blinds rolling down. At once. Every damn one of them.

Fucking weird, but appreciated.

Except the headache hadn't lessened; in fact it accelerated. Apparently it wasn't fed by the sunlight. More's the pity.

"Targets acquired." Wolf's voice came through the radio.

"Where?" Mac asked, trying to listen over the pounding in his head. Fuck, what he wouldn't give for some Excedrin.

"Deck three. Midpoint."

Which put them two levels down and a hundred feet away—give or take. According to the ship's blueprints, there was another flight of stairs just past the dining room on the bow. They headed in that direction and descended two flights of luxuriously carpeted stairs.

"Moving. Deck three, on the bow," Mac said before they entered the hallway. No sense in letting some trigger-happy Shadow Mountain warrior plug them when they stepped into the open.

The room Wolf had mentioned was easy to spot, even with the headache, which was quickly escalating into excruciating, fucking with his vision. Several huge men were stationed along the hall beside an open door.

As they headed for them, Mac tried to blink the black dots from his eyes. With each step the pressure in his head seemed to expand until his brain felt like it was banging against his skull and beating itself to mush. What the fuck was going on? Had the hit to his helmet been worse than he'd thought?

Except he'd had concussions before, and this didn't feel like any concussion he'd ever experienced.

He stepped through the door to find half a dozen dead men sprawled around the room and two bound men in business suits shoved against the wall. One of the men had a bloody lip and some ugly bruises, as though someone had coldcocked him. According to James Link, there were eight men and one woman on the council.

Six dead men and two alive. The men's numbers match up, but the woman's missing. We need to take pictures of the dead, show them to Link, make sure everyone on the council is accounted for.

He turned to ask Wolf if they'd located the woman when nausea crashed through him, surging up his throat. He bent, tensed his belly, and locked his throat, trying to hold back the vomit.

Jesus . . . Christ.

His vision blurred, refused to focus.

He straightened and carefully turned to Rawls to ask if he had anything in that magical first-aid kit of his that would knock back the headache and nausea.

"We have a problem." It was Wolf's voice, grimness lacing the words.

Wolf's tone distracted Mac. He couldn't make out the Arapaho warrior's expression; the black dots floating across his eyes were affecting his vision. But he'd never heard the bastard sound so ominous before.

Wolf waved a hand at the spherical object sitting on the huge table that dominated the room. Mac squinted, trying to concentrate past the splinters of agony shooting from his head into his eyes.

"This looks like the design Faith sketched of her clean energy prototype. The device these bastards rewired to make a clean bomb. And judging by that red light pulsing around its base, I'd say it's been activated. I can't find a way to turn it off."

The news rolled through Mac on another surge of nausea.

Clean bomb . . . activated.

Vomit burned its way up his throat. He froze, trying to force it back down, but the burning acid refused to recede.

"How the fuck can it be active? The EMP blast should have fried its circuits," Cosky said.

Good question. One Mac would have asked himself if opening his mouth had been an option.

"Not sure that matters at this point, dude," Rawls said. "The damn thing's lit up like a Christmas tree. Obviously it's active. Question is whether it's armed."

"There's no timer." Zane spoke this time, and he didn't sound relieved by his observation.

Mac swallowed carefully, forcing down the bile. He didn't have time for this shit, damn it. He needed to focus. If that motherfucker went off . . .

"Doesn't really need a timer, now does it?" Rawls's voice sounded even more urgent than before.

Gingerly Mac turned, zeroing in on the hazy image of the men huddled against the wall. These were the bastards with the answers. Hopefully there was enough time to force the information out of them.

He made a grab for the asshole closest to him and missed by a mile. Vomit surged. Agony exploded in his head.

Jesus fucking Christ.

This time he couldn't hold the groan or the vomit back. He hurled what little contents his stomach held all over their closest captive's chest. The guy made a gagging sound and cringed against the wall.

Well, that was a new interview technique for the books.

"Shit! Mac?"

He recognized his name but couldn't identify the voice through the ringing in his ears. As he started to sag, someone grabbed him and hauled him back up again.

They didn't have time to worry about him, damn it.

"Cut the wires." His order came out garbled but apparently clear.

"No access to the wires," Wolf said. "The device is smooth. Uniform. No screws, bolts, latches. The wires must be inside."

There was a fatalistic tone to Wolf's words. As though he were facing his death, which he was. They all were. It didn't even matter how much time was on the clock. If that thing went off, it would kill every living creature for hundreds of klicks. They wouldn't be able to avoid the blast radius.

"Turn it off," Mac said, gently turning his head toward the men against the wall.

"I can't," the council member he'd vomited all over said in a clipped British accent. "I crushed the remote and threw the pieces in the ocean. The remote was the only way to access the timer and the on/off mechanism. There is no way to stop the countdown now."

Fuck. The device cannot go off. I have to shut it down.

The fresh surge of agony that rolled through his head almost knocked him out. His vision darkened.

"Did you see that?" Rawls's voice was a dim echo in his ears.

"What?"

"The red light. It blinked a few times."

Something niggled at Mac's memory. Something important. The recollection of the blinds all rolling down replayed through his mind, but the grayness taking over his concentration couldn't quite grasp the connection.

"Long on . . . clock?"

The words were so distorted Mac couldn't tell who'd asked the question.

"Not long. Maybe a minute?" The same crisp British accent.

That he heard clearly, and it managed to knock some of the haziness aside.

They had to figure out how to turn the damn thing off. If they didn't, the blast wouldn't just kill his team and most of Shadow Mountain's warriors, it would take most of humanity with them. There were warehouses full of these devices, and sure as hell these eight men had scores of people tapped to distribute them.

With his team and most of Shadow Mountain's warriors dead, there would be no one to stop the mass extermination of humanity. They wouldn't just fail themselves and the people they loved; they'd fail the entire human race if they didn't *turn the thing off.*

Something *pushed* in his mind, followed by buzzing static and then searing pain. The agony brought him to his knees and loosed another bout of vomit.

Dimly he heard Zane say, "What the fuck. The lights have gone out."

Faith's voice suddenly echoed in his head. *In one experiment, the subject turned on a microwave just by thinking about it.*

The blinds had gone down.

Someone rolled him over, distracting him.

"Mac? Mac? Can you hear me?" Hands removed his helmet, straightened out his body.

"The device appears to be dead," Wolf said, relieved.

"What the hell's wrong with him?" Cosky asked, his voice so close he had to be bent over him.

"An aneurysm? Hell, I don't know. He's got blood coming from his nose. Where are the healers?"

An aneurysm?

Ah hell, apparently the universe wasn't done fucking with him.

As Eldon, Eagle Two's medic, prepared the truth serum for injection into their NRO captives, Wolf studied the metal object on the table. The pulsing light had vanished. Was the sonic bomb inactive? Or had it entered the final stage of countdown?

It was strange. It was flashing one moment, dead the next, as though someone had flipped its switch to off even though nobody had been near the device.

But maybe you didn't need to touch it to deactivate it.

He stared down at Mackenzie, who was stretched out on the carpet with Rawlings hovering over him. Faith had said certain people's brain waves could connect with her clean energy distributor, that it enhanced their minds and allowed them to mentally manipulate objects. The NRO's sonic distributor had been reverse engineered from Faith's prototype. Was this machine capable of supercharging certain brains too?

Had Mackenzie turned the sonic bomb off with his mind?

How would they even know?

He stepped forward, invading the space of the English *nih'oo3oo*—Manheim, judging by pictures he'd seen of the man. "The device has gone dark. Why? Is it still counting down?"

Manheim exchanged puzzled glances with the *nih'oo3oo* they'd captured on the lower deck.

Wolf turned away. He suspected they didn't know themselves, but even if one of the men answered, he couldn't afford to believe them. He couldn't afford to assume the device was dead. They needed to proceed as though it were fully operational and about to blow.

Which meant they had mere minutes to interrogate their captives and obtain the locations of the warehouses where the NRO was housing these things. Once they had the coordinates, he'd send the information via radio to Shadow Command. Neniiseti' could move on the locations before Wolf and his warriors even left the *Princess*.

Of course, Manheim and the other man would not volunteer such information easily. Which was where the truth serum came in.

He pivoted, zeroing in on Eldon. "How much longer?"

"The doses are ready now, Commander." The medic set the second of two syringes full of clear liquid on the table.

"Do it," Wolf said.

It would be two minutes before the serum would take effect. If the device was armed and counting down, as Eric Manheim claimed, they might not have those two minutes to spare, but they had to at least try to force the information they needed from their captives.

While the SEALs played nursemaid to Mackenzie, and his warriors held the struggling NRO operatives so Eldon could inject the serum, Wolf collected the Glock sitting on the table and waited for the world to end—or at least his world, his life.

If the device was going to blow, it would be any moment now. Which meant the death of him, his men, Mackenzie, and his SEALs, and also the unfortunate masses who made their homes along the coast of California. Assuming Link had been truthful about the bomb's range, it would take out Coronado naval base too—along with all of San Diego.

He fought back the burgeoning regret. The worry. The concern for Jillian, for his mother, for Shadow Command. How would Neniiseti' rebuild with the most experienced warriors gone?

No time for such fears.

Focus.

He ejected the magazine from the Glock and passed it, along with the gun, to one of his men. At least a minute had passed. The strobe on the device remained still. The bomb had not detonated. One more minute, and they could begin the interrogation.

If one were to believe the Englishman, the device should have gone off by now. They were well past the minute he'd claimed was on the timer. Which should have reassured him but didn't. Perhaps the council member who'd set the timer had miscalculated. Perhaps he'd transposed the numbers or added an extra zero. There were too many variables, and without access to the control clock, they had no clue whether the damn thing was counting down to detonation.

At the two-minute mark, Wolf turned to his warriors. "Samuel, John, write down everything they say. Jessup, David—you're on recording detail. Mikael, you broadcast the interrogation live to Command central."

Even though the entire interrogation would be broadcast live to Shadow Command—he'd still send notes and recordings with each helicopter after evac. In the unlikely event the live broadcast didn't patch through or one of the Eagles went down, there would be a backup copy. The information they were about to extract was too crucial not to take second and third precautions.

If the circumstances had been different, he would simply drag both men aboard the birds and haul them back to base—interrogate them there. It was too dangerous to loiter around in the open like this. While the Eagles' pilots were monitoring the local law enforcement and military channels, there was always a chance a team from one or both of those entities had gone off the com and was ghosting in on them.

However, they wouldn't be able to interrogate their captives aboard the Eagles. The noise of the rotors made that option impossible. Nor could they leave the bomb on the boat when they evacuated. If it went off, it would kill millions. It had to be removed.

The NRO council members had flown in on helicopters, two of which were perched aboard right now. He would pull one of the copilots from the Eagle and fly the bomb far away via the most unpopulated route he could find. If the device went off before he got it to safety, it would kill a lot fewer people that way. Most of his warriors would survive.

But first he needed to acquire the warehouse locations and send them to Shadow Command. If the device blew before he flew it to safety, those locations had to be in safe hands.

If it didn't blow . . .

Wolf glanced at Mackenzie and frowned thoughtfully.

William had his fingers pressed to the commander's head, and the silver glow of healing was climbing his arms.

Maybe Mackenzie *had* connected with the device and mentally turned it off.

Maybe the cerebral exertion had caused the pain in his head, along with the vomiting and the bleeding from his nose and eyes. Faith hadn't mentioned any side effects from mentally connecting to her prototype, but this was not the same device. Perhaps the rewiring had resulted in Mackenzie's symptoms.

Neniiseti' had insisted the commander be fully healed in time to join this mission. Was this why? Had the *beesnenitee* known that without Mackenzie the mission was doomed to fail, and millions of people would die?

Rawls looked up, caught his eye, and arched a sandy eyebrow. "We're not dead yet. I'm taking that as a good sign." He nodded to his CO, who was sprawled out next to his knees. "How much you want to bet he's the reason we're still breathing?"

"You think the machine synced with his brain? That he's the reason the damn thing went dark?" Cosky asked.

He didn't sound like he disagreed, more like he was asking to confirm his own suspicions.

"It makes sense." Rawls shrugged. "Something was sure as hell affecting him, and it got worse the closer we got to this room."

Black Cloud and his beniiinenno will fight beside you. The spirits have spoken. It will be so.

Neniiseti's cryptic comment blazed through Wolf's mind.

If what they suspected was true, and Mackenzie had synced with the NRO's bomb and turned it off before it could detonate, then he'd saved all their lives.

Wolf grimaced. It didn't sit well to owe this particular *nih'oo3oo* anything. Let alone his life or the lives of his men. Hell, the lives of the entire world.

However, it was impossible to ignore the fact that according to Eric Manheim, who should know, everyone on this boat should be dead by now.

Perhaps the spirits had had good cause for their demand after all.

Chapter Twenty-Nine

MAC AWOKE WITH DOZENS OF QUESTIONS.

On the plus side, he was alive, the nausea and headache were gone, and he was already aboard the Eagle—which was one way to avoid climbing the caving ladder. On the downside, he had no idea what the fuck had happened on that boat, but judging by the reaction of his men, who were eyeing him with varying degrees of concern, it must have been bad. Hell, Rawls's constant blood pressure and pupil checks were a clear indication that things had turned ugly back there. But the roar of the engine and rotors made conversation impossible, which meant he wouldn't find out the details anytime soon.

By the time the bird landed for refuel, he'd already filled in some of the blanks on his own. He was alive, as were the rest of the men on the bird, so the device hadn't detonated. He'd been miraculously restored to full health; even that bloody graze along his arm sported tender new skin. Ergo, one of Shadow Mountain's healers had gotten their hands on him.

Obviously someone had shut down the bomb, regardless of Manheim's insistence that the countdown had been locked and unalterable. If Manheim hadn't lied, if the device really had been sealed in countdown mode, who had turned it off? He flashed back to the blinds in the boat's dining room.

He might know the answer to that question too.

He waited for the rotors to power down on the Eagle before hopping to the tarmac. The smell of jet fuel stung his eyes and burned his nose.

Rawls joined him twenty feet from the fuel tanks. "How's the head?"

"Fine," Mac said impatiently. There were more important matters to discuss than his health. "Did we get the locations to the warehouses?"

"Yep," Rawls said. "Wolfie sent the coordinates to his big bad boss while we were still on the *Princess*."

"Shadow Command already has teams moving on the warehouses," Cosky added as he and Zane joined them.

"The council members?" Mac asked.

"Manheim and Coulson are on Eagle Two. The others are dead. Except for Manheim's wife. She wasn't on board."

Well, that was good news, at least on the first two counts. He stared at Rawls, then Cosky, and finally Zane. "What the fuck happened back there?"

Rawls scanned Mac's face, his blond eyebrows arching. "How much do ya recall?"

Mac thought back. "Not much. Manheim said the device was armed and counting down. Considering we're alive, the bastard must have been lying."

Or . . .

He didn't mention the other option in case he was way off. No sense in sounding the fool.

Zane cocked his head. Narrowing his eyes, he studied Mac's face closely. "The damn thing just shut down. Out of the blue. For no apparent reason. You wouldn't happen to know anything about that, would you?"

Okay, so obviously Mac wasn't the only one mulling over that other option.

"See, the thing is, Skipper, the bomb shut off at the same time you went down. We're thinkin' the two might be connected," Rawls added.

Time to stop playing dumb. "You're thinking I mentally connected with the damn thing and turned it off, and that's what caused the headache and nausea."

"Did you?" The point-blank question came from Cosky.

No surprise there.

"How the hell would I know?" At the rash of disbelieving looks, he shrugged. "I don't know, okay? Maybe? Before I crashed and burned, I was thinking I had to turn it off." He hesitated. "Plus—some weird shit happened in the dining room on the deck above."

"The blinds?" Rawls looked at Mac for confirmation.

"Yeah." Mac blew out a breath.

"What about them?" Zane asked, looking back and forth between Rawls and Mac. Zane and Cosky had departed the room before the incident had happened.

"My head was killing me, and that damn room was so fucking bright . . . I remember thinking it was too bad the blinds weren't down, and next thing I know—"

"The blinds are rolling down," Rawls broke in.

"Yeah." Mac rocked back on his boots. "Could just be a coincidence. The blinds, the bomb—hell, both malfunctions could be caused by faulty wiring, crossed circuits."

"It doesn't matter," Cosky said. "What matters is the damn thing didn't go off." He glanced at Mac. "Even if you did connect with it, the minute the device shut off, that connection broke. Your superpowers would be long gone by now."

"I dunno, Cos." Rawls casually scratched his chin, but his eyes were gleaming bright blue. "We can't know that for sure. We need to test him. Make sure he's not a danger to himself and others." He cocked his head at Mac. "How 'bout you try to levitate Cos? I know for a fact he's always wanted to fly . . . you know, like Superman."

Cos shoved Rawls hard enough to rock him back on his boots. "Or you could turn off this bastard's mouth. Christ knows that's an impossible task without superpowers."

Mac was regretting his lack of superpowers by the time they climbed on the Eagle and the sound of the engine and rotors washed away his teammates' remaining suggestions. It would be sweet to send the whole lot of them to Antarctica.

Six hours later Mac was on his feet, impatiently waiting for the cargo lift to draw the Eagle into the belly of Shadow Mountain. Shifting his weight from foot to foot, he glared at the men surrounding him—all of them still sitting on the bird's floor. Was it too fucking much to get off their asses and out of his way? He had places to be and people to see.

Or at least one place and one person.

When fate gave you three chances to get it right, and you blew those first two chances—the smart man grabbed on to that last one with both hands and clung like a motherfucker.

Evidence suggested he might not be the smartest of men, not with those first two chances washed down the shithole. But he'd never been called a stupid one either.

He wasn't fucking around with this last chance.

"Still no headache?" Rawls asked, rising to stretch beside him, piercing blue eyes scanning his face.

"I'm fine," Mac said curtly.

"I'm serious, Mac. You need to go to the clinic and get your noggin checked out."

Fine, he would . . . later. "Stop being such a damn mother hen."

As soon as the last of the Shadow Mountain warriors jumped down from the Eagle, Mac made his escape. Without waiting for his team, he headed—at a good clip—for the hangar's exit.

"Where you headed in such a hurry?" Rawls asked, catching up with him. The intense scrutiny in his eyes gave way to something sly and even more unwelcome.

"None of your fucking business." Mac kept walking.

Rawls smirked. "You realize it's oh-three-hundred, right? The lady will be fast asleep."

Fuck. Mac stopped walking. Planting his hands on his hips, he scowled across the bay. Rawls was right. Amy would be asleep, and she damn well needed that sleep.

Rawls slapped him on his shoulder. "You look like a man in need of advice."

"You need your eyesight checked," Mac said. Now that Rawls had shot down his plans, his adrenaline was fading fast.

"Not sure if you're aware, Commander," Rawls drawled, "but your interactions with the ladies can come off as somewhat"—he lifted his eyebrows delicately—"hostile." A wicked grin broke over his face. "'Course, if you don't care that they run off screamin' when they see you comin'."

Mac showed his appreciation for his corpsman's concern by giving him the middle finger salute.

"Why don't you two get a room," Cosky said, walking up behind them.

Well, look at that. Cos is talking to me again.

Deep inside him a hard little knot of regret eased.

"Can't." Rawls shot Cosky a conspiratorial wink. "Mac's in a *relationship*."

Cosky gave Rawls a no-shit glare. "Fuck, that's news to you? Anyone with eyes could see that."

Mac scowled. It was news to him.

"I'm thinkin' he needs the wisdom of the big boys." Rawls gave Mac a taunting shove. "Otherwise he's liable to lose the girl."

Zane, who'd approached on Mac's right, paused with a thoughtful look on his face. "Rawls has a point."

Ah fuck.

Cosky stopped too, his face deadpan. "How much time we have?"

"Seven hundred?" Rawls's grin was blinding white. "She should be up by then."

Lifting his arm, Cosky consulted his clock. "Hell—" He shook his head, the flat expression never leaving his face. "Not sure we'll be done by then."

With a laugh, Rawls slung an arm over Mac's shoulder. "Don't you worry, Mac my boy. We've got your back. Everything you wanted to know about the birds and the bees and the Amys is coming right up."

Oh for Christ's sake.

But Mac followed them out of the hangar. The hazing the bastards planned to unleash on him was better than sitting in his quarters all by his lonesome, stewing over what he was going to say to Amy. Or what she was going to say back. At least it would keep him occupied for the next few hours.

As they headed through the maze of corridors to the personnel quarters, Mac stopped at one of the phone stations along the wall and rang the clinic for an update. Both boys were doing well. Still admitted but due to be released in the afternoon. Amy wasn't there.

Relieved that shit hadn't hit the fan in his absence, he rejoined the loose huddle of his team, ready to kill some hours until it was time to take back his streak of cowardice.

"First thing to remember," Rawls said fifteen minutes later around Mac's table as he filled everyone's tumbler with two fingers of Johnnie Walker, "is you don't demand anything of her. Ladies don't appreciate that. You ask her." Setting the bottle down, Rawls sprawled out in the chair next to Mac.

"Without yelling," Zane added, taking his dose of Johnnie by throwing back his head and tossing it down his throat.

"Or swearing." Cosky slid a dry look his way.

"You wanna make eye contact," Rawls continued.

"Without trying to glare her into submission." Zane's slight smile told Mac he was enjoying this way too fucking much.

"Oh for fuck's sake," Mac said, picking up his tumbler. "I'm not a fucking nub here. You forget I've been married before?"

Three sets of eyebrows climbed, but Cosky was the one to clear that land mine. "And we all know how well that turned out."

He had a point. Mac grimaced.

"Remember," Rawls said. "If she nods at what you're sayin', it doesn't mean she's agreein' with you, just that she's listenin' to you."

Zane turned to stare at Rawls. "Where the hell did you hear that?"

"*Psychology Today*. They had this article on body language."

Zane's face wrinkled. "That sure explains a fucking lot."

"Remember to smile at her." Rawls's attention shifted to Mac. "Smiling is your friend."

Cosky froze for a second, then slowly lowered his glass to the table. "Not sure about that. Hell, with the way the muscles of his face are fixed in a perpetual scowl, trying to smile might scare the fucking shit out of her."

Before Mac had a chance to respond to that taunt, Zane stepped in with more helpful advice. "For fuck's sake, don't try to *solve* one of her problems. They don't want you to actually solve it. Apparently they just want to know that you're *listening* and that you *know* about it."

"Right?" Rawls's shoulders cinched up. "What the sweet Jesus is that about?"

By the time 0700 rolled around, the convoy had shifted from advice, to women, to sports, to weapons, back to women, and from there into shop talk. As the hour marched closer, Mac's earlier nerves returned. When the guys finally rose from the table, he was so fucking tense he felt like he could rip apart just by moving.

"Good luck, buddy," Rawls said, pounding the hell out of his back. As he stepped around him, Rawls suddenly stopped dead and flicked the flex-cuffs hanging from a belt loop on Mac's BDUs. "Oh, and, Commander. FYI, you never want to bring handcuffs to a first date."

Asshole.

Although in this case the flex-cuffs might come in handy. It was a hell of a lot easier to keep his hands to himself if they were bound together.

Before heading out he rang the clinic again. Amy wasn't there.

The walk over to Amy's quarters went way too fast. He still had no idea what he wanted to say when he arrived at her door. Fuck. He'd wing it. Before he could chicken out, he knocked on the door and waited—his skin crawling, his heart pounding, his gut trying to worm its way into his chest.

Christ, being brave was damn uncomfortable.

When there was no response to his first knock, he tried again. Was she still sleeping? In the shower? Had she left for the clinic while he was walking over? He should have rung her instead of the—

The door opened.

Her hair was wet and tousled, her face scrubbed and shiny. The scent of cocoa butter and peaches clung to her. The nerves rumbling in his belly stilled as primal hunger rose.

"Mac," she said, her eyes cool and blank.

"Can I come in? We need to talk."

Obviously the wrong choice of words, as her eyes narrowed.

"Sure." She stepped back, opening the door wider. "But I can't talk long. The boys are being released today."

"I heard." Mac stepped through the door. How the hell would he recover from that first misfire? She'd already erected an invisible barrier. "I called the clinic when we landed."

"That was kind of you," she murmured, throwing another billion miles of cold front between them.

Son of a bitch, he'd just tripped over another land mine. He could sense it. What the hell had he said this time?

"Look." He rolled his shoulders, ignoring the sudden punch of nerves. "I'm sorry about taking off without waking you up the other morning. You were exhausted. I figured you needed the sleep more than you needed the goodbyes."

She nodded, her head tilting, as though she were waiting for something. "I understand."

Did she really?

Was she nodding because she agreed with him or just to show she was listening?

Damn Rawls's fucking hide for putting that bug up his ass . . . like he needed anything else to worry about.

"We secured the council and the location—"

"I know. Neniiseti' told me yesterday." Amy's eyebrows drew together. Yeah, she was obviously waiting. Then she took the tiger by its tail, in typical Amy fashion. "Why are you *here*, Mac?"

Ah hell . . . time to shit or get off the pot.

The nerves swelled, tried to grab the words from his tongue. "I'm here because . . ." He dug deep and coughed the emotion out. "I think I love you."

Think? You think?

Dumbass.

She looked like she'd been poleaxed. Obviously his suave sophistication had impressed her speechless.

He squared his shoulders, grabbed his big boy britches, and tried again, hoping like hell that fate would give him a fourth chance.

"Amy, I love you."

Her blank expression fragmented in front of his eyes. Her face softened, her eyes widening. She stepped toward him, raised her hand, and . . . punched him in the stomach.

What the hell?

At least all those workouts with the boys had paid off, judging by the way she was shaking her hand.

"Why didn't you lead with that?" But the softness on her face was infiltrating her gaze.

"Because I'm an idiot." He rubbed his chest. Although her response didn't exactly equate to "I love you too," it was a long way from "Get the fuck out of my quarters." He'd make do with that . . . for now.

"Why did you say we have to talk?"

So he'd been right; those words had set her off. He'd have to tell Rawls to add that to his list.

"Because we do . . . we are."

She nodded slightly.

Was she agreeing? Or just listening? Damn, he need to exorcise that tip from his brain.

"Why didn't you come to me as soon as you landed? Why check on the boys but not come to see me?"

That's what that last withdrawal had been about? Hell, conversation was going to be a minefield with this woman. Damn good thing he was up for the task.

"Because you were sleeping. Because you needed the sleep. Because I didn't want to wake you up." Had he covered all the bases?

Oh fuck, he was scowling. He wiped the scowl and tried on a smile.

Amy took a giant step back.

Yeah, fuck this shit.

He let the smile go and watched the woman he loved more than he'd ever believed possible relax. She edged forward again.

"You love me too, right?" he demanded.

There he went, breaking another one of Rawls's stupid-ass rules. But the woman knew what she was getting. No sense in white-washing it.

"What are you going to do if I say no?" she asked with a lift to her eyebrows.

Mac couldn't tell whether she was teasing or serious. Pulling one of the flex-cuffs free, he dangled it in front of her eyes. "I'm going to rock your world so hard you'll never want to let me go."

Her face stilled, sudden anxiety in her eyes. "Mac, I don't think I'm ready—"

Ah fuck . . . something else he should have worded differently. "Sweetheart, they're not for you. They're for me."

Understanding brushed the fear from her eyes. "For you?"

"Yeah." He glanced toward the bedroom. "I figure we can cuff me to the headboard. Make sure I can't reach for you."

He'd managed to keep his hands to himself the night before last, but just barely. She got him so damn revved and ready to go . . . this time he wasn't counting on his self-control alone. Not when one wrong move could ruin the moment.

"That would be great"—her hazel eyes glinted—"if I had a headboard."

He scowled at that news. "Fuck."

"Absolutely." She slid up to him and stroked his arms.

He breathed deeply, awash in her clean, fresh scent. The grounding was back.

She took the flex-cuffs while he yanked off his T-shirt. Once the shirt was gone, he crossed his wrists and held them out to her.

She hesitated again, this time stroking his bare chest, her fingers leaving a trail of fire. But her eyes had lost some of their sparkle. "Mac, we don't need—"

"We do. Trust me." Mac shook his head. "Babe, you have no clue how hard it was to keep from grabbing you last time. I came way too close way too many times."

"But now that the first . . . time is over, maybe it wouldn't hit so hard if you do reach for me," she said.

Her voice was so tentative; he knew she was wondering whether that was wishful thinking.

"Why don't we stick to the status quo a few more times before experimenting?"

Apparently she was good with that counteroffer, because she wrapped the plastic cuff around his wrists and pulled until it was tight.

The flex-cuffs locked his wrists together, but they left his hands free, which gave him plenty of opportunity to touch her.

He started by grabbing the hem of her shirt and dragging it over her head. Her hair emerged ember bright and tousled. Sexy as all fucking hell.

She wrapped her arms around his waist and pressed in, but, damn it, his arms were in the way. He bent, his mouth searching for hers, but again his fucking arms were in the way, and the position was damn awkward.

It was time to rework the logistics of this plan.

"How 'bout we take this to your bedroom?" More specifically her bed. So he could lie back, his arms above his head, and let her have her way with him. That strategy had sure worked well last time.

It took half a dozen steps for him to realize that securing his hands in the living room had been a major miscalculation. The trip to the bedroom was endlessly awkward with his hands bound in front and at an angle that made it impossible to touch her, soothe her, caress the nerves jumping under her skin.

As soon as they reached the bed, he kicked off his shoes and dropped ass-first on the bed. He fell back and reached his arms above his head, fisting the blanket. "Come here, babe."

She crawled onto the bed, straddled him, and stretched out flat.

Christ, this was what he was talking about. She felt so fucking perfect pressed against him like this. Her warm, soft body melted into his. He arched up slightly, moving his body beneath hers, grounding her without his hands.

She purred, her mouth finding his and sipping at his lips. The hunger burning in his gut spread out, heating flesh and skin, hardening his muscles.

He opened his mouth, encouraging entry, but her lips moved across his face and down his neck instead, leaving a steady stream of nibbles and nips down his neck and across his collarbone. When she reached his nipples, she stopped to suck, and Jesus H. Christ, he about came off the bed.

Her mouth was so fucking hot and so fucking wet and so fucking sexy.

Then it moved on, trailing those same nipping, licking, sexy kisses down his ribs and across his abdomen to the waistband of his BDUs.

Jesus . . . Jesus . . . Jesus.

She backed up a bit, stopping to suckle the tight muscles of his abs.

Ah shit. Disappointment crested until he realized her fingers were at the waistband of his BDUs, unbuttoning and unzipping.

Oh . . . yeah.

He lifted his hips, and she dragged his pants and boxers down his thighs all the way past his knees. Released from its cotton prison, his cock sprang up, all but begging for the touch of her mouth.

Her mouth slid down again. The kisses wetter. The hot suck of her lips hotter. The wicked nip of her teeth sharper. A whoosh of lust hit his blood—the kick as potent as Jack and Johnnie mixed together and shot back straight. Christ, she was *killing* him.

Her mouth enveloped his cock, slid down and back up. Down and up. She added the light scrape of her teeth and the wicked glide of her tongue to the hot suction of her mouth. A deep, rumbling groan erupted from him.

Electrified, he arched his back. His arms came up, and his bound hands dived into her hair. Squeezing his eyes shut, he tried to think past the urgency boiling in his blood. This wasn't supposed to be about him. It was supposed to be all about her.

"Babe. Sweetheart," he ground out, forcing himself to let go of her head. "Enough. Take me inside you."

Another long, slow glide and suck of her mouth over his straining rigid cock. "I am."

He lost his breath when her talented hand closed over his balls and squeezed. The pressure built, throbbed through his cock and sac. A tingling started in his spine. Christ, he was running out of time. "Not like this. Not in your mouth. This is supposed to be for you."

Fuck, he wasn't making any sense . . . but then his head was about to explode . . . both heads.

"The boys won't be released until this afternoon. We have plenty of time for me." Her voice was husky.

While his brain was still processing the implications of that, her mouth went in for one final up and down before stopping to nibble at the tip of his cock.

Son of a bitch.

His hips arched off the bed.

He may have shouted. He may have screamed.

And then the pressure was loose, boiling up and out, carrying him away.

Chapter Thirty

HER CHIN PROPPED ON MAC'S HEAVING CHEST, AMY WATCHED HIS face. His sweaty, content face. His eyes were closed, his hair clinging damply to his forehead. The hard thump of his heart pounded against her slick hands.

He looked like a man who'd been utterly satisfied.

The hot rise of emotion rushed her chest, swelled until it flooded every cell, every nerve, the very breath she drew. She swallowed to ease the ache in her throat and concentrated on the steady beat of his heart against her palms.

It beat strong and steady and sure, this heart beneath her hands. The heart he'd given to her. The heart he'd protected so carefully through the years. He wasn't a man who loved easily. Nor would he be a man easy to love. She knew both these things. Knew they didn't matter.

She drew his sweaty male scent into her lungs, filling herself with him. A sense of peace, of belonging took hold. It felt like forever since she'd belonged to someone or since someone had belonged to her—someone other than her children, anyway.

The heaving beneath her hands slowed as his skin cooled. She waited.

When his eyes finally fluttered open, they were still hazy, the pupils dilated. She'd never seen them so soft—like black velvet. It didn't take long for them to sharpen—just the time it took for them to focus on her face.

"Hey." He pulled his bound hands forward, using his fingers to stroke her face. "You okay?"

Her clenched throat grew so tight it ached. The ache spread through her chest and into her heart. His first thought always was of her and the boys. Never of himself.

For a man so determined not to love, not to hold responsibility for anyone other than himself—he sure did it well. He'd put himself, his life, on the line for her so many times she'd lost track. When she'd been captive back in the very beginning. When he'd insisted on going with her to pick up the boys. When he'd used his body as a shield to protect her at Clay's house. He'd argued on her behalf for going after James Link and Leonard Embray. Over and over again, he'd stepped up to the plate for her. Almost died for her.

"Amy." A hint of sharpness entered his voice. He lifted his head off the bed, worry lighting his eyes.

She'd waited too long to respond.

Leaning her face into his hands, she smiled at him. "I think you're the one who should be answering that question." She waited a beat and offered him a slow, satisfied smile. "Just who rocked whose world?"

He laughed and dropped his head back to the mattress. "You didn't have to try to kill me to get out of answering the big question." He wiggled his eyebrows meaningfully. "I can be patient."

"Now *that* might just kill you." She was only partly kidding. For a SEAL, a commander no less, who must have had patience drilled into him from BUD/s onward, he was an odd dichotomy of extreme patience and explosive frustration and anger.

The frustration and anger weren't directed at her much these days . . . and it had *never* been directed at the boys. If it had, she wouldn't be lying on top of him right now.

His silence registered, and she refocused on him, catching the fleeting glimpse of vulnerability in his eyes.

He needed to know that she loved him. He might hide it behind his cranky, alpha, misogynist facade, but he was as vulnerable to her as she was to him.

His admission that he loved her had surprised the crap out of her. She hadn't expected the weighty *I love you* discussion so soon. Sure, she'd sensed he might have those kinds of feelings for her, mostly because his actions spoke volumes. Most of the men she knew tended to show rather than verbalize their love. Like her dad shoveling snow out of the driveway and warming and deicing her mom's car during the winter. Or Mac telling Embray to give him the antidote in his misguided quest to protect her.

Mac was as closed off emotionally as a man could get—or so it had seemed. She'd resigned herself to rarely, if ever, hearing those three powerful words. Then he'd dropped them on her at the very moment she'd girded herself to let him go. She'd been so certain he'd regretted their night together and intended to call them quits, she'd steeled herself to get through the discussion without letting him know that she cared.

Perhaps she'd steeled herself a little too well. Perhaps that initial instinct to protect herself from hurt when she thought he was abandoning her had tangled her up inside. Was that why she hadn't said "I love you" back? Had she been protecting herself in case he changed his mind? Was she still protecting herself?

She'd always prided herself on facing events head-on. On not taking the cowardly way out. But wasn't that exactly what she was doing now?

She did love him. She'd suspected it since the night he'd almost died in his quest to save Benji. It wasn't fair to keep him in the dark about her feelings when he'd been so surprisingly open about his.

She shuffled herself forward to brush a kiss across his lips. "I love you too."

His mouth hardened under hers, forcing her lips open so his tongue could surge inside. There was something wild and uncontrolled in his reaction, in the urgent sweep of his tongue, as though her words had unleashed the beast he kept locked inside.

As their mouths locked and their tongues dueled, her passion roared up to tangle with his. Heat flashed through her like a forest fire. She undulated against him, her breasts and thighs on fire.

For the first time, she resented the cuffs binding his wrists, keeping his arms from her. She wanted them around her, locking her to him. She wanted all of him over her, inside her, pressing her into the mattress.

She jerked her mouth from his. "Mac, take off the cuffs."

Although she knew it wasn't as easy as that. Flex-cuffs were designed so they couldn't be broken. They had to be cut. Which meant going to the kitchen and grabbing a knife—which was bound to break the mood.

He stilled beneath her, his concerned gaze stroking her face. "We agreed—"

"I've changed my mind."

The instant, emphatic response must have registered, because he gave her face one last searching scan and held his bound hands out to her. "There's a knife holstered to my right ankle."

He has a knife on him? Well, of course he does; he was still in his battle clothes.

She scooted down and pushed his pant leg up, freeing the knife from its holster.

"Be careful. It's sharp."

She almost rolled her eyes but caught herself in time. Of course it was sharp. Who'd want a dull knife strapped to their calf? She carefully sawed at the cuff between his spread wrists until the plastic gave way.

Hands free, he took the knife from her and set it on the bedside table. Damp hands cupped her cheeks; gentle fingers swept her hair behind her ears. "You're sure about this?"

She nodded. She wasn't just sure, she was determined. No way was she giving this man half measures. He deserved better than that.

She deserved better than that.

"If anything changes, let me know." He drew her mouth down to his. "Anything," he reminded her between kisses.

She murmured an agreement. The heat was already rising, stoked by the thrust of his tongue. Vaguely she felt his hands slide from her head to the clasp of her bra, and the fabric fell away. The feel of his chest against her breasts as she rubbed herself against his bare skin acted like accelerant on fire. Passion exploded, a flash of tingles and heat and electrical impulses that liquefied her. Her skin tightened and dampened.

Fingers unhooked her jeans and eased down the zipper. She sat up, lifting her hips so he could drag them down her legs. The moment she shimmied out of them, his hand was between her legs, slipping into her wet, swollen depths.

She groaned, frozen there above him, completely focused on his hand and on the slow, teasing glide of his finger. He moved faster and faster, adding a second finger until she was locked at the precipice, ready to fly.

"Let go, babe. Come on. Let go."

The gravelly rasp of his voice was rougher than ever and drew Amy's eyes. He was watching her face, hot urgency in his eyes.

"Not like this," Amy said, aware of the oddest sense of déjà vu. "I want you inside me. On top of me." Her urgency climbed with each word, echoed in her voice. "I want to feel your weight pressing me into the mattress. Please. I need you on top."

He froze for a moment, and she could sense the hot scrutiny of his gaze, but he didn't question her decision. Instead he drew her down, one arm between her legs, the other around her back, anchoring her to him, and he rolled.

They were exactly as she'd wanted. His hard, hot weight pressed her into the mattress; his arms were around her, holding her close to his heart; his breath was hot and humid against her neck—and the nightmare slammed into her with the force of a hurricane, blasting the passion from her veins.

She barely had a chance to stiffen before he was rolling again. Sitting frozen above him, drawing deep gulping breaths, she fought the urge to flee.

"I got you, baby, I got you. Breathe. It's me, Mac. You're safe. Breathe." Light, skimming caresses stroked her arms and hips. Rough hands cupped her breasts and squeezed. "Concentrate on me. My touch. On my voice." His voice was grittier than ever, but when she unlocked her eyes and focused on his face, all she saw was concern.

The terror faded beneath a flood of guilt.

"Oh God . . . oh God . . . how can I do this to you again?"

She wasn't aware she'd said it aloud until he replied, "You're still here. Your breathing is less gulpy. You're talking to me. I don't think we're done yet."

Less gulpy?

Some of her tension eased, allowing her to focus and assess. He was right. There was no longer an impulse to flee, not like there had been before. The horrific images weren't even an echo in her mind. Even more important, the feel of his hot, thick penis pressed between her thighs was nudging the heat levels back up.

Without thinking, she squeezed her thighs, raised herself up, and slowly lowered herself back down.

"Jesus." The sound was more groan than word. "I'm going to take that as an excellent sign."

She did it again, gasping at the surge of heat. The gasp turned to a groan as his hand returned to the damp flesh between her thighs. With each thrust of his fingers, her passion spiraled. Closing her eyes, she rode the wave, rising higher and higher, closer and closer . . .

Vaguely she was aware of his hand retreating, of him lifting her, of the thick, swollen length of him filling her aching, empty depths. Then his hands returned to her hips and moved her against him.

She took over the rocking, the lifting and falling, taking him harder and harder and deeper and deeper. His groans joined hers until they were moving and groaning in tandem, hurling over the cliff together.

She returned to awareness completely satiated. She collapsed across his chest. His hands were still at her hips, his penis still lodged inside her. She propped herself up to stare at him.

"What?" he asked without opening his eyes, his face relaxed and sated. The palms that glided across her hips were soothing.

"This isn't fair to you." Guilt started eating away at the contentment.

"You're fucking with me, right?" He finally opened his eyes. "Trust me. There is no place I'd rather be."

"You can't even touch me." Her throat closed.

"Give it time." He stroked her hip again and slowly advanced his hands up her spine, caressing her. But he didn't try to pull her down. "Barely over a week ago you couldn't even stay in the same room with me when the memories hit. This time, not only did you stay *on top* of me, but also minutes later you took me inside. I'd say that's a hell of an improvement. The memories are losing their hold. We just have to give it time. And, hell—it's not like we don't have plenty of time to spare."

She thought about that as she snuggled down.

He was right. This time, after the memory had fled, they'd rebuilt the passion. The memories were losing their hold because of him. Because of his patience and caring. They were banishing them together.

He sighed contentedly. It was a sound she'd never heard from him before. Maybe she wasn't the only one changing here.

"What time do we get the boys?" he asked.

We.

She basked in the warmth the word engendered.

"We have a while yet." She nuzzled his chest, feeling and hearing the sound of his heart accelerate.

Where they were headed, she had no clue. They needed to talk things over, and then they'd have to talk to Benji and Brendan—the boys were a huge part of her life. They had time for all that.

They had all the time in the world now.

A week later, Amy smiled and stretched lethargically, the sheets sticking to her damp skin. "I probably should have waited to jump your bones until you'd had a chance to shower and eat."

The fingers fondling her right shoulder paused. A raspy laugh sounded next to her ear. "Do you hear me complaining?"

No. Mac looked far too satisfied to complain. The normally hard planes of his face were lax with contentment. His black eyes were lazy. His big naked body was relaxed and sated.

As Amy's body cooled, a chill took hold. She rolled over and cuddled against his hot, bare chest—her own personal in-bed furnace. It was such a relief to have him back and in one piece, although this last mission hadn't held much danger. The warehouses had already been secured and the bombs were inactive. The focus had been on destroying the devices.

"I take it Leonard's spray dissolved the sonic distributors?" she asked, draping an arm across his hard chest.

Mac stirred, giving a disbelieving shake of his head. "You should have seen it. A few squirts of that shit, and those damn metal eggs were a sticky puddle of goo eating through the floor."

Locating the devices had ended up being the easy part. Destroying them had been much harder. The alloy the NRO had used for the outside shell had been almost indestructible.

Almost.

Until Leonard Embray had whipped up a cocktail of chemicals that would melt any alloy known to man. He'd finished the final version two days ago, after which Mac and his men, along with the rest of the Shadow Mountain operatives, had headed off to dispose of the sonic bombs and save the world . . . again.

"What do you think Neniiseti' and the elders are going to do with Eric Manheim and David Coulson?" Amy asked idly, rubbing her cheek against his tanned chest.

His heart pounded in her ear, its previously urgent rhythm slower now.

"They'll drain every ounce of useful information from them and execute them." His voice was flat. Cold. Full of agreement. The lazy fingers caressing her drying skin stilled as though he were awaiting her response.

She wanted to protest that the Shadow Mountain brass had no right to take such action. Like it or not, Shadow Mountain was within the borders of Alaska and as such bound by the United States Criminal Code. Neniiseti' and the elders had no right to play judge, jury, and executioner. Manheim and Coulson deserved a fair trial, except—

There was no way they'd receive a fair trial.

Their influence and capital made that impossible. They'd be released on bail pending their trial, which would leave them free to bring the NRO back to a full boil. The only way to safeguard the planet from their Machiavellian agenda was to make sure they never had another chance to influence anyone or anything.

The two men really did need to die.

So did Esme Manheim, if what Link had told them was true. The woman was as entrenched in the NRO as her husband had been. But for some odd reason Neniiseti' had declared her off limits . . . at least for the next year. As with all things Neniiseti' decreed, he hadn't explained why. Regardless, Shadow Mountain had eyes on her, and they'd intercede if she tried to start up the New Ruling Order again.

After a moment the lazy caresses started up again. She sighed. His arm was beneath her and curved up to her shoulder, almost holding her. They were getting closer to actual cuddling every day, although Mac still liked to call it grounding.

"How did the boys' checkup go yesterday?"

She was close to certain he already knew. That he'd questioned the doctors during the trip back home. If he hadn't, he'd have quizzed her about the test results before now. But that was okay. The inquiry gave her a chance to say the good news out loud. Maybe if she repeated what Dr. Zapa had told her enough times out loud, she'd actually start to believe it. "The N2FP and reversal isotopes are absent in both boys now. The test results came back picture perfect. We couldn't ask for better."

He leaned over to kiss the top of her head. "That must have been a relief."

"Yeah," she said slowly.

A rumbling half laugh, half snort worked its way up his throat. "Having trouble believing it, huh?"

He was getting to know her a little too well. But she was getting to know him too. This next piece of information was of vital importance to him. "Leonard has set up the press conference."

His entire body went still. Sudden tension vibrated in the muscles pressed against her cheek. "When?"

"A week from today. All the major newspapers and news stations will be there. You, Zane, Cosky, and Rawls. You'll all be exonerated in front of the entire world. John and Admiral McKay's killers will be exposed."

"If he's believed. If *we're* believed." Grimness flattened his tone.

"James Link is going with him to corroborate Leonard's account. But Leonard wants you there too, to tell your side of what happened."

His muscles twitched as he pushed himself up slightly. "Link? No shit. Have the two of them talked yet?"

"I don't think so. Leonard's still avoiding him." She glanced up as a frown worked its way across his face. He was having as much trouble believing his nightmare was over as she was believing hers was past.

What a pair they made.

"Is Link aware he'll be arrested by the FBI the minute he opens his mouth?" Mac asked, dropping his shoulders to the bed again. The tension in his torso slowly released.

"He must be. Leonard has said repeatedly that he's going to press charges." Amy went back to snuggling, soaking in the heat his body gave off along with his intoxicating, musky scent.

It didn't look like Leonard was going to forgive James anytime soon. The memory of James's betrayal was still new and raw. Although he was spending more time on his feet and less in the wheelchair, Leonard's continuing lack of mobility was a constant reminder of James's betrayal.

Amy doubted Leonard would ever forgive him.

In some ways Leonard's venom toward James reminded her of Mac's hatred of his mother, but in Mac's case it sounded like the emotion was tied to how his brother had died.

"How did your little brother die?" she asked without thinking and then froze.

She'd wanted to ask him what had happened since the night he'd told her about Davey, but she hadn't quite wrestled up enough courage. The subject was obviously a painful one, something he kept buried.

His chest stilled beneath her cheek, and the hand lazily gliding up and down her shoulder fell to the mattress.

"I'm sorry." She stumbled back into speech, kicking herself for ruining the mood. "I shouldn't have asked. It's not my business."

His ribs rose and fell, rose and fell. "Anything that's my business is your business." A long, raw pause, and then—"He was hit by a car."

The grit was already returning to his tone. The simmering rage. "See, Mom liked to have her fun, but she had two kids. If she hired a babysitter, people might talk. So she'd take us with her. Lock us in the car for hours at a time. The Civic was our own personal day care."

"Oh, Mac." Amy fought to keep her voice even and the shock from her face. "What about the summer, when it was hot? Or the winter, when it was cold?"

He looked down at her with eyes glossed by cynicism and a rigid jut to his chin. "That's what windows were for. She'd crack them in the summer. Close them in the winter."

Anger rose on his behalf. "That's criminal."

His nostrils flared slightly. "Maybe if someone had bothered to turn her in . . . Hell—I should have turned her in. If I had, maybe Davey would still be alive."

He fell into a brooding, vibrating silence.

"You were ten. Give yourself a break." She strove for a matter-of-fact tone even though her heart ached for him. "What happened?"

"She forgot to lock the fucking car. Too anxious to get her party on, I guess." His voice suddenly went flat. "There was a highway a klick away. He got hit by three fucking cars. Three of them. One after another. He'd been dead six hours before she returned to the car and discovered he was gone."

Amy leaned over and wrapped her arms as far around his chest as she could manage with him lying down. If ever a man needed a hug, it was him—now. "She was arrested?"

He sighed, and his arms slowly moved to stroke her back. The tautness in his big body eased by increments. "Eventually. His death was all over the news. She heard about it on the radio on her way back home."

"Back home?" Amy jerked up in disbelief and shock. "She just went home? She didn't go find him?"

"Yeah, she drove straight home. To shower the stench of booze and sex off, or so I assume." The rage was still there but muted now, simmering rather than boiling.

A comfortable silence fell between them. Amy pressed a kiss to his chest just above his heart. "I have to say, Mac. I really hate your mother."

That nudged a ghost of a laugh from him. His arms tightened around her waist, tugging her closer. "Join the club."

"What ended up happening to her?" she asked, lying down across his chest.

"I don't know." His hands started that lingering slide up her spine again. "She skipped bail. Was found and dragged back to jail. Went to prison for a couple of years. I heard she moved to the East Coast after release."

"You haven't seen her since your brother died?"

"Nope." His heart rate picked up speed as the rage stirred again. "Don't want to either."

"Don't blame you." She waited for his heartbeat to level out. "What about your dad? How did he handle what happened?"

"By falling into the bottle. He was drinking heavily even before Davey died. Started drinking himself into a stupor afterward."

He'd been only ten years old. A year younger than Brendan. A ten-year-old child with one parent gone and the other comatose drunk most of the time. "How in the world did you survive?"

When she lifted her head, he brushed a kiss across her lips, and she felt his lips curve. As though he liked hearing the horror and rage on his behalf. "I started taking odd jobs. That's why I wasn't in the car with Davey that day. I was mowing the neighbor's yard, trying to earn enough money to buy us some food."

He was earning money to buy him and his brother food, which must mean they'd been going hungry. A combination of wrath and grief rolled through her. If his parents were standing in front of her, she'd wring their necks without hesitation.

He'd been a child, for God's sake.

A giant fist plunged into her chest and squeezed her heart. Tears pricked her eyes. Her arms closed around him.

Suddenly he froze. She heard the rasp of his breath catch.

"Uh . . . Amy."

His voice was careful enough to bring her head back. She scanned his face and found the oddest expression. A mixture of . . . well, she wasn't really sure. "What's wrong?"

"Nothing." He paused a beat, his arms lightly cinching around her waist. "In fact, I'd say things are looking quite promising." Another gentle squeeze of his arms.

It took her a moment to realize what he was referring to. When it did, her breath caught, and her mouth fell open.

"Your arms are around me." Wonder turned her insides all fluffy and warm.

"They are." This time he remained perfectly still, his gaze searching her face. "How are you doing with that?"

Because it was important—crucial, really—she took a few seconds to assess her reaction. Nothing but blue skies and sunshine floated through her mind.

"I'm doing perfect." She wondered if her smile looked as happy as she felt. "Everything is perfect now."

Epilogue

Mid-June
Nine months later

LEANING A HIP AGAINST LEONARD EMBRAY'S STATE-OF-THE-ART BARBECUE station, Mac tossed his head back, savoring the icy slide of the Chuli Stout. "I sure as hell didn't expect this little Podunk Alaskan town to brew some of the finest beer I've ever tasted."

Embray punched the button to fire up the propane grill before looking up. "For a town of only eight hundred and seventy-some souls, Talkeetna has some damn fine restaurants and breweries."

Damn straight. Hell, the Single Engine Red and the Twister Creek IPA brewed by the Denali Brewing Company made settling here worth it. Well, that plus the proximity to Denali and the wild, remote wilderness—and the chance to start a new life with the woman he loved.

It wasn't often a man got a second chance at life.

At peace with his choices, he addressed Embray. "Appreciate you hosting the reception for us."

Embray nodded. "Least I could do."

Mac figured the guy had paid back any perceived debt he'd owed them last fall during the press conference. Not that he'd be able to convince Embray of that.

"How's the ring fittin'?" Rawls asked, ambling up to settle beside him against the brick. "Starting to chafe yet?"

After two hours?

Asshole.

"Has yours?" Mac countered, eyeing the plain gold band circling Rawls's ring finger.

"I should have saved that question for Amy. Bet she'd answer differently." Rawls's teeth flashed white.

Zane and Beth had married first—way back in November, three months before baby Ginny was born. Rawls and Faith had followed in the dead of winter, with Cosky and Kait tying the knot in the spring.

It had taken longer for him and Amy to reach that point, but then they had the kids to consider. Hell, if it had been up to him, he'd have hauled her to the altar after that first night in bed instead of waiting until June.

After a long pull on his can of Twister Creek, Rawls took a meandering look around them. His gaze lingered on the single-story, medium-size log cabin. "Have to say, dude"—he turned to Embray—"this wasn't what I expected when you said you'd bought a place out here."

"No?" Embray looked up, curiosity on his face. "What were you expecting?"

"I dunno." Rawls scanned the place again. "Just somethin' different."

Mac knew exactly what Rawls had been expecting—the same thing he'd been expecting. Something huge, something grand, something expensive. Something full of special features, security enhancements, and security guards. Something that signaled that one of the richest men in the world lived there.

Instead they'd arrived to find a house that any one of them could have lived in.

Embray shrugged and turned up the gas on the grill. "It suits me."

It did at that. Embray had filled out since leaving Shadow Mountain and returning to Hawaii to reclaim Dynamic Solutions. The hollows in his cheeks and eyes had smoothed out as well. He'd put some meat on his bones.

Back in October, when Embray had set up the press conference to tell the world what had happened to him along with everything he knew about the NRO, his face had still been stretched tight. His body taut with tension. His muscles weak and rigid thanks to all those months in bed.

Of course, getting up there on the world stage and admitting he'd been assaulted, held down, and drugged, or that he'd been betrayed by his best friend—none of that could have been easy. That alone must have added to the tension on his face and the exhausted look in his eyes.

Fuck, it must have been galling as hell.

Other than exonerating the men who'd rescued him, there had been no reason for him to go public with what had happened. It had been easy enough to step back into his role as Dynamic Solutions' CEO and quietly rid himself of the ciphers the NRO had planted on his board. With the capture of Manheim and Coulson, followed by their executions, there had been no reason to expose the organization because there was no longer a threat to humanity.

Yet Embray had done it anyway.

He'd stood up there and exonerated Mac and his boys. Because of that sacrifice, the four of them could walk free again. All the charges against them had been dropped. They didn't have to worry about the police or the FBI or the sheriff's department sweeping down on them.

Too bad their careers in HQ1 hadn't been as easy to save.

"At least we got the bastards who ordered the hit on McKay," Mac said, thinking out loud.

Zane, who'd just joined them, raised his beer in a salute. "To McKay."

"To McKay," Mac and Rawls echoed.

A few seconds of silence fell, and then Rawls stirred, and a flicker of bitterness crossed his face. "Nothing like being left to twist in the wind by your own command, though."

He had reason for his bitterness. They all did.

They'd been kicked off the teams by the brotherhood they'd spent their lives serving. Sure, they'd each been given a hero's retirement and full pension, but they were still out on their asses.

"Admiral Townsend made the right call," Cosky said, pulling up next to Zane. "You want to be pissed about it? Turn it on the press. We were too much of a liability with our faces plastered across every television screen and newspaper in existence. We're damn lucky Shadow Command would have us."

Though there was truth to his lieutenant's view, Mac still nursed his grudge. Or tried to. It took more effort than it would have in the past. There was just too much to be thankful for these days.

"You getting used to the daddy thing?" Cosky asked, turning to Mac.

Mac's gaze easily found Brendan, who was helping Marion set out the plates on the dozen or so tables on the lawn. Faith was distributing the glasses, while Beth, with baby Ginny strapped to her chest in an infant sling, was adding napkins and silverware to each of the place settings.

With Brendan located, his gaze went roving for Benji, who'd spent every moment since arrival chasing Embray's dog. He relaxed upon finding the boy collapsed on the ground next to the black Lab. It was one of the few times he'd seen Benji not energized. The realization narrowed his eyes.

Hell, they should get the kid a dog.

"They're good kids. But this whole dad thing—" He frowned and shook his head. "I've no fucking clue what I'm doing. Amy, thank Christ, is great with them. If it was just me . . . hell, they'd end up being serial killers or some shit." He checked on Benji again. The kid and dog were both rolling around on the freshly mowed grass, their legs waving in the air. He shook his head. Christ, the kid's new clothes were going to have grass stains everywhere. The washer and dryer that had come with their new digs were bound to get a workout. "Brendan's doing great at his new school, already made some good friends, aces both grades and sports. As for Benji, the teacher says he has trouble focusing." As though that were a surprise. He shook his head wryly and glanced toward the boy. Instantly he went on high alert. Both kid and dog were gone. Before he had a chance to get worried and start investigating, a shriek lit the air. At least you could usually track the boy by his lungs. "It's hard to believe he was at death's door nine months ago."

Muttered agreement went around the group.

Rawls shot Zane an innocent look, but pure mischief glistened in his eyes. "When are you and Beth givin' that little darlin' of yours a little brother or sister?"

Dread darkened Zane's eyes. "Never, if I have any say in it."

Rawls threw back his head, howling with laughter. After wrestling his mirth under control, he reached out to smack Zane's shoulder. "Never took you for a pussy, Skipper."

With no discernable embarrassment, Zane shoved Rawls back. "Call me all the names you want, asshole. I've been shot. Stabbed. Broken a couple of bones. My face has been used as a Goddamn strike bag too many times to count. Hell, even had a bad case of road rash back in the day. But nothing—and Christ as my witness, I mean *nothing*—hurts as fucking bad as giving birth. How the fuck they do it once and then step up to do it again—" He shook his head, his expression dumbfounded.

This time the eruption of laughter was thunderous.

The account of Beth's labor had already reached legendary status. Not because there had been anything unusual about the birth itself, but because Zane had gone through it with her. Not by way of holding her hand, or encouraging her to breathe, or any of the other ways husbands had supported their wives through the ages.

Oh no, he'd been right there beside her at the Shadow Mountain clinic, panting and groaning and screaming every time she did—pushing out a phantom baby next to her real, live squalling one.

The poor bastard had looked completely wrecked when the rest of them had been allowed to visit. Beth, on the other hand, had been glowing.

"Beth wants another one. Can you believe it?" Zane shook his head and took a long pull on his can of Twister, that earlier look of dread returning to his face.

"It's all those bedrooms in that new place of yours," Cosky told him dryly. "It's a natural impulse to fill them."

"You have one more than we have," Zane countered.

Cosky offered a small, sly smile. "We turned the smallest into a massage room."

After they'd agreed to join Shadow Command, they'd started looking for someplace to stash their families. Someplace close enough to Denali so they could commute—via chopper—when they weren't out saving the world.

Talkeetna had been perfect.

It was close to Shadow Command—ninety-five klicks as the crow flies, which equaled a thirty-minute flight by chopper. It was big enough to have a school and local clinic but small enough that strangers stood out. And the place boasted some damn fine pubs and restaurants. The only downside had been the lack of rentals or property for sale. Shadow Command had stepped in to clear that obstacle out of the way. They'd bought a huge private swath of land several klicks out of town and started building houses. The last of the new homes had been finished the month before.

While they were waiting for the houses to go up, they'd remained in the Shadow Mountain personnel quarters—at least in between trips down to the States to visit family and friends.

"How's your wife like working for Shadow Command?" Embray asked Rawls as he picked up his beer and took a long, slow swallow.

"Happy as a clam." Rawls gave him a you-don't-fool-me smile. "Ya ain't gonna tempt her away."

Mac listened idly as he took another long swallow of the stout. Faith and Kait were both working out of Shadow Mountain, taking the chopper in beside him and the boys and returning home with them each night.

Embray looked disappointed. "Has she found out how they keep the airstrip hidden? I've flown over it a few times, and I can't find even a hint of it. What technology are they using? How in the hell do they keep it clear of snow?"

A very good question, and one he and the boys had been mulling over for months. Wolf and Shadow Command remained cagey as hell about some things—the airfield up there on the mountain just one of them.

The other thing they'd questioned since accepting Wolf's offer of employment was why Shadow Command had reached out to them. The NRO was neutralized—well, except for Esme Manheim. Not long after Neniiseti's hands-off order regarding Eric Manheim's wife, they'd discovered the woman was pregnant. Killing a pregnant woman didn't sit well with anyone.

For the time being she walked free, but they were keeping an eye on her.

When he'd asked Wolf why they were adding to their teams when they'd just defeated their enemy, Wolf had simply said, "Earth has many enemies."

What the fuck that meant was open to interpretation.

Maybe they'd find out the answers to all these annoying questions when they officially joined the Shadow Command teams next week. Their long vacation was almost over.

Thank Christ. Nine months of free time had been enough to drive Mac crazy. But they'd wanted to make sure the media storm died so they didn't inadvertently expose Shadow Mountain.

Things had gone completely fucking crazy after Embray's press conference, followed by James Link's arrest and the complete disappearance of the NRO Council. Just as things had finally died down, Link had been assassinated. *Whoosh*—the media had swarmed in again.

It still made Mac uneasy that someone had stepped in to terminate Link. Who? Why? There wasn't anything that Link could say now that would make a difference to anyone. The NRO had ceased to exist.

Unless it had been a revenge hit, and someone had killed him as payback for betraying them . . . someone like Esme Manheim?

Maybe—but they hadn't had any luck tracing the hit back to her. Still, it was the only thing that made sense.

The distant sound of rotors beating the air pulled him from his musings. Their Shadow Mountain guests were arriving.

When the patio door to Embray's house opened, and Amy stepped out, balancing a platter piled high with steaks, Mac set his beer on the counter of the barbecue and headed over to intercept her. After relieving her of the heavy tray, he brushed a kiss across her lips. Side by side, his free arm around her shoulder, they converged on Embray.

"Doesn't seem fair that the bride should be working at her own reception," Embray said as he took the platter from Mac and started dropping steaks on the grill.

Amy smiled calmly. "We wanted to keep it private, which leaves out catering."

More like secret.

The safety of their families relied on keeping their locations secret. A catering service could have exposed them all. So they'd furnished the event themselves, with Embray's help. They hadn't even invited Amy's family and friends to the wedding, although they'd fly down to Bellingham for a second ceremony at some point the following month.

"We're taking the kids fishing for the weekend. Leaving tomorrow. Won't be back until late Sunday," Mac said as Amy excused herself and disappeared inside the house. "We're making a camping trip of it."

"No shit? What river?" Zane asked.

"The Little Susitna. King salmon are biting." One by one, Mac nailed his buddies with a dry look. "And no, none of you are invited."

He, Amy, and the kids needed some time alone.

"The salmon won't be the only things biting. The mosquitos will too." Rawls grimaced.

Mac scowled back. The damn bloodsuckers were everywhere. He could only hope that the locals weren't fucking with him when they claimed the mosquitos were light this year.

He twisted to check on Benji and found his new son—he still had trouble wrapping his head around that—dipping his finger in the potato salad and licking it clean.

"Hang on," Mac said. He handed his beer to Zane for safekeeping and headed off to intercept the boy before a third or even fourth dipping and a lecture about common courtesy and hygiene from his mother.

"Mac," the little guy said, dipping his finger into the bowl before Mac could stop him. He lifted his arm to Mac, a healthy dollop of potato salad on his index finger. "We're supposed to test it. You know, to make sure it tastes good enough for our guests."

Mac's lips twitched. The diction and tone had been pure Amy.

Catching Benji's wrist in case he decided to test the salad again, Mac grabbed a napkin and wiped the gooey mess from the kid's hand.

"That's right. Testing is imperative when you're throwing a party." He picked up a spoon and put it in Benji's hand. "But only with spoons or forks. Never with fingers."

Benji looked down at his hand and then up at Mac's face. "But why?"

"Because that's the polite thing to do. You wouldn't want to eat someone else's dirty finger cooties, would you?" Mac asked, instantly realizing his mistake. Benji's eyes flared with curiosity and excitement.

"What are dirty finger cooties? Do you have them? Do I have them? Are we supposed to eat them?" Bouncing up, Benji craned his neck, trying to get a better look at Mac's hand.

"Yes, Mac," Amy asked from behind him, laughter throbbing in her voice. "Do you have the dreaded finger cooties?"

From the excited fascination on Benji's face, he suspected they'd be hearing about finger cooties for a very long time. He needed to do a better job of censoring himself in front of the kid.

Not the first adjustment he'd made since moving here. Or the worst, for that matter. The dark, snowy months of winter, when the sun barely crested the sky—or the endless days during the summer, when the sun never left it—had taken much more of an adjustment . . . and then there were the mosquitos. He shook his head.

All in all, he wouldn't trade this move for anything, and he knew Amy and the boys felt the same.

He walked back to the barbecue to retrieve his beer with Amy under his arm and Benji bouncing beside them. His men shifted aside, allowing them into the loose huddle of bodies. As Zane returned his beer, he tightened his arm around Amy's shoulders, drawing her tight against his side. The move felt natural these days. Normal. As necessary as breathing or the beat of his heart.

Christ, she fit him just right.

As she leaned into him, not just accepting but reveling in the clasp of his arm, he inwardly smiled. The hold those monsters had had over her was gone. Terror didn't follow the tightening of his arms. She came as hard and as long beneath him as on top of him.

She'd won herself back.

She was a strong one, this woman of his. A stubborn one too.

Benji's shriek climbed the air, and Mac sighed. A deep sense of serenity claimed him. He hadn't realized how explosively dissatisfied he'd become with Naval Special Warfare Command, and his life, until Amy had entered it and he'd been cut off from HQI. Until he'd been welcomed into a new life.

A better life.

One that he'd kill to keep safe.

"A toast." Rawls lifted his glass of beer. "To Amy and Mac."

"To all of us," Mac corrected, his gaze drifting to Kait and Beth and Faith, who were laughing next to the table buried under mountains of potato salad, baked beans, and platters of corn. "To all the good things to come."

Glossaries
SEAL Terms

BUD/s (Basic Underwater Demolition training): a twenty-four-week training course that encompasses physical conditioning, combat diving, and land warfare

bullfrog: a nickname given to a highly respected retired SEAL

CQB (Close Quarter Battle): a battle that takes place in a confined space, such as a residence

deployment: active combat or training; deployments last generally between six and ten months

HQ1 (Naval Special Warfare Group 1/the West Coast Command): HQ1 has naval bases in Coronado, California; Kodiak, Alaska; Pearl Harbor, Hawaii; and Mare Island, California. Among other naval units, HQ1 houses SEAL Teams 1, 3, 5, and 7.

HQ2 (Naval Special Warfare Group 2/the East Coast Command): HQ2 has naval bases in Dam Neck, Virginia; Little Creek, Virginia; Machrihanish, UK; Rodman NAS, Panama; and Norfolk, Virginia. Among other naval units, HQ2 houses SEAL Teams 2, 4, 8, and 10, and DEVGRU (also known as SEAL Team 6).

insertion: heading into enemy territory, whether it's a house or a territory

JSOC (Joint Special Operations Command): A joint command that encompasses all branches of special operations. This command ensures that the techniques and equipment used by the various branches of the military are standardized. It is also responsible for training and developing tactics/strategy for special operations missions.

klick: kilometer

LC: lieutenant commander

NAVSPECWARCOM (Naval Special Warfare Command): The command for naval special operations. This command is under the umbrella of USSOC and is broken into two headquarters: HQ1 and HQ2.

NVDs: Night Vision Devices

PST (Physical Screening Test): The physical test a prospective SEAL has to pass. Minimum requirements: 500-yard swim in twelve and a half minutes, rest ten minutes, fifty pushups in two minutes, rest two minutes, fifty sit-ups in two minutes, rest two minutes, ten pull-ups in two minutes, rest ten minutes, 1.5-mile run in ten and a half minutes.

SEAL Prep School: A crash course in preparing to take the BUD/s challenge. Prospective BUD/s candidates are put through a physical training program meant to prepare them for BUD/s. This includes timed four-mile runs and thousand-meter swims. If the candidates are unable to pass the final qualifications test, they are removed from SEAL candidates lists and placed elsewhere in the navy.

SEAL Teams: Each SEAL team has 128 men, of which twenty-one are officers and 107 are enlisted. Each team has ten platoons, and each platoon has two squads. There are sixteen men per platoon and eight SEALs per squad.

SQT (SEAL Qualification Training): SQT teaches tactics, techniques, and special operations procedures.

USSOC (United States Special Operations Command): Beneath the umbrella of JSOC, the USSOC is the unified combat command and is charged with overseeing special operations command from the army, air force, navy, and marines.

Zodiac: A rigid-hull inflatable boat with 470-horsepower jet drives. It can reach speeds of forty-five-plus knots and has supreme maneuverability (also known as the beach boat).

Arapaho Terms

3ooxonouubeiht: crabby

be3ees: testicles/balls

bee'ice'ee' (singular); bee'ice'ei'i (plural): apple, a derogatory term for children who want to leave the res—red on the outside, white on the inside

beesnenitee: elder

Be:he:teiht: the creator

beniiinenno: soldier

beniinookee: general or highest-ranking official

betee: heart

betee3oo hohe': Shadow Mountain

bexookee: mountain lion

bih'ihoox: mule

biitei: ghost

bixoo3etiit: love

boh'ooo: thunder

ceece'esbeniiinenitiit: armed forces

ceeyoubeiht: talking foolishly

ciibehbiiwoohu: don't cry

ciini'i3ecoot: grief

heebii3soo: bastard

heeteinono'eino': the Arapaho people in the beginning of time

heinoo: mother

heneeceine3: lion

heteiniicie: the Wind River reservation

hiihooko'oet: bewitched

hiihooteet: death

hiinooko3onit: golden eagle

hiixoyooniiheiht: charm

hinono'eiteen: Arapaho

hisei: woman

hisoh'o: brother

hiteseiw's: sister

hitesih'o: his wife

hookecouhu hiteseiw: little sister

Hooxei: Wolf

houu: old word for God

houuwoo'oot: ceremony

hoxhisei: bitch

koo3eincecnise: age-old or ancient

nebii'o'oo: sweetheart

neecee: chief

neehebehe': younger sister

neenii3o'neihi: behave well or be quiet

neihoowuni'ixooni: bad attitude

neihoowuni'oubeih: sick

neniiseti: One Arrow (weapon of the people)

nesi: uncle (mother's brother)

netesei: my sister

nih'oo3oo: white men

nih'oo3ounii'ehiiho': white man's bird

niitouw hiine'tiihiiho': Indian people here, now

noniiteceenoo'oot: temporarily crazy

noonsoo: it is chaos or a mess

noo'uusooo': storm

notonheihii: medicine man

teeteeso'oot: apologize

teittooneihi: be quiet

tei'yoonehe: baby or infant

tei'yoonehihi: very young child

tei'yoonoh'o': children

woh'ooo': badger

wo'ohno: moccasins

wo'ouusoo: kitten

Author's Note

Dear Reader,

I hope you enjoyed *Forged in Ember*, the final installment in my Red-Hot SEALs series.

If you'd like to read more books set in my Red-Hot SEALs world, or sign up for my newsletter, please visit my website at www.trishmccallan.com.

Newsletter subscribers receive new-release information and free Red-Hot SEALs novellas.

For a full list of my available books, you can visit my website or my Amazon author page: www.amazon.com/Trish-McCallan/e/B006GHSSI2/ref=ntt_athr_dp_pel_1.

If you enjoyed *Forged in Ember*, I'd appreciate it if you'd help other readers find this book by sharing the title and book description with your friends, reading groups, book clubs, and online reading forums.

Additionally, leaving an honest review on Goodreads, Amazon, or any other retail site would be appreciated. Reviews help cue other readers in to what they might like or dislike about a book and enhance book discovery.

I love to hear from my readers and make a point of answering every email I receive. If you have any questions or comments, feel free to email me at trish@trishmccallan.com.

As always, thanks for reading!

Best wishes,

Trish McCallan

Acknowledgments

To Alison Dasho, you have the patience of a saint! Thank you for putting up with me these past few years and helping me get *Ember* out to my readers.

To Charlotte Herscher, my books are always so much stronger after passing through your keen eyes and sharp mind. You bump my writing up to the next level. Thank you!

To my readers, thank you so much for reading! I appreciate each and every one of you. Without you, there would be no Red-Hot SEALs!

About the Author

Photo © 2013 JK Steele

Trish McCallan was born in Oregon and raised in Washington State, where as a child she sold her first crayon-illustrated books for a nickel. This love of writing led her to study the craft at Western Washington University. She worked as a bookkeeper and a human-resources specialist before trading in her day job for a full-time writing career. Her Red-Hot SEALs novels include *Forged in Smoke* and the Romance Writers of American RITA Awards finalists, *Forged in Ash* and *Forged in Fire*. *Forged in Ember* is the fourth book in her series. She currently resides in eastern Washington with her three golden retrievers, a black Lab mix, and a cat.